For Jean —
I treasure our friendship
of so many years —
Enjoy !

Indian Winter

Best,
Jane McDonnell

Indian Winter

a novel

Jane Laura
Goldsmith

Full Court Press
Englewood Cliffs, New Jersey

First Edition

Copyright © 2012 by JaneLaura Goldsmith

Published in the United States of America
by Full Court Press, 601 Palisade Avenue
Englewood Cliffs, NJ 07632
www.fullcourtpressnj.com

ISBN 978-0-9849536-7-7

Library of Congress Control No. 2012949111

*Editing and Book Design by Barry Sheinkopf for Bookshapers
(www.bookshapers.com)*

Author Photo by Lawrence Lauterborn

Cover Photo courtesy istockphoto.com

Colophon by Liz Sedlack

"To live life fully is not just crossing a field."
—*Russian saying*

PROLOGUE

DURING THE NIGHT, BACK at the Montana ranch where I grew up, I dream the air is full of iridescent blue and green fish. They don't dart back and forth like the tiny ones you find in aquariums but glide slowly, magically, through the sunlight in stately lines: a fish parade. I watch them, run after them like a child, laughing, reaching out to touch them. But without turning they evade me, slipping smoothly by my fingers, their eyes revolving to watch me as they pass.

Suddenly I panic: Oh! I think, how can they breathe? They need water! I rush to find something, a pail or bucket, a large pot, anything I can fill and then put them in, to carry them to the river where they will be safe. But though I look and look, I can't find what I need. And meanwhile the fish keep gliding by serenely, watching me, smiling their secret smiles.

I wake up, my heart racing, sit up in bed, and switch on the bedside lamp. The room is familiar yet doesn't quite fit, as if I'm dreaming it instead of inhabiting it. The sky through the dirt-streaked window is a deep blue-black. Across the room stands the chipped wooden dresser my older sister Jess and I used so many years ago. I can see myself yanking open a drawer, riffling impatiently through piles of underwear, scarves, and socks to find the pair I want, Jess shouldering past me to get to the drawers on her side.

The soft too-whoo of an owl on its last round before settling into sleep sounds faintly in the distance. In reply, some tiny creature--a mouse, perhaps--rustles behind the baseboard next to the bed, instinctively scurrying for cover. I get up, throw on an old pair of jeans and a shirt I found yesterday in the closet, make myself a cup of coffee in the pale light of the kitchen lamp, and carry it through the parlor, down the dark hall, and into the tacked-on back room, the one Mom always planned to convert to a sewing room for herself but never did.

Now, as always, it's crammed with junk: three threadbare lumpy mattresses, a rocking chair with a broken cane seat, Mom's old black Singer, a small pile of moth-scarred deer and elk hides, cartons of canning jars and fabric remnants, stacks of dusty books, a rolled-up rag rug. And in the corner, the small black trunk with rusty metal edges, the one I've been meaning to open since I arrived, the one she's guarded from all of us as long as we've lived here.

From my pocket I slide the bunch of keys I found last night in Mom's treasure box and try several until the lock clicks open. Slowly I lift the lid, not realizing until I exhale deeply that I've been holding my breath. On top of piles of musty clothing lie several bulging manila folders, bundles of rubber-banded yellowing envelopes, and a collection of decorated metal and cardboard boxes, as well as some unidentifiable mounds covered with tissue paper and tied with cord.

From a manila envelope I pull out a faded photo of a very young woman--a girl, really--in a lacy summer dress and short veil, standing stiffly next to a grinning young man in a high-collared shirt, elaborately knotted tie, and dark suit: my parents on their wedding day. Then from its nest of tissue paper, a beaded, quilled multicolor leather bracelet falls into my lap: the one Mom's lost father guarded for her and that I brought back to her from the past.

Carefully I untie another bundle and unfold the paper: a child's sneaker, about the size that would fit a five-year-old, grimy white, dotted with faded pink and green circles like washed-out confetti. Lorrie's shoe. I open another: a lopsided ceramic clown Pete had made for Mom when he was six, and next to it, a blue plastic barrette, a tiny silver child-sized ring, and a dented Matchbox racing car. Underneath the bundle lies a black-and-white-spotted Composition notebook, the kind we used to use in school. I flip the pages, filled with Mom's rounded back-sloping writing, in navy blue ballpoint ink now faded to a reddish purple. It's a journal, one I never knew she kept. The entries are sporadic, each covering many pages. I catch a phrase here, a sentence there, and immediately I know I won't sleep again tonight, not until I've read it cover to cover and have met my mother in a place I've never seen her before.

Finally, at the very bottom, a flat square box. I open it to find a spooled reel of eight-track tape. I know what's on it: myself, at fifteen, playing Chopin. As I stare at the reel, lift it from its box, and turn it so the coppery rings catch the gleam of the lamp, I can hear in my mind the sinuous melody supported by the plangent chords, feel my hands find the phrases and shape the notes into a living, breathing world. In an instant, the space between now and then, a space I'd thought of as quiet and still, begins to move and vibrates like the air after the last gong of a cathedral bell.

CHAPTER I

I N 1970 WE WERE all living on our ranch on the eastern front of the Rockies in northern Montana: my mother, my stepfather Randy, my older sister Jess and I, and my little half-brother and -sister, Lorrie and Pete. The ranch was a half-starved, overgrazed outfit, ten miles outside Redmond, where we'd been living for six years, raising breed cows and selling the calves. Even in the good years, it barely supported us, with its sparse wheat and hay crops and the herd of scrawny cattle nosing its rocky acres for food. It took enormous amounts of work from all of us just to keep from slipping deeper into debt. Every spring, Randy would whip himself into a frenzy of optimism, and every winter he'd sink into self-pity laced with bitterness at the world for not having come through for him. Why did my mother tolerate him? All I could figure out at the time was that it had to do with money, and with a fourteen-year-old's certainty I pronounced this contemptible. It would be many years before I saw that my judgments of them, and of our life, were harshly simplistic.

But back then, all I wanted was to get away, to live somewhere else, to have a life totally different from the one I was living. The best I could do, though, was to escape to my favorite hiding place in the hayloft and read myself into another world. I could do this for hours if no one stopped me. On that particular early October afternoon, I'd only been there for what seemed a few minutes when I heard Jess' voice.

"Win! Dammit, where are you?"

I could tell she must be standing at the back door, looking over the weedy yard towards the dilapidated barn. If I kept quiet, maybe she'd give up. I knew she wanted me to help her with one of our list of endless chores. She hated the ranch even more than I did, but at sixteen, at least she had friends who could drive out and rescue her on weekends. I was stuck out there under the enormous sky, trudging back and forth between the house and the clothesline, out to the barn or the chicken coop, lugging a ten-pound pail of oats or a sack of chicken feed, assaulted by the odor of manure and chicken shit, pushing through snowdrifts or slogging through mud, wanting to be anywhere but there.

"Win?" Jess stood in the barn door. By raising my head, I could see her slim body backlit by the warm sunlight. She knew where I was; she'd only stopped using my hiding places herself a couple of years before. So I stood up and put my book under my arm.

"I thought so. What are you reading?"

"Jane Eyre." I held it up.

"Bet you're drooling over Mr. Rochester, huh? 'Oh, Winona, marry me, I must have you!'" She clasped her hands together and wrenched her face into a parody of a entreaty.

"Oh, shut up!" I didn't want to share the world I'd mixed from images sketched by the story and filled in with my imagined desires. Besides, I was only on Chapter 4; I didn't know who Mr. Rochester was, and I didn't want her to give away the plot.

"Well, come on and bring in the laundry. I've got to get supper started before they get back." She turned and walked out. I flopped back down and opened the book.

"And don't start reading again!" My skin prickled as it always did when she read my mind. I climbed down the ladder and crossed the stretch of pounded-down weeds between the barn and the clothesline. As I threw the sun-warmed sheets and towels into the clothes basket, inhaling their delicate smell, I looked back at the barn. The late afternoon light had turned the battered, colorless boards a golden bronze, the only time it looked beautiful to me. A wire fence marked off the barnyard behind it, and beyond stretched fields of yellow stubble, then the open rolling prairie, ending in a hazy range of bluish hills. A flock of crows croaked their way across the sky, lilac and gold where the sun was just dipping out of sight, darkening to sapphire at the far edge.

A few cows stared mournfully at me over the fence. I stuck out my tongue at them as I hoisted the basket against my chest, just under the small breasts I was still proudly self-conscious about, and lugged it into the big, high-ceilinged kitchen where Jess was wrestling with the rickety ironing board, coaxing it into the one position in which it wouldn't fall down. My heart sank.

"Jess, I'll do the potatoes if you'll iron."

"Forget it." She hated ironing as much as I did. "Come on. I warmed up the iron for you."

She sat down at the table, pushed her long, sable-brown hair behind her ears, and began peeling. Her dark eyebrows pinched momentarily into a frown, then smoothed out over her green-flecked hazel eyes. She was the pretty contrast, I knew, to my plumpish, freckled, frizzy-red-haired self. My body had finished its last three years of awkward changes, but I was still adjusting to my newer self. I kept wishing I'd turn into someone who looked like Jess, but I didn't hold out much hope for it.

I sighed and crossed over to the board, detouring the fifteen feet to the counter to flick on the radio. Mom complained you could get five miles of exercise easy each day just by cooking three meals in our kitchen.

"Oh bury me not on the lone prairie
Where the coyote howls and the wind blows free."

It felt like the coyote was wailing right there in the room.

"Put on something else." Jess flicked a long snake of potato skin onto the table and dropped a naked lump into the chipped blue bowl in her lap.

I went back and twirled the dial. Hank Williams on one station; Lawrence Welk on another. I settled on Loretta Lynn and snapped a shirt onto the ironing board. Suddenly Jess marched out of the room.

I didn't ask her why. In the last six months she'd become temperamental, her familiar easy-going self taken over by a touchy, eccentric witch who could be summoned by nothing more than an innocent question or an insignificant demand. I went on ironing. A few moments later, she came back, holding her portable phonograph. I let out a whoop and helped her set it up. The album she'd chosen unleashed a rhythmic subversive beat into the room.

> *"Looking for a job in Memphis*
> *Working for the man every night and day....*
> *Rollin', rollin', rollin' on the river."*

We both swayed in place, hypnotized, chanting the words with half-closed eyes, like ancient priestesses.

> *"Heard it through the grapevine*
> *An' I'm just about to lose my mind,*
> *Honey, honey ...."*

Jess' feet began to form unfamiliar patterns as her body broke into a dance, turning one way, then another. I gaped at her.

"Want me to teach you?" She took my hands. I imitated her movements, slowly at first, then catching the pattern, slipping into the beat like a foot into a comfortable shoe. Touching my hand, then my shoulder, she guided me, approaching then receding. Giddy with movement, we laughed, jigging our hips from side to side, tossing our heads, Jess' hair flickering in the light from the overhead bulb shaded by a pink glass half-globe.

"What the hell are you doing?"

We froze in mid-step at the clang of Randy's voice. We hadn't heard the front door open, and now Randy's flushed face stared at us from the living room, his eyes half-covered by the V of his frowning eyebrows. Behind him Mom peered anxiously at us, shaking her head warningly in slow motion. Lorrie and Pete held onto her dress, Pete's thumb in his mouth, Lorrie tugging nervously at her hair.

"You're back early," I stammered.

Without glancing at me, Randy crossed to the phonograph and snatched the arm away with a scratchy rasp that raised the hair on the back of my neck. Jess cried out as if she'd stepped on a piece of glass. I knew how many hours of weekend work that album had cost her, and I ached to scream insults at Randy, to punch him in the nose. Instead I clutched Jess' hand. She pulled loose.

"Leave my record player alone!" She stared at him, eyes blazing. Randy's gray-grizzled sandy hair seemed to rise from his head like electrified shavings.

"I told you not to play that trash in this house, didn't I?" he barked. Jess said nothing. He took a step toward her. Immediately Mom crossed over to him and put her hand on his arm.

"She didn't mean to upset you, honey." I could feel her golden voice like a warm bath on my skin. "Did you, Jess?" Her eyes pleaded with Jess: Do this for me. Jess' body stayed rigid as a taut wire.

"I can play my own record player if I want to!"

"Not in my kitchen, you can't!"

Randy's head jutted forward toward Jess, and his bared teeth glinted. Mom put her arm around him and gently tugged him toward her.

"Come on, honey. Let's go in the other room. I'll get you a beer, and the kids can watch *Gunsmoke*."

At this, the Lorrie and Pete statues came to life and rushed past us into the hall. Randy's shoulders began to drop slightly.

"Get that thing out of here." His voice was still harsh, but his body had surrendered to her before he realized it. "And what about the cattle? They have to be fed."

"The girls will do it."

They moved toward the door and disappeared. I became aware that I was shaking with rage, as much at Mom as at Randy. At that moment, I hated the honey in her voice, her cowardly fawning on him, her craven disregard of his obvious injustice. Capitulation to a tyrant was worse than the tyranny itself, in my book.

I glanced at Jess, waiting for her signal: revolution or retreat? Her face was turned away toward the still-open back door. We could hear Mom murmuring to Randy over the crackly TV voices, and Randy's growled answer. Jess hadn't moved. Her cheeks were wet, her eyes hard, distant. I wanted to hug her, to put my hand on her shoulder like tough guys in the movies did when their buddies had lost someone they loved. Instead I switched on the radio.

"What do you want to hear?"

She sat down slowly at the table, staring at the half-filled bowl. When she finally spoke, her voice was firm.

"You choose." She picked up the knife and began to peel.

I bypassed KCOW, Randy's favorite station, and settled for a top 40s out of Billings, turning the volume so only we could hear it. Then I unplugged her record player and carried it back to our bedroom, centering it carefully in its place of honor on her side of the dresser. Through the window I could see the bright white fingernail-clipping of a moon hanging low in the blue-black sky, waiting to disappear.

CHAPTER 2

W INONA! ANSWER THE DOOR!" It was two weeks later, and I was practicing a Bach fugue on the piano, grimacing at each wrong note. I sighed and stopped playing, listening to the agitated knocking at the front door. As I sat there, Mom passed by on her way from the kitchen, giving my shoulder a push.

"Why can't you ever do what I say when I tell you?"

She walked to the door, skirting the nubby brown tweed sofa and kicking down an upturned corner of the braided rug, quick on her feet for a heavy woman, her tail of dark hair hanging down between her broad shoulders. I watched the green-striped cotton pants stretched tight over her big rear end, her heelless blue Keds flopping against the floorboards, wishing she'd lose weight, would wear pretty black flats; would vanish into the stratosphere.

"Why, hello, Zip."

There on the doorstep was Zippy Purdue, holding an envelope. Usually we picked up the mail down at the P.O. in Redmond, but whenever something interesting arrived, Zippy would find some reason to drive out with it in person. I knew he was in high school, in tenth grade, the class below Jess and two above mine, that he'd grown about two feet in the past year, and that he liked to stare at boobs—anyone's, including my mother's. When I saw the slicked-back dirt-blond hair topping his pimply face, I felt a surge of burning rage for him that I didn't fully understand, and contempt for my mother for being nice to him.

Zippy grinned hopefully at the white lettering on Mom's sweatshirt and held out the envelope.

"Thought you'd want to see this right away, Mrs. Daggett," he gloated, as if he'd done something heroic.

"Why's that, Zippy?" Mom smiled at him.

"The postmark's California!" Zippy beamed as if he'd sent the letter himself. "You ever been there, Mrs. Daggett?"

"No, I never have." Mom turned the letter over, squinted at the return address, then looked up.

"Well, thanks for coming so far out of your way, Zip. And tell your folks hello. I'll be seeing Verrie next week at the Lodge meeting."

Mom closed the door on his crestfallen face. I followed her into the kitchen and sat down at the Formica-topped table as she opened the letter and read it. I didn't bother asking her about it yet, knowing that she never told us anything until she was good and ready. She shook her head once, then pursed her lips and raised her eyebrows, so I knew she was surprised. She folded it, put it back into the envelope, got up and left the room briefly. When she returned, I couldn't hold back any more.

"Who was that from?"

She shook her head firmly.

"It's about a private matter, Win. I don't want to hear any more about it from you."

I opened my mouth to protest.

"And I'd like you not to mention it to Randy."

There wasn't a chance in hell that I'd talk to him about it, and she knew it. I didn't even deign to answer her, I was so insulted. I turned and stomped out indignantly to water the stock. When the cold drove me back to the house, I found a note from Mom saying she'd taken the old Chevy and gone with the kids down to Redmond to get some stuff she needed for supper. Instantly I seized the chance to run to her room and open the box in which I knew she kept her private papers. Lying on top was the letter. I had to reread it twice before I could make any sense of it.

Dear Mrs. Daggett,

You'll probably be surprised to get this letter. It wasn't hard to find you once I figured out how. My father, George Reynolds, was your first husband Lee's brother, so you are my aunt and your daughters are my cousins. I'll be visiting my mother in Helena sometime this summer, and I could drive to Redmond and meet you then. I would very much like to know the rest of my family.

Please let me know you got this letter.

Hoping to hear from you soon,

your niece Marilyn

Fragments of feeling and ideas whirled through my mind. My real father had died when I was three, so of course I hardly remembered him. Jess remembered only a little more, including something unpleasant about what must have been the funeral: lots of people crying, a screaming argument, then nothing more. I'd tried unsuccessfully to dig some information out of Mom, but she never seemed to want to talk about him, and we never heard from anyone from his side of the family. The only pictures in which he appeared were the ones of their wedding. The year before I'd actually gone to the county courthouse to try and find his birth certificate, but it wasn't there. Mom had gotten angry at me when she found out. She'd said that Randy, whom she married when I was six, had adopted me and Jess, so he was our father now, and then they had Lorrie and Pete, and *that* was our family.

This letter felt like a message from a distant world, from another lifetime. I kept staring at it. The handwriting was dark and clear. An image of the writer swam into my mind: an elegantly dressed young woman exuding the odor of expensive perfume, knees crossed, leaning back on the soft cushions of her green velvet sofa, her eyelashes darkened with the mascara I wasn't allowed to use.

I checked the postmark: Berkeley, California. Berkeley! Maybe

Marilyn was a hippie. Long flowered skirts, leather-strapped sandals, hair down to her waist, smelling of sandalwood incense and pot. Of course I didn't know what either one smelled like: sandalwood as a mixture of nutmeg and burning leaves, and pot like heady mulled cider was the best I could imagine. The closest I'd come to a hippie was at the Bijou, watching *Monterey Pop* and *Easy Rider*.

I roused myself and put the letter back, only a few minutes before Mom and the kids returned. She didn't say a word about it as I peeled the inevitable potatoes and she stirred the lumpy beef stew. I kept stealing little glances at her, then staring out the window at the range of hills we used to run through, playing explorer, castaways, cowboys and Indians. I wanted to ask her about Marilyn: Had she ever met her? What was George—my uncle—like? Why hadn't she stayed in touch with them? My chest clamped down on the words.

When Jess came home in time to set out the silverware and plates on the kitchen table, Mom gave me one warning glance: if she wasn't going to talk about it, I'd better keep quiet, too. A few minutes later, when Randy stomped in from outside, Pete and Lorrie exploded at him from the back room where they'd been playing, throwing themselves at his legs and wrapping their arms around his waist. He stood there like a tall pole, heavily built, with well-used muscles under his shirt, while the kids tried to climb him. I watched him hoist them up to sit in the crook of his arm and was torn by two wishes at once: to be back in their small, happy bodies, nestling my face into his warm neck; and to be utterly sundered from him, from this family, from this bright room steaming with green beans, and out alone in the dark mysterious waiting world.

AT DINNER, AS LORRIE and Pete chattered artlessly with Randy and each other, Mom seemed preoccupied. Randy joked with Petey about the fishing rod he was going to buy him, and Lorrie begged for one, too. When Mom put a bowl of steaming ears of corn on the table, Lorrie and Pete cheered. The bowl emptied as it passed from hand to hand until it reached me. I passed it on without taking any. Randy squinted at me.

"What's the matter with you?"

I was silent.

"Answer me!"

"I don't like corn." I'd developed an aversion to it during the previous year.

"You'll eat it whether you like it or not. We pay good money for food!"

"I don't have to."

The room became completely silent. Mom turned away from the stove.

"Don't, Win."

"Don't what? I don't want any!"

"Just eat it."

I could hear Petey and Lorrie's breathing and the ticking of the clock. I looked over at Jess. She was staring at her plate, her face rigid. Her eyes flicked sideways at me, and she shook her head imperceptibly. All she wanted was to smooth things down until she could get her other foot out the door. No help there.

Randy picked up an ear of corn and threw it onto my plate.

"I said, *eat* it! All of it!"

I stared at the corn without moving.

Randy leaned forward, shoved my plate so close to me it touched my chest.

"You'll sit here 'til you eat it."

I pushed the plate away, lifted it and dumped the ear back into the bowl, staring at him with all the hate I could muster, daring him to cross the line he'd never crossed before. Suddenly he picked up the bowl, held it a second, then flung it down with a grunt of contempt, jumped up, grabbed his coat, and disappeared through the door. We heard the truck door slam, the motor race to life, the tires hiss in a circle, the truck drone away into the distance. Then we all breathed deep and giggled with relief. Except for Mom. She looked at me soberly.

"You're going to have a tough life," she declared.

I WAS LYING ON the bed, reading, when Jess came into our room later, getting ready for bed. She had some kind of cream on her face. "Trying to scare the horses, huh?" Randy had said after he came back within a half hour of his abrupt departure. Now I watched her wipe it off and smooth her skin carefully. Would I be doing that myself soon? I wondered skeptically.

"Jess."

"What?"

"Did you ever meet any of Dad's relatives? I mean *Dad*, not Randy. Like, Dad's brother George?"

She stared at me. She looked so puzzled I had to laugh. That annoyed her, and she started to give me the cold shoulder. So, swearing her to secrecy, I told her about the letter. I could see the shock of it hit her, drawing her concentration inward until she seemed oblivious to anything outside herself. Finally she noticed me again.

"Isn't it strange we don't know any of them?" I asked. "Dad's family, or Mom's either?" I kept my eyes on her face, but she didn't move a muscle.

"Maybe we wouldn't want to know them."

"Why not? *I* do. They *have* to be better than Randy."

She snorted. "That's not saying much." She picked up her hairbrush and attacked her hair. "Don't count too much on this Marilyn. Let's wait and see if she ever really shows up."

"She will."

"Why?"

"She just has to."

Jess smiled at me pityingly. I hated that.

"Jess! Sometimes I wish we were Indians."

She stared at me, stunned. Now I had her full attention. "Are you nuts, Win?" Being an Indian in Montana was not something you wanted to be if you didn't have to. I sat up.

"Then we couldn't be related to Randy at all. We wouldn't be anything like him."

"We're *not* related to him, Win. Remember that."

"And we could get those special scholarships for Indians and go to college."

"I don't want to go to college. I just want to get out of here and go somewhere and get a job."

"Where?"

"Anywhere. Bozeman or Missoula or Great Falls."

"Well, *I* could go to college, then. I want to."

She got into bed.

"You *should* go, Win. You're always reading anyway, so you might as well read there. Get yourself a scholarship and go. I'll move to Missoula. You can live with me when I get my own place."

So we told each other our bedtime story, about how we'd escape one day, painting all the details—the apartment we'd decorate with bright bedspreads and hanging plants, the exotic dishes we'd cook, the friends who'd drop in on the spur of the moment to eat with us, the movies we'd see whenever we wanted— until one of us fell asleep and the other turned out the lamp between our beds.

Almost as soon as the light was off, Jess was asleep, her breathing slowed and deep. I lay awake, forming an imagined life in Berkeley, college, huge libraries full of books. I was halfway asleep myself when I heard familiar sounds from Mom and Randy's room, soft at first, then louder, her panting gasps, his grunts. I put my hands over my ears and hummed loudly to myself to block the noises that made my own body hatefully hot and prickly.

Suddenly I remembered the first time I'd heard them, when I was six. They'd gotten married only a few weeks before. I'd been terrified and run crying to their door.

"He's hurting you," I'd sobbed. "I heard you yelling!"

Mom had come out, a blanket thrown around her, and had taken me back to my room.

"It's just the opposite," she'd laughed when I told her what had scared me. "Sometimes we get so excited about loving each other that words aren't big enough, and we start growling and yelping and making funny noises." She tucked me in and stood up, studying my doubtful expression.

"You know, if we could sing better, that's what we'd do," she smiled. "Yes. I think we're just trying to find the right song." She leaned down and kissed me. "You'll sing it yourself when you're older."

Then she went out, closing the door. And during the next few years, when I heard them at night, I'd imagine them like two animals, two elephants maybe, singing in their snorting language, and go back to sleep happy.

Not any more. Now I needed to drown them out with my own humming, with my own body's roar, until it was safe to take my hands away and let the translucent silence fold me into sleep.

MARIE

January 23, 1968

    God, I love him. I'm pulled toward him by his heat, the waves of heat rising from his skin, as if he's got a furnace inside him. If I hold my hand right next to him, not quite touching, I can feel heat radiating out from him, like a volcano that churns molten lava until it boils over into the air. If I touch his skin in bed, he'll twitch away from my icy hands or feet. But then he'll push himself back towards me and pull my hands under his armpits, and I'll tuck my feet between his calves and lay my nose on his back, and I'll burn from the heat of him.

    Don't they say, "Cold hands, warm heart"? He says the reason my hands and feet are so cold is that all the fuel in me goes to stoking the fire between my legs. When he slips into me, he groans as if I'm burning him, which I can't be, because his own cock is so hot. It makes everything that's happened during the day—my yelling at the kids, his pissy moods—fade away, as if someone turned a spotlight on our bodies, and all the rest slips into the dark.

    His heat was the first thing I ever noticed about Randy. I was sitting by myself at the counter at the Two Elks Cafe. I'd gone there after work, just for half an hour, even though I knew I should have headed straight home. It was the one time in the day I could be alone, no customers, no kids, no one yapping at me, telling me what to do, or what they needed from me. I had my eyes closed, inhaling the steam from my cup, thinking as much about nothing at all as I could, when all of a sudden my whole back got warm, as if someone had built a big wood fire behind me when I wasn't looking. And at the same moment I felt a puff of air on my cheek. My body knew what was happening before I did: my nipples crimped up and my face got all flushed.

I looked over my shoulder and saw a man standing real close to me. He took a step back, so I could see him better. He had sandy-colored hair, kind of kinky-wavy, and a reddish face. But what held my attention was his eyes. I only registered their color later—a deep gray speckled with brown—but right away I could feel their hot life reaching out for me, pulling me into him.

It turned out he'd only been in town a few weeks. He'd been working a while on a ranch near Lakeville when the owner let him go because he took a day off without asking permission. So he'd come here and convinced Angus MacLean to let him help stuff the deer and elk the rich dudes shoot during the season, when they decide to take the heads home to show off to their friends. He told me he planned to take off for El Paso as soon as the season was over, where a friend of his had a trucking job lined up for him.

That's what he said, but his eyes kept slipping down to my boobs. That was nothing new. Most men can't seem to get their eyes off my chest. But instead of making him lose concentration and stutter, like most, it seemed to speed his words up, as if he'd swallowed three cups of coffee in about two seconds. He told me all the details about digging out deer brains, about tanning hides and preserving antlers, and I kept nodding as if I'd waited all my life to learn about taxidermy. When all I could think was, I want him. I want him. I want to feel his big hands, with those short wide fingers, running up my sides, slipping into the crease between my breast and my ribs. I want to feel his teeth gently nipping my neck from my earlobe to my collarbone.

I was so embarrassed to be thinking thoughts like these, thoughts I'd never had before about any man, not even Lee, that I sat stiff as a nun in church, nodding and nodding like one of those fake dogs people put in the back windows of their cars that nod with each bounce in the road. *He must think I'm a dumb idiot for sure, I thought, but it didn't seem to matter much in the end. When he invited me to get a drink at the Rainbow, I heard myself say yes before I could think, and we went and I got drunk on one beer, and we laughed and told silly jokes, and he said maybe El Paso was going to have to wait 'til summer.*

Then I told him I had to go, that my two little girls were being babysat by the elderly neighbor whom I'd have to pay fifty cents for each hour I was late. He didn't object, just drove me home. I hadn't thought he'd really paid attention to my telling him I had kids, but the very next day I found a box on my doorstep, and inside were two big dolls, with a card that said "For Jess and Win." And my heart just opened up.

But that night, when he stopped his truck in front of the house, and turned toward me, I'd opened my mouth to say goodnight, and then, with neither of us making any move I could sense, we were at each other so fast and hard I could hardly grab a breath.

It was all hands, mouths, noses bumping, knees between legs, some-one's shirt tearing, hot flesh on flesh, breath heaving, tongues licking, curling, pushing, pushing harder. Sounds like in a barn, grunts and moans, and I lost all sense of who he was, who I was. It was all feeling and touch and the dark straining into each other, over and over, until I ripped open and the lava in me burst and spilled over into waves of pleasure.

When I could look around, the windows were fogged with drops of water, as if it had been raining inside the cab. I heaved myself up, not daring to look straight at him as he lay on his back, his arms under his head, his eyes following every move I made. I'd suddenly become someone I no longer knew, and I was dizzy with trying to put myself back inside the picture I'd lived in all my life, until three hours before.

I began to fish my clothes from off the floor and under the seat and pull on what I found. When I slipped my breasts into my bra, he reached out and stopped me.

"Don't put them away yet," he said, and ran the back of his hand gently across my nipples, to and fro, watching me watch his cock get hard in time to their swelling. And wouldn't you know, we were at it

again, as hot and eager as if we'd never touched each other at all.

And what I know is this: In the seven years since that first night, it's never gone away. Turns out that wasn't all there was, either: Under his strutting maleness that sometimes drives me crazy with wanting him, and sometimes just drives me crazy, he's got that soft heart. No one gets to really feel it but me, and the kids when he plays with them. But it's always there. And I know that, no matter what, if I can just get him alone, in our room, I can touch it and make everything all right. I can take his scalding thoughts and pour the fire from them into his body, and we can burn it all away. I want my girls to know that they have this power in them, a power as great as an earthquake, as rain in a drought, and just as mysterious. I want them to know that we have in us a power that helps run this world, and the whole starry universe.

CHAPTER 3

FOR THE NEXT FEW days I thought almost constantly about the letter from Marilyn: as I sat in class, during breaks from doing homework and chores, practicing the piano. I could recall every word of it, and the return address was seared into my brain.

As I rushed around on Saturday morning, getting ready to drive into Redmond with Mom, it was still on my mind. Mom was scrutinizing the shopping list in minute detail, making absolutely sure she hadn't forgotten anything. You did that when each round trip to the supermarket involved a half-hour drive in good weather over thirty miles of rough road, and used up three gallons of gas. I almost always went with her, for my piano lesson, and usually Jess came too, supposedly to help Mom, but really to get another chance to escape the ranch for a few hours.

That day Randy had gotten Lorrie and Pete up at six o'clock to go fishing; their enthusiasm of the previous evening had pretty well leaked out overnight, but by the time he got them dressed and into the pickup, they were pumped up again, waving their poles like banners and shaking the worm jar every ten seconds to make sure the worms had survived the night. I could barely remember a time when I had loved to thread a glistening worm on the hook, and stand next to Randy, shivering in the growing light, watching for the telltale dark roll underneath the surface of the water. You couldn't have paid me to go now.

After a few false starts, Mom and I settled into the old Chevy that smelled of sour milk from six years' worth of spilled baby bottles. Various dolls, playing cards, and shreds of paper littered the back seat. Jess had decided to stay home and spend endless hours setting her hair and painting her fingernails in preparation for a date that evening. She was doing this more and more, and I'd given up ribbing her about it.

As Mom plopped onto the seat, she tossed some envelopes onto the space between us, and I leafed through them curiously. She turned the key, and the car lurched to life and lumbered onto the county road. I decided to stick a toe in the water.

"Did you answer that letter?" My voice sounded too high to me, shot through with duplicity. Mom glanced briefly at me, then went back to staring through the windshield at the brown-stubbled fields whisking by, blue-dotted with late asters. She was silent.

I tried again.

"You know, the one you got on Tuesday, from California."

"Why is that letter so important to you?" Mom pushed her body briefly backward against the seat, then relaxed. "You're too curious for your own good, Win. You shouldn't go poking around looking for trouble. We're all fine right here."

Something rose up from my chest and filled my head with a reddish-black noise.

"It may be fine for you, but I hate it!" I realized I was nearly yelling, and tried to calm my voice. "All I ever do here is take care of the stupid cows and the stupid chickens, and we never go anywhere! I can't wait to get out of here!"

"Oh, really?" Mom's lip curled. "And just where will you go? You won't find it easy to get on with people, what with your temper and your weird ideas."

"*You're* weird, not me!" Now I was yelling unrestrainedly. "You're weird to even want to stay here and be married to a weirdo like Randy!"

Mom took one hand off the wheel and backhanded me on the breastbone. Surprise knocked the breath out of me, rather than the blow, which didn't really hurt. I gasped, and though I tried not to, I began to cry. Mom seemed to sink a few inches into the seat.

"I'm sorry, Win." I pulled as far away as I could and hunched over toward the side window.

"I wish you wouldn't aggravate me like that, Win. I hate it when I lose my temper."

"Oh, now it's *my* fault you hit me!"

Her eyebrows drew into a frown; then she took a deep breath and let it out slowly, smoothing her expression into inscrutability. She pulled the car to the side of the road and stopped. I could feel her staring at me the way she used to do when she was deciding if I was old enough to do something new and risky.

"There's something you should know. We may lose the ranch."

At first, sunk in my self-righteous sulk, I didn't register her words. Then I sat up straight, my mouth open, shocked out of crying. I tried to speak but couldn't. Much as I was sick of ranch life, the possibility that it could be pulled out from under us, whirling us into the unknown, disturbed me profoundly.

"Randy's applied for a loan at the bank to tide us over 'til the spring wheat crop comes in, but it's very iffy," she went on. "That's why he's so edgy lately. If we get the loan, we may be all right. If we don't. . . ."

Her voice hesitated.

"I try to calm him down when he gets upset. But sometimes . . . ."

Again she stopped. In my mind's eye I saw her reach to touch Randy, steering him away from his own monsters toward the peaceful calm of her voice, her smile, holding his red-hot fear against her wide body and cooling it with soothing breaths. But what did she do with it then? How long could she carry it before it flew out at me?

As if she could hear my thoughts, she reached over and put her hand on my arm.

"I could use your help on this, Win."

"How?"

"Don't be so hard on Randy. Just try and be nice to him, okay? Remember, he's had a hard life, with his mother dying so young and his stepmother hating him so. And his two little sisters pushing him out of their lives, too."

I sighed in exasperation. I'd heard this plea for my sympathy from

Mom so often it had no more meaning to me than the pledge of allegiance we recited every morning at school.

"So it's supposed to be okay when he yells and blows up at nothing because he's had a hard life?" I snorted. "Forget it."

"Win, I need you to help me. I'm not saying it's okay. He's better with little kids than with teenagers, I guess. But the way things are right now—"

She looked at me pleadingly. Exhilaration mixed with fear began to percolate through me: My mother needed me to be strong. She, on whom I'd leaned blindly all these years, now needed to lean on me. Pride pumped me up. I could do anything.

"Okay."

She squeezed my arm lightly, started the car, and we drove the next five miles in silence. As we rounded the last curve of road before Redmond I felt full of virtuous intentions. Then the letter floated back into my mind. I saw it lying in Mom's treasure box, white and gleaming. And I knew suddenly and absolutely that I was going to answer it myself.

WHEN WE GOT BACK to the ranch, I began putting the groceries away, shoving things into the cramped freezer compartment and stowing boxes and bottles on the pantry shelves as Mom washed the lima beans for supper.

"Mom. How come you don't have any relatives?"

She stared at me, puzzled.

"I've told you, Win. My family is dead."

"But how can that be? There must be someone, some great-aunts or something."

She shrugged. "Why are you so interested in this all of a sudden?"

"I don't know. I just thought about it. You've never told us anything, where you came from, what it was like, who were your mother and father. Why they died."

"You don't have to know that, Win. You're here, and I'm here, and that's all in the past. It's not part of your life."

"But, Mom!" Why did I want to know? I was struggling with a new thought: If something had been part of her life, then inevitably it was a part of mine. I couldn't tell her that I was about to reach toward someone connected to her invisible past, the same one that tugged on me. As I groped for something to say, she interrupted me.

"That's enough. Subject closed."

From the way she bent over the beans, I knew she meant it. I watched her a moment, then finished putting the food away and marched to the piano, pouring my confusion into Bach's intricately interwoven strands of harmony.

Later, after Jess had left for the evening with three of her friends in Bonnie's rattletrap Studebaker, Mom and Randy decided to go back to town and see a movie. Seizing the opportunity, I offered to baby-sit Lorrie and Pete, and after an endless game of War, six books about various talking animals, and twelve choruses of "Puff the Magic Dragon," they fell asleep. Immediately I retrieved Marilyn's letter and set about composing an answer.

Dear Marilyn,

Thank you for your letter. I'm your cousin Winona Daggett. I'm fourteen years old, and my sister Jess (short for Jessamine) is sixteen. My mother is thirty-four, and she is married now to Randy Daggett, my stepfather. They got married in 1962, eight years ago, when I was almost six. Jess and I have a half-sister Lorrie, who is five, and a half-brother Peter, who is almost four. If he was alive my father (your uncle Lee) would be thirty-six. We have lived on our ranch for six years. Before that we lived in Redmond, which is a little town not too far from Great Falls. I'd like to live in a big city like you, even though Montana is very pretty. I'm in ninth grade, and I like to read and play piano, and to travel a lot.

With best wishes, I remain,
Your cousin Winona (Win)

P.S. I am writing this letter to you privately, meaning no one but me knows about it. I hope you can keep a secret.

P.P.S. Are you a hippie?

I stared at it a moment, then crossed out the P.P.S., even though I really wanted to know the answer. I knew I'd exaggerated about traveling. What I meant was that I *wanted* to, with a fierce longing I couldn't explain. And I had my doubts about the closing salutation, which I'd copied from a novel I'd read in which the characters spent all their time writing letters to each other. I knew, if I let myself, I could brood about each sentence for weeks, so I grabbed a clean piece of stationery and an envelope, rewrote and addressed it, and slipped it into one of my schoolbooks.

The next evening I showed it to Jess, first making her swear she wouldn't tell Mom. She read it carefully, taking a long time, then refolded it and handed it back.

"Are you really going to mail this?"

"Sure. Why not?" I bluffed past my disappointment at her cool reaction. "Don't you want to find out who she is?"

Jess was quiet for so long I was about to prompt her.

"Don't get your hopes up too high, that's all."

"What do you mean?"

"She probably won't ever show up. She might not even answer."

"She will."

Jess smiled at me pityingly from her two years' superior understanding.

"She will because she has to!" Enraged, I snatched the letter back, put it in the envelope, and sealed it. Jess picked up her hairbrush and attacked her hair, staring gravely at herself in the mirror, like a general studying the terrain of a coming battle that would decide the fate of nations.

CHAPTER 4

T HE RICKETY SCHOOL BUS jerked to a stop in front of Redmond Elementary and Middle School. Across the yard loomed the non-color stucco walls and steel-framed windows, faded yellow shades rolled up for the day. We piled out, carrying book bags and lunch boxes, the younger kids running for the door, Corinne and I lagging behind.

The school, a one-story L-shaped building, was so familiar to us we'd stopped registering its utilitarian gloominess. We no longer noticed the packed-down dirt in the yard that turned to mud in the rain and lay buried for months under snow in winter. Over the summer, when the school stood empty, a hodge-podge of weeds—crabgrass, dandelions, prairie grass, Indian paintbrush, clover, and lupine—would spring up, flourish, and fade there, only to be mowed down a week before the first day of school in September.

Now we climbed the four concrete steps, walked through the doors, and sauntered into the wide entrance hall. The brown linoleum floor, with its ugly pattern of random green and white squiggles, gleamed dully, mopped overnight by crumpled-faced Mr. Peasley, who'd been janitor since the Ice Age when our friends' parents went to school there themselves.

We passed the two glass-fronted wooden display cases, the one on the left exhibiting school trophies and pictures of teams of fresh-faced boys in crew-cuts and uniforms holding footballs and basketballs, the one on the right filled with a mixture of the lower-graders' paintings in neon-bright colors, supposedly coordinated with the ever-changing large seasonal mural next it, produced by the middle-schoolers. As the year unrolled, September's collection of autumn leaves was replaced in succession by October's pumpkins, witches, and ghosts against a black background, then by turkeys and Pilgrims, Santa Claus and his non-aerodynamic reindeer, lopsided Lincolns and Washingtons in ill-fitting stovetop hats and pigtails, leprechauns and four-leaved clovers, and spring flowers among weeping clouds and impossibly fat robins of a size never seen within a thousand miles of Montana. We upper-graders scorned what we'd once loved: the special project afternoons of large-scale planning, task-dividing, drawing and cutting out the pieces, then carefully assembling everything under the joint supervision of the fourth-, fifth-, and sixth-grade teachers.

Once, in third grade, having read a story about Pocahontas and being fascinated at the time by weddings, I suggested a November mural depicting a Thanksgiving feast being held in an Indian village in honor of Pocahontas' marriage to John Smith, the Pilgrims seated cross-legged on the floor of a long-house, being treated by the welcoming tribe to a feast of venison, maize, and pemmican. This idea drew a warm response from some of the students. Our teacher, a thin, gray-faced woman named Edith Sprewell, registered absolutely no reaction and said she'd check with the other teachers about the subject. A few days later she assigned us our mural tasks: ten dancing turkeys for a multi-animal panorama of "Harvest Home on the Farm." I considered asking her what had happened to my idea, but the lines around her pinched mouth stopped me.

Corinne adjusted her steps to fit mine, pushing her lanky, mouse-brown hair behind her ears, as we turned right into the long corridor which connected all the middle-school classrooms. At five feet two she was a couple of inches shorter than I, and weighed about two-thirds of what I did. No matter how much she ate, she never gained weight, and next to her I felt like a football linebacker. Her skinniness wasn't helped by the too-big clothes her mother bought her in the hope she'd be inspired to grow into them. She and I had been best friends since the first day of first grade, when we'd been seated by chance next to each other, both of us trying to hide how scared we were by the school, which seemed enormous because it was so unfamiliar. Now, in our last year there, we treated it with affectionate contempt. Next year we'd be going to the high school down the road. The idea was exciting and frightening. First we'd be the new kids, then the cheerleaders would be our friends, and even eventually ourselves. Our boyfriends—even more exciting—would be the basketball and football stars the whole town watched on Friday nights.

In the greenish-yellow-walled homeroom, which was also Mrs. Belser's English and drama classroom, we slipped into our adjacent seats, and waved and called to our friends, who included almost all the thirteen white kids. Against the back wall, five Indian kids—three boys and two girls, alike enough in our eyes to be cousins—sat in a quiet row, murmuring now and then to each other, part of the background like the posters tacked to the faded paint ("Frontier Days, Fort Peck," "Turkey Trot, Redmond High School, November 23"). Abruptly it struck me that they might have been dropped there from another planet. They never raised their hands, speaking only when the teacher called on them, and then in short sentences and low voices, fading immediately back into silent observers of an alien, unpredictable species.

"What are you staring at?" Corinne asked.

I jumped; was I staring? I fished around for something to say. Until that year Corinne and I had told each other everything. Now, for some reason, I'd begun to hold some things back, toying with them, often deciding not to talk to her about them, to keep them secret. Not from shame, exactly, but from a desire to fashion a secret life for myself, an extravagant tapestry whose colors, I knew, would fade with the telling from rich purple, emeralds, and scarlet to washed-out pastels.

As I hesitated, the bell rang sharp and loud, and Mrs. Belser, her gray-white pompadour fluffed into immobility like a marshmallow, stood up as the class fell silent for the morning ritual: the Pledge of Allegiance, the list of announcements, again the low hum of murmured gossip, rustling pages, scribbled last-minute homework. Another bell, and everyone was on their feet, piling books together, shuffling into the aisles and into the hall, and the day was launched.

OUR FIRST CLASS AFTER lunch was my favorite, American History with Mrs. Isaacson. This was her first year teaching in Redmond. Her husband had taken over the forest ranger station outside of town from Ed Beidecke, who'd retired to Arizona because of his wife's arthritis, and the Isaacsons had moved here during the summer.

You could tell at a glance that Sarah Isaacson didn't come from around here. She had almost pure-white skin with a sprinkle of beige freckles across her nose, and short blond-gold ringlets which made her look as if she hadn't graduated from high school herself more than a year ago, though she was actually in her mid-twenties. She wore tailored suits with trim white blouses, instead of perky dresses, and talked to us levelly and without condescension, instead of in the high-pitched monotone most of the teachers used. She was a little taller than I, five-five, delicate-looking, her green-gray eyes serious under startlingly dark eyebrows.

She looked so young and delicate, we'd wondered if she might be easy to intimidate, but she handled us on the first day of class. Straight off, she told us to take out our notebooks and write an essay about our families' history: When had our first relative come to this country? to Montana? to Redmond? and from where, and why? When Jamie Ross protested, voicing for all of us the complaint that this was history class, not composition, and that we didn't know that much about our families, anyway, her voice grew sharp.

"You should," she uttered. "History is the story of what really happened, not just to kings and presidents and generals, but to ordinary people like you and your parents and grandparents. It's not just about wars and treaties. It's about how people lived, and what they worried about, why they moved from one place to another, where they worked and why they lost their jobs, and their farms, and sometimes their lives." She looked around, meeting the eyes of each of us, taking her time.

"You can't understand yourselves," she finally said, "until you understand how you got here."

Many of the kids looked puzzled, their expressions tinted with scorn that warded off the sting of incomprehension. But her words buzzed and expanded in my head. I'd never thought of history that way before, and afterward I could never think of it any other. As for the importance of knowing where I came from, that I'd learn soon enough.

She had us each create an imaginary family which experienced every era we studied. Mine were the Warners: Peter, who arrived in Massachusetts with his wife, Prudence, on the next ship after the Mayflower; Thomas, who fought in the Revolutionary War and served as secretary to Alexander Hamilton as he helped write the Constitution; Rebecca, who married a farmer and set off with him in a wagon for the green hills of western Kentucky; and so on through the decades. It brought everything alive, as if I were living through the impassioned debates about an unjust government; the decision to rebel and risk all we had; the anxiety and hope of pulling up roots and setting out with nothing but a carefully-loaded cartful of goods into wild, untamed lands no one had ever seen.

No one white, that is. When Mrs. Isaacson described the slaves captured in Africa and packed for weeks into tiny spaces not much bigger than coffins and finally unloaded onto Southern auction docks, we grew silent, fascinated. Such cruelty seemed distant, foreign. Redmond had only one black family—my piano teacher and her husband—and no one treated them with anything but courtesy. When Mrs. Isaacson pointed out that the very land our families settled had been already occupied by a culture that had been there for centuries, we shifted uneasily in our seats, suddenly conscious of the back row.

Instinctively we knew better than to talk about what she said to anyone outside of class, but some did. Corinne, for instance, reported to me shamefacedly that, after she let something slip, her mother and father threatened to complain to the principal about "scaring the children" with "wild exaggerations," but as far as we knew, they hadn't. Our whole class felt as if we'd been let into a secret society, privileged with classified information, initiated into arcane and crucial knowledge possessed only by the chosen few, and we guarded our closed circle jealously.

THAT DAY WE WERE to begin the next section on settling the West. As we took our seats, Mrs. Isaacson pointed to a cart filled with books, which had been rolled next to her desk.

"As part of our next topic," she said, "you're going to work in pairs. Each pair will use a report on one of these books as the main part of a class presentation on some aspect of the migration west. The books are from the library, and a few are my own."

Several boys groaned, among them Simon Rudolph and Seth O'Rourke, who hated reading, but Mrs. Isaacson frowned at them and went on.

"Who's going to work together? Win and Corinne." She didn't have to make it a question. People shouted out their names and those of desired partners, sometimes giggling if a girl and boy were put together. Mrs. Isaacson wrote until everyone's name was on the board.

"Now I'm going to hand out the books." She began to read titles with a short explanation of the contents: the Louisiana Purchase, the annexation of Texas, farming on the Great Plains. Corinne, as usual, waited for me to choose. None interested me, until:

"*Cheyenne Autumn.* It's about..."

"Me!" I heard my voice before I knew I'd said anything.

Mrs. Isaacson raised her eyebrows.

"Are you familiar with this book, Win?"

"No."

"Really? Why are you so eager to claim it, then?"

"I—I like the title."

She looked at me quizzically. "My, I didn't realize you were such a romantic."

Several people laughed as Mrs. Isaacson handed me the book. Corinne threw me a puzzled frown. My face felt hot as I glanced at the cover, flipped quickly through the pages, seeing nothing, and slipped the book into my desk. Mrs. Isaacson watched me intently. Suddenly she turned back to the names on the board and began erasing several of them.

"Hey, what're you doing?" Seth whined in his cracking tenor. He'd managed to get himself matched up with pretty Liz Tennant and didn't want that accomplishment jeopardized.

"That book gives me an idea," Mrs. Isaacson said. "We need some variety, so I'm going to shuffle people around a bit."

Other protesting voices rose. Mrs. Isaacson turned and lifted her hand, and we fell silent.

"Win, you and Corinne could benefit from a fresh point of view, especially on that book. Marjorie doesn't have a partner yet, so she can work with you." She turned and added Marjorie's name next to Corinne's and mine.

My mouth fell open: Marjorie was an Indian. I snuck a look at the rest of the class; they looked as dumbfounded as I felt. Didn't Mrs. Isaacson know that the Indian kids always worked together, that the white and Indian kids, like oil and water, never mixed?

"Look what you've done!" Corinne hissed at me. I shrugged helplessly. One by one, Mrs. Isaacson added the names of the remaining Indians to other singles and pairs, then turned back to us.

"We all need to be shaken up now and then," she said. "I guarantee we'll all learn something."

She said it easily, and it sounded pithy and reassuring: a promise and a binding compact. It would not be long before we found out that the old saying, that learning comes at a high price, can be true not only for the pupil but for the teacher as well.

WHEN THE BELL RANG, Corinne was standing over my desk before I'd put all my books in a pile. She was chewing her bottom lip, something she did when she was upset.

"What are we going to do?" she half-whispered to me.

"About what?"

"You know! Why'd you pick that stupid book, anyway? Now we've got to work with a dumb Indian!"

I stood up and stared at her. Her face with its blazing eyes, her flared nostrils, seemed shrunken and distasteful to me, and I hated seeing her that way.

"She's not dumb. She's pretty smart." I moved toward the door.

"Oh, who cares? We don't want to work with her." Mrs. Isaacson glanced up as we sidled past her desk.

"Well, we've got to, don't we?" Mrs. Isaacson smiled at me as I pushed through the door and walked into the hall. Marjorie stood on the far side, waiting for us.

I stopped so abruptly that Corinne bumped into me from behind. Other kids moved past us, watching from the corners of their eyes.

"So we're doing the project together." Marjorie's voice was high and clear, her gaze level and fierce.

I nodded. Corinne stood frozen, gazing at a point somewhere to the right of Marjorie's head.

"We should get together and talk about it."

I nodded again. As Corinne's elbow dug painfully into my side, I felt a jolt of rage hit my chest.

"How about Study Hall tomorrow?"

"*What?*" Corinne exploded. Marjorie's mouth clamped into a line, then relaxed.

"Okay." She turned and began walking away, her back straight, her glossy hair shining under the hall lights.

"Now look what you've done!" Corinne scuttled alongside me as I marched as fast as I could to our next class, trying not to listen to her attacks on my idiocy and her moans about our terrible fate. My own head was whirling. I had had almost none but the most superficial contacts with Indians. Though they lived in our town, on scattered farms nearby, their existences were carried on in a parallel universe.

As we reached the classroom, Corinne pushed in front of me and stopped.

"I'm not going to go." She paused, waiting for my reaction. "I just won't do it."

I took a deep breath.

"Well, I will."

Her mouth rounded, and her eyebrows drew together. She looked ready to cry.

"Come on, Cor. How bad can it be?" I pushed past her through the door and felt her following me to our desks, waiting for something more, for me to step off the boat I'd boarded, leaving her on shore while I watched her grow smaller and smaller.

AFTER SCHOOL, I TOLD Corinne I'd be taking the late bus home, making up an excuse involving having to go by Roone's to pick up some music. Ordinarily, Corinne would have assumed she'd hang around, but she seemed as uncomfortable with me as I felt with her and got on the bus without any discussion and didn't look at me as it drove away.

I walked down Spruce and turned right at the corner of Main, past the Two Elks Bar and Cafe with its splintered half-log siding and its two separate entrances, one for those who wanted a drink, the other for those who aimed at what passed for a meal; then Woolworth's, where Corinne and I spent hours cruising the aisles, eying cosmetics and candy, trying on scarves and headbands and glittering jewelry. I turned into Reynolds Drugs and Sundries, slipped onto a stool at the soda fountain, and ordered a vanilla Coke.

From my seat I could look through the store window across Main at the gray post office huddled into in the narrow space between Swensen's Food Mart with its big window full of hand-lettered signs on the left, and the daunting stone facade of the Montana State Bank on the right, like a puny child dwarfed by a stern grandmother and a gaudy aunt. When, after fifteen minutes of observation, I'd satisfied myself that it was clear of customers, I left, crossed the street, and pushed through the door.

Zippy grinned at me from the counter window. Behind him I could see the rows of boxes with letters and newspapers and a couple of sacks of mail waiting for his attention.

"Hey, Win. What's new?"

I pulled out the envelope I'd stuck in my History book and handed it to him. He looked boldly at the address.

"You're answering that letter from California, huh." He glanced at me for confirmation; I didn't move. "What's the matter, can't your mom write?"

He gave a snort of laughter at his brilliant joke. I gritted my teeth to stop an angry retort, and took a deep breath.

"Can you keep a secret?" I lowered my voice as if there were an invisible spy lurking by the table in the corner. Zippy's eyebrows shot up, and he leaned so far forward I took an involuntary step back.

"Try me." I could smell the sharp sweetish smell of Wildroot, the same tonic Randy used on his hair.

"I'm answering the letter, and I don't want Mom to know. She— I'm kind of setting up a surprise."

His grin broadened.

"What kind of surprise?"

"I can't tell you. Not yet."

Where had that come from? I hadn't the slightest intention of ever telling him anything about Marilyn.

"When?"

"I don't know. Soon, maybe."

Without my wanting to, my words were beginning to create an intimate bond with Zippy, a guy I didn't even want to walk down the street with. But I couldn't see how to get out of it then, so I took another step in.

"So can you hold any letters I get here, for me? And not tell my mom?" I stared at his greenish eyes, his shiny forehead dotted with tiny bumps, and smiled at him, willing myself not to move back any further.

"Sure!" he boomed. I felt myself relax as I turned, ready to leave.

"Thanks, Zip, that's great." I walked toward the door.

"Hey, wait a minute, Win." Something in his tone made me stop as if I'd heard a police siren.

"What?"

"Ya wanna go to the Harvest Ball?"

I turned. *Every* middle-schooler wanted to go to the Harvest Ball, the first big dance of the high school year. Most didn't get asked, since the high school kids looked down on us as too babyish.

"Do you mean, go with *you?*" I hadn't meant to let that much incredulity into my voice.

"Yeah. Since we're friends and all."

My mind raced. Favor for favor; quid pro quo. My friends would be amazed and envious at this coup. Jess might feel embarrassed to have her little sister at a school dance with her. But Zippy as my escort! I tried to picture sitting next to him, dancing with his hands around my waist, his chin grazing my temple. It was about as appealing as putting on cold underwear in winter. Oh, well, I thought, I could stand it for one evening. I pulled my mouth into a smile.

"Sure, that'd be neat."

He leaned back, a self-satisfied smirk on his face.

"Great! Maybe I'll ask Collie if I can ride out to your place with him."

"Collie? Collie Burns?" Collie was a junior, star of the basketball team, a legend to those of us who looked to high school as a promised land toward which we strained as hard as we could. "Why would he drive you out there?"

"Don't you know? He's going out with your sister." Zippy shook his head at my ignorance.

I put on a look of sudden recognition.

"Oh, sure, *Collie*. I forgot for a minute." I could tell he didn't buy this, so I hoisted my books and turned away before he could say anything more.

"See you later, Zip."

"Hey, wait a minute." I waved at him as I pushed open the door. "I'll call you!" The door closing behind me muffled his voice. I walked slowly down Main, chewing over what had happened. Why hadn't Jess mentioned Collie? Was he her boyfriend? She must have talked to her friends about him; why not to me? Another secret I had been excluded from!

Well, now I had secrets, too. I cradled this newest one, shaping and reshaping the events of the last minutes, the dance to come, dressing it in the spangled outfit of my imagination. If Collie and Zippy did pick us up together, it would be as if Jess and I were double-dating, like characters in a story in *Seventeen*. I felt myself rushing headlong toward my future, impatient yet terrified, as if I'd just loosened my grip at the top of a waterslide, my body beginning to gather speed in its inexorable descent toward the dark water below.

THAT EVENING, I KEPT sneaking glances at Jess when I thought she wasn't looking. I tried to see her as a stranger, as Collie, would: her cheeks flushed from the heat of the kitchen, her long eyelashes throwing shadows on her smooth olive skin, the curves of her mouth turned upward into a smile, her lips generously arched in repose. Her face reminded me of a ripe peach. She was more than pretty, much more. No wonder, I thought, that Collie liked her.

Mom must have picked up on something, because she began looking at Jess, too. After dinner, in the kitchen, as Jess and I put away the dishes and Mom was setting beans in the big blue bowl to soak overnight, she said, out of nowhere, "Jess, it's time you went to see Dr. Wright."

Jess blushed to the roots of her hair. Dr. Wright was Mom's doctor, a gynecologist in Great Falls. Jess, like me and all the kids in town, had been tended at Dr. Elwood's clinic in Redmond. When girls began seeing Dr. Wright, it meant they had crossed the line from childhood to womanhood. Now Jess looked as if she'd been caught stealing money from the collection plate. She glanced at me and frowned.

"Can't we talk about it some other time?" She dumped the spoons in the drawer and walked out of the kitchen. I felt as if she'd slapped me.

"I didn't mean to embarrass you," Mom stated at her retreating back, then sighed and looked at me. "You might as well come too, Win. I should have taken Jess a year ago. She's more than ready, and you'll be soon enough."

I didn't want to ask what she meant, but I knew it had to do with my changing body, with the monthly periods I'd been getting for over a year by then. Why was I so embarrassed now with this woman, so familiar with every part of my physical being, who'd bathed me, wiped my bottom, cleaned the fold between my legs? She was staring at me now as if she'd never seen me before, and I couldn't meet her gaze.

"You both grow so fast. Jess is a full woman, and you're just about there. I don't know why I didn't see it as clear before, but there it is." She stood up and put her arms around me.

"Jess is beautiful," she whispered, "but don't be jealous. You will be, too, in a different way. The boys'll flock to you like bees to honeysuckle." She held me at arms' length, studying me. "If they haven't started already." She raised her eyebrows at me questioningly. I squirmed my right arm loose. She held my left hand a moment, then let me go.

"Fly away, then," she nodded, holding the bowl in front of her like a votive offering. "About as smart to try and stop you as to keep a bird from flying south in the fall."

I LAY IN BED, reading, while Jess brushed her crackling hair. Her reflection bobbed in the bumpy glass of the dark window.

"Jess, I heard something today. About you."

The rhythm of her brush never changed, but I could tell she was listening.

"Someone said you were going out with Collie Burns."

"Don't believe everything you hear."

"You mean it isn't true?" I felt a keen disappointment, almost as if I'd been told I couldn't go to a party I'd wanted desperately to attend.

"I didn't say that." Jess turned to me. "Who've you been talking to?"

"Oh, just someone."

"I hate being talked about. You know that. What I do is nobody else's business."

"Hey, Jess, this is *me*. Why can't you talk to me anymore? You used to. It's—oh, never mind."

I turned my back to her and pretended to read, so she wouldn't see the tears that prickled my eyes. After a moment she spoke softly. "We've been hanging around together, I guess. The last two months. Nothing very special."

I flipped over to face her again.

"It *is* special. He's so handsome!" I could see Collie's shoulder-length brown hair, still fairly unusual where we lived, pulled back into a pony-tail during a game, his athletic body gliding, jumping, running on the basketball court, the wide, white flash of his grin as he turned to slap the palm of the nearest teammate. A suggestion of a smile hovered around her mouth, and she shrugged lightly.

"Are you going to the Harvest Ball with him?"

"I guess so."

"How'd you get him to ask you?"

She sniffed. "I didn't have to get him to. He wanted to."

"How'd you know?" The minds of boys were a mystery to me. I assumed you had to have some kind of mental X ray to penetrate their thoughts.

Jess laughed. "I just knew."

I thought of telling her I was going, too, then decided to wait. Maybe it wouldn't happen; I wasn't even sure if I wanted it to.

"What are you going to wear?"

She put down the brush and got into bed, her eyes shining.

"There's the loveliest dress at Starr's. Green silky cotton. I've been saving up for it. I have almost enough, and I don't want to ask Mom. I don't want her to have to ask Randy for money." A shade of anxiety passed across her face.

"Why not?"

"I just don't want him to know."

"Know what? He never notices clothes."

Jess stared a long time out the window at the blue-black sky. Finally she lay back on her pillow.

"It'll be all right," she murmured to herself. "It has to."

I wanted to reassure her, but about what? She was so far away I'd have to shout to get her attention. So I stayed quiet as she stared up at the ceiling. Finally she turned off the lamp and rolled away from me.

"Jess."

"Hmmm?"

"Do you—" I started again. "What's it like when you kiss him?"

A long pause.

"Nice."

"Do you—touch tongues?" I couldn't imagine wanting to do this. I think I really wanted to ask her: Do you make love? Do you lie down and open your body for him, let him crouch over you, invade you, fill you up? I held my breath. When she spoke, I could tell she was smiling.

"Leave me alone, Win."

I knew she wouldn't say anything else. So I lay there in the dark, listening to her breath growing slow and deep in sleep, imagining Jess and Collie's mouths pressed together, their hands moving purposefully over each other's bodies, his face bending over hers, over mine, drowning my vision in sensation. The space between my legs seemed to expand, to wake into a life of its own. Its pulsation caught me by surprise, then sucked me into its power, pulling my hand down to touch, to stroke myself. I tried to quiet my breathing, to keep this as secret from Jess as her life with Collie was kept from me. Was this what she felt with him? And had she ever, thinking of him, given herself over to these waves of pleasure while I lay in the next bed, oblivious, stupefied, asleep?

CHAPTER 5

got up the next day already late for breakfast. I wanted to be alone—something impossible in our house on weekday mornings— so as to cradle the secret world I'd discovered. Instead, Mom yelled at me over and over to hurry or I'd miss the school bus. My skirt zipper jammed; I dropped my toast on the floor, butter side down; and I couldn't find my book bag.

"Here." Mom shoved the bag at me.

"Where was it? What were you doing, hiding it?" I scowled at her.

"Don't blame your troubles on me!" She held out a paper bag. "Here's your lunch. It's lucky someone around here's organized."

I snatched it and raced out the door and down the lane to the road. Jess was leaning against the fence post, watching the yellow rear end of the bus recede in the distance.

"Oh, shit! Why didn't you tell him to wait?" Furious, I threw down my book bag, then looked at her. "Why aren't you on the bus? What's the matter with you?"

"I'm getting a ride," she answered. "And if you calm down, you can come with us." Jess did this sometimes, when she felt particularly generous. It didn't happen often. For one thing, no one lived very near us, so anyone picking her up had to come considerably out of their way; for another, I was too young to hang around with her friends. I'd protested at first when she began to exclude me from her social life, but I'd gotten used to it by then. Why was she being so nice today?

"I felt sorry for you, rushing around like a maniac." As if she'd read my thoughts again. "Here he comes."

A speck on the road bloomed into an old green car trailing white smoke as it approached and lurched to a stop in front of us. Dark eyes flashing in his wind-burned face, eyebrows raised inquiringly, Collie Burns leaned over and pushed the front passenger door open. Jess slid in and motioned toward the back.

"It's okay, isn't it, Col? She missed the bus."

"Sure, why not?" Collie grinned at me as I eased into the seat. As I met his eyes, I felt myself blush, last night's images springing into my mind. *He* couldn't know how we'd kissed, or what I'd felt because of it, I reminded myself. I wasn't so sure about Jess, though, so I pulled a book out of my bag and opened it, muttering something about a history test that day.

"Then you better study history, not geography," Jess smirked. I glanced down and quickly changed books. Did she have to notice everything? I shot a venomous glance at her, but she'd turned toward Collie. She spent the rest of the ride chatting and laughing with him, and ignoring me. I took the hint and used the time to watch them, to try and uncover another piece of the mysterious world toward which I was headed.

We were a couple of miles from Redmond when Collie turned the car down a dirt road. What was this? No one ever went here. Jess didn't say anything but looked at him quizzically.

"Picking up Bell." She nodded, as if this explained it.

But this was Indian town! We slowed, bumping past ramshackle box-houses with tar-paper roofs, their yards full of the rusted hulks of cars, refrigerators with no doors, piles of torn truck tires, broken bottles, and other discarded junk. Here and there a dark-skinned man sat in front of a house, or a woman hung clothes in a back yard, or a child played with a brick. Poverty and defeat hung over everything like a sour mist.

I shrank back into my seat as Collie stopped in front of a house-trailer set on concrete blocks and honked the horn twice. A tall boy in jeans and a denim jacket, carrying a pile of books, burst through the door, yelled something over his shoulder, and ran toward the car. I almost forgot to move over before he shoved his long body into the back seat with me. Collie gunned the motor, and we raced off.

"Hi, guys." Bell stared at me, then at Collie. "Hey, who's this?"

"That's my sister, Winona," Jess answered. It sounded as if she'd named a previously unnoticed species of insect life. I figured I wasn't supposed to talk, so I half-smiled at Bell, then dropped my eyes to my book.

"Hey. You don't look much like Jess, do you?" He was talking to me! "You in tenth grade? I haven't seen you around." What was I supposed to do? If I answered, Jess might get mad or make fun of me, but if I didn't, Bell would think I was rude or, worse, a creep.

"I'm in ninth." And almost fifteen, I was about to add, but his eyes turned away.

"Oh, junior high." He'd dismissed me. "Hey, Col, we set for next Friday?"

"All set." Collie grinned at Jess. " We'll show 'em how to have fun, huh, Squinch."

Squinch? What was that? It didn't matter. The word, the way Collie looked at Jess, the same smile on her face as when she told me about him, opened a window onto a scene of intimacy between them as intense as any I'd imagined the night before. I had to look away. My eyes fell on Bell's profile. He was grinning at them. He'd been there, too. And suddenly the window turned frosty and I was standing out in the snow, looking through it into a bright, cozy room full of dancing couples, knowing I wasn't invited—yet.

I WAITED IN THE school yard for Corinne to get off the bus. She spotted me as soon as she got out and walked over.

"Where were you? I thought you were sick or something."

"I got a ride with Jess and Collie."

To my satisfaction, Corinne's mouth flew open. Before she could form the question, I answered it.

"He's taking her to the Harvest Ball."

"You're kidding!" Excited pleasure suffused her face, and I let my own reflect it. She began asking me the details as we walked up the steps and down the hall: How long had they been dating? Did Jess really like him? What was she going to wear? I realized how happy I was to regain what we'd always had, to talk without guarding myself, without judging or shaping my words into a conscious pattern, without worrying about what she'd think of me for saying them.

I was just about to tell her about Zippy's invitation when she stiffened. I followed her gaze to our homeroom door, with Marjorie's stolid figure standing next to it. Faded blue jeans, a green tie-dyed T shirt under an army fatigue jacket with a long rip down one sleeve. She stared at us, then turned and let the door swing closed behind her.

"We're supposed to meet her in Study Hall," I reminded Corinne.

"Forget it." Corinne could be bullheaded when she felt like it. "My Mom says I don't have to do anything with her." We stopped at the door. "What did your parents say?"

"I'm not a baby. I don't run to them with every little problem."

Corinne shot me an outraged glance, then pushed through the door. "They're gonna know soon enough, whether you tell them or not."

"What's *that* mean?" I hissed as we slipped into our seats. But she shook her head and stayed silent as the bell rang.

As FIFTH PERIOD STUDY Hall began, I went up and asked Mrs. Hilyard for a library pass. Corinne stubbornly stayed in her seat and wouldn't look at me. As I walked down the empty hall and past the closed classroom doors, listening to the drone of a teacher, the buzz of children's chatter, the first graders singing a song, I felt as alone as I ever had. My resentment began to build with every step, against Mrs. Isaacson for creating the situation, against Corinne for forcing me to confront it by myself, against Marjorie for challenging me to live up to the best image I had of myself, rather than the easiest or most familiar. Over the next few months, then years, I would come to know this sensation intimately, until it became a part of who I felt myself to be.

Now, though, as I reached the library and peered through the glass-paned door, I was hoping so intensely that Marjorie wouldn't be there that the sight of her round black-haired head bent over a book startled me. I stood for a moment, my muscles gathering themselves to turn around and flee. Then, in one of the small random events that send a life down a particular course, like a train passing over a switch, the shift in direction barely noticeable at first, then gradually widening into an immense divergence, another student pushed past me, threw open the door, and Marjorie turned and looked around, straight at me.

She smiled briefly, her eyes questioning. I walked over, plunked my notebook down, and lowered myself into the chair across from her. For a moment we stared at each other blankly. Somehow I sensed she was as empty of any clue about what to do next as I: comrades in confusion, explorers equally lost on an unknown continent.

"Corinne had to study today," I said. "She's failing algebra." Why was I lying for her?

"She doesn't want to do this project," Marjorie stated matter-of-factly. "You don't either."

I opened my mouth to protest, but she got there first.

"Do you think I do?"

We looked away. Sunlight peppered the holes in the yellowing window shades with spots of brightness, and gleamed on the wooden tables polished by years of sweaty shirtsleeves. The room echoed with silence, with our breathing, with the tick of the clock and the creak of the librarian's chair. I opened my notebook and wrote *Cheyenne Autumn* in big letters at the top of the page.

"Did you bring the book?"

"I left it at home. Sorry."

"That's OK. You can read it first, then give it to me." She fell silent. Was that it? I felt stupid. We could have settled that much in the hall. So we must be here for something more. I stared out the window, at the library assistant shelving books, at the two students reading at the other long table.

"I know what it's about, anyway." Her voice was barely audible. She was staring at her hands lying on the table in front of her, broad hands with short, square nails and weathered skin, hands older than she was.

"What?"

"Genocide."

I felt as if I'd stepped off a cliff into empty air, and I grabbed for the first thing I could think of.

"You mean the Nazis?"

I'd heard about World War II from Randy's stories about his father's battalion helping liberate the concentration camps, burying enormous piles of bodies, herding the starving prisoners, so weak they could barely hold the plates of mush that meant the difference between life and death. Now I know these stories hadn't actually happened to Randy's father, who sat the war out on a Section 4-F. Instead they had been gathered from others, from newspapers and books, and borrowed to impress his small son with his own importance.

Marjorie raised her eyes and stared at me with a look of angry disbelief. Not Nazis, then. I didn't dare tell her that, for me, the title had concocted blurry images of cowboys singing as they rounded up for a cattle drive from Wyoming to some far-off destination down the Rio Grande.

"Just read it." She stood up. "Then you'll see."

She walked away, tall and straight-backed, leaving me staring at her invisible wake.

THAT NIGHT I BEGAN reading *Cheyenne Autumn*, and for a week I picked at it like a sore. I'd read a chapter, then put it down, sickened and angry, sure I couldn't continue. An hour later I'd be at it again, the next few pages stoking my helpless fury until I'd throw it across the room or kick it under the sofa, only to pull it out an hour later for another go-round. Images from the book replayed themselves over and over in my mind: Indian men, women, and children yanked from their homes, forced to walk endlessly without enough food or firewood to fuel themselves against the lethal cold; growing weak; freezing, dying, the living not allowed time to stop and bury the dead.

When I tried to imagine Marjorie reading it, I hit a blank wall. Had there been, among the slaughtered, people of her own tribe? Had her own great-great grandfather suffered like that because of other soldiers, other settlers, others like me? What did it feel like to be on the losing side of history, watching helplessly, suffused by impotent rage? I had no idea how I could ask her these questions, yet I knew that, to conceal them, to act as if they weren't there, was beyond my power.

I wanted to believe the book was a lie. Many years later I would read about skeptics who were convinced all the stories about the Nazi death camps, the efficient Holocaust machines, were wild exaggerations, a giant myth invented to vilify an honorable nation. Right then I wanted to believe that this book was lying like that, but I couldn't. Its words struck sparks, lit fires in me that illuminated the obsidian silences, the willed unresponsiveness and blank watchfulness of those dark faces that had walked at the outskirts of my conscious life.

Whom could I talk to about this? Not Mom, somehow. Certainly not Randy. Corinne would just wave it away, grimacing and refuse to look at it. Jess? Maybe. But she was staying in town with Leila that weekend.

The one person who I knew would understand my reaction and would honor it with serious attention was Mrs. Isaacson. Yet the idea of approaching her made me nervous. Would she think I was criticizing her choice of books? Would I be disappointing her faith in my ability to deal with what she'd given me to read? I decided to wait until Monday. If circumstances provided me with an opportunity to talk to her privately, I would. Until then, I wanted to shove the whole mess out of sight, but the book pulled me onward like an undertow in a threatening sea.

CHAPTER 6

THAT SATURDAY, AS USUAL, I drove into Redmond with Mom, for my weekly piano lesson. As the Amoco station came into sight, signaling the beginning of town, I leaned into the back seat and shuffled my music together, holding it in my lap as we passed the station, the Catholic church, then turned off Main Street into Elm.

Redmond, which had seemed like a big place when I was a very young child, was really barely more than a village. That was where we went to school on weekdays, and to church on holidays and occasional Sundays. Our social life was spread among Rotary Club potluck dinners and Women's Auxiliary swap meets in the church basement, high school football games and Elks dances in the drafty hall decorated with trophies shot over the past half-century by town residents, moth-eaten animal heads in various states of dilapidation. We bought our food at the brightly lit Food Mart, picked out new fall clothes at Starr's Style Corner, browsed the counters and lingered over Cokes and ice cream sodas at Woolworth's, and yearned for the combination hi-fi record player and radio at the hardware and appliance store.

Mom stopped the car in front of a small wooden house, like all the houses in Redmond, but painted an odd smoky blue with bright red trim. Roone always joked that it was too bad it didn't snow on the Fourth of July (although once it actually had) because they would have had the most patriotic house in town without doing a thing to decorate it.

I jumped out and ran up the two steps to the narrow front porch set off by a railing.

"I'll be back at twelve," Mom yelled. I didn't answer as I turned the round metal handle in the middle of the door. Above the jangling clash that sounded more like keys banged together than a doorbell, I heard the clicking of high heels. The door opened, and there stood Roone.

She loomed over me, five feet seven in bare feet, five nine in her red pumps with straps over the instep. Flamenco shoes, she told me. In a town and an era when women wore either prim cotton dresses with Peter Pan collars if they were expecting someone to see them, or blue jeans and their husband's flannel shirts if they weren't, Roone dressed like a gypsy on acid, in long, full skirts, blouses handmade from squares of brilliantly colored silk scarves, and big hoop earrings. Her long wiry hair, drawn behind her neck in a haphazard bun, was mostly still black, shot through with gray; one thicker streak of white flowed back dramatically from the middle of her forehead. Her dark brown eyes—in some lights, you couldn't tell where the iris left off and the pupil began—gleamed, and her teeth cut a brilliant white swathe in her chocolate-colored skin. She and her husband Selby were the only Negroes in Redmond, and the only ones I'd ever seen.

"Win!" She sounded as surprised and pleased, as if I were a beloved cousin who'd arrived for a long-awaited yearly visit.

"Win's here," she called over her shoulder, then stepped aside and let me precede her through the hall into the parlor, moving in quick spurts from one place to another, talking the whole time. Only when she listened to music did she sit completely still, her whole body focused and intent.

The parlor was bursting with books and lamps and stuffed armchairs, underlaid by a thick patterned carpet. A stuffed owl sat on the mantelpiece, its glass eyes glaring balefully. But the baby grand piano, its dark wood glistening, dominated everything else. Just seeing it, anticipating the sounds it made, I felt happy.

As I walked over and placed my music on its stand, Selby walked in, smiling broadly at me, waving a wooden spoon in greeting. In his way, he was as exotic a sight as a Balinese dancer: thin, wiry, gray-haired, skin the color of dark butterscotch syrup, and wearing a white chef's apron. No man I'd either come across or seen pictured in magazines or movies would be caught dead in an apron, doing anything productive in a kitchen. But there he was.

"I'm stirring up something for you, Win. Just you wait," he smiled me. Roone claimed she didn't spend much time in the kitchen; Selby was the cook. After every lesson he'd present me with a slice of warm bread, fresh butter melting into its crumbly surface, or a plate of thick venison cobbled with chunks of potatoes and peas, steam rising from its rich brown surface, or whatever other dish he was concocting. My stomach rumbled in anticipation as I caught the tang of cinnamon and nutmeg.

"Later, honey. She's got more important things to do first." Selby waved his spoon again and disappeared. Roone sat down in a straight-backed chair across from the piano. "What do you want to do first?"

I'd started taking lessons from Roone when I was seven, when Randy sent Selby a bunch of rich dudes he'd met in a bar in Great Falls who wanted a hunting guide. Selby led them on a week-long trip during which they bagged four elk, six deer, and a mountain goat, then tipped Selby more money than he'd seen in his life. Selby was desperate to do something for Randy in return. Mom had noticed that I could sing back any tune I heard on the radio, and she persuaded Randy to let Roone give me lessons and an old rickety second piano they'd kept in a spare room.

I learned to read music with simplified versions of "Moon River" and "April Showers," then moved on to pop hits and show tunes. One day when I walked into the house, Roone had been playing the piano and I'd stopped, thunderstruck by the bass arpeggios and staccato chords rippling from her hands.

"What's that?" I had breathed, when she stopped.

She's stared at me a second, startled by my obvious awe.

"Beethoven."

"Who?" I'd never heard classical music.

Instead of answering me, she had resumed playing and kept going to the end of the piece. Then she's turned to me.

"Would you like to learn to play this?"

I couldn't answer, just nod. She had grinned.

"Child, you look like you've seen the Holy Ghost. Let's get started."

I'd gone home that day with Mozart's Sonatina in C, and we kept on going, through Bach's Inventions and Schubert's Musical Moments, right up to the same Beethoven sonata she'd played that day, which was what I was working on.

I opened the music and began to play. Roone sat completely still, leaning slightly forward, her eyes closed, her whole being focused on what she was hearing, the air around her humming with suppressed energy. When I stopped, she opened her eyes, cocked her head, and raised one eyebrow at me.

"Well?" she asked.

"It felt too fast, maybe. Especially those octaves."

"Have you been doing the exercises I gave you?" She shook her head, already knowing the answer. "If you strengthen your wrists and arms, they'll come easier, and they won't sound so rushed and cramped. Keep your wrist steady instead of flopping it, like this." She sat on the bench with me and touched the keys. She smelled very faintly of vanilla and smoke. I imitated her movements.

"Try it again, just a little slower. Try to feel the shape of each section, opening up and then closing." She went back to the chair.

I played again, breathing with the phrases. As the last note faded, Roone jumped up, clapping her hands.

"Bravo! Very good! You're ready for the competition!"

Roone wanted me to enter a statewide contest for young musicians held every year in Missoula. At first I had been reluctant, but Roone was persistent: She brought it up every lesson, though she made it clear it was my decision whether or not to enter. As time went on, I'd become more and more interested. What really lured me was the prospect of a stay in Missoula. Seeing my expression, she handed me a printed form.

"Fill this out, and bring it back next time." I glanced at it: the application. I put it with my music, and we went on to a Bach suite that I was just beginning to learn. After forty minutes of hard work, we stopped.

"That's fine for today. Let's do some listening."

She motioned me to the cushioned sofa, crossed to a big cabinet, and threw open its doors, revealing a hi-fi and hundreds of records lined up in orderly rows. She selected one, placed it carefully on the turntable, then came and sat next to me as the record dropped and the needle hissed.

Roone had an eclectic collection of classical, jazz, and blues records, most of which she brought back from her frequent trips to Chicago, where she'd grown up. I knew she'd sung at jazz clubs as a young woman. She'd studied classical piano with a teacher she'd had in junior high school who, like Roone with me, kept her on for the talent and love of music she saw in her. On the way home from her lessons, Roone had told me, she'd stop off at Alonso's Nite-Brite Club, to listen to Al play honky-tonk and to soak in the current singer's repertoire, humming it under her breath as she walked home shivering, late for supper as usual. She'd hung around the Chicago Lyric Opera, charming the manager into allowing her to usher at Saturday matinées, until she'd heard all the great operas and most of the great singers. When she put on a record, I never knew whether to expect *Carmen* or Carmen Mc-Crea, Beverly Sills or Bessie Smith.

Now the sounds of Sviatoslav Richter playing Chopin's *Etude in G* filled the room.

"Listen to that cadence," she whispered once, holding up her hand. I concentrated, hearing with her the lilting downward turn at the end of the phrase.

"That was great," I said as the music stopped. I could never find words that corresponded to what I felt when I listened, so I simply fished out the handiest.

Roone laughed. "Time for your reward!"

She led me into the sunny kitchen, where brightly colored pots hung from hooks on the wall and Selby stood in front of the big ungainly

Wedgwood stove, which seemed old-fashioned even back then. Roone and I sat down at the yellow wooden table.

"Finished already?" Selby asked. "It sounded real nice." He put a plate with a round, spicy-smelling loaf in front of us.

"Pumpkin bread. Try it."

Roone handed me a thick slice, then cut herself a thin piece.

"Take more, gal. Don't you like my cooking?"

"I like it too much. See?" Roone patted her stomach. She was delicately-boned, still slender at forty-seven. Selby gave a mock howl.

"What you know about cookin', city gal? You been raised on fried chicken and greens!"

"I know plenty. I've eaten in the finest restaurants in Chicago, and I know a good dish when I taste one." She took a bite of her slice. "Mmmm-hmmm! This is it!" She finished her piece and cut another as Selby beamed.

"Honey, you know what? I've got a real hankering for duck *á l'orange*, but we don't have a duck."

"I'll get one, don't you worry. I'm going out with Randy tomorrow—right, Win?"

I dropped my eyes. I didn't keep track of Randy's schedule and had less than no interest in it. I hated that he'd been brought into the kitchen, even as a ghostly presence.

The friendship between Randy and Selby was a mystery I didn't even try and solve. Randy's antipathy toward Indians seemed not to extend to Negroes, or at least not to Selby. Possibly one of a kind was easier to deal with than a whole regiment. Actually they saw each other only on joint hunting and fishing expeditions. Selby never appeared at social events —Roone showed up at the more public ones—and had little to say outside his home. He worked in the carpenter's shop set up in a shack behind their house, and people came from all over the county to buy the tables, armoires, and bookcases he made, or to hire him to make and install cabinets and built-in shelving in their kitchens and parlors. But he dropped everything whenever an out-of-town hunter came looking for a guide. It was this passion for hunting and fishing that he and Randy shared, that transcended their enormous differences in temperament and background.

He'd come on several of the those childhood expeditions I remembered taking with Randy, and the two of them could stand for hours, barely moving, exchanging only a few low words about where the deer was likely to appear, or whether the fish were getting ready to move to the shady side of the stream. On the way back, in the truck, they'd swap tall tales of game tracked and missed, huge fish almost landed, falling rocks narrowly avoided, sudden lightning storms outwitted. I'd stopped going with them shortly after I stopped believing every word they said.

On one of the last of these trips, when I was eight, Selby had mentioned his cowboy days. This had startled me, as all the cowboys I knew were white or Indian.

"How can *you* have been a cowboy?" I was too young to have a clear sense of what my question sounded like. Shelby had shrugged.

"There was plenty of black cowboys around back then," he's finally said. "You just don't hear about them much. I worked on all kinds of spreads."

"Where? Why did you stop?"

Before Selby could answer, Randy had barked at me, "Shut your mouth! You look like a dead fish!" He's glared briefly, then snapped on the radio.

"She didn't mean nothing by it, Ran. She's just curious, like a kid."

"She'll be quiet when I tell her to be," Randy had grunted. "Always yammering on about some dumb stuff. Half the time I don't know what she's talking about."

I'd stared straight ahead, halfway between fury and tears. Selby had patted my hand but said nothing. I'd poked at a question in my own mind: What had I said that made Randy so angry? It had something to do with Selby being black, but what? I thought about this now, and wondered: Were the questions I'd been asking ones that Randy would have wanted to ask? Did Randy not want to look too directly at contradictions he didn't fully understand?

Selby poured coffee from a chipped blue enamel pot into heavy white mugs and handed them to Roone. One—mine—was only half full. He added steaming hot milk to it. "*Cafe au lait*," Roone announced, sipping hers coal-black.

The harsh jangle of the doorbell startled us. Roone left the room, then returned with Mom behind her.

"I can't stay more than a minute," she protested as Selby offered coffee, then sat down and nibbled a slice of pumpkin bread. "I've never seen the market so crowded. I should have remembered it's time for food stamps. I swear, it makes me hopping mad how they can get good food for nothing, while the rest of us've got to sweat or go hungry."

I'd heard this complaint so many times from Mom, it had become a familiar recurring event, as regular as the full moon, or Jess' crankiness before her period. Roone nodded.

"They just aren't raised to take on responsibility," she agreed.

"Who wouldn't rather take it easy than work?" Mom went on. "*I'd* love a free vacation, sitting around all day and get my groceries paid for."

"If they didn't get handouts," Roone added, "they'd have to go out and find jobs and earn their way."

Selby looked up briefly from his coffee.

"Someone'd have to hire them first," he said quietly. His eyes turned toward the window, through which I could see the weathered boards of his shed. There was an uneasy silence. I'd never heard Selby disagree with Roone before, except in their bantering play. This was different.

Mom looked back and forth from Selby to Roone, then shook her head.

"I don't know. Whenever we've hired one out at the ranch, he just up and leaves after a day or two. You can't depend on them."

And who wouldn't quit? I thought. Shoveling manure and collecting chickenshit in the middle of nowhere can't be anyone's idea of a dream job. But I said nothing; better not to aggravate Mom before I got my weekly allowance.

"Well, maybe we'll get a chance to find out," said Selby. "I've hired one to help me in the shop."

Mom's mouth dropped open. I stared hard at Selby. Roone

swiveled her body around in her chair and faced the door. I could tell this wasn't news to her.

"Who'd you hire?" Mom asked.

"Guy named Bell Youngman. He's in high school. He'll work three to six, learning the trade. He had to give up basketball to do it, too. Seems like a nice kid. You know him, Win?"

Startled out of my spectator role, I shook my head before I could consciously make a decision about what to say, then shifted ground. "I think I met him once. Jess knows him better. And everyone knows he's a good player," I said, trying to help Selby. I always felt sorry for the underdog, and I automatically assumed this was Selby, since whenever I'd been there, I'd felt the full power of Roone's personality, while he'd always stayed in the background. Now I know how the private dance between two people can be very different from the one outsiders are allowed to witness.

Mom was still shaking her head.

"It's a bad idea, Selby," she worried. Something in her voice didn't sound right, like when I was trying to convince her I hadn't forgotten to feed the chickens when I had. "You'd better be real careful. Keep your eyes on him when he's in the house."

A look I'd never seen before passed like lightning over Selby's face, a look of outrage. Then it was gone so fast I'd have wondered if I'd imagined it, except for the way my heart was pounding. He smiled, his expression bland. "I'll have to let him in to use the bathroom, I guess."

Roone turned back to face him.

"You know you need one in the shed." Her voice was higher than usual. "Peter Johnson just put their first one in for the Carrolls last month. He's got extra pipe left over. Why don't I talk to him tomorrow? It wouldn't cost —"

"I guess we don't need more than one, Roone," Selby interrupted. "Don't want to get too far ahead of the Joneses."

Roone picked up her mug, although it was empty. Mom got up from her chair.

"Win, let's get going. We've still got to stop by Woolworth's. That's wonderful pumpkin bread, Selby. Be sure to have Roone bring some to the church bake sale."

She marched down the hall with Roone. I lingered behind, wanting to say something to Selby but not knowing what. He slipped what was left of the loaf into a paper bag and handed it to me.

"Tell Randy I'll be ready at six," he said. I nodded, then suddenly held out my hand. His eyebrows shot up; he grinned and shook it firmly. I turned and ran out to the porch and down the steps, waving goodbye to Roone, falling in next to Mom as she padded determinedly toward Main Street, gazing straight ahead.

I TOLD MOM I wanted to walk down to the library to get some books while she shopped at the drugstore. As soon as I saw her go in, I scooted across the street post office. Zippy wasn't there, so I had to explain to Ralph Anderson, the manager, that I was expecting a special letter I wanted held for me. He gave me a fishy look but checked and turned up nothing. Then I ran over to the library and pulled two novels off the shelf, barely glancing at them. Knowing Mom would probably take her time, I sifted through the subject categories in the card case: *Cheyenne Autumn* (nothing); Western history and U.S., settlement of (several books each). I chose one from each category, checked them out, and ran back to the drugstore where Mom was waiting for me.

"What did you get?" She never chose any books for herself but sometimes read the novels I borrowed as I finished them. She frowned at the novels, *As I Lay Dying* and *The Hamilton Woman*, and raised her eyebrows when she saw the history books.

"They're for a paper I've got in American history," I explained. "Nothing *you'd* be interested in."

"Don't sass your mother," she sniffed. "I've got interests that'd scare the pants off you. How was your lesson?"

I rattled on to her about the competition, keeping her mind off any third-degree about the application. I hadn't meant to mention it, but I still hadn't completely outgrown the easy talkativeness I'd had with her when I was small, and things would sometimes pop out before I realized I wasn't standing behind my protective fence. This time it was easy: Mom didn't much care what I learned at school, as long as I got good grades.

"I don't know about you going to Missoula," she said. "When is that contest?"

"The *competition* is in February." We'd reached the car, and I opened the door and threw my books in the back seat.

"The roads will be real bad then. And where will you stay? A hotel is expensive."

"Roone has friends there we can stay with."

Mom shot me a quick look.

"You can't stay with strangers."

"They're not strangers. Roone has known them forever." I slid into the front seat alongside Mom.

"It's not a good idea." Just what she'd said to Selby. I saw her features set into planes of stubborn finality. Usually when this happened, I'd pull back and wait until she'd had time to digest the new idea, until it settled into her imagination the way a new shoe worn a few times eases onto your foot. This time, though, I lost patience.

"You just don't want me to go, do you?"

She turned to me, frowning. Instead of seeing the warning, I chose to take up a challenge.

"What are you afraid I'll do, decide to stay there and not come back to this dumb hick town?"

"Win, be quiet." Her voice told me I'd hit close to the target but not in it. I readied my next arrow.

"It's because she's a Negro, isn't it?"

At my words, her eyes narrowed and she sucked in a quick breath. I didn't know what to do with what I'd discovered. We stared at each other, frozen, like two enemy soldiers who'd taken cover under the same bush. Then she shook her head and started the car.

Questions I'd never considered poured into my mind. Why didn't Selby come to the social events in town, or Roone to any but the public ones? Where did they go to church? Who visited them, hung out in their kitchen, invited them to dinner? I remembered Roone telling me she taught classes in Missoula every week. I'd always thought she did it for love of music. Maybe she had to drive a hundred miles just to relax and be herself with someone beside Selby. The thought seemed unbearably sad, yet Roone herself was so alive, radiated so much love of life, that pitying her seemed ridiculous.

"I'll ask Randy about it," Mom said finally. I'd gone so far into my own thoughts that I had to trace backwards and calculate that "it" meant my trip to the competition. She waited for me to ask questions, to thank her, but I kept staring out the window, punishing her with silence.

I'D NEVER BEEN MORE relieved to see the open gate and the rutted driveway to the ranch. As the car turned in, we both spotted a green truck parked in front of the house, *Gregory Appliance and Hardware, Great Falls* lettered on its side.

"What in the world?" Mom slammed on the brakes, yanked the door open, and practically ran up the front steps. I pulled out a sack of groceries and followed her into the kitchen, where she stood still, watching two men propping up a huge white porcelain rectangle upended on a slanted dolly. Lorrie and Pete stood to one side, their eyes riveted on the balancing act.

"In here," Randy's voice called from the pantry. "If it'll get through the door."

His compact bulk danced through the doorway, his hair glowing around his head like reddish dandelion fuzz. When he saw Mom, he stopped short, reading the anxious question in her eyes.

"Here it is, ma'am," he shouted, sweeping his arm toward the dolly. "The best freezer money can buy. It'll hold three hundred pounds of venison and elk, not to mention enough frozen corn and peas to get us into the next century."

He stopped and took a breath.

"Well, what do you think? Is it big enough?"

"But, Randy. . . ." Mom squeaked, disconcerted.

Before she could go on, Randy held up his hand. "We got the loan."

For an instant, Mom didn't move. Then she leaped across the floor and jumped at him, throwing her arms around his neck with so much force he staggered back and bumped against the wall. The two men, still holding the dolly, rolled their eyes sideways at each other and smiled as Mom kissed Randy full on the mouth. Randy's hands clamped onto her backside, then squeezed hard enough that she cried out. Lorrie and Pete started jumping up and down, hooting and pointing.

"They're kissing, they're kissing!" they cried, then launched into "I Saw Mommy Kissing Santa Claus" as they ran full-tilt around the table. The two men lowered the dolly to a standing position, popped cigarettes and matches out of their pockets and lit up. Even Jess, lured to the door by the noise, hands on her hips, couldn't keep a grin from her face. Randy pulled Mom against him and began to two-step with her, bumping into Pete, who attached himself to their legs, while Lorrie threw her little body at me.

"Dance! Dance!" she yelled, so I lifted her up and twirled her around, my usual resistance melting like ice cubes in hot coffee as I let myself slide into the celebration.

AFTER THE FREEZER HAD been ceremoniously installed in the pantry corner; after Lorrie and Pete had rummaged through the refrigerator and the pantry shelves for items to put into it, items Mom would salvage later, when they were asleep; after a dinner made special by Jess' crumb cake topped with canned peaches from September's county fair, Randy pulled out his guitar case from behind the recliner.

"What'll it be?" He played country and gospel tunes when he felt good. That night he played everyone's favorites, "Turkey in the Straw" for Lorrie and Pete, "Shall We Gather at the River" for Mom, "House of the Rising Sun" for Jess. Then he turned to me.

"Come on, Win. You play, too."

I sat down at the piano and joined him. He didn't have to ask what I wanted.

> Oh the Tennessee Stud was long and lean,
> Color of the sun, and his eyes were green.
> He had the nerve and he had the blood.
> There never was a horse like the Tennessee Stud.

Jess' clear soprano rose over my alto and Randy's tenor, while Pete and Lorrie rocked in Mom's lap, the golden lamplight falling on us like a veil, as outside the field of night sky expanded over the house in an infinitely widening arc, studded with galaxies that stretched on forever.

CHAPTER 7

THE WEATHER TURNED MEAN on Monday. Gray, ugly clouds hovered over the hills and settled on the ranch and the town like a heavy blanket. It wasn't quite cold enough to snow, so we were drenched every few hours with rain that made the skin under my sweater feel like a damp layer of clothing I couldn't take off. By sending kids with notes first requesting, then pleading, then threatening, the teachers finally got Mr. Peasley to turn up the heat a notch or two, just before half of us came down with our first winter colds.

I kept avoiding Marjorie, conscious of *Cheyenne Autumn* sitting in my book bag like a thermos of old milk I didn't dare open for fear of its rancid stink. On Wednesday she finally confronted me in the hall outside the lunchroom.

"Well?" Her dark eyes held mine; I couldn't meet them.

"Well, what?"

"Have you read it?"

I thought for a second about playing dumb, but that would only prolong my misery.

"Most of it. About two-thirds."

"So?"

"We can't use it."

"Why not?" She spit this out as if she'd anticipated my judgment.

"It's too—ugly."

That didn't quite convey what I meant. I'd tried more than once to picture us standing in front of the class, describing the scenes I'd read to a roomful of slack-jawed kids, their eyes at first bored, then slowly alarmed as they struggled to fit what they were hearing into the familiar stories of heroic Western pioneers versus savage, pitiless warriors. I saw them then, infuriated, picking up books, pencils, desks, hurling them at us, defending the world they knew against the barbarian horde of two who would destroy it.

"They won't listen." The insufficiency of my words overwhelmed me even as I said them.

"We can make them listen!"

We? I almost threw out Tonto's reply to the Lone Ranger, "Whaddya mean *we*, white man?"—Randy's favorite dumb joke—but caught myself in time. Marjorie seemed two inches taller than she had a few minutes ago, her eyes snapping with fire.

"Mrs. Isaacson will back us up. She knows what the book is about, and she wants us to do it."

Just beyond Marjorie's voice I could hear kids laughing and chattering in the lunchroom, and a tide of envy for their innocence, their uncomplicated lives and easy choices, filled my chest. Whose side was I on? Was I supposed to kick everyone I knew in the teeth, rub their noses in the manure their grandparents had left for them in the corners of their houses, under the stairs, in the back of the closets, the muted stench familiar now as their own sweat? And if I did, where would I live afterwards? I didn't want to be ostracized, yet I couldn't unknow what I now knew. I could choose to keep it to myself, and if it were up to me, I would have. Marjorie was part of it, though, and I knew she wouldn't disappear or be silenced.

"Look, let's ask Mrs. Isaacson for a new topic," I suggested in a low voice. "We just can't do this one."

"You mean *you* can't." Her look was a challenge, a condemnation. I imagined her alone, in front of the class, her voice clear and angry, picking up speed, trying to finish without faltering.

"Come on, Marjorie. She'll change it."

"No." Why was she so stubborn?

"Don't you get it? No one wants to hear about this!"

"No one?" Now I heard "Who's *we*, white man?" in *her* voice. "If you don't want to do it, I'll do it myself."

I snatched the opening she'd made.

"Fine!" I dug into my bag and handed her the book. "Have fun." I pushed past her and marched, fizzy with relief, toward the laughter beyond the glass-paneled door, my hand ready to push it open.

"Coward."

The word pinged in the air like the after-buzz of a tiny metallic bell, so faint I couldn't tell if Marjorie had actually said it or if my own thought had crystallized into sound. I whirled to confront her, but she was already walking away from me down the dim hallway.

"Hey, look at these!"

Corinne stopped in front of a display of hair ornaments in Woolworth's, where we'd come on a reconciliation outing after school. She'd greeted the news that Marjorie was on her own with a smile that mixed self-righteous smugness with just enough welcoming delight to allow us to agree without words to work together again. I decided not to say anything to Mrs. Isaacson until the following week, giving us time to come up with a new topic.

"What do you think?" Corinne slipped a blue headband over her hair and turned her head back and forth in front of the counter mirror.

"It's okay." With her hair yanked back from her pale face, she reminded me of a wet cat, but I knew that, just then, that was as close to the elegance she longed for as she'd get.

She glanced at me suspiciously.

"Well, I think it looks great!" I hadn't sounded enthusiastic enough. She pulled the headband off, paid the saleslady, and marched down the aisle.

"No, really, Cor, it's slick. It makes you look kind of like a *Seventeen* model." That fib would actually become reality in a few years, as Corinne acquired a knack with blow-dryer and hot curlers, and sleek curves replaced her bony angularities.

She slowed down, soothed. I helped her adjust the headband to the perfect angle, and we ambled past the multicolored scarves, the fake pearl earrings and necklaces, and turned into the cosmetics aisle. We'd often tried samples of lipsticks, pink and peach blusher, mascara, and exotic shades of eye shadow, then wiped most of it off with tissue before we left the store.

"Why don't you get some for your big date?" Corinne snickered. As part of making up, I'd confided to her my dilemma about Zippy's invitation.

"Oh, sure, I really need to be beautiful for him." I fluffed out my hair, parodying primping. Corinne chose a purplish-red sample lipstick and carefully spread it over her lips, then puckered them at me and squeezed her eyes shut.

"Kiss me, Zippy!"

She bent over, dissolving into contagious giggles. Suddenly defiant, I selected Revlon's newest coral-pink shade and waved to the woman at the counter, pulling out my wallet.

"You're going to *buy* it?" Corinne's purple-rimmed mouth had fallen open. Ten minutes later we left the store with gold-tone tubes of instant adulthood in our pockets.

As WE WALKED BACK toward the school, I saw Collie and Jess turning into the Two Elks Cafe. Jess spotted me and waved.

"Let's go in." Junior-high kids usually had sodas at the counter in Woolworth's, while the high-school crowd filled the Cafe, but I was feeling unmoored from my usual routine and, buoyed by my daring purchase, was ready to break the rules.

The door closed behind us, and we surveyed the sea of crew cuts, denim shirts, pony tails, and rivers of brown and dishwater-blond hair covering the backs of girls with fuzzy sweaters and leather jackets, animated faces grinning and sparring, wreaths of smoke rising from burning cigarettes. I felt out of my depth.

Jess and Collie had stopped next to a table full of boys with broad shoulders and lanky legs, clean-lined jaws, most with a faint hint of beard visible only in indirect light. One ruddy-faced, stocky guy sported an attempt at a mustache, which he stroked ostentatiously. Collie turned a chair backwards and straddled it, nodding to Jess to sit down next to him. Jess glanced briefly at me, then sat without any gesture of invitation in my direction. I looked around for an empty table.

"Let's get out of here," Corinne whispered, shifting from foot to foot. I took her by the arm and marched her, so fast she almost stumbled, toward a table in the middle of the room, two over from Collie's. I knew, if I didn't do it right then, I'd lose my nerve.

As we lowered ourselves into our seats, the ruddy-face guy's deep bass voice rumbled behind us, carrying over the general murmur. One of the high-school-girl waitresses came and took our order—two Cokes, one cherry and one vanilla—and sauntered back to the counter. Carefully avoiding looking in Jess' direction, I scanned the tables for a friendly peer and came up empty. A loud burst of laughter, then the bass voice again, and suddenly Collie was on his feet, his chair banging onto the floor.

"Shut up, you prick!"

Collie's head, neck veins bulging, was thrust forward toward the ruddy guy, whose face was now a deep red, his lips frozen in a caricature of a smile. Jess stood up, put her hand on Collie's arm, and tilted her body slightly toward his in a gesture so familiar I had to remind myself I wasn't seeing Mom soothing Randy. For a moment neither boy moved.

"Take it back," Collie hissed.

Ruddy-face sat back in his chair.

"Okay, you're not. But you're next door to one."

"To *what*?"

The whole cafe, already listening intently, fell even deeper into silence, all eyes on Collie. Jess tugged gently on his arm, murmuring in his ear. He jerked his arm away, and she put it back so lightly she was hardly touching him.

"Come on, Col." Jess tried again.

Collie turned toward her. "Stay out of this!" She took a step backward and stood still. Collie faced his opponent. "You too goddamn scared to say it when everybody's listening?" No reply from ruddy-face. "Go on. You think I'm a Chey-lover?"

Ruddy-face broke their locked gaze and muttered something in the direction of his glass. Collie's head eased back. Jess let her breath out and put her hand again on his arm. This time he let it rest there, glancing slowly one by one at the other boys, who were staring at him, waiting for a signal.

"Get a new joke book, you jerk." He turned and wove through the maze of tables, Jess immediately behind him. As the door closed, a hubbub of voices erupted like a crowd of children let loose after school.

"What was that all about?" Corinne asked me. "Who's a Chey? He can't mean Jess, can he?"

"Of course not! He must mean Bell."

Corinne looked blank, then puzzled.

"The Indian guy in the car?" I'd told her about the ride I'd gotten from Collie. "Are they friends?"

"What if they are?" Suddenly the tension that had been building in me spewed out at Corinne. "They play on the same team, don't they? What's the big deal? You're just like everyone else in this stupid backwater town—if your great-grandmother didn't like someone, you won't like them either."

Corinne snapped her body upright.

"What's the matter with you?" she sputtered. "I didn't do anything!"

"Oh, leave me alone," I mumbled. "I'm worried about Jess, I guess."

Corinne glared at me but decided to accept this as a token apology. We drank our Cokes and avoided any further discussion of what we'd just witnessed, which strained our conversation. Soon we left to wait outside the school for the late bus. By then the rain had stopped, and a few shafts of late afternoon sun were filtering through the dank air from behind the steel-gray clouds, like a promise I couldn't quite believe.

AT HER KITCHEN TABLE, after my next lesson, Roone leaned forward, poured me a second cup of tea, then sat back, scanning the application form I'd filled out during the week. She handed it back, nodding in approval.

"If we leave that Friday morning, that should give us plenty of time, even if the roads are bad. If they predict a blizzard, we'll leave a day earlier, or Selby can drive us." She grinned at Selby, who was buttering a cranberry muffin hot from his oven.

"Woman, that's four months away! Who knows if I'll be here or in South America, playing with the young gals on the beaches in Rio?" Selby winked at me and popped a steaming fingerful into his mouth. Roone played at whacking in his direction with a spoon.

"You've got the money for the entry fee?"

I pulled a twenty-dollar bill from my pocket. I'd had about eight dollars saved up, but thought I'd have to wheedle the rest from Jess, or even Randy, much as I'd hated the idea. But, still bursting with generosity from the loan, he'd listened to Mom's unenthusiastic description of the competition with a grin.

"He told me, 'Go get 'em,' and handed this to me," I reported.

"Good for him!" Roone smiled. "He must know what it means to you, because he sure doesn't know Beethoven from his butt."

Selby pretended to be shocked.

"Honey, watch your language around the child!"

I looked over my shoulder.

"You've got a child in here?" I exclaimed in mock surprise. "Hiding in the closet maybe?"

Selby grinned.

"That's right, we got a half-dozen all waiting to get at that piano as soon as you leave."

Someone knocked quietly at the kitchen door.

"There's one of 'em now." Selby waited a moment before raising his voice. "Come on in."

The door opened. Not a child, but a tall, black-haired, umber-skinned boy, maybe sixteen, with thick eyebrows over deep-set eyes that glanced quickly around, then fixed on mine: It was a second before I realized I'd already met him.

"Sorry." His voice was deep, clear, yet tentative. He took a step back. Selby motioned him forward.

"Hell, Bell, I told you a million times you don't have to wait. Just knock and walk on in." Selby gestured toward me. "Do you know Win here?"

Bell hesitated as if searching my expression for a signal about his answer, then decided for himself.

"Yeah. Hi, Win."

"Hi."

He took a few steps into the kitchen, his head seeming to graze the low ceiling.

"I just need to—use the facilities." His cheeks began to flush; I could feel sympathetic heat in mine.

"Go ahead. You know the way."

Bell disappeared into the hall, and I heard his footsteps recede and a door close. Selby turned to me.

"He's working out real well. Only been here a week, but he works hard, never late. Wants to help me on hunting trips, too, but I tell him he can't miss any school."

"You're too good to him, Selby," Roone added in a low voice, then turned to me. "Selby would let him skip work for basketball practice, but then he'd hardly be here at all."

"Playing ball is real important for boys, woman," Selby frowned. "How you think they ever learn to get on with each other if they don't share all that stuff?"

"He's here to work for you, not be your do-good project." Roone sighed. "I know I'm whistling Dixie, for all you'll listen to me. Don't think I don't know you've made a deal with him."

"Now, honey, don't be like that." Selby put his arm around her and shook her shoulders gently. "You're no different than me, and you know it."

He glanced briefly at me. I saw Roone nudge him with her elbow.

A wave of embarrassment rose like a hot tide into my face. A few months before, Randy had begun to complain that he was fed up with Roone's charity, that three years of free lessons had more than paid off Selby's debt to him. I'd hated pleading with him to let me keep taking lessons, but I'd done it. I knew I was Roone's best and most advanced pupil, and I sensed how much satisfaction it gave her when gleaming strands of music unrolled from my hands, the hands she'd guided.

But each week, as I knocked at their door, I felt less like a scholarship student and more like a charity case. I was counting on winning the competition and using the five hundred dollars in prize money to become a paying pupil. Otherwise, I vowed, I wouldn't continue, even though stopping would feel like cutting off the air I breathed. My world had become inconceivable without music, and that never changed. Later on, in college, I started asking people which, if they had to choose, was worse: a world without art, or one without music? Many chose art; many agonized, declaring the choice impossible. I never had a moment's doubt. A world without music would be cold and empty, like a dead star.

To cover my emotion, I reached for another muffin, though I wasn't hungry. Selby got up and had removed another batch from the oven just as Bell walked back into the room.

"Sit down and have a bite," Selby said. Bell hesitated, then pulled out the chair next to me. I passed him the butter plate, watching his long, slender fingers, his delicately boned wrists. He ate carefully, neatly, and quickly, trying, I intuited, to conceal how hungry he was, as Selby asked him about the team's prospects, the lineup for the coming season.

Everyone went to the Friday night games, huddled in the crisp night air for football, our breath making puffs of white steam as the season marched to an end, then crowded into the indoor gym bleachers for basketball, emerging from the steamy hall, our heads still reverberating with echoes and shouts, into a silent snowy world. I knew the players by sight and by reputation, but I'd never paid much attention to details of positions and plays. What I could tell now was that Selby was aware that Bell was better than good, and that admiration for Bell's skill formed part of Selby's warmth toward him.

As Selby finished describing a near-miraculous win in which Bell had played a crucial role, Bell, clearly uncomfortable, turned to me.

"You're really good."

I stared at him, not sure what he meant.

"The piano. You're almost as good as Mrs. Grafton." He must have been listening to my lesson. My dismay must have shown on my face, because his words came out faster.

"I couldn't help hearing you. I was working right outside the window. You play like—I don't know what, like a record or something."

"No, I don't." I snuck a look at Roone, convinced she'd been insulted at this downgrading of her own talent. She smiled at me, but I wasn't soothed; instead, I grew more uncomfortable.

"You don't know much about music, do you?" I snapped. "I'm nowhere near as good as Roone is. Anyone can hear that."

Bell pulled back as if I'd slapped him, and his face hardened into immobility. In one fluid motion he pushed back his chair, got up, nodded to Roone, and walked out the back door, leaving me in a whirl of irritation, as much at myself as at the rest of them.

Selby raised his eyebrows, and his mouth twisted into a line of exaggerated bewilderment.

"You got something against compliments, girl?"

Roone shook her head at him and looked at me seriously.

"Don't you know he doesn't hear what you hear, Win?"

She chuckled at my confusion but turned serious again.

"What he said sounded ridiculous to you because you're comparing yourself to what *you* know. Compared to Richter or Van Cliburn, you know you're a beginner. But what *he* knows is that, when you play, music comes out, and when he's tried to do it—and he has—it sounds like a cat chasing a mouse down the keys."

She raised her eyebrows at me.

"Don't you see? To him, you're a magician."

I shifted my gaze to the window. Through the open door of the shed, I could see Bell's shadowed figure bent over a table, his right arm moving back and forth. For a moment, I stepped inside his head, imagining him hearing the Bach fugue I'd been playing, its bright notes weaving themselves into an intricate web of sounds, rising and falling in the still air like a pattern of light and shadow, and then realizing, astounded, that someone I knew, someone entirely real and ordinary, was creating this. And I felt the same awe that I'd felt as a four-year-old watching my mother produce a dress out of random pieces of cloth, or as, last year, I'd watched Bell himself leap into the air, improbably twisting his body and flicking his wrists at exactly the right moment to send the ball into the net. Maybe we are all magicians, I thought. To someone else, what we do, who we are, is magical and mysterious.

I MADE UP AN excuse to leave Roone's before Mom arrived, and ran to the post office. The air was frosty against my tingling skin, and in the west clouds were piled up behind the hills, promising snow. I pushed open the door, grateful for the warmth of the musty room. Zippy's pale face looked up from the table where he was sorting stamps.

"Hey, Win, I got something for you."

He disappeared and re-emerged holding a white envelope.

"It's from California, like the other one." He held it out but pulled it back as I reached for it.

"We're still on for next week, right?"

I nodded.

"Good. Collie said no sweat, we can go with him and Jess. We'll come and get you at seven-thirty, okay?"

I barely listened, stuffing the envelope he relinquished into my pocket.

"Aren't you gonna read it?"

"I don't have time. My mom is waiting." I turned to leave.

"She was in here earlier."

I stopped and turned back, opening my mouth.

"Don't worry, I didn't tell her." Zippy grinned, leaning toward me. "Your secret is safe with me."

As soon as I got outside, I ripped open the envelope and pulled out the letter. The bold black script glowed against the white paper.

Dear Cousin Winona,

Thank you so much for your lovely letter. I'm so glad your mother got mine. I'd love to meet you all. It's so exciting to find a whole corner of your family you didn't know existed.

I grew up in Montana myself. We lived first in Choteau, then moved when I was eight to Great Falls. My father was in the forest service, and my mother taught English in high school. They're retired now. I'm twenty-nine, and my sister Joyce is twenty-seven. She lives in Helena and is a lawyer. I went to the University of Montana, and then I went to graduate school in Oregon and got a master's degree in psychology. Two years ago I moved to California. I work in a mental hospital, helping people who are seriously disturbed.

I love it here—California really does have good weather all year long, so I do a lot of hiking and camping. Since you like to travel, maybe one day you'll come and visit me! Meanwhile, I'll be in Montana at Christmas, to visit my parents and sister, and I hope we can all get together and meet each other then.

Love, Marilyn

I stared at the letter, trying to imagine Marilyn's life. What was it like to work with crazy people? I pictured zombies with twisted faces lurching down dark corridors, their hospital gowns flapping behind them, while Marilyn stalked them carefully, a hypodermic poised like a gun in her hand. Or, like the doctor in *The Snake Pit*, did Marilyn sit in an office, wearing a white coat, nodding sympathetically as a sobbing patient poured out her woes? In either case, she probably didn't spend her days strumming a guitar or stringing love beads.

And only two months from now I might get to meet her! The thought filled me with a sense of expansion, as if I were rising in a hot-air balloon, about to soar over the hills that hemmed in the horizon, out into the vastness of an unknown land. How I could manage a meeting apart from my family I had no idea, but I decided I'd worry about that later. Just then I reread the letter one more time as I walked back toward Roone's, then put it away, gathering myself behind a wall that

Mom wouldn't be able to penetrate, one so smooth and bland she wouldn't even know it was there.

As soon as we got back, Mom set me to carrying the jars of the beans and tomatoes she'd been canning down to the cellar, then sent me outside to help Randy stack cake for the cattle to eat during the long winter storms ahead. After supper, when I thought I'd be free to plunge again into *Forever Amber*, which I'd snuck past Mrs. Cunningham, the librarian, and was hiding under my mattress, she insisted I stand and let her measure me for a new skirt I'd picked out of the pattern book. As soon as we were in her room, she closed the door and faced me with a look that told me she'd been hiding behind a wall as thick as mine.

"Where's the letter?" She put her hands on her hips. I backed up and sat down on the double bed's green-and-white floral patterned bedspread.

"What letter?"

"Don't play dumb with me, Winona."

"Honest, I don't know what you—-"

"Just show it to me. I mean now."

I drew my head down as though I were running through an ice-cold thunderstorm. Mom grabbed me by the shoulders and shook me hard.

"I won't have you acting sneaky like this and then lying about it. Do you hear me? I ran into Mr. Anderson at Starr's, and he said there was a letter from California waiting for you in the post office. That's where you went after your lesson, isn't it?" She didn't wait for an answer. "Go get it for me."

I pulled the envelope from my pocket and handed it to her, watching her face as she read it, hating her broad turned-up nose, her thin dry lips, her reddened hands that shook with anger or fear. She looked up at me as if I'd turned into someone she didn't know and didn't particularly want to meet.

"What have you told her?"

"What do you mean?"

"I mean, how many letters have you written her? What does she know about us?"

"This is the only one! I answered her letter, and then she wrote this one back."

"You haven't answered this one yet?"

"How could I? I just got it today!"

Mom exhaled slowly, deeply.

"You will not write her again."

A hot wave rose in my chest, and my heart beat wildly.

"Yes I will! She's written *me* now, and I'm going to write back!"

I stood up and turned to walk out. Mom grabbed me and jerked me back to face her.

"Why can't you understand?" Her face was flushed. "Nothing good can come from her. She's just got you all wrought up, expecting things to change, and they won't. She's just pretending to be interested in you, in us, can't you see that?"

"She is not! She wants me to visit her, she says so!"

"She's just being polite. People promise all sorts of things to your face, and then they treat you like dirt!"

"You don't even know her!"

"I know enough." She sat down gingerly on the edge of her bed, as if she'd suddenly hurt herself.

"Win, I'm only trying to save you from being disappointed, that's all. People hurt you even when they don't mean to, and most of them get a kick out of it when they do."

"I don't believe that! You're trying to scare me, and I don't know why."

She looked at me oddly. All the anger suddenly drained from her face, replaced by a mixture of pity and distance, as if she were watching a child from a tribe so alien she could hardly label it as human, whose cry she nonetheless could interpret instantly. She reached out as if to touch my face. I flinched, and instantly her eyes filled with tears. I wanted to throw myself into her arms, to cry with her, rocking together in a sorrow I didn't understand, but my pride held me back. Instead, I picked up the letter from the bed and walked out, listening through the sound of my blood swishing through my veins for her to call me back, but she let me go.

MARIE

April 19, 1969

 My god, Win reminds me so much of Mama when I see that furious snap in her eyes like a dam about to burst, and me waiting for the icy water to knock me off my feet. Not that Mama hit me: She did it all with words, hateful, unforgivable words that I carried with me for days, for years, that I've never completely forgotten.

 Jess is different—she holds it inside, pushing against you, stubborn and slow like a glacier. Win flares up in a second, and then suddenly I don't see her any more. Instead I see Mama, those same freckles and reddish-brown hair that frizzes up in the damp air, lashing out at whatever is there, shooting up like a rocket, out beyond where anyone can reach her. I want to yell, "Stop!" I want to reach out and call her back before she disappears, but my body gets there before I find the words. And then I've pushed her, or sometimes I've shaken her so hard her teeth rattle. And then it's Win again, not Mama. Something in me shrinks up at what I've done to her, at the hatred I see in her face, and I know I deserve it. But I want to cry out: It wasn't what you think. It wasn't really you I hit at all.

 I never knew what to expect from Mama, that's for sure. I had to watch her like a farmer watches the sky for signs of the weather in tornado season. When she felt good, she could be funny and charming, sweeping you into a world of wonderful adventures. Before I was old enough to go to school, in the morning once my father was gone, she'd teach me to dance. She'd put on the radio and I'd stand on her shoes, and we'd waltz around the kitchen, singing the words to some old song as loud as we could, until we were dizzy, and then we'd collapse on the floor, laughing our heads off. And she'd tell me stories, exciting ones about murder and revenge, and scary ones about vampires and werewolves. Sometimes I'd wake up screaming from nightmares about the creatures in her stories, and then she'd come and lie down with me on my bed, and hum a sweet hymn, in her voice as beautiful as a silver bell. "Shall we gather at the river, where bright angel feet have trod?" And I felt sealed with her inside a magic circle, where nothing bad could ever get at me.

But then something would set her off, some little thing, a dish you broke or a drawer that stuck. And then, in a flash, everything changed. It's as if Mama disappeared and someone else, someone I didn't recognize, stood there in her place, screaming and cursing. "The Fiend has come to drag you down!" The words the minister yelled at us in his hellfire sermons, they're what I heard again in my head as I cowered before her. I'd hold my breath and shut my eyes and pray, over and over: Come back, Mama, come back. And sometimes she would, and sometimes she wouldn't.

It was Papa who seemed to set her off worst, doing something she didn't like or not doing something he was supposed to do, like picking up something she'd asked him to get at the store, or coming home two hours later than he said he would. He didn't feel time the way she did; he didn't measure it by the clock.

She gave him a watch one Christmas to fix that, and he wore it for a month or two, and then he lost it. He took it off, I guess, and left it somewhere, and when he came home one night there was no watch. When she discovered that, oh Jesus, she reached out and grabbed a pot from the stove and threw it at his head. He ducked just in time, and the pot burst against the wall, and macaroni exploded everywhere. He turned so pale under his dark skin, his face looked like cement.

For a second he didn't move; then he took two steps over to her and grabbed her wrists and dragged he to the door and threw her out. It was pouring rain, and she started pounding on the door, screaming for him to let her in, but he wouldn't. He yelled at her, "Go sleep in the barn with the other animals!" She kept on screaming and pounding, but Papa wouldn't open the door. She came in the next morning, filthy, with straw stuck all over her clothes, and went straight to bed.

I waited a while and then I went in quietly and slipped up next to the bed. Her eyes were shut; her face was so white it looked like part of the pillow. I thought she was going to die.   "Mama, when are you going to get up?" I whispered to her. She didn't answer. "Please get up, Mama. Let's make cookies." She turned her head away and started to cry without making a sound. I climbed onto the bed and snuggled up close to her. "Don't cry, Mama, please don't cry." I patted her shoulder like you'd pat a baby. She let me stay there, and after what felt like hours, she got up and went back out like nothing had happened. Afterwards, whenever she went to bed like that, I'd be the one to go in after her. And Papa let me do it.

Later, when Papa had left and we lived with Aunt Beulah and Uncle Harold in Billings, there were the tight clothes she started wearing, her skimpy, silky skirts, and the bright red lipstick and big circles of rouge on her cheeks. She'd spend whole evenings in the Roundup, coming home smelling of beer and whiskey, her makeup smeared and her stockings lopsided. Sometimes some man we didn't know would be with her as she staggered up the steps, laughing and talking, the man looking half-confused, half-excited. He'd let go of her as I opened the door, and she'd fall against me, and the man would walk away while I got her to come inside and not sleep on the porch where everyone could see her the next morning on their way to work.

She'd write checks for money she didn't have. I'd sneak stuff she bought out of her room and go and beg the storekeepers to take it back. But sometimes I didn't get there fast enough, and the store would have put her on their list. And when they refused her next check, she'd blow up and they'd call the police, and we'd have to run down and try and fix that, too— until the day when I'd gone, tired of trying to fix everything, and no one could fix it any more.

She never spoke about it to me, that's for sure. The times when she was Mama, I thought I could read in her eyes what she could never say, that she was grateful and that she needed me. But the real truth was that nothing I did could make her happy; nothing was enough to make her pleased to just be where she was, there with me. That's what drives me crazy, when I see Win desperate to be anywhere else but with us, here and now. I see her, a wild horse, fighting the bridle, a bird beating the sides of its cage with its wings. And then I see Mama, screaming, frantic to get out, to escape from what she can't get away from, her own self.

CHAPTER 8

L OOK AT MY HAIR! It's hideous!"

"What's wrong with it?" Jess turned toward me, holding the can of hair spray she'd been using. Her new green dress hung on a hook on the door and shone in the light of the dresser lamp.

"It looks like a rat's nest!" I wailed, clutching a hank of my auburn frizz and tugging on it. I hadn't realized how anxious I was about the dance until I found me making faces at myself in the bathroom mirror and brushing my hair so hard my scalp still tingled from the dig of the bristles. Zippy and Collie were coming to pick us up in just over an hour. The pleasure of fantasy had long given way to worry about what I should wear and horrified contemplation of various disaster scenarios that, I knew, were bound to take place.

"Don't do that. You'll just split the ends. Let me see." Jess motioned for me to turn around.

"What did you do to it?"

"I was trying to tease it, like you do, but it just poofed up like a sponge or something. I can't go looking like this!" I sat down on the bed and dropped my head into my hands.

"Calm down. How much time do we have?" Jess looked at her watch lying on the dresser in front of her. "Get it all wet, and I'll set it for you. You can use my dryer."

Ten minutes later, my hair slick with conditioner and looped over giant rollers, Jess struggled to fit my grotesquely enlarged head into the plastic bonnet at the end of her dryer hose. Then she turned on the motor, and my ears filled with the roar of a combine in high gear. Twenty minutes later, Jess skillfully disengaged the rollers and carefully combed my now-silky hair into waves. She slapped the hand I automatically reached toward my brush.

"Don't touch it. If you leave it alone, it'll stay."

"How do you know all these things?"

"Trial and error. Reading articles and trying stuff out. Seeing what looks best." She caught my eye. "It takes a lot of work to look good, you know."

I sighed, knowing that, in that case, my impatience doomed me to a life of plainness interspersed with occasional moments of assisted beauty. I'd watched Jess apply small daubs of blush to her cheeks, a touch of mascara and eyeliner to her eyes, outlining her mouth with reddish lip pencil and filling in the lines with lipstick, bringing her already pretty face into clearer focus until it shone like a pearl.

"Here." She approached me, eye pencil in hand. I shrank back but leaned forward when she put her hands on her hips.

"Go ahead. It can't make me look any worse," I said, and gave my face up to her hands. Half-hypnotized, lulled by the silkiness of her brush, the sweet fragrance of powder, her fingertips on my skin, the warmth of her hands near my cheek and on my eyelids, I sat before her, an initiate being prepared by an older priestess for a mysterious ritual.

"Look."

I opened my eyes. It was still my face, but older, more knowing, more seductive. The ends of my hair were turned under; my lips seemed fuller. The small pearl earrings she'd fastened to my earlobes glistened in the lamplight. I felt ready for anything.

"Do you like it?"

For an answer, I hugged her tight.

"Hey, don't wrinkle my dress. I think I just heard Collie's car. They'll be here in a minute. Come on. What are you going to wear?"

I gestured at the black-and-brown striped taffeta, with its rounded collar, lying on my bed. "It makes me look like a sad sack!" I meant it made me look like a kid, not the grown-up I wanted to be.

"What else you got?"

"Nothing."

Jess rolled her eyes, riffled through our closet, pulled out something blue, and threw it at me.

"Try this. It's a little small for me."

I slipped the dress over my head. The neckline was cut lower than I was used to. When I tried to pull it up, Jess laughed. "Cut that out. You're meant to see something. Here, let's pin the shoulders so your bra straps don't show." She fished around with the straps, and stepped back, looking at me like a horse trader scrutinizing a prospective brood mare. I heard the front door slam, male voices growling at each other, Mom's laugh.

"Jess! Win! Your Romeos are here!" Randy boomed.

I winced and threw myself on the bed.

"I can't go. Tell them I'm sick. Tell them I'm dead."

"Don't be ridiculous. You look good, *really* good. Come on, where's your bag? Here." She stuffed a lipstick, a scarf and a dollar bill in a paisley string bag, threw it at me, grabbed her own black velvet one, and pulled me up.

"Cheer up. It happens to the best of us." She shoved me from the back out the door, stopped, and whispered in my ear, "I'm glad you're going with us." Then she frog-marched me, half-panicked, half-elated, down the hall.

As we walked into the living room, Collie and Zippy looked up from the sofa where they were sitting awkwardly side by side. The light glinted off Collie's black hair, slicked with pomade and caught into a small ponytail at the nape of his neck. His cheekbones stood out above cheeks hollowed by muscles rippling in his jaw. Zippy, in a shirt so brightly white I couldn't look at it directly, pulled nervously at his polka-dotted green tie. When they saw us, they both scrambled to their feet. I could see Zippy's eyes widen and his mouth fall open. Collie grinned briefly at Jess before he smoothed his expression into blankness.

"Don't you girls look nice!" exclaimed Mom. She was standing behind Randy as he reclined in his armchair, Lorrie and Pete keeping silent watch on either side.

"They took long enough getting all gussied up," said Randy. His eyes inspected me as he frowned and took a sip from his beer. "That's quite a dress. You look ready for a night on the town. Better watch her close, Zip."

I felt my face grow hot. I wanted to run back to the bedroom and hide, or to smash in Randy's face with a baseball bat. Mom came over and put her hands on my shoulders, adjusting my neckline by pulling at it.

"Don't!" I whispered. Her hands fell away and she took a step back, smiling at me tentatively. I saw Jess cross over and stand next to Collie.

"So what kind of heap are you going to ferry my daughters around in?" Randy asked.

"We're *not*—" Jess stopped herself and took a deep breath. Mom's face contracted. I scrambled for something to say before Jess could resume, but Zippy got there first.

"It's a Mustang, and it's terrific." The words rushed out of him. "You should see it. It does zero to sixty in six seconds, and it's supercharged. He's souped the engine, and it runs smooth as. . . ." His voice died as he noticed Jess' warning look and Collie's raised palm directed at him.

"Well, you be extra careful, then." Mom was watching Randy's eyes as she tried to forestall him, but he wouldn't be overridden.

"Your father must have money to burn," he said. "Give me a good solid pick-up anytime. Mine goes 200,000 miles, and she's still humming. A Mustang's an expensive gas-hog next to that."

"It's not my dad's, it's mine." Collie's voice was cool and strained, like a stretched rubber band. "I do all the work on it and I pay for it myself." He didn't want to antagonize Randy, I sensed, but he couldn't let this slip by. Jess' eyes burned with pride.

Once again Mom soothed Randy's flame.

"You better get going, kids, or you'll be late. You all look so fine, you'll be the hit of the dance." She bustled toward the hall. "Take your warmest coats, girls. It's awfully cold out there."

Randy kept his eyes on us as we bundled up.

"Hold it," he barked as we opened the front door. "Remember, back by midnight, you Cinderellas."

I nodded reluctantly.

"Enjoy yourselves." A smile spread across his face, mirrored by Mom.

We turned, ran out the door, and burst into the frosty air, relief exploding from us in white-breathed gusts of laughter that launched us into the car, through the gate, and on the road at last.

As we drove through the dark, I kept at least a foot of distance between me and Zippy, who looked almost as uncomfortable as I felt. His forehead was dotted with tiny beads of sweat, while my hands were so clammy I kept wiping them—secretly, I hoped—against my coat. The interior of the car—black leather, gleaming glass, and chrome—was so immaculate I sat on the edge of the seat, afraid to lean too heavily on it. In front, Collie and Jess talked in easy voices about their friends, school events, harmless gossip. I couldn't think of anything to say. I ran sentences through my mind in silent rehearsal, but they were all sure to sound stupid to Jess and Collie.

Finally Jess turned around. "Everything OK back there?" she asked. "You both speak English, don't you?"

I threw her a dirty look.

"We—we're practicing yogic breathing." What had possessed me to say that? The previous year I'd read an article on yoga, which had led me to spend a week sitting cross-legged, staring at a candle flame, humming, "Om". I'd ended up with gray spots dancing across my field of vision, no nearer enlightenment than before.

"Well, at least you're breathing. I'd begun to wonder."

Zippy looked puzzled. "What's yolk breathing?" he asked. Some help *he* was.

"*Yogic.* It's what the big Indian gurus use to reach a state of nirvana." I hadn't known I remembered all that.

"You mean medicine men?" asked Collie.

"Not that kind of Indian. *Indian* Indian."

"What's nirv—nirva? Kind of like nervous?" Zippy again. I turned away, exasperated at his ignorance. Submerged in my own self-consciousness, it didn't occur to me he might be an anxious as I was.

"I've got something better for nerves than breathing funny," said Collie, reaching into the glove compartment and pulling out a small bottle. "Here you go."

With one hand, he unscrewed the top, took a gulp, and offered it to us. Zippy reached for it and took a long swallow. I watched his Adam's apple bob up and down like a disoriented rodent tunneling back and forth just under the surface. Smacking his lips, Zippy held the bottle out to me. Jess squealed.

"No! She's too young!"

That did it. I glared at her, snatched the bottle, filled my mouth and swallowed hard. Intense heat filled my throat and sank slowly toward my stomach as fire pricked my nose. I coughed reflexively, spraying liquor at Zippy, my eyes watering. He pulled a handkerchief from his pocket and handed it to me. I wiped my face carefully and blew my nose, catching Collie's amused eyes in the rearview mirror. Zippy swallowed another mouthful and handed the bottle to Jess. She took one ladylike sip and gave it back to Collie, who replaced the top and shut it back in the glove compartment.

My head felt loose and tingly, whether from coughing or the liquor I wasn't sure. Zippy slid along the seat until his leg touched mine, and draped his arm along the seat back, just grazing my neck. In my ordinary frame of mind, I'd have slid away, but right then I didn't care. He leaned close and put his mouth next to my ear.

"You look real good," he whispered. "Are those real pearls?"

Before I could answer his lips closed around the tiny globe on my earlobe and tugged gently on it. I jerked my head away abruptly and felt a pinch. Zippy, looking surprised, sat there with my earring hanging from his mouth.

I doubled over with laughter as Zippy spit the earring into his hand. He threw me an angry glance as I howled, unable to stop.

"You—you—" I tried to explain. "The earring—" I howled again, clutching my stomach. Collie and Jess, who'd been watching, were laughing, too.

"Do you take ketchup or mustard with your earrings?" giggled Jess.

"Hey, Zip, if you're that hungry, we can stop at the cafe for a burger." Collie smacked the steering wheel with his hand and guffawed. Zippy's frown slowly dissolved into a grin of good-natured embarrassment. Then he licked his lips in a parody of hunger, playing to our laughter. I could see his future unrolling in front of him as he slid into the role of a clown, earning acceptance by consenting to be ridiculed.

Zippy handed the earring back to me and held the hair away from my ear as I screwed the earring back in place. The car turned into Valley Street, and at its end loomed the brightly lit high school, glowing like a giant lantern against the ink-black sky.

THE PACKED GYM LOOKED huge and felt unfamiliar, no longer the shining arena in which I'd sat dozens of times. The usual bright lights had been replaced by strings of softly shining colored paper globes, illuminated by the small round bulbs inside. Faces took on a mystery, a glamor that made them hard to recognize. Music swirled from the speakers overhead, soft and sinuous, gently rocking the dancers in its flow.

As soon as we put away our coats, Jess and Collie had joined their respective groups of friends, laughing and talking, then joining to form couples, arms melding as they headed onto the dance floor. Zippy and I stood on the side for a while. The ice that had been broken in the car seemed to have us back in its chilly grip. Several of Zippy's friends came over and made half-suggestive, half-envious remarks.

"Aren't you guys going to dance?" asked one finally, just as "Black Magic Woman" started playing. Zippy reached for my hand without looking at me.

"Yeah, let's go." He pulled me towards the mass of couples, now moving their hips in separate, mirror-image gyrations. We found a spot, and Zippy closed his eyes, planted his feet, and wiggled his pelvis back and forth, holding his arms stretched out loosely. This wasn't what Jess had taught me a month before. I looked around, panicked. Everyone seemed to be undulating in a separate bubble of space, alone yet aware of everyone else by virtue of some new sense I was only beginning to realize existed.

"I—I can't do this." Zippy didn't seem to hear me. I could walk off the dance floor, I told myself, and he won't know until the music ends. I turned to leave.

"Hey, where are you going?" So he was using that mysterious awareness, too. Or perhaps he'd kept his eyes half-open. That was repellent, as if he'd been spying on me.

"I don't know how to do this."

"Doesn't matter what you do. Come on." He grinned encouragement and closed his eyes again. Oh, hell, I thought, what's the difference? No one was watching anyway.

I pretended I was alone in my room and let my body slip into the rhythms of the music. Slowly I became a Minoan dancer from *The King Must Die*, swaying in torchlight, golden serpent-shaped bracelets twining around my arms, the temple courtyard filled with incense, intoxicating and pungent. I circled and turned, exhibiting my half-clad body, oiled and burnished in homage to the goddess of love. The muscles of my hips loosened, my arms moved sinuously, beckoning and enticing. I couldn't believe how seductive I felt or how much I was enjoying myself.

The music shifted into a slow dance, and Zippy pulled my arms up to his shoulders and pressed his body against mine, gripping my waist with his hands. His heat surrounded me like a heavy blanket. I knew I was supposed to stand against him, swaying from side to side, our clothes and our skin stuck together, but instead I pulled away involuntarily. His startled expression began to darken into hurt resentment.

I fumbled for an excuse. "It's really hot in here," I said, hating myself for smiling. "Let's get something to drink."

He hesitated, turned, and led me toward a table covered in colored crepe paper weighed down by a huge punch bowl half-filled with pinkish liquid, surrounded by paper cups decorated with black cats and orange jack-o'-lanterns. Zippy dipped two cups in the bowl and handed one to me, then glanced around.

"Wait here." He walked over to the bleachers, where three of his friends sat hunched over, snapping jibes about the dancers out of the corners of their mouths. Zippy said something to them, and they stared at me and smirked, rose, and filed out the gym door. When they returned a few minutes later, their grins were wider and their eyes glittered. I could smell the liquor on Zippy's breath as he grabbed my hand and pulled me back toward the dancing couples.

"Come on." He draped my arms around his neck and locked his own tightly around my waist. I could feel the swelling in his groin against my pelvis. I tried to pull my hips back, but Zippy tightened his grip.

"Hey, cut it out," I protested. "I can't breathe."

"So don't." I'd become an enemy to be subdued. I gritted my teeth; the song couldn't last much longer. The music didn't seem in the least appealing any more. All I could think about was getting myself free from Zippy's chin against my forehead, from the lump in his trousers pushing insistently against my skirt. As the song ended, he relaxed his hold slightly. I was beyond trying to save his face, so I turned away as hard as I could. He kept his hand on my arm as I marched over to the punch bowl and let go when I shook it free, then signaled to his friends to join him outside. This time they didn't wait; one of them pulled a bottle from his pocket just before they disappeared through the door.

Jess came over to me as I was downing my second cup of punch.

"Having a good time?"

I glared at her and shook my head.

"We're sitting over there." She nodded toward a table. Collie, and another fellow facing away from me, were leaning back in their folding chairs, laughing. Jess jerked her head from me to them as she started walking toward them.

"Come on."

I hesitated but followed her. As I reached the table, Collie's friend pulled out a chair for me.

"Hey, it's the piano player." He grinned at me, and I recognized Bell. "Are you going to provide the half-time entertainment?"

"She's having a rough time," said Jess.

"Your date looked like he was using you like a fence to hold him up," laughed Bell. His faded denim shirt was open at the neck, and his skin glowed like burnished copper. In the low light, the blue and gold of his letter jacket had faded from their usual neon brightness to softer tones.

"Or maybe he got weak knees when he saw you," added Collie, putting his hand on Jess' shoulder.

"Weak knees from a bottle," snorted Bell. "Where'd he go, to sleep it off in the bushes?"

"You shouldn't have gotten him started, Col," scolded Jess. "He's probably totally loaded by now."

Zippy appeared in the doorway, scanning the crowd, his friends behind him. As he spotted me, his beet-red face gathered into a frown and he started in my direction. I shrank down into my chair.

"Here he comes," I muttered. "What'll I do?"

Bell stood up and held out his hand. For a moment my mind didn't follow; then I jumped up, took his hand, and hurried toward the dance floor.

"Thank you," I whispered as he put a hand on my waist and turned me around. This time his dance steps resembled the ones I'd learned with Jess. His movements were graceful, and he led me lightly, pushing and pulling with the gentle tugs of an experienced horseman putting a colt through its paces. I followed in a half-circle, turning away, then back. I began to enjoy myself again, in spite of the glimpses of Zippy's sour face beyond the moving shapes of the dancers. As a new song began, Bell hesitated.

"Let's dance some more," I proposed. "You're a really good dancer."

I didn't know which I wanted more, to dance with Bell or to keep Zippy at a distance, but as the same action accomplished both, I didn't have to choose. We went back to the undulating mutual seduction of the dance I'd just discovered that night. Bell, though, didn't shut his eyes. He watched me closely, a half-smile on his face, his body swaying with an easy grace that made it impossible for me to take my eyes off him.

When the song segued into a much slower melody swirling over an almost melancholy bass rhythm, Bell stepped back and stood for a moment, eyebrows raised, giving me the choice: stay or go? I didn't have to think. Willingly, I put my right hand in his, my left on his shoulder, and rested my head lightly on his chest.

> *I don't know if it's cloudy or bright*
> *But I only have eyes for you.*

His hand felt very large and warm on the small of my back. I inhaled his scent: something pungent and spicy mixed with the scent of clean cotton and a metallic undertone of fresh male sweat, heady and intoxicating. I kept my feet close to his as we shuffled and swayed. I could feel his chest vibrating softly as he hummed the melody. I knew he was smiling. I raised my head and looked at him, his deep eyes under heavy eyebrows, the dark crimson of a fresh shaving nick on his chin.

"Nice song," he said. "Kind of sad, though."

"A lot of love songs are sad." I thought a moment. "This one makes me sort of homesick. Even though I haven't gone anywhere." I wasn't sure what I meant by that, but the word was right. To my surprise, Bell nodded.

"I know. Homesick for somewhere you haven't been yet."

Exactly. I smiled at him, and he pulled me closer so I could no longer keep his face in focus, and rested his cheek lightly on the top of my head.

"Hold on." Suddenly he spun around, keeping me tight against him, moving us quickly across the floor. I barely managed to keep my feet even with his. "Hope you don't mind. Your date was headed this way."

"That's OK." Over Bell's shoulder I saw Zippy glaring at us, then turning to walk off. "This is a lot better than I thought it would be."

He looked amused. "You mean my dancing?"

"No. Just being here."

He touched my face briefly and put both hands on my waist. We stood, swaying very slightly, as if a wind were blowing two ways at once against both our backs, pushing us toward each other. The lower half of my body was tingling, and I felt as if the seams of my dress had grown too tight. The music faded slowly. Neither of us wanted to move. Finally Bell pulled back and looked at me.

"Let's get some air."

He walked toward the door, keeping one arm around me. Other couples were sitting down at the tables, perching on the bleachers, clustering around the punch bowl.

I felt a hand on my arm and turned to face Jess, her forehead creased with worry.

"Hey, Win, you need to fix your hair."

I opened my mouth to protest, but she was pulling me with her in the direction of the girl's bathroom. I pulled back.

"What do you think you're doing?" she hissed into my ear. "Do you think people didn't notice?"

"We're just going outside for a minute. What's wrong?"

She glanced around. No one was paying us any attention. I yanked my arm free and began walking away.

"Win!" I walked back to Bell and out through the open door. The cold air hit my face without seeming to drop my temperature at all. Bell pulled off his jacket and arranged it around my shoulders. We walked beyond the elongated oblong of light stretching from the doorway and passed into the deep blackness of the night sky, the autumn stars so thick overhead they merged into a milky carpet that stretched overhead from one end of the horizon to the other.

Bell stopped and turned me toward him. I didn't know what I wanted to happen, but my body did. He put his hands on either side of my face and slowly lowered his head. I felt his breath warm my skin as he touched his mouth to mine. The softness of his lips shocked me. I hadn't realized that I'd expected the clenched hardness of teeth pushing against my mouth, instead of this velvety touching that made my own lips tingle and swell.

Over and over, he grazed my lips with his, stroking my neck with his thumbs. My mouth opened, and I realized I was arching my body against his. Embarrassed, I drew back slightly. Bell opened his eyes and looked at me.

"You want to go back in?" I shook my head. He pulled his jacket closer around me, fumbling the snaps closed, his gaze level and serious. Then he stood a moment before he pulled me toward him again.

This time I kissed him back, ran my hands along his shoulders, breathing quickly. Currents of sensation seemed to be connecting parts of me I never imagined could be linked: my earlobes and my nipples, my lips and the inside of my thighs. Half-formed images galloped through my mind, whirling, stretching, collapsing. I tightened my arms around his neck.

Suddenly I felt a blow against my back, and I was pulled away from him so brutally I fell hard onto one knee. Bell's silhouette had become a dark mass of moving shadows bobbing up and down, flailing from side to side. I heard the sound of blows, grunts, the abrupt outrush of breath, the sickening thud of boots against flesh and cloth. I threw myself onto someone's back, kicking and clawing, but was immediately thrown to one side and landed on my ass.

"Keep her off!" I recognized Zippy's voice, thickened and ugly with rage. Someone loomed over me—one of his friends, a tall, heavy boy named Tim. As I started to rise, he pushed me down, hard.

"Stop it!" My voice emptied into the blackness, tiny, thin, useless. Again I was pushed down. Two figures held Bell's arms, as Zippy punched him in the stomach, in the chest, in the face.

"Fucking Indian! Keep your hands off white girls!"

I screamed, and my guard pulled me up and clamped his hand over my mouth. I twisted and pulled, trying to bite his hand. He squeezed his other arm around my throat, cutting off my breath. I kicked out backwards and heard him yell as my foot landed against his shin. But he didn't let go. My head was swelling grotesquely.

"That's enough!" I could barely hear the voice and didn't know whose it was. My chest was on fire. Then I was free, the gripping arm gone. I fell to my knees and pulled air into me in stabbing lungfuls, tears and snot running down my face. When I could breathe, I looked around. They had disappeared, and Bell lay immobile, face down in the dirt a few feet from me.

I tried to get up, but my muscles trembled and my knees buckled. A sharp pain ran up one of my legs. I managed to crawl over to Bell. He was breathing in shallow gasps. The stillness of his body frightened me, and I touched his shoulder tentatively.

"Bell?"

His breathing paused, then resumed as he turned his head slowly toward me. Blood was oozing from a large cut in his forehead and trickling from his nostrils. When he opened his mouth, his teeth were rimmed in red.

"Fucking cowards." He coughed deep from his lungs, bringing up more blood.

"Don't talk!" I looked around into the blackness, then back toward the gym door. Music drifted out, peppered with laughter. Why couldn't I bring Collie and Jess out here through the urgency of my need?

"Don't move." As if he could have if he'd wanted to. "I'll go get help."

"Hey." Bell reached his nearer hand toward me. I took hold of it. "You shouldn't have had to see this." Another fit of coughing. Tears rose in my eyes. If I let them out, I knew, I might dissolve in helpless rage.

"I'll be right back." I staggered to my feet, took a few steps without falling, and limped as fast as I could toward the bright refuge of the doorway.

CHAPTER 9

G ODDAMIT, I KNOW YOU'RE there!"
Collie's fist pounded over and over on the door of the home
office where Dr. Elwood saw patients when he wasn't working
at the hospital in Great Falls. Bell had begged Collie just to take him
home, but as soon as we had bundled him into the back seat of Collie's
car, he'd passed out, and we'd decided to bring him there.

The office was dark, but there were lights on in the upstairs bedroom.

The porch light blinked on, the door opened, and Dr. Elwood's long
face peered out at Collie. He was clutching the lapels of his blue
bathrobe together with one hand and smoothing his thinning gray hair
with the other.

"What's the matter?" Dr. Elwood's deep voice always startled me,
emerging as it did from his rail-thin body. "Someone hurt?"

"Yeah." Collie pointed toward the car. "Got beat up at the dance.
He's hurt bad."

"Can he walk?"

Collie shook his head. "He keeps passing out."

"Let's get him in here." Dr. Elwood hurried down the walk and
over to the back door window, which I'd rolled down. Bell's body was
slumped against me, his head lolling against the back seat. Large
smears of dried blood crusted his face and shirt. His lips were white.

On the way, he'd come to and drawn his legs up to his chest, but he couldn't keep them there. As they slipped down, he'd groaned as if someone had kicked him in the belly, and lost consciousness again.

As Dr. Elwood leaned through the window, Bell's eyes opened. They stared at each other for a moment. Then Dr. Elwood drew back and straightened up.

"I can't treat him."

The words seemed to fall into the air like pebbles, into widening circles of silence in which no-one moved or breathed. As their meaning hit me, my heart kicked against my ribs. Before I could react, Collie took a step toward Dr. Elwood.

"He's hurt, goddamit!" The light from the door glinted in his eyes.

Dr. Elwood, his face stiff and expressionless, shook his head. "I don't treat Indians," he said. "You know that, Collie. You'll have to take him to the hospital in Great Falls. Or the Indian doctor on the reservation."

"That's forty-five miles away, you bastard. He could die on the way."

"He won't die."

"How do you know? He's been coughing blood."

Dr. Elwood frowned and looked toward the car window, then seemed to make up his mind. "Let me take a quick look."

He slid in next to Bell, peered into his eyes, turned his head to inspect the cut on his scalp, pushed at his chest, and leaned his ear against it. Bell groaned in pain. Dr. Elwood nodded and climbed back out of the car.

"He's not seriously hurt. No sign the lungs are punctured. It looks worse than it is. I can't keep him here, though. Just take him home and let him sleep it off."

"He isn't drunk!" The sound of my voice shocked me, shrill and harsh. Dr. Elwood looked at me, then at Jess, registering us for the first time. He shook his head.

"Take the girls home, Collie." He turned and walked back toward the house. Collie's hands clenched. He took three long strides toward him, grabbed his shoulders and spun him around. As Dr. Elwood lurched off balance, the long bray of the car horn screeched through the air. I jumped. Jess was pressing with all her weight on the center of the steering wheel. As Collie twisted his head around to see what was going on, Dr. Elwood tore himself away, ran to the door and slammed it behind him. Bell, roused by the noise, raised his head and opened his eyes.

"What's going on?" His voice was hoarse and rasping, scarcely recognizable. I didn't know what to answer.

Collie opened the driver's door and slid behind the wheel. He looked at Bell and slammed the dashboard once with his fist, his mouth clamped in an ugly line. He turned the keys in the ignition and sat back, the motor shaking us as if it had caught my fear and Collie's frustration.

"Fuck it! It'll take an hour to get to Great Falls!" Collie turned to look at Bell. "How're you doing, man?"

"Hey." Bell didn't open his eyes. "I'll live. Just take me to Aunt Frances' house. She'll fix me up."

Collie and Jess looked at each other. I could see them hesitate, question each other, then come to a decision, and Collie eased the car into gear and hit the gas.

WE RACED DOWN MAIN Street as it dwindled, stores giving way to little box houses with carved woodwork trim, their bare yards exposing darkened facades. We made a sudden right turn and rolled past shabby cottages and rusty mobile homes, two or three skeletons of long-dead cars scattered in almost every yard.

There too most windows were dark, only one or two lit by the flickering blue white light of an out-of-sight TV, pulsing and bobbing like a captured ghost. The night seemed blacker, denser and threatening, reluctant to let us pass through. Though I knew the road was level, it felt as if we were slowly dropping. I shrank into myself, shivering with cold, drifting into a country where birds might fly backward and I no longer knew the language.

We jolted to a stop in front of a cottage neater than the rest, surrounded by a wooden fence made of boards of different widths and colors. Collie slipped out of the car, ran up the steps, and knocked. In a moment the windows lit up and the door opened, revealing a dark silhouette. Collie and she exchanged a few words and hurried toward us, Collie opening the door to let the woman lean in. We recognized each other at the same instant: It was Marjorie.

The same question flared in our eyes: What are you doing here? As I pieced together an explanation, her gaze shifted to Bell, her brows drew together, and she forgot me.

"Help me get him inside." She retreated to let Collie slip in. He slid his arm under Bell's shoulders, pulled him gently through the door, then placed his feet on the ground and helped him gain his balance, swaying like an old man after a bender.

"Can you walk?"

Bell nodded.

"Hey, Marj. Sorry about this." Marjorie had slipped his other arm around her waist, and with each supporting half his weight, the three of them made their way slowly through the door. Jess and I shuffled after them.

I didn't realize until I stared curiously at the room and felt my body relax that I'd been harboring a nightmare image of what it would look like: dirty dishes and greasy pots crusted with burnt food packed on the table and in the sink, roaches scurrying in the corners, empty beer bottles half-visible under the shabby furniture. This room was like a crisp daytime print of that false negative, bright and orderly, full of homely objects placed neatly and gleaming with obvious care.

A brown-and-orange braided rug covered the middle of a wooden floor scoured to near-colorlessness. On one side of the room, a worn armchair and sofa faced a large television set, and on the other six rickety-looking wooden chairs, all of different colors and shapes, stood around a worn Formica table covered with a checkered blue-and-white plastic tablecloth. The walls were dotted with photos of Indians in outfits ranging from turn-of-the-century long skirts and stiff high collars, to cowboy gear, to jeans and T-shirts and brightly patterned dresses. It wasn't much different from our own living room, only quite a bit neater.

Marjorie and Collie eased Bell onto the sofa. At first he struggled to stay upright, but Collie pushed his shoulders down as Marjorie lifted his legs, and they settled him lengthwise. He let his body relax into limpness.

"Let me see him."

The words were clipped and emphatic, the voice soft and deep, unfamiliar to me. Everyone looked toward the doorway to the back of the house. A very tall, thin woman of about forty was standing there. Long, dark hair, shot through with strips of silver, hung over the shoulders of her purple nightdress and down her back. Brown leather loafers, so old they had softened to shapelessness, sagged around her feet. Her skin was the color of a copper bowl that had darkened to a deep umber with only a hint of sheen. She stared at us from keen eyes shadowed by thick black eyebrows.

"A bunch of rednecks jumped him," Collie explained as she moved to the sofa. "We took him to the doctor's, but the bastard wouldn't touch him."

"I told him not to go!" Marjorie's voice was tight, aggrieved.

"You can't keep a buck penned in with the women." Frances' hands probed Bell's head, his chest, his legs.

"But look what happened! I was right, wasn't I?"

Frances glanced up briefly at Marjorie. A hint of a smile flickered across her face, a brief lift of the corners of her mouth. "You are always right, my daughter." Her slight emphasis on *right* brought a flush to Marjorie's face. "Now I need you to help me."

She rose and looked at Collie, Jess, and me where we stood clumped together near the armchair.

"They must have kicked him hard, many times." Marjorie's body drew together in shock at Frances' words. "Some of his ribs are cracked, I think. His nose may be broken, and he has a bad cut on his scalp."

A surge of rage mixed with shame rose into my face as she continued.

"I know what to do. Thank you for bringing him here."

Collie mumbled something. Frances nodded.

"Come and help me, Marjorie." She turned and left the room. Marjorie went to the front door instead.

"You'd better go."

"Wait a minute." Bell raised his head. Marjorie halted, and we all leaned toward him.

"Forget all this. You hear?" He stared intently at us, one by one, pausing at Collie. "I mean it, man. Leave it alone."

I must have looked stricken, my face betraying the tears just behind my eyes, because he grinned briefly at me.

"Hey, Win. We'll really show them how to dance at the Turkey Trot, huh?" The next big dance at the high school.

At this point I didn't know what I wanted, mostly not to have any more to deal with right then, so I nodded mutely and, from the corner of my eye, saw Marjorie frown. She marched to the front door and threw it open, avoiding our eyes as we slipped out. I looked back one last time at Bell, Frances bending over him, touching his forehead, now creased with furrows of pain. He lay quiet and still in the pool of light cast by the lamp, stretched out as if on a funeral boat, gliding slowly away from me.

I DIDN'T SAY MUCH on the way back to the ranch. My neck was still throbbing where Tim had squeezed it. The adrenaline that had galvanized me for the last two hours, pumping my heart at double speed, had vanished, and I was overcome by drowsiness, nodding off, then jerking myself awake, only to drift away again as the car plowed a wedge of light through the blackness ahead of us. Behind my eyelids I saw Bell running, dribbling a basketball, leaping and turning, tossing the ball in a high straight arc to me. I caught it and tried to bounce it as I ran, but my legs got tangled in my skirt, my zipper broke, and my dress slipped down, exposing my breasts. I wanted to pull it back up, but I knew I couldn't let go of the ball. Suddenly I was surrounded by men with dark, sinister faces slowly approaching in a tightening circle. I clutched the ball, my only protection, against my chest, trying to cover myself with it, as one of the men reached and slapped it out of my hands, and I stood naked as they grabbed me, a dozen hands reaching for my defenseless breasts.

"Win!"

Jess' voice kicked me awake, gasping, disoriented, then relieved as the dream slipped away, but hit by a new wave of anxiety as I looked at our house, where every window was blazing with light.

"Do you think they're awake?"

"Looks like it." Jess' voice was flat, carefully expressionless.

"I thought they'd be asleep. We're not really late, are we?"

Jess gave me the look I was so familiar with, the one that put me back in diapers.

"Dr. Elwood probably phoned them when we left there." I sat still, a picture of Randy's reactions to this news pulling into focus in my mind.

"Come on, let's face the music." She pushed the car door open. Collie was already waiting for her. I made myself get out and join them.

"Col, don't come in, okay?" Jess whispered. "We'll handle it."

Collie didn't look happy but walked heavily alongside Jess toward the door. It burst open, and Randy stepped onto the stoop. I could see Mom hunched over, clutching her coat around her, trying to edge past him. He put out an arm to stop her, and she peered over it at us.

"Are you okay?" Her voice was tight with worry. "We didn't know if you. . .all the doctor said—"

"What the hell happened?" Randy had spit out the words with a steely precision behind which I heard fear. "We've been sitting here beating our brains, trying to figure out where you were. At least you could have called! And where's Zippy? The poor pussy run out on you?"

No one answered. Randy gestured to Jess and me.

"Come in here." I climbed the three steps. Jess, behind me, lifted her hand in a small, tender gesture to Collie.

"You too, you piss-poor excuse of an escort," Randy snapped. Collie looked uncertain. "What's the matter with you, can't fight your own battles? Have to let a girl do it for you."

"Don't talk to him like that." Jess sounded as tightly furious as Randy. "He doesn't have to follow your orders, and I don't either."

Randy's nostrils flared.

"Just go on inside. At least you're home safe. Your boyfriend can go home. You won't be seeing much of him after this."

"I'll see him as much as I want to. It's my life!"

Randy reached out, grabbed Jess' arm and pulled her up the steps. She sagged onto her knees to break her momentum, hitting her kneecaps on the step with a thud that made me wince. She yanked her arm free.

"Leave me alone, you asshole!"

Randy's face, already flushed, turned dark red. He lifted his hand as Jess stood up and backed down the steps.

"Don't!" Mom yelled and surged against Randy's back, scrabbling for his hand. As they wrestled, Jess pulled herself upright, staggered over to Collie and sagged against him, hiding her face in his coat. He put his arms around her.

"Let's get out of here." Her voice was muffled, urgent. Collie turned with her and they hurried toward the car. Randy struggled down the steps, Mom's arms still wrapped around his torso as she leaned her weight backward to try and stop him.

"Keep your Indian-lover hands off her, or I'll kill you!" Blue-purple veins stuck out on Randy's neck, and spittle flew from his mouth. "You tramp! If you open your legs for him, don't you ever come back here!"

I covered my ears as Mom cried, "No!" again and again, screams that scrambled and obscured Randy's words, as Collie's car jerked into motion, jounced out the gate, and tore down the road.

CHAPTER 10

ARTS OF THE REST of night and the next day have jumbled together in my memory. I remember Mom dabbling the cuts on my
knees and hands with alcohol, and how I welcomed the sting and
the tears it brought to my eyes, while Mom's face brimmed with a mixture of tenderness and exhausted impatience. She said nothing about
Bell, so I guessed they were linking him more to Jess and Collie than to
me. And I remember Randy bringing me a cup of mint tea as I sat in
his armchair.

"You okay?" he asked gruffly, adding at my nod, "Hope you
learned a lesson," thus dousing the tentative spark of warmth his unexpected attention had lit.

I remember Lorrie and Pete sensing, with that radar children have
about things they don't understand, the unease radiating from Randy's
body as they alternately sidled up to him and pulled away, Randy barking at them when they asked for Jess, their mouths turning down like
the pumpkin they'd carved and placed on the stoop for Randy to stum-
ble over and shatter with one furious kick.

I remember Mom at her most obsequious, making Randy his favorite dishes, whisking the kids out of earshot when he wanted to rest
or watch TV, stepping between him and me whenever he flicked a sarcastic remark in my direction.

I remember, too, how images of Bell's face as it approached mine would flash through my mind, of the feel of his lips, the warmth of his hands, leaving me flushed with embarrassment and pleasure. Then a rush of anxiety: Was he all right? Had they taken him to the hospital? Did he blame me?

I know I didn't want to go to Redmond, didn't want to face the curious looks, the solicitous questions. But I wanted even less to stay alone in the house with Randy, so on Saturday I went in with Mom for my piano lesson, the kids fidgeting behind us. Mom's determined cheerfulness vanished as soon as we hit the highway.

"What's Daddy so angry about?" Lorrie asked, leaning over the seat back.

"He stepped on my truck!" Pete threw in. "I want a new one!"

"You can't get one till your birthday," Lorrie stated self-righteously, flopping back to make a face at him.

"But he broke it!" Pete protested. "He's mean."

"Maybe he misses Jess," Lorrie said. "Where is she, Mommy? I miss her."

"I want her to come back!" Pete said emphatically. "Make her come back, Mommy."

"Will you kids shut up!" Mom yelled suddenly, turning to swat the air in front of Lorrie's startled nose. "Just be quiet, or I'll dump you out of the car and let you walk back to the ranch!"

For a few minutes they subsided into awed silence, then lapsed into a whispered dialogue between their respective dolls, a G.I. Joe and a tattered Bridal Barbie.

When we reached Roone and Selby's, to my surprise, Mom got out of the car and walked me to the trunk of the car, ordering the kids to stay put. I knew she must want to tell me something out of earshot.

"Jess is at Leila's." No surprise there; Leila was her best friend. "She's probably going to stay there for a while." I kept my face impassive. "Give her this." She pulled two bulging grocery bags from the trunk and shoved them into my hands. Her face was stern, as if I'd protested her command. "We'll meet you at Reynold's at three." She turned back to the car door, then looked at me. "I can't go see her, because of the kids."

She scooted back into the front seat, leaving me seething. She wanted to see Jess, I knew, but wouldn't because the kids would tell Randy. The pity I felt for her ran into a surge of anger: Why did *I* have to do her dirty work? Why did she always have to sneak, pander, cater to his flashing temper? Why couldn't she, for once, just stand up to him?

I seldom played worse than at that lesson, but Roone didn't utter a word of criticism. Nor did she comment on the bags or ask me anything about the dance, even though I could read in the few glances I caught her taking at my face when she thought I wasn't looking, in the ever-so-slightly heightened formality of her manner, that she'd heard something about it.

At the end, when she handed me a letter, I stared at it without comprehension, my mind arranging and rearranging the typed letters into random combinations. Finally she took it back.

"It's from the competition committee. You've been accepted as a contestant," she announced. "Congratulations."

Was she being sarcastic? I could swear I heard a teasing tartness in her voice. "I've seen you more excited by Selby's cooking than you seem to be about this letter." She raised her eyebrows at me questioningly. I started gathering my piano books, avoiding her eyes. "I guess you've got other things on your mind." Her voice was gentle.

She went on matter-of-factly to outline the arrangements we'd have to make, the schedule of practice and preparations I'd have to adhere to. I kept nodding mechanically, unable to bring any sense of reality to the pictures she painted. My utter indifference to this letter, which I'd daydreamed about receiving, which had made my heart jump with excitement only a few days ago, seemed bizarre. I thought of how I'd read that the hand of a person who'd had a stroke no longer seems to them to be part of their body. The letter seemed like that to me, an object so fully imagined as to be completely familiar, yet utterly alien.

"Maybe you'll feel different in a few days, when everything settles down." Roone smiled at me. Again I nodded, not believing her.

"Roone." I didn't realize where I was headed, only that there was something I had to find out. "Do you—I mean, why do people. . . ."

That wasn't right. "What do you think about Indians?" That wasn't right either, but it was said. She looked at me quizzically, and I tried to explain. "I mean, people hang out with people who are the same as them. Indians don't come to meetings or parties with whites, or to the Two Elks. But *you* do. Sometimes."

She was silent. I was suddenly terrified I'd offended her.

"People here like you and Selby. They're glad you live here."

"Are they?"

"Sure they are. Mom is. Randy likes hunting and fishing with Selby. People come from all over to buy Selby's stuff."

"Win." Her cool voice cut through my awkward fumbling. "We're tolerated, we're not really accepted. Because there's only two of us, we're not much of a threat. But if there were more of us. . . ." She hesitated. "Lucky for Selby and me, there aren't. They've never felt threatened by us, like they used to be by the Indians."

She started gathering my music together.

"People are funny. The more they feel guilty about what they've done to you, the worse they treat you."

She stood up and handed me my music. I knew she wouldn't say any more.

I declined my usual post-lesson treat, and as soon as I could, pleading a pressing errand, headed out the door.

"WHERE DO YOU SLEEP?"

Jess and I sat on the edge of the narrow bed, careful not to muss the pink-and-white bedspread. Leila's attic bedroom was cramped and dark, the ceiling low and steeply pitched. Leila had tactfully stayed downstairs.

I felt awkward, as if Jess were a stranger. As soon as I saw her, I'd sensed a subtle alteration in what I'd learn later to call her "aura," some mysterious shift in the invisible scintillation of the atoms surrounding her. She seemed suddenly much older. She sat very straight, her hands nested in her lap, looking at me with gentle abstraction, as if from a great distance. I fought off a wave of sadness.

"On a mattress, there." She pointed to the narrow strip of floor between the bed and the chipped blue dresser. "I've done it before, lots of times." True, but that had been just overnight.

"Will you be back tomorrow?"

Jess looked at me a moment, then gazed out the window at the crumpled leaves hanging from the oak tree in the yard. "I'm not coming back."

I breathed in sharply, as if someone had hit me on the back of my neck.

"What do you mean?"

"What I said."

"Not ever?" I heard the quiver in my voice.

Jess reached over and put her hand on mine. I pulled away, afraid of crying. She sighed. "I'll come and get my things when he's not home." She twisted a hank of her hair around her fingers. "You can come visit me here, Win. It'll be fun. Kind of like our plans."

"You can't just leave us and hitch onto some other family!" Indignation felt much better than grief. "They don't want you! Do you think they'll adopt you, or what?"

"Don't be silly, Win. I'm not looking for a new family. I'm leaving home, that's all." All? "I'm going to get a job and help pay the Evanses room and board."

"A job where?"

"I don't know yet. Somewhere." She clasped her arms across her chest. Suddenly she didn't seem as grown up.

"Jess, you can come home. In a few days, Randy won't be so mad. Mom will get him calmed down. All you have to do is apologize."

"For what? I'm sick and tired of groveling in front of that creep! I'm tired of tiptoeing around to make sure that some little thing we say doesn't send him off the deep end. Jesus Christ, I'm sick of it!" Her eyes blazed, and she breathed fast. I edged away from her. Some part of me had known for a long time this day would come, but now I fought to push it away. After a while she looked at me again.

"It's better for everyone if I stay here."

"Not for me," I muttered. Tears pricked my eyelids again. Before Jess could speak, I handed her the grocery bags I'd been crushing in my lap.

"Here. Mom told me to give you this."

Slowly Jess opened one bag and pulled out a nightgown, several sweaters and skirts, underwear. The other contained her hairdryer and a flowered plastic zipper bag with her cosmetics. A small envelope fluttered out with her hairbrush. I watched as she tore it open and pulled out two crumpled ten dollar bills. We both stared at them. We knew how Mom, longing for a new sewing machine, had saved months of dimes, quarters, and dollars in the black tin box in her dresser so she could trade them in at the bank for the money in Jess' hand. For a moment, Jess' eyes gleamed with tears. Then she stuffed the bills into the envelope and handed it back to me.

"I can't take this."

I put the envelope on the bed between us.

"What if you can't find a job?"

She shook her head. "I don't need the money."

"So what? Keep it anyway."

"I don't want it."

I realized I was trembling.

"You have to keep it!" To my chagrin, I felt tears stinging my eyes. It seemed so clear to me that this was Mom's way of telling Jess it was all right to leave, that the money was her hand reaching out to steady Jess on her way. I tried to organize my words around what I knew, but they burst out with the indignation of the child I no longer was. "I won't take it back, and you can't make me!" The inadequacy of this so appalled me that I jumped up. "I gotta go."

Before I could reach the door, I broke down, sobbing in earnest. Jess took the envelope and put it in her pocket. Then she put her arms around me and held her wet face against mine, as we sat huddled together, watching her leave forever the room we'd shared for so long.

CHAPTER 11

I LAY LOW ON Monday, deflecting questions as best I could. Kids stared at me, tossing remarks like "Where's your shiner?" and "How does an Indian taste?" my way. I concealed my discomfort with smiles that made my face feel frozen. I could tell, from the way people asked about the fight, that they knew very few of the details. I kept my tone light and held my sadness tight inside my chest, numbing myself and waiting for the school day to end.

In the middle of history class, Mrs. Isaacson had us put down our pens and notebooks. Her first words made my stomach cramp. "I want to know how your reports are coming," she said, picking up her list of student pairs. "Liz and Anna? Let's see, you're doing 'Ways West.' Tell us one or two things you've found out so far."

Liz ducked her head until her dark-brown hair fell like a curtain around her face. She hated to talk in class. Anna, still almost tow-headed and bolder, spoke up.

"Well, we've read *Frontier Trails* and a couple of entries in the encyclopedia. We're learning about the different wagon trails, and how they build forts along each one so pioneers could get new supplies, and to get protection from the Indians."

"Very good. Seth and Billy? The annexation of Texas?"

Silence. Mrs. Isaacson looked around. Seth was glaring at the top of his desk, while Billy Ten Horse stared out the window.

"Well? Aren't you guys deep into the Alamo yet?"

Her smile got no response.

"What's the problem? There are plenty of books on the subject, even in this little library. Have you read the one I gave you?"

Still no answer. I could hear the students on all four sides of me breathing as quietly as they could, and the sharp clicks of the clock's second hand. Then, in an undertone, Seth muttered, "I don't want to work with him."

Mrs. Isaacson stared at Billy's immobile profile, started to say something, and stopped.

"Well, you've got to, and that's that." She looked down at her list, made a note, and read another set of names.

"Judy and Rich? How's the Gold Rush and California?"

"Great!" At the sound of Judy's perky soprano, rigid bodies relaxed and faces broke into smiles, as if a movie scene caught in freeze-frame had melted into motion again.

"There's lots on it, all about Sutter's Mill and people pulling dirty tricks on each other to get hold of mining claims. And how the people who got rich weren't the miners. They were the people who sold miners supplies and food. Most miners went broke."

Mrs. Isaacson nodded approvingly.

"Good! It sounds like you're well on your way." Again she consulted her notes.

"Win, Corinne, and Marjorie?" My heart jumped once, hard, then slowly evened out. I wanted to turn and look at Corinne but willed my eyes to stay still. The room seemed even quieter than before. Several kids darted sidelong glances at me. I read everything on their faces: pity, excitement, fear, barely concealed eagerness.

"Well?" Still no response. "Have you read *Cheyenne Autumn*?"

"Most of it," I said in a low tone.

"Corinne?" Corinne barely shook her head.

"Marjorie?"

"I read it." Her voice from the back row was loud, clear, carrying a ring of prideful defiance.

"And what else have you read?"

"*Black Elk Speaks* and *The Man Who Killed the Deer*." Beneath my fright, my curiosity was aroused. Where had Marjorie found those books? And what were they? Mrs. Isaacson looked pleasantly startled.

"I'm glad to hear our library is well stocked."

"Not *this* one." Now Marjorie sounded scornful. "At home."

"You had those at your house? Then Win and Marjorie are lucky to have you as a partner. What else have you found, Win?"

Silence again. Shame coursed through my body. I'd always looked forward to the glint of pleasure on Mrs. Isaacson's face at my accomplishments. I hated to imagine how disappointed in me she must be.

"Corinne?" I saw Corinne drop her head, her face scarlet. Mrs. Isaacson looked from her to me.

"How many times have you girls met to work on the project?" She stared at me.

"Once."

Another long pause. The air was humming with currents of panic zipping from one student to another. I stole a quick look at Marjorie. She was sitting straight in her chair, her chin jutting forward, a tiny smile pulling at the corners of her mouth. She actually looked happy.

Suddenly Mrs. Isaacson slammed her notebook onto her desk with a loud bang that made everyone jump.

"I will not tolerate this." Her voice bit into my ears like a false note on the piano. "You kids have to understand that this is an assignment. Your reports are due in three weeks. You do not have a choice about whether or not to do them. You *will* do them, and that is final."

"My mom said I don't have to do it." Who had said that? Mrs. Isaacson gazed in the direction of the low-pitched voice somewhere near me on my right.

"Please repeat that." Nothing. She walked over and stood between Simon Rudolph and Seth O'Rourke, looking first at one and then the other, then at the kids on all sides of them. Still no one spoke. Her eyes filled with contempt.

"So on top of being disobedient, one of you is both insolent and a coward." Now there were frowns, and several people shifted uneasily in their seats. Her expression softened slightly, and she sat on the edge of Seth's desk.

"Look, kids. I know the way I've set it up isn't easy for you. I'm asking you to do something you're not used to. But that's exactly the point. How can you grow, if you only do what's easy?"

She leaned forward, letting her eyes rest on each one of us, and when she spoke it was with piercing seriousness. "No matter what, no matter how hard it is to do it, you must get the work done. That's what it means to be an adult."

She rose and returned to her desk. "I expect you all to do the best work you're capable of. And I won't stand for any delays. Now open your books to page 93."

Without a sound we all did as she said. My heart was pounding as if I'd been jerked out of sleepwalking to find myself on a high cliff, one foot already half over the edge.

A scattering of students sat hunched over the library desks when I walked in during last period study hall. Corinne had only agreed to meet me and Marjorie, and start working on our report, after I pointed out that her only alternative seemed to be to fail History. Since she was already perilously close to failing math, she let fear of her mother's wrath carry the day. But now, although I was a few minutes late and spotted Marjorie bent over a book at the far end of the room, Corinne was nowhere in sight.

"Hey."

Marjorie looked up and nodded as I sat down across from her. This was the first time since the dance I'd been able to approach her outside of our classmates' scrutiny. I leaned closer and spoke in an undertone.

"How's Bell?"

Marjorie was silent. I felt uneasy under her piercing gaze. Just as I was about to repeat the question, she spoke.

"He's OK."

"OK? What about his ribs and his nose?"

"He'll get better."

"Is he still at your house?"

"Yes." Again her silent scrutiny. I fumbled through my mind for something to say.

"Tell him—tell him I said hello."

She raised her eyebrows and continued staring at me. I couldn't tell if she was expecting me to say something more. She made me feel like one of those clacking wind-up toys that chatter their way mindlessly across the table.

"Hello to you." She smiled wryly at my puzzled look. I felt stupid, trapped in a dialogue with someone speaking a foreign language.

"From Bell," she clarified. I felt my face grow hot, and my eyes shifted involuntarily away from hers. I reached for the book in front of her and riffled unseeingly through the pages.

"He wants to see you."

As soon as she said it, I realized I'd known it was coming, just as I knew my answer from the jump of pleasure in my chest. It didn't seem to matter whether I wanted to go or not, not because I had no choice but because the issue seemed already beyond choice, as if I'd already argued and analyzed and come to a decision without knowing I'd done so. Marjorie looked at me without sympathy or judgment as I nodded. She had done her own arguing and made her decision, too.

"We've got to get to work on this," she said, looking at our book. I forced myself to stop sifting images of Bell lying in bed, propped up on a sofa, sitting at the kitchen table, and tried to concentrate.

"What do you think?" Easier to let her take the lead, especially as I hadn't thought about the subject for a week. She opened her notebook and handed it to me. As I began reading her notes, I sensed her body tensing, contracting in on itself. Was she nervous, I wondered, about my reaction to her ideas? To reassure her, I smiled and looked up, to see her staring at something behind me. I turned and saw the brown-suited, bulky body of Mr. Sajarsky, the principal, two feet from my chair, his face smoothed into a facsimile of pleasant interest.

"What are you girls doing?"

We were so taken aback by the obvious insincerity of his tone that we stayed quiet. The lines around his mouth deepened, though his smile didn't budge.

"I understand you're preparing for your History class reports?"

I nodded, as he seemed to expect a response.

"Were you told—are you working on one together?"

Again I nodded. A few moments went by. He looked away, seemed to consider, and said, "Please come with me."

He turned, not waiting to see our reaction, with small bouncing steps to the door. Marjorie and I glanced at each other, gathered our books, and followed him out of the library and down the hall, tracked by the curious glances of the few students who passed our odd trio.

In his office, Mr. Sajarsky lowered himself gingerly into his wooden swivel chair and motioned to us to sit across the desk from him. He cleared his throat portentously. "You girls are in Mrs. Isaacson's history class, correct?"

Again we nodded.

"How is it that you two are working together?"

"Mrs. Isaacson assigned us to be partners." My voice sounded more assured than I felt. I thought briefly of mentioning Corinne but decided to let her off the hook.

"Did Mrs. Isaacson do that with everyone?" He leaned slightly on "that." I decided to play dumb.

"Do what?"

"Assign partners."

"Yes, she did." I smiled out of nervousness. Mr. Sajarsky's face creased into a frown.

"I'm surprised she didn't make an effort to pair people up with their friends, instead of with people they don't know."

Some contradictory impulse, touched off by his all-knowing manner, took hold of me.

"But Mr. Sajarsky, we know each other. I mean, we're in the same class and all. We've been in classes together all fall."

Mr. Sajarsky's frown deepened. "I think you know what I mean, Winona."

"I do?" I widened my eyes in an attempt at puzzled innocence. There was a moment's silence before he swiveled toward the window and rested his teepeed fingers against his chin.

"I imagine people aren't very happy with this arrangement." He swiveled back to face us. "In fact, I know it. I've had complaints from many students and parents. I imagine you two would prefer different partners as well." He looked at us questioningly. "If you don't want to work together, you don't have to. You can tell Mrs. Isaacson that she should assign you to other partners. In fact, I'll give you a note to take to her."

He pulled a yellow pad toward him and began writing. Marjorie stared at him, her expression blank. She shifted her gaze to me, and I knew exactly what she was thinking: *I'll do it if you do.* I nodded imperceptibly.

"Mr. Sajarsky." He looked up at Marjorie's voice and back at his scribbling hand. "It's okay for us to work together."

His hand froze as he stared at us.

"I don't think you understand. I'm releasing you from your teacher's arrangement."

"We want to work together," I said.

Mr. Sajarsky's features drew together in puzzled frustration; his eyes widened in shock and blood rushed into his face, rising from his wide neck to his cheeks and suffusing his forehead with a scarlet burn. I stopped breathing as his eyes bored into me.

"Is this true?" His tone contained a trace of uncertainty that unnerved me. The very thing I wanted, his discomposure, frightened me.

I looked down at my fingers, my nails still covered with the now-chipped pink polish I'd worn to the dance. Out of the corner of my eye I could see Marjorie's straight body, her hands gripping the edge of the seat of her chair. I took a deep breath. "Yes."

He seemed to be waiting for me to say something comprehensible, and this wasn't it. The silence expanded like a huge soap bubble blown up beyond the laws of physics. Suddenly Mr. Sajarsky jumped up, his feet hitting the floor with a thud.

"You'd better watch your step," he hissed at me, ignoring Marjorie. "Now get back to your class. I'll handle this."

Marjorie and I didn't need to hear anything else. We shot out of our chairs and ran out of the office, bumping shoulders as we jostled against the doorway, startling the school secretary into pausing at her typewriter to stare at us as we tumbled past her into the corridor, and doubled over with giggles, helpless before the relieved outrush of pent-up tension.

When we recovered, we started down the hall, breaking into fits of laughter every time we looked at each other. As we passed the metal-handled front door, I stopped. "It's not really worth going back to the library," I said. "It's almost three."

Marjorie nodded. We retrieved our coats from our lockers and slipped out of the building, my blood fizzing with the forbidden pleasure of defiance. In the pale autumn light the breath puffed out of our mouths in tiny white bursts. Marjorie began to walk away, toward the junction of Main and Spring.

"Want to go get a Coke at Reynold's?" I asked.

For the first time that day, Marjorie looked truly startled. I remembered then that Indians never went into Reynold's. If they wanted a soda, they bought one at the market or from the machine outside Fletcher's Garage. Marjorie hesitated, shook her head, and kept walking, turning at the corner up Spring Street. I followed her, catching up so we were side by side. I couldn't think of anything to say as we trudged the long blocks past the same houses I'd rushed by in the car Friday night.

My thoughts whirled back and forth. What was I getting myself in for, going to Marjorie's to see Bell? I imagined Bell glancing up as I walked in, his surprise, the rush of pleasure filling his face, mirroring my own. Then a wave of doubt: He'd be cool to me. Or he'd be undressed and I'd embarrass him. I imagined the sculpted muscles of his bare chest, the contours I'd felt against my skin as we danced, and I knew I wanted to see him without his clothes. I cringed, irrationally sure that the intensity of this image would somehow be transmitted to Marjorie's awareness. I almost turned around, but pride kept me moving forward.

Finally, we reached Marjorie's home. It looked shabbier by daylight, the white paint in front spattered with rain and mud, the dried-out stalks of chrysanthemums and daisies in the flower bed shriveled and brown. But the yard was neat, the windows gleaming with reflected mid-afternoon sun. Marjorie pushed the door open and motioned with her head to follow her in through the living room and into the kitchen, where Bell sat at the table, shelling peas.

When he saw me, he jumped up, knocking over the bowl in front of him, peas rolling across the table. He swore and leaned over to scoop the peas back into the bowl. I dropped my books and ran to the table, reaching out to help him.

"It's okay." He shook his head, and I drew my hand back. I felt a pinch of disappointment. He didn't seem as tall as I remembered. His eyes were deeper set, his skin paler. Without the gleam of ironic amusement that usually played across his wide features, his face seemed tired, flatter.

Then he drew himself up and smiled, and his white teeth lit his face into beauty. I felt my own face open in response, and we grinned at each other for no reason except our pleasure in looking at each other.

"Tea."

We both turned our heads to Marjorie, to the rush of water from the spigot that rattled the battered kettle in her hands. As she clapped on the lid and placed the kettle on the stove, I searched for words, finding only trite ones, hesitated, and said them anyway. "Are you feeling better?"

Bell nodded. "I'll be back at school in a few days."

"Ma said not till next week." Marjorie faced us, two mugs in her hands. "Where is she?"

"In the shed."

Marjorie put the mugs down.

"Watch the kettle." She left the room.

Instantly I felt the air between Bell and me solidify and stretch like a rubber band pulled to its limit. He looked at me unwaveringly. His black hair, liberated from its usual ponytail, hung loosely to his shoulders, glistening in the light the way melted tar shimmers on a hot summer road.

We moved toward each other, stopping when our bodies were so close I could feel the heat from him radiating toward me. I heard his breathing quicken, saw my hand lift, felt the heavy smoothness of his hair fall across my fingers. Then my body was pressed against his, his hands around my waist, my face against the curve of his jaw, his lips at my ear, the roar of his breath drowning out my words.

Just as quickly we were apart, staring at each other, the space between us suddenly icy, as if my clothes had been ripped off during a winter storm. I couldn't understand what was happening, how my body had betrayed me by its waywardness, by the power of its willful responses. A wave of anger at my helplessness welled up in my throat. Bell must have seen it in my expression, because his own face closed down as thought a heavy curtain had been pulled over a glowing window.

I wanted to explain, to tell him I wasn't angry at him, although maybe I was. I wanted to turn and run and hide somewhere so I could examine what I'd found, caress and befriend it. Even more, I wanted to see his face open again, wanted his eyes to spark with pleasure.

As I took a step toward him, he turned away and scooped herbs from a jar sitting on the counter into the teapot. I felt as though I'd been shoved hard in the chest. I went over to the window and leaned my burning forehead against the cold glass.

"Saturday."

His voice was so low I barely caught the word. He poured the water from kettle to teapot, his eyes fixed on the steaming arc between them. My heart pounded. Saturday was my piano lesson, when Bell would be working with Selby. I'd forgotten. Now, I knew, it was all I'd think about until then.

FOR THE REST OF the week, between bouts of daydreaming, I forced myself to concentrate alternately on my piano and the books Marjorie and I had decided we needed to read for our report. Pride and fantasy took turns claiming me. I didn't want Roone to turn away from me, so I had to practice. I didn't want to disappoint Mrs. Isaacson, so Marjorie and I had to prepare a report that would knock the collective socks off our history class.

I signed up for the late bus, which gave me time to work at the library, then back to the ranch to help Mom do laundry or mending, or

Randy fix fences or milk the cows, dodging his double-edged comments and Mom's anxious inquiries. After dinner I'd play Bach and Beethoven until Randy bellowed, "Turn that highbrow stuff off! We got enough culture for one day."

I'd retreat to my now-single room to do homework on Jess' bed until I nodded off and climbed into mine for the night. Then came the time I treasured, when finally I was free to let Bell's image, colored by all the romantic novels I'd read since I was ten, fill my senses: his smoky scent, his silky-smooth hair, his curious, exploring hands and tongue. Inevitably I'd use my own hands as substitutes for what his might do, guiding myself ever deeper toward the release that left my body temporarily sated and the rest of me lonely. At that moment I would have traded in an instant my treasured privacy for Jess' return, the soothing murmur of her breath nearby in the dark.

SO FOR THE NEXT few weeks I fell into this rhythm of quickening anticipation laced with increasing anxiety as each Saturday grew closer. I never saw Bell except after my piano lesson; seeing him might have lessened my fear that he'd no longer appeal to me, or I to him. At fourteen, a week feels like a year, a huge span of time in which to develop a crush on Monday only to have it flip into repulsion by Thursday. Yet the absences gave our meetings a luster of excitement they might otherwise not have had. The time between them stretched out like an elastic cord dotted with rare, glittering beads.

Roone and Selby must have guessed how we felt and decided to tolerate, if not outright approve, what was happening. Bell was invited to share our post-lesson treats, which I could barely swallow but which Bell, his rail-thin body brimming with energy, ate steadily, carefully, to the last crumb. Then Selby would suggest he and Bell show me their latest piece of work, and once in Selby's shed, Selby would find some reason to visit the back room with its piles of curing lumber, its racks of fishing tackle, leaving us alone.

Bell and I would sit down, our knees barely grazing, our words giving way to touches, to mouths pressed quickly together, tongues darting, dizzy with each other's ragged breath. The knowledge of Selby's presence just behind the thin plywood partition corralled our desire, reined it in. Though I'd never have admitted it, I was actually glad I didn't have the freedom to decide whether to go further. My body was galloping ahead of my judgment, mixing with resentment at being still confined to the remnants of childhood to form a potent brew of rebellious excitement I wasn't sure I could control.

I WAS SURE MOM would sense some change in me, and I became an expert in finding reasons to avoid being alone with her. Fortunately she was preoccupied with Lorrie, whose chronic asthma had flared up early that year, as well as with helping Randy prepare the cattle for market.

It was Jess who noticed. "You look different," she remarked one afternoon. We were sharing a soda in the back storeroom of Reynold's while she took a break from her after-school job behind the counter. Sitting on a stool, amid the boxes and bottles of malt, chocolate syrup, straws, and detergent, she pulled a cigarette from her pocket, struck a match, and narrowed her eyes at me over her cupped hands, ignoring the murmur of voices and bursts of laughter from the store.

"Since when did you start smoking?"

She shrugged, exhaling a stream of smoke from her rounded lips, and frowned.

"Is it your hair?"

I touched my curls self-consciously. I'd begun letting my hair grow longer, taming it as best I could with barrettes and bobby pins.

"Here, let me try something." She removed the pins, rummaged through her purse, produced a gold-tone hair clip, pulled some of my hair from each side of my face, and fastened it together at the back of my head with the clip, fluffing and patting the remaining curls. I closed my eyes.

"Remember when I helped you get ready for the dance?"

Again that intuition of hers, an integral part of the childhood I was so eager to leave behind. Right then I welcomed it with the ache we reserve for things we know we are seeing for the last time. I opened my eyes and found Jess staring at me.

"There's something else." A smile spread across her face. "You're in love."

"I am not!" My pleasure was drowned in indignation, as if the door had been thrown open as I stood naked in front of my bedroom mirror.

"Don't you have to go back out front?" I stood up.

"It's okay." Her face was soft. "Sit down. I know all about it."

"There's nothing to know!" Panicked, nonsensical questions raced through my mind. Had Bell talked about me to Jess? Had she been spying on us, peeking through the shed windows at our explorations? Was she able to enter my mind whenever she wanted?

Before I could say anything, she answered me. "I got Collie to ask Bell if he'd seen you. He told Collie you'd visited him while he was at his aunt's." She noticed my agitation. "He tried to cover up at first, but Collie can read him like a book. He got the whole story out of him."

"What story?" I pretended to look for something in my purse.

"That you see each other at Roone and Selby's, with them as chaperons. How you never get a chance to be alone."

Her look was sympathetic, without any sarcasm. I sighed with relief and nodded, grateful for Bell's diplomacy. Jess straightened, stubbing her cigarette out in the ceramic ashtray with *Souvenir of Glacier Park* painted in red against a blue sky and impossibly green mountains.

"Do you know what you're getting yourself in for?" Now she sounded severe. "Bell is one neat guy, but he's still a Chey."

"So what?" My voice had a thin, dangerous edge to it.

"Don't be like that, Win. I'm not trying to pull a Randy on you." She poked at the cigarette butt. "It's just—you wait and see the shit you'll get from people if they think. . . ." She let her words trail off. "Collie gets plenty just for being his friend."

"I know." The scene in the Two Elks Cafe flashed into my mind, Collie's clenched face, his bitter words.

"So just be. . .just take it easy. Don't do anything stupid, okay?" Jess leaned back against the wall, brushing her hair from her face. "I'm not there now to help you if Randy or Mom finds out."

"Mom wouldn't mind." Where did my certainty come from?

Jess' eyes widened. "Are you crazy? She'd go nuts!"

"Maybe she's different than you think."

Jess shook her head slowly.

"I wouldn't count on her."

"What about you?"

She frowned at my question, comprehension slowly filling her eyes as she weighed it. I knew with complete certainty where her sympathies lay. But I was really asking something else. "I'll stick up for you, Win, no matter what. You know that."

She glanced at her watch and stood up. I followed her toward the door. As we reached it, she pulled me toward her, put her arm over my shoulder and bumped her forehead gently against mine, a gesture of solidarity we'd borrowed as eight- and ten-year-olds from some long-forgotten movie and used ever since.

"Goddamit, Win," she half-whispered hoarsely. "Why can't you, just for once, do something the easy way?"

"You mean like you do?" I countered.

A grin flashed over her face, then faded as she pushed me away abruptly and walked out the door.

CHAPTER 12

*T*HE HISTORY OF THE *settlement of our continent is the history of one people, by superior force of arms and the weight of numbers, subduing, suppressing, and displacing another. It is the story of newcomers who used justifications built from the beliefs of their own culture to condemn the inhabitants of the land they coveted with the familiar sentence: You are less than truly human, and thus you deserve exile, removal, or extermination.*

No one moved or spoke as the last syllables of our report faded into an after-sound, the ghost of a hum, then nothing. I imagined lifting my hands from the keyboard at the end of a concert, suspended for a last moment before the music dissipated. Whatever we had created with our words had held the class captive, and now, slowly at first, then in a rush, they were released.

"Where'd you get all that stuff?" Seth's voice was shrill. "It doesn't sound real." Of course they'd already heard the story, but as a jigsaw puzzle whose pieces were forced into a distorted picture in which the whites were the heroes and the Indians the cruel tyrants.

"Yeah, a bunch of sob stories!" Simon, as usual, echoed Seth. I saw frowns and angry looks on the faces that had stared raptly at us a few moments before.

"Indian lover!" There they were, the words I'd dreaded. All the articles, the entries, the books I'd read flashed through my mind, their stories of promises broken, treaties betrayed, oaths that were never intended to be honored merging into a flood that I'd fought until it pulled me under. Now I could not un-know what I knew: A great wrong had been committed, over and over, and nothing could make it disappear.

Fourteen pairs of eyes fastened on us. Many were hostile; some, like Liz, avoided our gaze, and some seemed to be in shock. I thought I saw in a few, like Josie Rennaker and Steve Harper, a hint of quiet sympathy, even admiration. Corinne was staring at her desk. In the back row, the Indian kids were looking past us, a kind of muffled exuberance on their faces.

"Stop it!" Mrs. Isaacson cut through the crescendo of voices. She rose from the seat she'd taken during our talk. "That was an excellent report. Class, if you have questions about the facts Win and Marjorie have included, then ask them for specific references."

"The whole thing is made up!"

"No way those soldiers acted like that."

Indignation rose in me.

"If you stupid idiots read books," I snapped at the seething class, "you'd know it was true." I pulled out the last page of the report and began to read the names of the books we'd consulted. The noise level rose by several degrees.

"Whaddya expect from an Indian and an Indian lover?" Girls as well as boys were yelling now, malice and resentment filling their voices.

Mrs. Isaacson strode to her desk and glared at the class, willing it into obedience. Slowly the noise subsided to uneasy mutterings.

"*Mitakuye oyasin*." From the back, first one voice, then another, then four together, then Marjorie too, joined in, neither loud nor soft, solemn, until the chant stopped as if by some mysterious vote. I looked at Marjorie.

"'All my relations,'" she translated.

Before the mutiny roiling just below the surface could break out again, Mrs. Isaacson intervened. "Everyone. I want you to spend the rest of the period writing down your reactions to this report. Put down everything, all your questions, what you think is wrong with it, and why it's upsetting. And—" she glanced at the back row— "what you agree with, and why."

For a moment the room teetered on the edge of a chasm.

"I mean *now*!"

With an exasperated snort, Simon slapped his notebook open, Seth followed his lead, and heads bent over lines of scribbled scrawls. Mrs. Isaacson turned to Marjorie and me, who'd hardly moved since the first outbreak, and handed us library passes.

"It's not every day someone swats a hornet's nest in here," she said to us in a low voice. "It sure makes life interesting." She motioned toward the door. "Go on. You've earned it."

We didn't have to be told twice.

BUT OF COURSE THAT wasn't the end of the story. While Marjorie was taken in by her clan, surrounded by and absorbed into them, I was cast out from what I'd thought of as mine. It wasn't unexpected, exactly, but it didn't seem much less painful for being anticipated. No one in eighth grade talked to me that day, other than to mutter epithets at my back. No one met my gaze, their eyes shifting to a spot about six inches above my head. Whispers followed me through the halls. During those two hours I felt more than alone, more than invisible. I'd become untouchable, something contagious to avoid, something grotesque to mock.

What, I wondered, would they do if I suddenly lurched at them? Would they draw back and spit? Hold up crossed fingers to keep me at bay? And what about tomorrow, and the next day, and the endless stretches of weeks, months until the semester ended, and I could go—where?

Time, when you're a child, is focused on the present; everyone knows this. Yet even a small child's past contains pain, which he or she tries to shove into the dark where it fades and droops into a mass that can be squeezed and tucked away. Then, as he or she grows older, the doorway of the future begins to reveal a road promising escape from the dark closet at the center of home. Far down my road I could make out a bright college town full of gleaming libraries and classrooms, peopled with readers eager for friendship and conversation. What I didn't know was how to reach the road, how to get through the door, how even to survive long enough in this room that had suddenly become a dungeon.

By seventh period I gave up and cut my last class—something I'd never done before—to walk over to the high school and try to intercept Jess. I leaned against the smooth trunk of a bare aspen, wet flakes of the first fall snow melting on my cheeks, watching boys and girls—men and women, nearly—their faces flushed with release, their excited anticipation so distant from my leaden misery that I turned away.

"Hey, Win!" It wasn't Jess' voice; a deeper, male one. Bell was gesturing at two other boys who slowed to wait behind as he loped toward me.

"What's up?" He peered at my face. "What's wrong?"

"I'm waiting for Jess." My voice was shaky.

"She left early."

"Then I'll go find her at Reynold's."

I began to walk away. Bell motioned to his friends to go on without him and fell in step with me.

"What's going on? You look like you're on your last legs."

"I'm okay!" I made myself fierce to stave off tears as I strode down the sidewalk, nearly running. Bell's sudden grip on my arm swung me around and I bumped against his shoulder.

"She's with Collie." He grabbed my other arm and held me captive in front of him. "They take off in his car every day for a couple of hours. All right?"

Going where, I wondered, doing what? But I was too preoccupied to follow that track.

Bell brushed a few melting flakes from my hair and raised his eyebrows quizzically. "Guess you'll have to tell me."

His words felt like a warm hand turning the knob on a bursting reservoir. As I began babbling to him, snatching phrases here, descriptions there, trying to shape a picture of what had happened, he walked steadily beside me, staring straight ahead. Up one street and down another, circling back, I talked and talked, and he listened intently in a way I'd never been listened to before. He said little—a question here, a word or sound there—but it was enough. As I talked and he listened, my soul turned toward him like a sunflower toward the light.

And all the while some small part of me repeated: He has to listen, he has to understand this, because he's an Indian.

"I don't know how you stand it," I faltered, at last. "You and Marjorie, all of you."

When he answered, he sounded as if he were speaking over an intercom that thinned his words to a bitter thread. "What you feel is yours, not ours." His face was rigid. "What you went through today, multiply that by a thousand, and throw in murders and rapes and stolen land, every month, every year, for hundreds of years, and you'll get a taste of what's ours." He threw me a brief glance. "You've opened it up, you and that crazy cousin of mine. She should have known better. I warned her."

I stopped, stunned, and grabbed his hand.

"But don't you want people to know? To think about it? They *should* know!"

"Why?" He pulled his hand away.

"So they'll understand how you feel, how unfair it is what happened."

"And what good will that do?"

I shook my head. His eyes blazed through me.

"Do you think we want your pity, even if we could get it? Look how those kids reacted. Did they cry and wring their hands and say they're sorry?" His lips twisted into a sneer. "They shut their ears, and they hated you for telling them about it!"

I stepped back, appalled at the rightness of what he said, and how it echoed what Roone had told me about the guilty resenting the ones they'd hurt. His eyes softened.

"I know your heart is in the right place. But what you did will only make things worse for us. And now they've come after you, and they'll get your teacher, too. You wait and see."

We walked on, slowly now, past the darkening, moisture-slicked gardens, past glowing windows in shadowed houses. What cage had I unlocked, I wondered, what mad dog was now prowling through the streets, seeking its prey?

"I'm sorry," I whispered. I felt as stupidly naive as Oliver Twist when he asked for a second helping.

"That Marjorie. Just like her." Was Bell trying to cheer me up by rolling the weight away from my shoulders onto hers? "She just can't let things alone. She's famous for it." He shook his head. "Here I am, finally, first Indian to make the team. And here we go again."

"Maybe nothing will happen."

"Maybe pigs will fly." He stopped and turned to face me. "What do you want to do? It might be better to lie low."

"What do you mean?"

"The Turkey Trot is next week."

"I know." I thrust my jaw forward. "So?"

"It could get ugly."

"I don't care. I want to go with you."

He smiled.

"You and Marjorie. Two of a kind." He ruffled my hair and leaned over slowly, giving me time to pull away. Instead I pressed myself, neck to knee, against him and opened my mouth to greet his lips, his tongue, wrapping my arms around his neck, reveling in the pressure of his arms at my waist.

When we released each other slowly and walked on, I knew something had shifted between us. He was as close now to me as anyone had been since the days when I lived inside the warmth of my mother's loving solicitude. And yet we were holding hands across a crevasse, struggling to keep our balance, listening to the receding echoes of the pebbles kicked in by our scrambling feet.

As SOON AS I came in the door, Mom swooped down and whisked me off to the kitchen.

"What in hell happened today?" she asked under her breath, although Randy was out in the barn. "I've had calls from seven different people, ranting and raving about your report. What possessed you to stir up such a stink? And with an Indian, too! Isn't Corinne good enough for you any more? When Randy finds out, he'll bust a gut."

"First of all, Mrs. Isaacson assigned partners for our reports. And I didn't know what the topic was about when I picked it." Something in me wrinkled up scornfully at my temporizing.

"You knew enough not to work with an Indian, didn't you?"

"No."

Mom shook her head in disbelief. I flared up. "What's so wrong with working with her, anyway? She's one of the best students in the class. Her mother is a medicine woman and took classes in nursing at the college. They keep their house as clean as ours."

Mom's eyes grew wide.

"Have you been going to an Indian house? Is that where you go after school when you say you've been studying?" Her face was flushing with rage.

"We've been studying together to write the report!" I threw my books onto the table. "All we did was do our work! Can I help it if she's actually nice? And if her house is fixed up better than ours?" I knew this would really hurt Mom. Sure enough, she seized my shoulders in a powerful grip.

"You don't have an ounce of sense! You've got the entire town up in arms, calling us names. And that foolish teacher of yours! Why didn't you tell me about her right at the beginning so we could have stopped it?"

"Maybe I didn't want to stop it! She's the best teacher I've ever had. Maybe everyone in this stupid place needs to be shook up. And that goes for you, too!"

"I will not have you sass me!" She shook me hard, my head snapping back and forth. She stopped abruptly when we heard Randy at the back door and dropped her voice to a muted hiss, rolling her eyes in the direction of his steps.

"You keep quiet about this unless you want a real smacking. You hear?"

I rubbed the back of my neck.

"What do you care if he smacks me? You hate me anyway." My voice rose despite her shushing motions. "Everyone in this house hates me, and I hate all of you!"

Randy's puzzled frown poked into the kitchen from the back entryway as I turned and ran to my room, slamming the door behind me.

CHAPTER 13

FOR THE NEXT WEEK intermittent rumblings shook the town, as if a sleeping volcano were nudging itself awake. I was ostracized at first; then, one by one, in groups of two and three, kids pulled me aside in school, wanting to know why I'd done what I had. Their parents did the same when they saw me in town, questioning me like a doctor probing for the cause of a mysterious ailment. I refused to rise to their bait, reciting a factual account without emotion, rendering no verdict, voicing no opinion.

The Indian kids nodded to me now when they met my eyes, where before we'd been mutually invisible. Marjorie didn't approach me, nor I her, in silent agreement to lie low, unsure whether we were protecting our delicate bond or letting it crumble.

Mrs. Isaacson, it was announced, had caught a terrible cold and would be out of school indefinitely. I was indignant but had no one to share it with. Kids labeled her ailment "Indian flu" and were uncharacteristically bland and co-operative with Mrs. Krauss, an elderly math and science teacher who was dragged out of retirement to substitute for her. The rest of the reports, as well as Mrs. Isaacson's last impromptu assignment, were quietly shelved until the hazy time of her return.

I don't know what explanations Mom came up with at home, but Randy left me alone, avoiding me as if I'd slipped beyond the pale of sanity. To my surprise, Mom even suggested I spend Saturday night at Leila's with Jess, which I was only too happy to do, as that solved the problem of how to get to and from the Turkey Trot without letting them know I was going. Since I was still in junior high and Zippy had become *persona non grata* since the Harvest Ball, the idea of my attending never came up. I knew, though, that I was enjoying the last moments of calm on the home front. Once I showed up at the dance with Bell, the cat would be out of the bag, the tiger uncaged. What the hell, I told myself with bravado, I always wanted to be in the circus.

WAITING WITH JESS FOR Collie in Leila's room, my hair once again smoothed by rollers and the dryer, wearing the same blue dress she'd loaned me before, I tried to calm my racing pulse. The girl who'd agonized about her frizzy hair seemed separated from the one I was now, not by five weeks, but by a century, as if I'd passed out of childhood into—not adulthood, exactly, but the rarefied air of a high mountain path between one world and another.

"Maybe they'll try to baptize us in the punchbowl," I joked nervously, trying to fool myself into calm. "Or hang us from the glitter globe."

Jess, leaning toward the mirrored dresser, rolled her eyes without moving the lashes she was stroking with mascara. Leila looked up from her bed.

"Calm down," she said, touching her carefully teased blond hair. "Half of them won't even notice, they're so self-centered."

"It's the other half I'm worried about." I smoothed my skirt for the dozenth time, trying not to think about what might happen to me, and even more, to Bell, trying not to remember his bruised face after the last dance. Jess swiveled around.

"You don't have to go, Win. Bell will understand."

I jumped up, exasperated. "Jesus Christ, why does it all have to be so important? You'd think I was Joan of Arc or something! We're just going to a dance. What can they do, stone us with cookies?"

"More likely, *get* stoned with brownies." Jess fished around a moment in her pocketbook and held up an embroidered change purse.

"Here we are. This'll make you feel a lot more relaxed."

Leila sat up straight.

"Stop it, Jess!" she snapped. "Not here. You promised."

"Don't worry, I'm not stupid. We'll wait till we're in the car." She waggled the purse at Leila. "And we'll save some for you."

For a moment I couldn't believe what my brain was telling me. Did the purse hold marijuana? Was Jess a pot-head? Did all the high school kids smoke it? And where had I been, not to have seen it?

A car horn honked, and Jess stuffed the little purse into her coat pocket.

"Let's go." She ran out, Leila at her heels. I followed slowly, negotiating a wobbly course down the narrow staircase in my first pair of high heels. Maybe they were a mistake, I thought. Maybe this whole thing was a mistake, but I was too far in to pull out now.

Once I saw Bell standing by the car, his hair slicked back, the tension in his eyes bumping against the strained smile on his lips, something in me loosened. As hard as this was for me, I thought, it must be harder for him. My heart expanded at his courage, his willingness to accompany me down the dangerous passage I'd bumbled into and from which I now refused to withdraw. This time we both knew what we were headed for.

Leila waved to us as we arranged ourselves in the back seat and Collie helped Jess into the front.

"See you guys there." She closed the front door behind her, then stuck her head out again. "Hey. *Illegitimati non carborundum!*" And the door banged shut.

"She's had Latin?" I asked, puzzled, as the car sped forward. Collie and Jess laughed.

"It's slang." Bell put his arm around my shoulder. "'Don't let the bastards get you down.'"

"And we won't." From her embroidered case Jess extracted a hand-rolled cigarette, lit it, inhaled deeply, and passed it to Collie. A sweetly pungent odor tweaked the inside of my nose. I stared at her, recalling her indignation at Collie's flask a month ago. Her profile seemed harder, more angular than I'd remembered, and when she turned her head to hand the joint to me, her eyes glittered like wet stones. I waved it away.

"Oh, come on, Win." Her voice was edgy. "Don't be a priss."

Bell reached in front of me, took it from her hand, sucked on it briefly, and passed it to Collie. I wanted to jump from the car; I wanted to arrest them all; I wanted to try some myself. Jess inhaled twice, three times, holding the smoke in her lungs, and softly exhaled an endless stream of smoke, thinner than cigarette smoke, giggling softly at nothing. Collie and Bell began to soften at the edges too, grinning, their muscles easing. Their easiness infected me. By the time we reached the gym, I felt almost happy.

The same soft lights, twisted brown-and-orange crepe paper garlands, swirls of soft music, walls festooned with cut-outs of turkeys instead of pumpkins—hundreds of dots of light cast by the revolving silvery globe circled the gym slowly, casting bouncing rainbows on walls, profiles, carefully combed hairdos, shuffling feet. Faces turned to us, greetings were called. Then, as they registered my presence next to Bell, double-takes, heads put together, eyes returned to us with raised eyebrows, mouths rounded in surprised.

"Don't let them see you notice," Jess hissed in my direction, her mouth scarcely moving, nodding and waving at a group of girls staring in our direction. "Let's go sit down. We'll see who's got any guts."

We pulled out chairs around a small circular table covered with a brown-and-yellow checked cloth. In the center stood a cardboard cartoon-drawing of a Pilgrim, musket over his shoulder, shaking hands with a near-naked, feather-hatted, inanely grinning, tomahawk-waving Indian. Three months before, I wouldn't have registered it. Now I cringed with distaste at its coarse exaggeration, aching to tear it to pieces before Bell could see it. And if I did? What about the ones on all the other tables? And the walls? And the store windows and posters and bulletin board and greeting cards all over town, in the state, in the world? I slipped away from the weight of responsibility beginning to settle on my shoulders and slid into my seat, averting my eyes from the decoration.

"Hey, want a Coke?" asked Collie, gesturing toward the long table at the side of the gym loaded with bowls of potato chips, bottles of soft drinks, and an enormous punch bowl.

"Not yet," Jess decided for us.

"Hey, guys."

Several grinning boys with starched shirts and pomaded hair loomed over us. Were any of them the ones from that day in the cafe? I couldn't tell. They greeted Collie, Bell, and Jess, and looked at me with eager curiosity.

"You Bell's date?" one asked suddenly. His words seemed to vacuum the sound from the rest of the room. To my horror I couldn't coax a single syllable from my throat, so I nodded over and over. The boys stared a moment, grunted a few words at Collie, shuffled their feet, and moved away.

"How long do you bet before every single person here knows?" Collie tilted his chair back and surveyed the room.

"Five minutes tops," Jess guessed, her fingers drumming against the table. "But why wait?"

She got to her feet and held out her hands, one to Collie and one to me.

"Let's get this over with."

We stood up and moved as a body onto the dance floor, the crowd parting like the Red Sea before Moses in *The Ten Commandments*. Why was Jess so impatient? I'd much rather have waited a while, preferably at a table in a dim corner, rather than so close to the dance floor and its loops of circling couples. But I didn't want to antagonize her, so I let Bell gather me close, let my body slip and sway in a now-familiar fit against his. I kept my eyes down. Whenever I raised them past his shoulder I ran into quickly averted stares, some frightened, some excited, most frankly fascinated. One dance, two, a fast one, another slow one, Jess and Collie dancing close to us.

"Fun, huh?" I looked up at Bell's words, met his wry grin.

"It's good practice, I guess," I mumbled.

"For what?"

I shrugged. "For whatever." For weeks and months of this, I thought. For the role I'd chosen: the rebel. The weirdo. His hand tightened on my shoulder.

"Would you look at that." His voice was awed, yet tight, apprehensive. I followed his gaze. Five Indian couples were dancing around the four of us, forming a loose protective net, swaying to the sinuous music, materialized as if by magic in a place where they knew they would find no welcome. I searched my memory: No Indians ever appeared at the junior high dances. No one had ever noticed their absence, because no one expected them. Where they might have been stood a blankness so profound that it too had disappeared, the way a pond, once the ripples die away, bears no trace of the vanished stone.

Where had they learned these dances? I thought of them listening to this very music, in dingy bars, in crowded shacks, dancing in tiny community centers to the blare of a tinny radio. They didn't look at us as I scanned their faces. The only one I recognized was Marjorie.

"I told you," whispered Bell in my ear. "Two of a kind."

He nodded at her, and she smiled briefly.

"What's she doing here?" I asked softly. "Is that her boyfriend?"

"All I told her was that we were coming. The rest must have been her idea. And she doesn't have a boyfriend." He glanced again in her direction. "The guy she's with, that's Bronson. He lives next door to her. First time he's showed up at one of these. Them, too." He gestured with his chin at another couple as the music faded. We began to make our way off the floor, the Indian couples moving in parallel with us, then melting into the shadowy corners of the hall as we sat down.

"Hello, Jess. Bell, Collie." A very pale woman in her forties, her dark blue dress garnished with a bright yellow collar, stood stiffly by our table.

"Hello, Mrs. Fergus." Collie nodded at her, unsmiling.

"I have to ask you to stop making trouble." Her voice had a brassy thinness that set my teeth on edge. "We don't want any unpleasantness tonight."

We looked at each other and back at her.

"We're not making trouble, Mrs. Fergus," protested Collie with such oily sincerity I almost laughed. "We're just here to dance."

Mrs. Fergus' red lipstick stuck out like a gash on her bloodless face.

"Please don't make it hard on everybody. You know what I'm referring to."

"No, we don't." Jess articulated each soft syllable like a threat. "We can dance with whoever we want. It's a free country."

"I'm sorry. Then I'll have to ask you to leave." She turned her head toward two men who had made their way silently toward us. One was the sheriff, Mr. Lundgren. The other was Mr. Sajarsky.

So they had received bulletins, prepared for us, laid plans, concocted a strategy. We were the enemy, the renegades, the troublemakers. The Indians in the woodpile.

Collie and Bell rose slowly, their faces suffused with dark blood. I shrank into my seat, my body pounded by my heartbeat.

"Sit down!" snapped Jess. "We aren't going anywhere!"

Mr. Lundgren stepped forward and put his beefy hand on her shoulder. She shook it off with a quick backward jerk of her upper body. He grabbed her arm and hoisted her up roughly. She pulled away violently, staggered against the chair and began to fall. As Collie reached down to help her, Mr. Lundgren shoved him backwards hard enough to send him careening into the wall of paralyzed onlookers. At the same moment, Mr. Sajarsky stretched out his arms in front of Bell, who hadn't moved, to fence him off. Jess, recovering her balance, threw herself at Mr. Lundgren, kicking his shins, pushing at his chest. Her chair banged over and the embroidered change purse fell out of her pocket, spilling rectangles of thin white papers, a hair clip, and two pencil-thick joints onto the floor at Mr. Sajarsky's feet.

I reached out my foot to push them unobtrusively under the table, but Mr. Sajarsky was too quick for me. He kicked my ankle painfully, then grabbed the purse and the joints and held them out to Mr. Lundgren, who was clamping Jess' arms behind her back. Mr. Lundgren studied them a moment, then looked directly at Bell.

"I'm going to have to take you in for this."

My ears roared.

"That's not his stuff." As soon as I spoke, my stomach lurched with fear. I stole a glance at Jess, who'd missed everything but the joints resting in Mr. Sajarsky's palm. As she opened her mouth, I announced loudly:

"Those are mine!"

"You shut up! They're mine!" Jess answered, glaring.

"Mine!"

"Mine!"

I fought back the wave of hysteria rising in me at the absurdity of our no-win contest. As we continued to hurl claims at each other, Mr. Lundgren let Jess go, put his hand on Bell's arm, took the purse and joints from Mr. Sajarsky, and stuck them in his pocket.

"Let's go." Without pause, he yanked Bell in the direction of the exit. Instantly five Indian guys materialized, blocking his path, while the girls, Marjorie included, flanked them, stone-faced. Mr. Lundgren slowed his pace.

"*Huka, hakamya upo.*" At Bell's words, the Indians melted to either side and Mr. Lundgren escorted him out the door.

"All right, people, everything's under control. Go back to dancing." Mr. Sajarsky waved to the deejay, and music poured into the air. Without a word Collie, Jess and I picked up our coats and, preceded by the Indian kids, left the gym and headed for our cars.

We followed the sheriff in a convoy to his office behind the public library. As he unlocked the door, we tried to crowd in with him and Bell, but he ordered us to wait outside, where we tried to keep warm by stamping our feet and walking in circles. Jess, Collie, and I stood in a huddle slightly apart from the others. After a few minutes, I heard Marjorie's voice raised in anger.

"You're crazy! Put it away!" Laughter and protests, some muttered curses, foreign words, and the clink of glass. Then Marjorie walked over to us.

"You should leave now."

Jess and I looked at each other and at Collie, who was frowning in the direction of the Indians. They were staring at us coldly.

"Whitey go home." A male voice.

"Leave our men alone." A girl's voice, bitter and fierce.

I turned to Marjorie.

"But I thought—" I stammered. "I m-mean, you all were protecting us. Helping us."

"Helping Bell." Her face told me nothing. "Go home now."

"Go on, you guys," I whispered to Jess. Without thinking I walked up to the sheriff's door and pounded on it. The crowd shifted uneasily as the door opened on Mr. Lundgren's frowning face. I pushed past him, fumbling for words, pleading sickness, dizziness, exhaustion, fear, anything to keep me inside. Bell had jumped from his chair as I entered, his eyes apprehensive, but made no gesture toward me. Mr. Lundgren pointed to another rickety chair against the far wall.

"All right, sit there 'til we're through. And keep your mouth shut." I sat, watching the bare light bulb sway slowly back and forth.

"Mr. Lundgren, please—"

"I said, be *quiet*." He turned back to his desk. The embroidered purse and the two joints sat accusingly in front of his paperwork. He finished writing Bell a summons for being drunk, then another for disturbing the peace in his cramped hand. As he began the third, for possession of an illegal substance, the words burst out of me.

"Mr. Lundgren, that isn't fair. The purse with the pot in it was mine, not Bell's."

Mr. Lundgren turned slowly toward me. His heavy gray eyebrows drew together as he examined my face keenly.

"Do you know what you're saying?"

"Yes." I drew a deep breath. "A boy wouldn't carry a thing like that. Look at it." We all stared at the dainty red, green, and yellow stitching, the gold-colored clasp.

"You sure you want this on your record?" Mr. Lundgren asked gruffly.

"Well—" I faltered. "I mean, no, but it's mine, so I should take the consequences, right?"

"Don't." Bell's voice was shaky but clear. "Leave it, Win."

Mr. Lundgren looked at us both, shook his head, and leaned back in his chair.

"This sure is unusual. Usually we have too few people confessing to a crime instead of too many." A smile crossed his face briefly. "Complicates things, though. How do I choose?"

"It's my fault," Bell repeated. Mr. Lundgren shook his head.

"Too complicated for me. I'm gonna confiscate the material, and let you both off with a warning this one time. But if I ever catch either one of you with this stuff again, it'll be the slammer for sure."

Bell and I glanced at each other, unsure if we'd really understood him. He handed Bell the two completed tickets.

"You'll have to appear in court on these two charges, probably pay a fine. Now get out of here."

We rose and edged toward the door.

"Thank you," I breathed as I groped behind me for the doorknob.

"I like people who stick by their friends." Mr. Lundgren's voice, low and resonant, followed us as we hurried into the night.

By then, most of the Indians were gone. Only Marjorie and Bronson were standing on one side of the street, Jess, Leila and Collie on the other. Bell conferred briefly with Marjorie, as I explained to an obviously relieved Jess what Mr. Lundgren had decided. Then they left us alone.

As Bell walked me back to Leila's, he seemed miles away, silent and aloof, almost angry at me. His silence finally silenced me, and my exhilaration at our escape evaporated, leaving me drained of hope, of ideas, of strength. He waited as I walked up Leila's steps, standing stolidly until the door opened for me. Ignoring Mrs. Evans' startled questions, I watched his back recede beyond the weedy lawn, beyond the glow of the street light, until he vanished into the darkness.

JESS AND LEILA DRAGGED themselves out of bed late the next morning to slouch to the breakfast table and smoke cigarettes as I pushed a fork at the remains of the eggs a cheerful Mrs. Evans had scrambled for me. Jess and Collie had returned to the dance only briefly, to corral Leila and her boyfriend off to a bar in the next town, thirty-five miles away. They'd sneaked back home at one-thirty, waking me with suppressed giggles, filling my nostrils with their boozy breath. Then they'd let me lie alert for endless hours while sleep refilled their faces with the plumpness of false innocence.

As soon as I could, I slipped away, before the phone could ring and fill my ear with Mom's worried questions and accusations. I walked up and down the streets, wondering what each occupant knew about last night, and what they thought of the figure, gliding past their windows, who resembled only in external features the Winona they'd known for so long. At least I was left alone; soon I'd be back at the ranch, where the shit would really hit the fan.

Either by chance, or guided by fragments of information I didn't know I'd remembered, I found myself on Brook Street in front of a gray house whose owner, I knew, had moved the year before to Arizona. True to the street's name, a tiny rivulet ran across the front yard, spanned by a wooden plank which connected the two halves of the path that led from the gate to the front porch. A plaque with the name *Isaacson* was fastened to the fence.

I pushed the gate open, jangling the bell that hung from its top. As I climbed up to the porch, Mrs. Isaacson appeared at the door, dressed in faded jeans and a blue-and-green striped shirt.

"Winona!" Her face broke into a smile that dimpled her rosy cheeks. "How nice to see you! Come on in." She stepped to one side and let me precede her into the house.

They'd worked hard on the place. The parlor had been recently painted a fresh near-white that glowed with a buttery tone in the pale morning light. The wooden floorboards had been scraped of years of dirt and covered with a clear finish that made them look like freshly hewn planks. A shaggy rug woven into muted, abstract lavender, green, and teal blue swirls lay near the stone fireplace. The walls were lined with books of all kinds, mostly paperbacks, obviously well read. Instead of ruffled curtains or heavy drapes, they'd hung plain sheer white gauze fabric over the windows, letting in as much light as possible, light that dazzled me as it bounced off the floor, the walls, the shiny white coffee table, making all the other rooms I'd ever been in seem gloomy by comparison.

At the same moment I registered the music. Bach. I'd never heard that particular piece—I later learned it was a Brandenburg concerto—but I was as certain of the composer as if he'd signed his name. This was a new world to me, new but familiar, one I might have dreamed up to live in, far down my own road.

"I'm glad you like it," Mrs. Isaccson answered, reading my expression. "You should have seen it when we first moved in." She sat down on the pale blue sofa and patted the seat next to her. "Richard's working out back in the garden. I'll make some tea in a bit. First tell me how you've been—how things have gone for you since the last day I was in school."

"Okay. No big deal." I sank into the plushly yielding cushions. The effort involved in telling her everything that had happened seemed so enormous that I switched the subject. "Are *you* feeling better?" I knew she wasn't ill.

"Me? I'm fine." A puzzled frown creased her forehead. "Did they say I was sick?"

"That you had the flu."

She shifted her eyes to the framed poster over the fireplace: thick brush strokes of vibrant pinks, greens, and purples formed themselves into the shape of a buxom woman reclining in front of a large window that opened onto a landscape of lush jungle palm trees and a turquoise sea, magical and intoxicating. For a moment the room contained only Bach and that seductive picture-world.

Then Mrs. Isaacson made a decision. "You should know the truth, Win. I haven't been sick. I've been put on what's called 'administrative leave.' That means—" She broke off.

"I know what it means. They fired you, didn't they?"

"Not quite. The principal has called a school board meeting for Tuesday, when they'll go over my record. My 'poor judgment.' My 'radical agitation.'" She laughed suddenly, a harsh, bitter sound, startlingly in contrast to the silky child's curls, the round face. "*Then* they'll fire me. But not before I give them a piece of my mind."

"Because of our report?"

"All the reports. Mostly, the way I mixed Indians and white kids together." She sighed. "Your report was just the final nail in my coffin, I think."

She looked directly at me.

"Don't feel bad for me, Winona. I feel bad for *you*. I should have known how much I was biting off by trying to change the world, even a small part like this."

"You *should* try." I fought against the cushions to sit up straight. "You have to. Things need to change."

"If you really see that—" she broke off and bit her lower lip— "then it hasn't been a total waste."

She rose abruptly and turned toward the hall. "I'll make us some tea," she announced, her back still to me.

"No, thanks, really. I have to go." I levered myself out of the sofa. She swiveled back toward me, rubbing something from the corner of her eye. Part of me longed to stay, to see the rest of that house that had fallen into Redmond from my home planet, to talk about books and music and painted jungle worlds. Another part, though, knew she'd gone far enough, had revealed almost too much, knew if she said any more she might never let herself reappear in our classroom as my teacher. And I was determined that she would come back, though I had only the faintest spark of an idea how to make it happen.

APPARENTLY THAT WAS MY day for unannounced calls. I plodded over to Roone's, rehearsing a sudden need to confer with her about a Chopin *Nocturne* that had been causing me problems at yesterday's lesson. She'd gone to Great Falls, Selby informed me.

"You look like you could use a bite," he insisted as he ushered me into the kitchen and cut me a slice of apple pie. "You need the energy, from what I hear."

I kept my eyes on my plate.

"You don't need to tell me about it, Win," he went on softly. "People talk. They can hurt each other pretty bad with their tongues, worse than sticks and stones, if you ask me. But it's amazing how quick they get tired of it if you don't give them what they want."

"What about when it's more than words?" I burst out. "They wanted to arrest Bell, did you know that?"

"That so? They didn't lock him up, though." No, they hadn't. For the first time, it struck me how differently Mr. Lundgren had acted at the dance from how he'd treated us in his office. For the first time, I got a sense of how, not only kids, but even secretly sympathetic white adults, might feel the temptation to show only that part of themselves that fit how others wanted them to be.

"He's right out back," Selby added, jerking his head in the direction of the shed. My heart gave a lurch but evened out.

"Selby, what do you know about the school board?"

"The board? Just a bunch of ordinary folks who haven't had a new idea in their lives. Mostly they rubber-stamp what the teachers and principals want to do. Roone was on it for a couple of years, but she got tired of trying to teach old horses new tricks."

"Who's at the meetings?"

"Them, and whoever shows up to listen to them waste time. And add their two bits, if they want to. Though no one hardly ever does."

I jumped up, thanking him so effusively for the pie that he looked at me askance, though he smiled.

"Go ahead and visit with Bell a while. He sure looks like he could do with some good words."

I ran out to the shed, my mouth dry. Bell was stooped over, planing the top of a desk, tiny oak shavings curling away from his hands onto the floor like a miniature snowfall. When he saw me he raised his torso slowly, his head almost touching the low plasterboard ceiling. Deep circles under his eyes, and lines pinched into the sides of his mouth, had aged him overnight, giving him the face he might have when he was a man.

"Bell." I stopped, appalled by the pain I glimpsed. Desperate to make sure he understood I wasn't begging for sympathy or support he no longer wanted to give, I made my own voice cool and clear.

"There's a school board meeting on Tuesday to discuss Mrs. Isaacson," I stated. "They want to fire her." I paused, trying to reach for his help without asking. "Anyone can come and say what they want."

He looked at me, some color now invading his sallowed skin. "All right." He picked up the plane and set to work again.

I hesitated but walked close enough to feel the heat of his body, smell the tang of his sweat. His hands slowed and stopped, trembling slightly as they gripped the plane. I put my hand on his wrist, feeling the bones and sinews under the skin. No intake of breath, no motion, no flicker of expression from him. Then he pulled his wrist away, staring at me intently a moment before averting his gaze. "You shouldn't have had to do that." It wasn't the injustice itself that bothered him, I intuited. That he was used to. It was his inability to get out of the situation without my help, without a white girl there to enlist the sympathy and conscience of white authority.

"I'm glad I could," I said.

He still wouldn't look at me. "I can't hurt you anymore." The words were so low I barely heard them.

"It isn't you," I breathed. "And *this* hurts more."

Still no movement. Then he looked at me again, the angles of his face losing their hard edges.

"You and Marjorie. More guts than a squashed groundhog." He was grinning now.

Relief flooded me so intensely that my bones felt loose.

"Now get out of here and let me work." Again he bent over the desk, shaking his head, still smiling, his hands moving across the board steadily back and forth, sawdust spraying around him like aromatic confetti.

CHAPTER 14

W E SHOWED UP AT the unfamiliar high school library five minutes before the school board meeting, Mom scurrying to keep pace with me, Randy trudging behind us. He had been ready to jump into the truck as soon as I mentioned that I wanted to go to the meeting, eager no doubt to throw me out of school along with Mrs. Isaacson. "I have to put the brakes on you, since you can't do it yourself," he'd declared, which only made me more nervous. Other than to announce that my weekly piano lessons were hereby suspended, he hadn't alluded to the dance or its aftermath.

"I wash my hands of you," he'd announced with disgust on Sunday evening. "I hope you get what's coming to you." Mom had flinched at that but said nothing. Since then he hadn't uttered a word directly to me, looking through me as if I'd become transparent, which was fine with me.

The crowded library, bigger than the one I was used to, was humming with subdued chatter and occasional bursts of laughter. The study tables had been shoved out of the way against the bookshelves and the large open space filled by rows of metal folding chairs. People shuffled in, parents and kids from my class—Seth, Corinne, Simon, and more —jostled past each other to sit with their friends, or leaned against the walls. A group of grave-faced teachers sat in the first row, separated by an empty chair from the rigid figures of Mrs. Isaacson and a tall man I assumed was her husband. Their profiles radiated calm assurance, but I could just make out their tightly clasped hands resting in the space between their chairs.

In the back, the last two rows were solid with Indian faces, dark, silent, staring straight ahead at the long wooden table at the opposite end of the room. There were Marjorie and her mother; Bell and Bronson; Billy Ten Deer and Sam Fire Hawk from my class, flanked by adults who resembled them, and others I knew by sight or not at all. If Bell had gotten them here, I fretted, that meant they supported Mrs. Isaacson. But if they felt the way the kids outside the sheriff's office had—my mind went blank. I could feel a tiny rivulet of perspiration making its way down my back.

The room quieted somewhat as six flustered-looking women and men, led by Mrs. Gruber, the school board president, filed through the door and made their way to the empty table at the front of the room. Only Mr. Hansen, the gray-haired, gray-faced high school principal, and rotund Mr. Sajarsky, moved with the deliberate pace of confident purpose. Mrs. Gruber spent several moments arranging a stack of papers she had brought with her, until Mr. Hansen coughed ponderously. Then she searched for something and leaned over to confer briefly with Mr. Hansen, who grabbed a book and banged it on the table. Everyone jumped, including Mrs. Gruber.

"The meeting will come to order," she announced, her too-loud voice cutting through air already thick with thousands of breaths and the smell of wet wool. "Could someone please open a window? We usually don't have so many, uh, *people* here."

What did they usually have, I wondered, Martians? A window creaked and clanked its way up its frame.

"We have quite a lot on our agenda tonight." She consulted a piece of paper. "Let's see, approval of the cafeteria menus for December; appropriation for new school uniforms; repair on the bus—"

"The teacher first!" a deep voice called out from somewhere in the back. Mrs. Gruber looked up, hesitated, and resumed her reading. "Repair for the team bus; the chaperon list for next semester's dances—"

"The teacher first!" The same voice, louder. Several others repeated the phrase. Mr. Hansen rose slowly as Mrs. Gruber's eyes flitted nervously around the room.

"Look, folks, settle down. We've got an agenda. All our business is important."

"The teacher! The teacher!" By then everyone seemed to be yelling at once, drunk with a sense of what might be the evening's last moment of unanimity. I looked around in amazement at the mottled skins, the excited smiles, the wet lips, remembering Seth and Simon and the angry cries of our class. This was worse, because these were our parents, adults, our supposed bulwark against the chaos of childhood.

At that moment the library door opened on a startled Jess and Collie. Simultaneously Randy popped to his feet from his seat next to Mom.

"Why do you think we're all here, Hansen?" he shouted. "It ain't to listen to you talk about buses and dances!"

Cheers and a ragged chorus of "That's right!" erupted from the crowd. Mr. Hansen and Mrs. Gruber whispered together as the chant of "The teacher! The teacher!" rose again from the crowd. From her perch on the end of a table, Jess flashed her raised eyebrows at me and glanced around the room with a sardonic twist of her lips.

This time Mrs. Gruber banged the book as Mr. Hansen and Randy both sat down.

"Very well, we will start with the contract between this district and Mrs. Sarah Isaacson, teacher at Redmond Junior High School," she resumed. "As I understand it, several parents have brought complaints against her teaching methods and the material she assigns to her class. Given the, uh, strong feelings about this matter, the board would like to open the meeting for general discussion. Who would like to start?"

A long moment of silence was broken by the creaking of chairs and a chorus of coughs; then several hands went up. Mrs. Gruber pointed to Seth's father, Andy O'Rourke.

He rose heavily, his square face turning beet-red. "This teacher don't teach what's in the history book," he breathed hoarsely. "She should stick to what they say, not go make up her own ideas about it."

"Do you mean she hasn't used the assigned textbooks?" Mrs. Gruber asked. Mr. O'Rourke looked at Seth, who whispered something to him.

"They read the book, but she gave them all kinds of other stuff, and told them all kinds of other crazy stories, too."

"'Other stuff'? What do you mean?"

Mr. O'Rourke's eyebrows drew together. "Some old books she dragged in on her own, Commie stuff, throwing mud on the U.S.A." He turned to Seth. "Go on, you tell them, son."

Seth's face turned as red as his father's, and he sank deeper into his seat. With a quick jerk, Mr. O'Rourke pulled him upright.

"Go on. What'd you have to read?"

Seth stood and shuffled from one foot to the other, then licked his lips.

"*Black Elk Speaks*," he muttered.

"What was that?" Mr. O'Rourke poked him in the side.

"Some book written by some old Indian guy, stupid stuff all about Indians being tromped on by the Army."

"I looked at that damn book," barked Mr. O'Rourke. "Bunch of bleeding heart stories. Didn't say nothing about how those Indians raped and murdered white women and children. Made it sound like all white folks were devils, instead of how they were defending themselves against a bunch of savages."

"She's trying to set them against us." Mr. Rudolph, Simon's father, his dark hair sticking up in clumps where he'd run his agitated fingers through it, had gotten to his feet. "We got everything quiet here, everyone gets on peaceful with each other, no one bothering anyone else."

Oh, really? I thought. What had happened at the dance, at both dances, didn't seem like peace and quiet to me. I turned around. The back two rows were silent, the dark faces expressionless.

"Who does she think she is, anyhow?" That was Mrs. Rudolph's treble twang, setting my teeth on edge. "She rushes in here, stepping on everyone's toes, not even getting to know us first."

A clamor of shouts and plaints blended together, a phrase here and there clear. Again the book slammed down. As the noise ebbed, I breathed hard and slow to steady myself and began to lift myself from my seat. Mom pulled me down hard just as Mrs. Gruber pointed to a waving hand.

Mrs. Harper, Steve's mother, stood up uncertainly, blushing as all eyes focused on her.

"I just wanted to say, this is America, you know. A teacher has the right to say what she believes, just like anyone else. Not everyone has to agree with her opinion."

"She's supposed to be *teaching*, not giving opinions!" Mr. Weaver, Corinne's father, called out. "She's filling our kids' heads with garbage and calling it facts! That's not teaching!"

Mrs. Harper look distressed. "But maybe she's got her own opinions about what the facts are."

"Her ideas are a bunch of nonsense, and worse than that, they're dangerous!" Randy had risen without waiting to be acknowledged. "What she's spouting out is tearing us apart. It's tearing up my own family."

He had the room's attention now.

"Until she got this teacher, my daughter Win was a good girl, a good student, did what she was told." This was definitely news to me. "Then this teacher gives her this report to do, has her work with some Indian instead of with her best friend. Next thing you know, she's gone crazy, won't listen to her parents, dumps her friends, and starts taking up with troublemakers." His code word for Indians, I noted.

His words had come fast, and he was perspiring. I saw Mom's hand tugging at his jacket, but he ignored her.

"The races don't belong together. Everyone knows that. But you let someone put these kind of crazy ideas in kids' heads, and they turn into Indian-lovers. Next thing, they'll be wanting to *marry* them!"

He looked around at the nodding heads, the indignant expressions on nearby faces, and sat back down, his face bright with satisfaction at his speech. Mrs. Gruber hurried to follow his lead.

"Well, it seems pretty clear that Mrs. Isaacson's teaching methods do not meet with community approval," she declared. "And community satisfaction is an important part of our standards. Usually we would terminate a contract at the end of the semester, but judging by the level of dissatisfaction here tonight, the board is inclined—"

"Excuse me." Everyone turned to look at the back row, where Marjorie's mother, Frances Manybear, was standing, her arms folded in front of her. The room jerked to a standstill. Mrs. Gruber's face froze.

"Some of us in this community are very pleased with Mrs. Isaacson's teaching methods," Frances went on in a clear, firm voice. "We believe she is trying to be fair. She is telling a part of the story that many people haven't heard before, though some of us know it well."

"We've been doing just fine with what we already know," shouted Mr. O'Rourke. "What we all learned in school, what our parents learned, that's the only story we need."

"Half a story is a lie." Frances stood up even straighter, if that was possible.

"Are you calling me a liar?" Mr. O'Rourke's hunched shoulders rose. His chest expanded and his hands balled into fists as he got up from his seat. The veins on Randy's neck were bulging. Without realizing I'd decided to get up, I found myself on my feet.

"Mrs. Isaacson didn't do anything wrong!" I practically shouted. "She didn't write what's in the books, she just gave them to us to read. Generals in the U.S. Army wrote them, and soldiers, and all kinds of people who were there when things happened."

I took a deep breath. What seemed like a thousand eyes had fastened on me. I felt like a circus tightrope walker without a net. "At first I hated reading those books, finding out what really happened, all the horrible things people did to each other. Sometimes I wish I'd never found out, because it doesn't feel good to know. But if it's true—"

I stopped, trying to sort what was whirling through my head into some sort of order: Adults always hide things from children. They want to protect us, but they're really protecting themselves. They're all scared of looking like fools, like cowards, like bullies. They're scared of finding out they don't belong on their little thrones, where they've always been comfortable.

"If it *is* true," I went on, "then I'm glad I know. You know why? Because now no one can fool me about it, ever again." I glanced briefly at Mr. O'Rourke. "*You* should have known. *All* of you. *You* should have told us. And you should give her a medal for doing your dirty work for you!"

With that I sat down. Mom was staring at me, open-mouthed, her eyes full of anxiety mixed with something close to admiration. My heart was pounding so hard I could hardly hear the silence in the room over the roar in my ears. After several seconds, Mrs. Gruber cleared her throat.

"Well. I promised Mrs. Isaacson she could have a chance to speak. This seems like a good time. Mrs. Isaacson?" She nodded at the red-gold head. Mrs. Isaacson let go of her husband's hand, rose, and turned to face the room. Tell them, I willed her. Tell them what they need to know.

"I was hired to teach your children," she said in a low, clear voice, "and that's what I've done to the best of my ability."

She paused and patted her forehead with a tissue crumpled so tightly it looked shredded.

"What I try to do is to get them not to accept blindly what someone else has decided they should think or know. They have to find out the real story and make their own judgments. And often that means examining different versions of a story, trying to analyze them to see how true they might be. That isn't easy, it isn't comfortable and—" she glanced quickly around the room, the hint of a smile on her lips— "it certainly isn't always popular. But I think it's worth it. Even more, I think it's absolutely essential. It demands that your children meet the greatest challenge anyone is capable of: thinking for themselves. And that's the biggest compliment you or I can pay them. I'm sure you wouldn't want me to do less."

She looked directly at me. "I'm grateful to you, Winona. Not just for defending me. But for having understood what I was trying to do."

She smiled at me, then at Mom.

"Mr. and Mrs. Daggett, I hope you're as proud of your daughter as I am. She makes me glad I'm a teacher."

She sat down.

For a moment the room was completely quiet. Then someone behind me began to clap, then someone else, then more, until a wall of sound rose and filled the air. I clapped until my hands stung. Mom and Randy were leaning their heads together, whispering. Mr. and Mrs. Tennant, Liz's parents, were clapping too, and so was Mrs. Ross, and the Harpers. Once again Mrs. Gruber banged the book and waited for quiet.

"All things considered, it seems appropriate that this matter be given further study," she barked. "Opinions are divided, and feelings are strong. Therefore, as chairman I'm proposing that the board table further action on Mrs. Isaacson's contract until we've had time for discussion. Any objections?"

She paused a moment, then hurried on. "All right, the matter is postponed."

A murmur began to swell as people stirred in their seats and exchanged remarks with neighbors. Mr. Sajarsky whispered something to Mrs. Gruber and turned to Mr. Hansen. The three conferred briefly, and Mrs. Gruber raised her voice over the babble.

"Until a decision is reached, Mrs. Isaacson will remain on administrative leave."

Cheers, some boos, a few protests. Then Mrs. Isaacson stood up.

"I can't accept that," she asserted firmly. "I want to do my job. Either fire me, or let me teach."

Again heads met, indistinct words were exchanged, longer this time as various board members were consulted. Finally Mrs. Gruber straightened up. "Until further action is taken, you may return to teaching," she announced. She held up her hand as a babble of protesting voices rose and mounted in volume. "If parents wish, they can have their children excused to attend study hall during the class, and the student can read the approved textbook."

A murmur, quieter than before, met this statement. I guessed at which parents would urge their children to drop out, which would insist, and which would support their continued attendance.

"And Mrs. Isaacson, please—" here Mrs. Gruber leaned toward Mrs. Isaacson— "remember that we have our ways, and they've worked pretty well until now. It doesn't sit right with us when someone tries to change them overnight."

She banged her book a final time.

"Let's take a fifteen-minute break before we go on to the rest of the agenda."

I sat stunned with relief. A tide of voices rose and swelled as people scraped their chairs, shrugged on their coats, and headed for the board table or the door, jostling, chattering, shaking their heads. It was clear the board would have the meeting more or less to themselves for the rest of the evening. I craned my neck, looking for Jess, but couldn't see her in the crowd. She, Collie, and Bell had all disappeared.

Randy was shoving his way past empty seats, his head jutting forward like a bull. Mom pulled at my sleeve, eager to follow him.

"I'll meet you outside," I muttered to her. She hesitated but hurried after Randy. I edged toward Mr. and Mrs. Isaacson, who were still sitting quietly in their seats, his arm now resting around her shoulders. Her head was lowered, and her cheek was shiny with tears.

I stopped abruptly as he turned and shook his head at me briefly, then bent toward her again. I backed away clumsily, stumbled over a chair, and turned and ran from the room, my face burning, as embarrassed as if I'd stumbled on them making love.

In the hall I found myself next to Corinne and her parents. Corinne wouldn't look at me.

"Well, Winona, that was quite a speech," said Mrs. Weaver gruffly. "You're certainly turning into a rabble-rouser, aren't you."

The sight of Mrs. Weaver's compact, wiry body, her familiar blue wool coat, her stubby work-reddened hands, flooded me with nostalgia for all the times Corinne and I had gobbled her home- baked chocolate chip cookies in front of their jumpy TV, or mixed homework with meandering gossip and pointless giggles in Corinne's pine-paneled bedroom. An ache for that world I'd lost burst in me like a flame, blazing up for a moment, sputtering, and finally flickering out. I searched for something to say and found only words that seemed so trite they stuck in my throat. After a moment Mrs. Weaver pushed Corinne in front of her, and they moved away. Corinne looked back once, her face forlorn, a reflection of my own.

In the parking lot, small groups of people stood staring at the smashed windshields of five parked cars, the broad sheets of glass cracked into crazed whorled spider-webs. The cars' owners, all Indians, gazed at them impassively, then one by one got in and drove away, sticking their heads out the side windows in order to see the road.

CHAPTER 15

SOMETIMES WHEN YOU LOOK back, you can see individual events merging into a pattern too close to recognize at the time, like big stones randomly scattered on a field you're crossing. Only later, once you've climbed to a hilltop high above, you can see that they spell "help" or "danger" or "this is it."

What could I have seen, if I'd only known? In the weeks after the board meeting, I was preoccupied with school. At first, five or six kids in each class opted for study hall instead of History with Mrs. Isaacson. Then, as the weeks went on, they trickled back, missing the others, the stimulation of her lessons, and worried in a few cases about the way their grade might appear on their record. I also maneuvered to keep meeting with Bell, and to continue my piano lessons, while concealing both from Randy.

The phone call fell out of nowhere, a message from the moon. And I wasn't even there when it came. "Get out the fancy tablecloth, Marie," Randy announced one evening a few days before the school Christmas break was due to begin. "We're having company for dinner next week."

Mom and I stared at him, bewildered. His voice was falsely hearty; his eyes glinted with malicious pleasure at our confusion. Not counting hired hands during harvest season, I couldn't remember anyone outside the family having a meal with us. Corrinne and Leila had sometimes eaten supper with us when they stayed overnight, but that didn't count either.

Lorrie and Pete, unfazed, voiced the question for us.

"Who, Daddy? Who's coming?"

"Win can fill us in." Now all eyes turned to me. My scalp prickled. "Go on, Win. Tell us who's coming to dinner."

"How should I know?" But suddenly I did.

"I'll give you a hint." Randy smiled at Lorrie and Pete. "It's someone no one's met, but who Win's been writing to."

"Sean Connery! Sean Connery!" Lorrie and Pete screamed, bouncing on their chairs so hard Pete's tipped backward and Mom caught it just in time. I'd kept posters of him as James Bond on my wall for the last two years; I'd seen all his movies at least four times.

"Here's another hint," Randy went on after Lorrie and Pete had recovered from their dashed hopes of a Hollywood visitor. "This person is related to some of us sitting here, but not all of us." He directed his needle gaze at Mom.

The look I'd dreaded spread over Mom's face: the shock of sudden comprehension, shifting into hurt surprise, then into righteous indignation. She opened her mouth to let fly, then immediately stopped herself: Should she blow up at me and so let Randy realize she'd kept information of my treachery from him? Would he assume she'd assented to my correspondence? What strategy would be least likely to stoke his fury? Could she get away with pretending this was the first she'd heard of Marilyn?

Too late. Randy had watched her as closely as I had.

"So." He sat back in his chair, nodding slowly. "Looks like this isn't as big news as I'd thought."

"What do you mean? I never invited anyone to dinner." Her attempt at naiveté made me cringe. Instead of innocent, she sounded stupid.

"I know that. *I* invited her, didn't I?" Randy sneered.

"You did? Why?"

"Because I'm real curious about these relatives of that dead husband of yours you've been hiding all these years. I'm wondering whether they have leprosy or something. Or whether they think *we* do."

"I haven't been hiding anyone! I didn't even know she existed until she—" Mom bit her words back in mid-sentence. Randy smirked in triumph.

"Until *she* wrote you out of the blue, and Win answered, right? What's the matter, you can't write a letter yourself?"

"I-I didn't know if you—I didn't think you'd want —"

Randy slapped the table so hard the plates jumped, and Pete's eyes began to fill.

"Why don't you let *me* decide what I want?" He leaned over to pull Pete up into his lap. "At least Win had the guts to do what you wouldn't."

He hoisted Lorrie, who had slipped off her chair and sidled up to him, on to one knee, shifting Pete to the other. The three of them stared solemnly at Mom and me like a pyramid of owls, Lorrie and Pete resting the backs of their heads against Randy's chest as he ruffled their hair. His eyes were full of calculation laced with the barest hint of enjoyment.

I knew what was coming next, and I decided not to postpone it. Sure enough, as I washed the dishes, Mom eased the kitchen door closed and walked over to the sink.

"Why did you do it, Win?" she asked in a low, tense voice, elbows out and hands on hips. "Couldn't you leave it alone when I asked you?"

"But why? I'd think you'd want to meet her."

"*I* don't, *you* do. And it's whatever *you* want, isn't it? I ask you, I *tell* you, to do something for me, but no. You never listen to me, and you never will. I'm sick of it."

"But Mom, why won't you explain? It doesn't make sense. Unless—" I stopped, not liking the thought I'd had.

"Go on. Unless what?"

"Unless you hated my father so much you can't stand even to be reminded of him."

Mom's mouth fell open, and she shook her head slowly, as if unable to believe what she'd heard.

"For God's sake, Win." She paused, searching for words, then gave up. "Think whatever you want. I'm through trying to get you to help me. You're on your own."

She turned and marched, not into the living room, but into the hall toward their bedroom, leaving me holding the dishrag as it dripped soapy tears onto the floor.

ALMOST AT ONCE IT was next week, and Mom was washing dishes and clashing pots while barking orders at us. Lorrie and Pete were picking toys up from the living room floor while I vacuumed and swept and tried to make the place look just slightly less shabby than it seemed in the dull gray winter light.

The chicken was baking in the oven, the table was set, the potatoes peeled, when I heard the car turn into the drive. Lorrie, Pete, and I ran to the front door, Mom and Jess behind us, and I threw it open just as Marilyn brought her blue Bel Air to a stop, stepped out, and turned toward us. Her mouth, bright with newly applied red lipstick, curved in a tentative smile, her shoulder-length auburn hair caught to one side by a tortoise-shell barrette. Dark sunglasses concealed her eyes, making her face remote and mysterious. She came toward the steps, clutching a white-wrapped package and a manila envelope in her red-gloved hands.

"Win?" She looked directly at me and grinned as she started up the steps. "You look just like I imagined you from your description."

Before I could answer, Mom pushed past me.

"I'm Marie." She reached out and briefly hugged Marilyn, whose eyebrows rose in pleased surprise. "You got here okay? Come in. You must be cold as anything."

She ushered Marilyn through the door, a suddenly shy Lorrie and Pete clinging to her legs. Introductions were made, Marilyn's duffle coat removed, the ceremonial box of candy presented and opened, Lorrie and Pete carefully selecting their one-each-before-dinner pieces and again retreating to Mom's side. Marilyn was ensconced in Mom's green armchair with a cup of hot coffee as she sketched in the details of her two-hour drive to Redmond.

"I was surprised it was so easy, but the road was clear," she said.

"Looks like we may have an open winter," Mom agreed. "Last winter was closed. Three feet of snow by Thanksgiving, and cold as the Arctic."

"I remember. Last year when I visited, we were housebound for three days. It happened a lot when I was growing up. Guess that's one reason I left." She laughed, a deep rich sound that made me smile.

The back door slammed. Mom jerked upright as if someone had jabbed her in the small of the back. Randy appeared in the doorway, his face scarlet with cold. He crossed the floor, pulling off his mittens and stuffing them in his jacket pocket, and held out his hand to Marilyn, who had risen to meet him.

"So this is the famous cousin from California." His voice was warm and inviting. "Welcome. I'm Randy. It's not every day we get to add to the family."

He sandwiched Marilyn's hand between his own and gave her the crooked, engaging grin that lifted one corner of his mouth and crinkled his eyes into crescents.

"Here, sit down." Still holding her hand, he eased himself into the brown armchair next to hers and leaned slightly toward her.

"Run it by me again, how we're all related." He shook his head slightly. "I guess I'm not really your blood relation."

"My father, and Jess and Win's father, were brothers," she said. "So I'm their first cousin. Now, Pete and Lorraine here —" Lorrie giggled at the sound of the name she hadn't been called since her christening— "let's see, we're half-cousins, I guess. They're your children, right? Yours and Marie's?"

"So I'm told." His voice had an icy edge. "And I guess I believe it."

Just as Marilyn's smile began to falter, he winked at her, and she burst into relieved laughter.

"That reminds me," Randy said to Marilyn, glancing at Mom. "You said you'd found something you wanted us to see."

My ears perked up. Mom drew back slightly, clasping her hands in front of her.

"I wanted Marie to have it. Maybe you already have a copy, but. . .

here it is."

She handed the manila envelope to Mom, who turned it over several times before carefully opening it and pulling out an old black-and-white photograph in a sparkling new matte. As she looked at it, her eyes softened and her face grew remote.

"I found it in our family album," Marilyn said eagerly. "I had it re-matted."

I edged closer to Mom and looked over her shoulder. A young, dark-haired woman in a white dress and a veil—my mother, so slender she was barely recognizable—stood next to an achingly young man with hair in an Elvis-style pompadour, his teeth flashing in a wide grin.

"It's your wedding picture. You and Lee, my uncle," Marilyn said proudly.

"Let me see," I said, reaching for it. Lorrie and Pete crowded round.

"You look pretty, Mommy," Lorrie stated. "Who's that man?"

"That's my father," I said firmly.

"No, it's not," Lorrie protested. "That's not Daddy. Daddy, that's not you. You don't have all that hair."

"That's the truth, all right," Randy said, patting his sandy fuzz as he studied the picture. "Funny, my hair and Win's are more alike than her and her father's, huh?"

"But *you're* her daddy, Daddy!" Lorrie protested, running to him and punching him with her little fist. "You're everybody's daddy!"

Randy ruffled her own string-straight strawberry-blond hair affectionately and pulled her onto his knee, whereupon she hid her face in his chest.

"You'd like that, huh, Funny-face? Me, too." His voice was odd: quiet yet tight, as if he were holding back something that threatened not only us but himself.

"Thank you, Marilyn," Mom said, slipping the photo back into its envelope and sliding it into a drawer of the end table next to the sofa. I made a mental note to check it out later on, but when I did, it had disappeared.

Mom stood up, the skin on her face stretched too tight over her cheekbones. "Dinner's probably nearly ready." She hurried out of the room. "Come on, Win."

"Can I help?" Marilyn had half-lifted herself out of her chair, but Randy touched her arm briefly.

"You stay right here and tell us more about California."

I followed Mom, keeping the door to the living room open and rejoining them as soon as I could so I could hear her describe the steep rocky coast falling down to the turbulent sea, the line on line of darkening hills receding toward the evening sky, the barren sandy desert of Death Valley that sprang into colorful bloom while here we were, still buried in snowdrifts five feet deep.

And as we sat down at the table, she recounted her bewildered, eager excitement at the multi-colored garb and variegated skin colors packed together in the redolent city that sparkled and hummed and throbbed at all hours of the day and night, the city whose pulsating dance and unpredictable beat formed as great a contrast as could be imagined with the slow cycles of plains and hills and clouds of her childhood.

"My parents were so upset when I moved to Berkeley," she recalled. "But I couldn't wait to go somewhere completely different. I've been to Hawaii too, and Mexico. I hope to get to Europe one day."

"Me, too." I couldn't hold back any longer.

"Win talks just like that all the time," Randy observed, lifting an eyebrow.

"Like Lee." Mom's words popped out like a jackrabbit from behind a bush. "He was always dreaming about traveling somewhere. One summer when he was in high school, he hitched over to the coast, right through Oregon and Idaho, to see that ocean he was always talking about. He said he liked being next to a horizon with no end in sight so much, he almost stayed put."

"Why'd he come back?" I asked. This was more than she'd ever been willing to reveal about my father before. She shrugged and waved a dismissive hand.

"More chicken?" She picked up the platter and held it toward Marilyn.

"No, go on, tell us more." Randy was smiling, but the icy edge was back in his voice. "What did your father tell you about Lee?" He leaned toward Marilyn, raising his eyebrows questioningly.

"I think they were pretty close as kids. Of course, my father was a lot older. They had some kind of falling out later on, when I was in junior high. I know they didn't see each other much when I was growing up. I kind of remember meeting Jess as a baby, but not Win." She frowned slightly.

"Then you all moved away, I think. I mean, Marie and you two kids."

"After Dad died," I said. "We never saw any of them—dad's family—after that."

Randy looked from Mom to me, then at Marilyn.

"Bad blood there, huh? That's a damned shame." His lip twisted in an ironic grin. "Course, I haven't had much to do with my own family. Happens like that sometimes. They go their way, you go yours."

"I always wondered about it," Marilyn added. "But my father died before I got the story from him, and my mother just completely lost track of you all, once you'd moved. She wasn't even sure if you were still in Montana."

"So how did you find us, then?" Randy sat back and folded his arms across his chest. "You're a detective?"

"I found Marie through the Bureau."

"What?" Such a small question, from one of us, or from everyone, as if we'd collectively drawn our breath.

"The Bureau. The B.I.A. They made it easy. They keep track of everyone who's Indian, or part Indian."

For a few seconds, Marilyn kept spearing bits of chicken and lifting them to her mouth. Then something in the silence alerted her and she looked up at our frozen faces. As her eyes moved around the table, the fear that had filled our bodies seeped into hers. She put her fork down.

"Didn't you—You *must* have known." She fixed her eyes, wide with embarrassed shock, on Marie. "Oh, my god."

Marie reached across the corner of the table and put her hand on Marilyn's arm.

"Of course I knew," she reassured Marilyn.

"Knew what?" Randy asked coldly.

Mom looked at a spot over Marilyn's head as she addressed us all. "My father was half Indian."

The room was absolutely quiet, as everyone waited for Mom to re-arrange the scattered pieces of the day into a whole. The same phrases kept running over and over through my head: the B.I.A. The Bureau. The Bureau of Indian Affairs. Indian. Records of Indians. Indian records. Our family is in the *Bureau.*

An image of all of us in miniature popping out of a bureau drawer in Mom's bedroom bubbled up behind my eyes, and I burst into snorts of laughter that I tried to suppress. Lorrie and Pete started giggling too, catching my hysteria, and soon their infectious glee, plus our know-ing they hadn't the slightest idea why they were laughing, had us all in stitches.

All but Randy. He was smiling thinly, grudgingly, eyes cold and calculating. As our laughter began to taper off, he rose abruptly and stomped across the room, pulled open the door of the small end table next to the sofa, and seized the bottle of whiskey he kept there for spe-cial occasions that occurred whenever he felt like it.

"Go get some glasses," he snapped. "Not *you.*" As Mom rose, he had motioned her down and nodded toward me. "We'll drink a toast. It's not every day you find out something about your wife and kids you never suspected."

I scuttled from the room, shutting the door behind me. As I pulled the jelly glasses that were our substitute for wine goblets from the shelves with shaking hands, I tried to orient myself. It felt as if the floor was tilted at a slight angle and I couldn't stand fully upright without staggering. I thought of Jess' darkly shining hair, the beautiful olive skin and prominent cheekbones I'd always envied; now they seemed ominous. I remembered a conversation we'd had years before about what she, but not I, could remember of our father's funeral.

"There was a big fight." Her words had been hushed, barely audi-ble. "They wanted you and me to go live with them. Dad's family. They wanted to take us from Mom. They hated her. I didn't know why." Now I wondered if I had the answer.

"Where're those damn glasses?" Randy barked menacingly from the dining room. I stumbled back with the glasses.

For the rest of the meal, everyone acted cheerful—even gleeful, led by Randy, who toasted his newfound niece-by-marriage and then steered the conversation to safer subjects: his own youthful adventures, his plans for the ranch, my piano and upcoming competition, about which I'd completely forgotten.

But just below the surface, another whole world was in motion. Mom's eyes kept darting to Randy, and her laughter at his witticisms was tense and brittle. I kept skimming backward in time over moments of revelation missed, information misunderstood, a self made willfully blind. At moments I was indignant: She had misled me! How could I have seen what was hidden from me so carefully? Then I'd remember a tiny fragment —a questioning look, a cool greeting at a church group, a veiled smile and two heads leaning together, speculative eyes fixed on Mom—and tingle with dread as I plunged into the cold water of where we were headed.

I pulled myself back into the scene we were playing around the table and slipped behind my brightly painted mask. I no more believed in it than in Santa Claus, but the false cheer felt distracting and safe. Years later, I would seek this same numbing comfort in smoky bars, with their twangy music and over-hearty laughter. Then, as now, I knew it was no more than a mirage, a shadow play that would vanish with the snap of a switch, leaving us defenseless against each other.

FINALLY IT WAS OVER.

Marilyn's red-gloved hand waved from the window, her last "good-bye" ringing in my ears as she turned her car toward the open gate, tail-lights glowing bright in the dusky air, then dimmer, then gone. I stood stone-still in the front doorway next to Mom, not quite touching her, feeling the warmth rise from her rigid body, her hands moving, rubbing each other over and over. I couldn't look at her. I couldn't keep my eyes off her.

My mother, the Indian.

She was still staring at the after-image of the car's lights shimmering in the dull gray air.

"I wish she'd never found us," I whispered. Mom's hands stopped their involuntary motion.

"It's not her fault, Win."

Then whose is it? I silently asked.

I knew. I'd answered Marilyn's letter. Everything that had just happened had flowed from that.

Now the enormity of what I'd done hit me like a sharp blow to my diaphragm, so sudden and intense I almost doubled over. A wave of anger at my mother rose from my stomach to my throat, to the back of my eyes, curling my lips back from clenched teeth. I wanted to scream at her, to rake my nails over her face, to tear her hair, my hair, to sink to the ground and howl.

She turned to me, her eyes opaque, as if hidden behind mirrored glasses. She touched my shoulder lightly. "It's not really your fault either, Win," she said, her voice like frost-crackling grass. "It's mine."

My anger fell away as if I'd stepped out of an ugly dress. I opened my mouth to ask: Who, then? Where are they? What am I, and where will we go? But she was already turning, taking a deep breath, crossing the threshold. I followed.

Randy was sitting in the brown armchair, staring at the floor. Lorrie and Pete were nowhere in sight. Mom walked carefully over to Randy's chair and stopped.

"Why?"

Had he said that? Slowly he raised his head and looked up at her, bewilderment twisting his eyebrows and cutting deep lines into his forehead. He stared at her for five, ten seconds, breathing in open-mouthed raspy gasps. He turned his head away. Slowly Mom sank to her knees and reached out a tentative hand.

"Don't touch me."

She drew back. Suddenly he seized her jaw with one hand and her hair with the other, twisting her neck and wrenching her head forward so her face was flooded by the light of the floor lamp next to him. She offered no resistance, though her position must have been horribly uncomfortable. He searched her face, his own so close to hers that for a moment I thought he was about to kiss her, or bite her. When he finally pushed her away, she rocked back on her haunches and lifted her hand to rub her neck. Randy stood up so quickly I couldn't see the transition.

"*You fucking squaw.*"

The blood drained from her face, leaving her skin the color of paste. All the air seemed to rush out of the room, the silence so complete I heard the gravelly thunder of my own heartbeat. Then he shouted loud enough that the lampshade shook, "Lorrie! Pete! Come here!" Mom looked at him pleadingly. He ignored her. "Come *in* here!"

Their startled faces appeared at the hall door. Randy yelled at them, "Get your tom-toms, you little Cheys! We're gonna have a pow-wow!" They didn't move. He rushed over, grabbed each of them by an arm, and dragged them into the center of the room. "Come on, do a goddamn rain dance!" He shoved them onto the rug. Bewildered, they began to cry. "Dance, you little suckers!"

Mom's body unfroze. Still kneeling, she reached for them, and they ran over to her and buried their heads in her neck, her hair. Randy bent over and began to stomp his feet rhythmically, letting out a series of grating whoops.

"*Stop* that!" Mom's eyes blazed. "Leave them alone! They're *your kids*, yours and mine!"

Randy straightened up, and a flicker of pain passed like a shadow across his face. Mom looked at him over their heads, her face so pale it seemed to phosphoresce.

"Don't you think I've wanted to tell you?" she whispered. "I've thought about it every single day I've known you. But I couldn't. Don't you know why?"

Randy stared at her with the intensity of a man listening for a reprieve from a death sentence, for the words that would erase the last three hours from existence. Her husky words ran like electricity toward him.

"I couldn't bear it if you hated me." Her head fell forward. "So I just let it be. And then, when nothing happened, I began to think I could forget, that no one would ever have to know. I thought I'd escaped, that we were safe."

She stopped talking, but her lips kept moving as if in prayer. I saw the words: *I love you, I love you.*

Randy hadn't moved. He swallowed convulsively, then shook his head violently, crossed to the front door and wrenched it open.

"No, Randy. Don't."

He froze, his hand on the doorknob. He held her gaze for a second, then turned and disappeared, slamming the door behind him. A moment later the pickup motor gunned, and gravel hissed under the tires as the truck roared down the drive and into the silent blackness.

I LAY FACE DOWN on my bed in the dark, listening to Mom put Lorrie and Pete to bed, soothing their frightened bodies and answering their insistent questions with murmured half-truths and equivocations. An image kept coming to me, one that would have seemed ludicrous if it hadn't made me cringe: I'd opened a bottle, and the genie who'd materialized from the escaping mist was angry as the devil on Sunday. I tried frantically to remember how Aladdin had tricked his genie back into the bottle. If I could remember that part of the story, I thought desperately, maybe I'd understand how to undo what I'd done.

But even as I turned this notion around and around in my head, picking at it like a scab, I knew I was avoiding the thought beneath: Everything I knew about myself, about my family, lay jumbled, exposed, like the remnants of daily life after a tornado has raged through a home. And it seemed so far beyond my power to gather up what was left that looking made me weak, made me turn to rush back to—what? There was no shelter now.

I began to replay the last few hours, as if envisioning them enough times would change what had happened, thinking over and over, Please make it different. Please.

I heard a tap on the door, saw a crack of light widen and stop. I rolled away from the door and stared at the wall.

"Win? Are you all right?"

I didn't answer. I heard Mom's steps, and the bed sagged as she sat tentatively on the edge. I waited for her to explain, to apologize, but she was silent, breathing slowly, deeply. Finally I turned over on my back and stared at her. In the light from the doorway, her profile seemed odd, alien yet familiar, as if she existed simultaneously in the world I knew and another that belonged only to her.

"Tell me." Until I spoke, I hadn't known I would ask.

She turned and looked at me carefully. Somewhere an owl hooted mournfully. The loose pane in the window rattled in a sudden gust of wind. Then, her voice so quiet it barely stirred the air, she began to speak.

MARIE

July 25, 1966

 It won't go away, no matter how I try. For days, weeks, I forget, and then there it is again. Maybe if I can put it down here, then it will shrink so tiny I can put it out of sight for good. If I remember it right, everything, just as it was, then it won't hurt me anymore.

 Everyone calls me Marie, but my name is really Singing Bird. That's what my father called me. Whenever my mother heard him, she'd yell at him, "Don't call her that! Do you want the kids to make fun of her?" My father's face would just close down when she said that. I could see his eyes turn away, even though he'd still be looking straight at me. He wouldn't say anything back to my mother. I wanted him to, but he'd just pinch his lips together, and then he'd reach out and put his hand on my head, very softly. And I knew for sure I would always be Singing Bird to him.

 He was three-quarters Cheyenne Indian and I was his favorite. Maybe because I looked the most like him: the same dark hair, even if mine was a bit wavy, not dead straight like his; the same brown eyes. His skin was much darker than mine, but I thought that was because he was so old. He seemed old to me, the skin scored with deep lines like the bark of a tree. His eyes were so deep-set I sometimes couldn't see any light in them, his eyebrows threw that much shadow. My brother inherited my mother's green eyes and her pale, freckled skin. Win has that skin too, and her hair. Jess looks more like me. Like my father.

Mama loved my brother and me fiercely; she never wanted us to go out with my father when he took off, just took off on our horse and stayed away all day. He'd come home, with fish he'd caught, or rabbits he'd shot, sometimes a deer. I was wild to go with him. For some reason, Mama didn't fight him as hard about me the way she fought about William, so sometimes he'd take me, riding in front of him, holding onto the blanket. When I see Win going off fishing with Randy, so eager and excited, like I used to when I was little, it was as if I get those hours with my father back for a moment—the early morning air so cool and thin, the light just coming up in the sky, my father's arm around me. I've never felt so happy since.

Sometimes relatives visited us. We never knew when they were coming; they'd just suddenly be there. His sister Moon came, with her husband and their son, Bob. We called her Moonface behind her back, her face was so round. Once, she brought us presents: beautiful bracelets made out of bits of porcupine quills and seeds dyed different colors. She said they were magic; they would make wild animals want to come close to us. As soon as she left, my mother took them away, and we never saw them again. I cried and cried. I kept asking her for my bracelet back, but she just said, "You don't want that old pagan thing. It's full of germs." I said, "Yes, I do want it, I don't care about germs!" Finally one day she got fed up and slapped me hard and said, "You can just shut up. I threw that stuff out. It's gone for good, so don't ever ask again." Oh, I was furious, but I saw it was no good saying anything.

But a few days later my father took me on a walk, and when we were well away from the house, way down near the creek, under the willows, he pulled a little packet out of his pocket and unwrapped it, and there were our bracelets, safe and sound. He let me put mine on for a bit, then took it off and wrapped it up again and slipped it back into his pocket. "I'm keeping it for you," he told me. "It'll be our secret. *When you're older, when you get married, you can wear it."* But of course, by then I didn't want to.

MY FATHER GREW UP *on the reservation over at Lame Deer. He met my mother by hiring out to work for her father in Garland during the season. A lot of the men did that, work for ranchers nearby. He'd gone to the Indian boarding school in Dillon and done real well, even thought about going to college, but back then for an Indian that was like going to the moon. These days it's just like going to China, I guess. Once he graduated and came back, he didn't fit into reservation life anymore. So he moved to Fort Peck and worked as a repairman—he could do anything with his hands. I guess he was a loner. He'd put aside most of his Indian ways, but the white folks didn't accept him either.*

Anyway, Mama came across him one evening sitting under a tree, reading For Whom the Bell Tolls. *She'd just finished reading it herself. It turned out he was reading her copy; he'd found it where she'd left it down by the creek.*

Well, she was floored, that's for sure. It had never entered her head that an Indian would want to read for enjoyment. He was different from any man she'd ever met, she told me, and he gave her the greatest gift anyone ever could: He made her take herself seriously. She'd always been kind of wild, saying crazy things without a thought to how people would take them, jumping from one activity to another, until everyone took her as flighty: "Oh, that's just Linda spouting off, you can't listen to her." And since no one listened to her, she stopped listening to herself, until Frank came along.

She loved books almost as much as Win does; sometimes she'd read two or three at once, picking up whichever one suited her mood at the moment. And here was my father, Benjamin Franklin Little Deer, who'd read any book he could get his hands on, which was never enough to suit him. At last, a match for her in the reading department. And even more important, he listened to her opinions about them as if she were a professor in that college he never went to.

So she started bringing him books she got from the library in Gar-

land—novels, stories, biographies. They'd both read them and then talked about them, and about what it was like in New York and Paris and all the romantic places they'd read about.

Then one day they started reading poetry, out loud. I'm no reader myself, but I know that when a man and a woman read poetry to each other, they're playing with fire, that's for sure. But they did it. She'd brought a copy of Tennyson, and they read "The Lady of Shalott." She read it to us, too, later, so many times I've got whole parts of it by heart.

Out flew the web and floated wide;
The mirror cracked from side to side;
"The curse is come upon me," cried
The Lady of Shalott.

I've imagined it many times, them sitting under that same tree where she first saw him, their imaginations tingling with the story of the beautiful woman locked in the tower, condemned to die if she looks full at the man she loves.

"I feel like that," Mama said. "I'm half sick of shadows too. I'm locked up just as tight in a tower as she was, and how am I going to get out?" And she began to cry. He reached out and wiped off her tears with his fingers, and she covered his hand with her own and pressed it against her face, and looked at him, her blue eyes shining, the lashes trembling with her tears —she who was so proud!—and his heart gave way. That's when it was done, when all our fates were sealed.

My mother had fallen in love with my father, and in those days that meant marriage. Of course, everyone warned her, but the more people lectured her, the more stubborn she got. And once she married him, she turned slowly more and more against his Indian side. The grief everyone gave them, she began to blame on him.

After they married, my father worked for seven years in Fort Peck for an old man, Mr. Abbott, who treated him real well. But when Mr. Abbot died, his son took over the business and decided he didn't want my father around. So he was out of work. My mother couldn't find a job either—there weren't many for women in those days, you know.

They'd fight about it, at first when they thought we couldn't hear, then right in front of us. She wanted to move us to a city, even go to New York or San Francisco, where he'd be more likely to get work.

But he didn't want to leave. He felt his soul would shrivel up if he were yanked from this land where his ancestors still held their spirit arms around us. When he talked like that, it drove her crazy, it turned her more and more against his Indian side. He usually let her have her way, but on this he wouldn't budge. She'd make digs at him, and then he'd pay her back for bad-mouthing who he was by refusing to touch her, and she'd get more and more upset. This would go on for days, and then finally she'd blow up, and really let him have it. He'd go stone-faced, and she'd end up in their bedroom alone, aching for him to come in.

I'd go and try to comfort her, but it should have been him. God knows, he should have been the one to lie down with her, and pleasure her like she wanted. I didn't understand it then, but I can see it now. It's like they were caught in a trap. And meanwhile, they couldn't pay the rent. So where could they turn? They went to his people, to the reservation.

It was a bitter blow for my mother, and for my father too, come to think of it. She hated it, though she tried not to let it show. It leaked out in the way she kept her skirt away from the furniture in people's homes, in how she sat on the edge of chairs, in the pinched look on her face, even when she smiled. People saw it, and in the end they just froze her out, ignored her, wouldn't speak to her, treated her like she was a ghost. Prejudice goes both ways, I've found out.

But they were wonderful to us kids. We could go into any house— they were more like shacks, really—and we'd be welcome, we'd be given something to eat, fried bread or fruit. We could climb into anyone's lap or sit down and ask for a story, and they'd tell us tales about the coyote and the eagle, about Buffalo Woman and Night Bear. William loved it; after a few months you could hardly tell he'd ever lived any-where else. He didn't miss going to school, either, the way I did; he got to run around with the other children all day, playing games and riding ponies and making up stories.

I was supposed to watch and learn from the grownups. The kids my age were mostly away at boarding school—the authorities still shipped them off to schools far away from their families, where they weren't allowed to speak their own language. I was pretty lonely, so I kept my mother company, and her misery wrenched my heart. I began to turn toward her, maybe because she turned toward me. She stopped getting angry; instead, it seemed more and more as if she'd locked herself in her room even when she was walking around outside. She'd talk to me, but the life had gone out of her eyes.

It all blew up at a big feast at the Community Center. Everyone was there; everyone brought different dishes. My mother made pineapple upside-down cake, my favorite. I don't know where she got the can of pineapple; she must have bought it back in Fort Peck and brought it with her. Well, everyone stuffed themselves, but wouldn't you know, no one touched that cake. I kept going back for more, hoping Mama would be fooled into thinking other people were eating it, too. But when I went for my fourth piece, she stopped me and said, "You don't have to make yourself sick just to soothe my pride, Marie." She took that cake and dumped it onto the ground, right there in front of everyone.

It got so quiet you could hear the flies buzzing. Mama looked around very slowly, staring hard, but no one would meet her eyes. Then she marched out the door, and I walked out right behind her. My father came after us, apologizing and explaining, but she didn't answer him. When we got to our shack, she pulled out a suitcase and said, "Pack your things, Marie, we're leaving." And we were on the bus to Fort Peck that night. Nothing he said could stop her. She told him he could keep William till she had a place for them, that it might be a while, and she'd have to live with the pain of that. But she took me. I felt wrenched into pieces to leave my father, but she needed me, and I couldn't turn away from her, even though my helping her never seemed to make her happy.

I can see now how people are always looking for someone who will make them happy, because they think that's what will satisfy them. But they're wrong. What's really important is finding someone who's made happy by you. I found that out then, and I've never forgotten it. I made my father happy just by being alive, and that was the most wonderful feeling in the whole world. But with my mother, no matter what I did, it wasn't me she wanted. And that was just about the worst. That's what I want my girls to know. Better to be the one who can fill somebody up than the thirsty one dying for water. I know that as well as I know anything at all.

ONCE THEY SEPARATED, *I saw my father only from time to time on weekends. My mother never got over her anger, and over the years she blamed him for just about everything that went wrong in her life. I got married partly to get away from her bitterness, but it turned out I just jumped from the frying pan into the fire, because Lee's family never let me forget for one second where I came from.*

When he died, I decided to put aside everything that came from my father, to take Win and Jess and run as far as I could, and pass as white. I didn't want them to go through what I had. And now that Randy's come along and we're married, and there's Lorrie and Pete, as far as I'm concerned the past has disappeared, not just for me but for all of us. The only place it exists now is in my head, and on this page.

CHAPTER 16

RANDY DIDN'T COME BACK that night or the next. During the four days between Marilyn's visit and Christmas Eve, Mom moved through the house like a zombie, her reactions two beats slower than normal. She'd forget where she'd put the car keys, what she needed to buy at the store, when we needed a ride into town. Lorrie and Pete were jumpy and irritable, whining at minor frustrations, pleading to decorate the tree that we didn't have yet, the cookies that weren't yet baked, bursting into tears when Mom yelled at them for any small indiscretion. Then she'd push them aside and run into her bedroom, slamming the door behind her.

I don't know what I thought about, at first, or even if I thought at all. As if I'd received a kick in the head, all I could do was reel around, trying not to fall down, trying to absorb the shock, to catch my breath when my chest wouldn't expand. Everything felt far away, then suddenly rushed toward me like a cannonball. Things didn't taste right: I'd bite into a hamburger and find myself chewing something dead.

Fragments of thoughts whirled through my mind, rising up from nowhere as, shivering with cold, I hung clothes on the line, dragged buckets of feed to the chicken shed, forked hay down for the cattle, spinning themselves into obsessive monologues:

Who am I? Am I some complex mix of my parents' traits, or am I, can I be, something totally new and unique? Can I make myself into something different through an act of will? What if my father and mother had lain together on a night different from the one that produced me, and a different sperm had reached her egg? Would I be half of me, and which half would that be? And what if it had happened on a different month? Then I wouldn't be here at all. Beyond that I couldn't go; imagining the absence of my consciousness felt like death.

Then the adoption fantasies I'd had as a young child popped up like mushrooms after a rain: Maybe I'm not hers at all. I don't look anything like her; maybe none of her blood runs in my veins. As I thought this, shame filled me like a hot fountain. I hated myself for wanting so badly to not be who I was. To not be Indian.

All the familiar images I'd seen before as picture-book engravings, smudgy photos in newspapers, seemed to enlarge, to spring to life and loom over me menacingly: Squalid shacks surrounded by rusted carcasses of trucks; wrinkled leathery-skinned drunks in torn jeans and threadbare jackets staggering into alleys clutching green jugs of Thunderbird; mothers with carefully impassive faces sitting in stuffy government welfare offices waiting for their interviews, their silent kids pressed against them. The cold angry eyes that stared at me outside the sheriff's office after the Thanksgiving dance—they didn't want me, and I didn't want them.

Then the image of Bell would rise before me: the darkness of his eyes, glowing with heat; the softness of his wide mouth; his skin warm against my cheek; his broad shoulders under the blue-and-gold felt varsity jacket he was so proud of. And the blue glint of his hair as it reflected the light that poured in through the window in Selby's shed. Did I want him near me any less, now that a giant hand had picked me up and set us side by side?

I hid out at the ranch. I was convinced that anyone who saw me would guess instantly that something had changed me profoundly, the way you feel when you've first had sex and are sure everyone can read it on your face. This drifted into an illogical conviction that word had spread about us through the whole town. Maybe Jess had told Collie in strictest confidence, and he'd let it slip to someone else. Or she'd told Leila, who'd told her mother, who'd told the Women's Church

Auxiliary. Or, more likely, Randy had spewed it out to a bunch of drinking buddies in late-night drunken self-pity that segued into belligerence, playing the betrayed lover who, when sympathetic listeners agree with him that his woman's a bitch, turns and releases his rage on them instead.

Whom could I have talked to, if I'd wanted to? School was on vacation, so I had no chance to see anyone. Corinne wasn't talking to me, and in any case I couldn't bear to imagine how she'd react to what I had on my mind. Roone wouldn't be available until my next lesson.

That left Jess. Jess, whose absence I'd thought I'd learned to accept, whom I missed so keenly now I tried pretending she'd moved to Canada, or died. It didn't work.

On the third morning, I broke down and called her. I'd already talked to her once, to tell her the bombshell Marilyn had dropped on us. It hardly seemed to surprise Jess.

"I think I've half-suspected for a long time," she's said. "I didn't want to understand, so I didn't."

"You never told me!" I protested.

"There was nothing to tell. I didn't want to know, and you didn't either."

Now I had to talk to her again. This time she was slow getting to the phone, and her voice, when she finally answered, was remote, uninviting. I decided to concentrate on the practical.

"Jess, things are a mess," I said finally, keeping my voice low so as not to be heard by Mom, who was in the kitchen, finally starting the cookies as Lorrie and Pete sorted out raisins, silver dragees and multi-colored sugar, spilling half of everything onto the kitchen floor. "The kids are monsters, and Mom's just making it worse. It's like she's not really here even though she's here. Like those people in *Invasion of the Body Snatchers*, remember? When the little boy yells, 'You're not my mother!'? It's spooky."

No reply. Maybe she'd been snatched, too. I wanted to spread open what had happened like a bloodstained sheet, to talk about the wound that had left its mark there, but I couldn't find the words.

"It's spooky," I repeated in a near-whisper.

Lorrie's voice suddenly rose in a wail, and Pete shouted back.

"Sounds like things are pretty rough for you." I heard a hesitation in her voice, a hint of the same anguish I was holding at bay.

"Oh, I'll get by somehow," I said with just enough brave stoicism to let her know I was staggering under my burden. What good are older sisters, I thought, if you can't play on their guilt?

I heard the snap of a match, the rush of exhaled air as she lit a cigarette.

"What do you want, Win?"

You, I screamed silently. I want you to come home.

"Win, I can't come back." *This* was spooky: she'd read my mind again. "You can come visit me here if you want."

"Please, Jess." Silence. Try harder, I told myself. "We need you." Still nothing. "*I* need you." My voice cracked.

She sighed deeply.

"Okay, okay," she breathed. "I can come and stay for a couple of days, if you want. Until he comes back." A pause. "Because he *will* come back, the creep."

"Thanks, Jess." Sudden tears filled my eyes, startling me.

"Hey, cut it out." She hid her embarrassment in gruffness. "Tell those kids to shape up, all right? Because I'll be there before they know what hit them."

THE INTENSITY OF MOM'S relief, her mumbled thanks when Jess walked through the door two hours later, made me turn my face away, half-angry, half-nonplussed. I wanted to whisk Jess aside, pull her into our room, run and hide out with her in the barn where we could open our hearts to each other as we had years before, while time backed up and stopped at an idyllic past.

Instead, Lorrie and Pete clamored to play with her, producing their latest paste-and-macaroni masterpieces for her inspection, while Mom consulted with her on what needed to be done around the house. Leila, who'd driven Jess to the ranch, made coffee, compiled a list of items we needed from town, and offered to go get them. Jess would be unavailable until later, I could see, and I felt suddenly stir-crazy, so I seized the opportunity to bum a ride. I had hardly touched the piano in the last few days, but I grabbed my music anyway. Roone's house might be a useful haven, if she happened to be home.

As Leila bumped over the rutted drive and onto the road, whipping past snow-speckled hummocks of dried grass stubble, she darted an appraising glance at me.

"What's going on, Win?" She fumbled in her purse for a cigarette and reached to punch the car lighter. Her blond hair fell in a silky sheet over the side of her face. "Something's been eating Jess for the last couple of days, I can tell, but she won't say anything."

I shrugged noncommittally, washing my face clean of the relief that flooded me as I realized that Jess hadn't talked.

"Conspiracy of silence?" Leila snorted. The lighter popped out and she snatched it. "She's avoiding Collie, and he's totally confused."

She lit her cigarette and replaced the lighter, glanced at me again, hesitated, and spoke. "Maybe she's pregnant." My mouth had popped open, about to overflow with protests, when I stopped myself. For all I knew, Jess was visiting motels with Collie on a daily basis, and what I'd gleaned from sniggered jokes about 'rubbers' and 'pulling out' didn't sound very effective. Yet I was completely convinced that Jess' secretiveness had much more to do with Marilyn's revelation than with her love life. Still, I realized, this could be useful. It was fine with me if Leila got it wrong, for now.

"How would *I* know?" I mumbled. "She *did* seem awfully quiet when she came out to the ranch for lunch. And then, Randy was really mean to her." A pang of shame ran through me at my deception.

"He is such a shit." Leila flicked ash out the window. "Sorry, but he really is."

"You don't have to apologize." Here was the perfect diversion. We spent the rest of the drive running Randy down, as I discovered how to use his crimes to elicit sympathy for myself and, at the same time, turn the spotlight away from what was really going on.

"How's Marie holding out?"

Roone slipped this in as I was marking the phrasing of the

Beethoven *F-minor Sonata* we'd chosen as one of the pieces I should play at the competition. The pencil jerked in my hand, etching a small diagonal zig in the paper.

"Okay." I kept my voice neutral. For the thirty minutes I'd been playing, I'd had to force myself not to speculate about what she knew and who she'd talked to. Now I didn't want to find out.

"It must be real hard on her. On all of you." I couldn't meet her eyes. "Don't worry, Win, he'll come back. Any fool can see how much he loves her. And needs her."

I made myself breathe again.

"How did you hear?" I asked.

"One of Randy's friends saw him in Fairfield and said Randy told him he was staying there for now."

"Did he—Randy—say why?"

Roone started to gather my music together.

"Win, all men get like this sometimes. They feel everything weighing on them like a ton of bricks, and they've got to bolt, just to prove to themselves they've still got an out. Even Selby's done it. Believe it or not."

She threw me a sardonic smile as she stood up.

"What I found is, if you leave them alone, they'll start missing you, and they'll come on home."

"Wagging their tail behind them?"

"Exactly." She handed me the pile of music. "Now I've got to finish packing. We're taking off first thing tomorrow for Chicago."

I looked around the room, at the antlers of the elk head, on the wall, festooned with red and green glass balls. That, the spreading aroma of cinnamon and nutmeg, and the rows of Christmas cards lining the mantel and covering the windowsills and end tables were the only signs of the impending holiday. She put a hand on my shoulder, and I could feel the heat of her fingers through the thick wool of my sweater as she began to guide me toward the door.

"Roone." I stopped and she turned toward me, tipping her head to one side. "Is—is Bell outside?"

"So that's it." She smiled again. "Nope, he's left for the day. Tomorrow's Christmas Eve, after all."

She noticed my crestfallen expression.

"Why don't you call him, honey?"

"I don't know his phone number." To my chagrin, I realized I hadn't imagined his home containing a telephone. Roone crossed to the desk, rummaged through a pile of papers, tablets, and notebooks, copied something down, and handed me a slip of paper.

"*Voila.*" Once again she steered me toward the hall. I shrugged on my coat. "Sorry to rush you. I'm real glad you came by. Tell Marie to keep her chin up—it'll all turn out fine."

Sure it will, I thought as I stepped into the blue-gray late afternoon chill, the door closing quietly behind me. Just like it always does.

I had a little over half an hour before I was to meet Leila. I spent the first ten minutes walking around, blowing on my hands and stomping my icy feet, working up the courage to call Bell. Finally, my fingers so numb I dropped my dime twice and the piece of paper once, I huddled over the public phone hanging from the side of the garage, staring at the collection of numbers, names and risqué phrases scribbled on the wall, and with the clanking and screech of metal on metal as a background, listened to the ringing at the other end go on and on. Just before I was about to give up, a woman's tinny voice came on the line.

"Hey?"

"Hi, is Bell there?"

"Who?"

"Bell Youngman. Is this the right number?"

"You want to speak to Bell?" The voice was high-pitched, unfocussed.

"Yes, please."

"Why?" How could I answer that? As I batted words around in my head, she went on.

"Who's this?"

"Win. Winona Daggett."

"Nona Dagger? What kind of name is that? He don't know anyone named Nona. He ain't here anyhow. You better—hey!"

Curses followed, then a familiar voice: "Win? Is that you?"

"Hi, Bell." A shrill stream of words in the near distance, and Bell's sharp reply, grew muffled, as if he were holding his hand over the receiver.

"Sorry. My mother's kind of—out of it. What's up?"

I shut my eyes to intensify the resonance of his voice in my ear, unable to say anything more.

"Hey, you still there?"

"Yes."

"How are things out in the boonies?"

"I'm here. In town." Silence descended as he absorbed what I meant.

"Where?"

"At the garage. I only have fifteen minutes."

"Stay there." Before I could answer, the line went dead.

FIVE MINUTES PASSED, FIVE interminable minutes during which I deliberately blurred the pictures my mind kept forming of what would happen next. Finally a battered green Chevy with yellowish-white fins turned into the garage and jerked to a stop, gray-black smoke billowing from its tailpipe. With a rasping crack, the door sprang open, and Bell unfolded himself to his full length and hurried toward me. He was wearing his team jacket over a dark green hooded sweatshirt, hands sunk into pockets, shoulders hunched forward. He stopped directly in front of me and scanned me for news. Then he tipped his head toward the car.

"Come on, get in." He walked over to the passenger door and opened it. As I slipped by him onto the seat, I rested my hand on his arm to steady myself with his reality, his solid presence.

He gunned the motor and rolled out of the garage and down the street pocked with patches of ice, turned right, left, then right again. The sun, low in the winter sky, seemed barely to illuminate the leaden air. At the far end, where the road came to a dead end against a field strewn with old tires, odd scraps of wood, planks, and tin cans, he stopped the car and sat silent, staring through the windshield, waiting for me to lead the way.

"Randy left." My voice sounded flat. Bell nodded and shifted so he was half facing me.

"Everyone knows, huh?"

Again he nodded.

"Do you want to know why?"

Bell lifted his eyebrows momentarily. The rest of his expression didn't flicker. "If you want to tell me."

"He found out something about us. We all found out. No one knew, except Mom. She'd kept it a secret all these years, ever since I was a baby. How could I know? Jess maybe knew once, but she forgot."

I was practically rasping, tightening my chest and throat against rising tears, turning instead toward anger. I pressed the backs of my hands against my eyelids and took a deep breath.

"And Randy got so mad he left. He can't stand knowing— about Mom, about us, about his kids."

I waited for the question that would change everything, but Bell sat silent. When I dropped my hands and looked at him, his eyes were filled with comprehension.

"Can *you*?" He'd spoken so quietly his words drifted into the hiss of the wind blowing through the cracks around the ill-fitting window frames.

"Don't you want to know what it's about?" My voice sounded harsh, unfriendly. I dreaded the curiosity I might hear in his answer, the readiness to take pleasure in the great blow that had leveled us. I searched his face, finding only the flat smoothness of water ready for the tossed stone.

"I know."

At first I didn't understand. Then I did.

"You *know*. . . ?"

He turned away and stared again through the windshield. "We've always known about Marie."

"How?" I croaked.

The corners of his mouth lifted briefly. "It's there for those who have eyes to see it." He ran his fingers through his hair. "With Jess, too.

Not so much with you." He looked at me again. "It's hard to tell, the way you look. But I know. I knew."

I could feel myself flushing. "Is that why you liked me? Because I'm—like you?"

He inhaled sharply and pulled his body back as if I'd hit him, his eyes narrowing into an expression I'd never seen before, scrutinizing me like a player on an opposing team, assessing me for weak spots he could use. Then he turned away, started the car and backed it up.

"I'm sorry," I whispered. "That was a stupid thing to say."

Suddenly he jammed on the brake, rocking me forward, and grabbed my shoulders. His eyes pierced into mine.

"Now ask the right question."

My mouth went dry. I was posed on the edge of a cliff where one wrong move would send me tumbling into catastrophe. My mind skittered frantically from word to phrase, faster and faster, discarding each one, until the gears jerked apart, and I gave up. "I don't know what it is," I whispered, shaking my head back and forth like a wind-up toy, watching the pulse beating in his throat. "I don't know anything anymore."

His grip on my shoulders relaxed, and he let go and leaned against the car door, staring at me.

"I'm late. I better go." My words sounded airless. "Leila's waiting for me."

Silently he restarted the car, drove back to the garage, and let me get out. I walked away as quickly as I could without running, not looking back, not wanting to hear his car pull away, to see him vanish.

CHAPTER 17

W E EMERGED FROM THE church into the frosty night air, carrying with us the echoing chords of Christmas carols and the pungent scent of the pine boughs heaped on the altar, Mom urging us to get our jackets on fast.

"I don't want to spend Christmas day dosing you with cough syrup," Mom puffed, struggling with Pete's zipper. "Win, button up Lorrie real good."

Already I could hear the tiny wheeze in Lorrie's breathing. I wound her blue scarf tightly around her little neck before squeezing the wooden buttons through their loops.

"I hate this," she whined, pulling at the wool. "It itches me."

"Keep it on," I insisted. "You don't want to get an asthma attack, do you?"

I glanced down and almost jumped when I saw her feet.

"Why are you wearing those stupid Keds?" I snarled. "You should have put on your boots! What's the matter with you, you dumb goofball?"

"Am not!" She tugged against my hand. I pulled her along for a few steps, then gave up and lifted her into my arms, carrying her to the Chevy. Mom hustled up behind me, carrying Pete, and we stuffed them both into the back seat. Jess had run out before us to start the car and was sitting in the driver's seat, coaxing the motor into a comfortable rumble.

As I was pushing the front passenger seat forward, Mom's eyes fastened on something at the other side of the parking lot, and her face grew rigid. Jess was staring through the front windshield at the same spot. I turned to see what had grabbed their attention.

Randy was standing there twenty yards away, his bulky body enlarged by his unbuttoned pea coat. As I watched, he began to approach us. Mom took a deep breath.

"Get in." Jess' voice was tight. She revved the motor.

Mom didn't move.

Randy's figure left the pool of light cast by the lighted church window and was lost for a moment in darkness but reappeared in the headlights of the car. He had his chin down, his red hands clenched. His face looked gaunt, unshaven. He stopped a few feet from Mom.

"Marie."

He must have read something in her expression, heard a password in her sharp intake of breath, because he seemed to grow by several inches as he seized the car door decisively and wrenched it open.

"Move over." He motioned to Jess to give him room behind the wheel. Instead she jumped out, pushing roughly past him. Randy grabbed her by the arm, but she tore herself free.

"Keep away from us, you bastard."

Her voice cut through the clear air like a gong, and I saw old Mr. and Mrs. Kiser's heads shoot up from beside their car to stare in our direction, like edgy antelope catching the scent of a predator. I stiffened, tightening my muscles in anticipation of a confrontation, but to my surprise Randy ignored Jess. He stuffed himself behind the wheel, reaching underneath the seat to yank it backwards. Lorrie and Pete screamed with pleasure at his sudden appearance and threw themselves over the seat back toward him. He pushed them away and they fell quiet, puzzled looks on their faces. The sour-sweet smell of alcohol began to fill the car.

As I was hesitating, ready to jump out and join Jess, Mom slid into the passenger seat and closed the door. Instantly, Randy floored the accelerator and the car lept forward, barely missing my sister.

"Jess, look out!" Mom cried out. Randy spun the wheel, catapulting us out of the lot and onto Main Street, tires screeching, the engine roaring. We caromed past the town and onto the open road, listing from side to side.

"Please slow down, Ran," begged Mom. "The road's icy."

"*Shut up!*" Randy turned his chalky, shadowed face to her. "That's all over."

Mom stared at him, a look of apprehension mixed with bewilderment in her eyes. She reached a tentative hand toward him but pulled it back. "I'm glad you're back, hon," she murmured. "We were all so worried, wondering where you were."

She laid her hand softly on his sleeve. For several moments he let it rest there. She sank back against the seat, taking a deep breath. I began to peel my body away from the upholstery against which I'd forced it in my effort to get as far away from them as I could.

Then Randy's voice lashed out: "Keep your fucking hands off me."

Mom's face filled with hurt perplexity. Then I saw something else take its place, a kind of fatalistic resignation, as if she'd been expecting this all along, and worse, was prepared to accept it without a struggle.

"I can't believe it," he hissed. "I don't give a rat's ass about your half-breed brats, but *my own kids*." He half-turned to glance at Lorrie and Pete, who were staring at him with the same puzzled fear.

"Do you know you're Indians?" he addressed them, watching them in the rear-view mirror.

"No, we're not," Pete protested.

"Goddamn right you are. Your mother here is, and if you're her kids, you're Indians, too."

"Mommy's not an Indian," whispered Lorrie. "You're not an Indian, Mommy!"

Randy bared his teeth in a caricature of a grin that made Mom flinch. "Go ahead, tell them." She kept quiet. "I said, *tell them*!"

She shook her head mutely.

"I want to hear it from your own lying mouth."

"I never lied to you, Randy!"

"You never told me the truth either, you bitch, but you'll fucking tell it now."

Everyone stared at Mom as she opened her mouth and closed it, her eyes brimming with tears. I held my breath, willing her to fend him off, realizing I wanted the story she'd told me to remain private, a secret that she'd held for so long that was now a bond between us, one she was about to break.

But she surprised me by choosing a different part of the story. "Lee knew," she stated. My real father. "He loved me anyway. It was his family who never let me in. They couldn't bear it that my father was half Indian." Her words barely stirred the air, yet they reverberated as loud as a scream. "I loved him very much."

Suddenly the car's rear end fishtailed to the right, and the vehicle began to twist out of control. Randy jerked the wheel and slammed on the brakes. We spun in a circle and slid to a stop, pointing straight ahead. Pete and Lorrie began to cry. Randy leaned over the top of the seat, scanning them with burning eyes, then settled back, eased the car forward, and floored the accelerator until we were flying down the road as fast as before.

"Randy, please slow down," Mom pleaded. The car slowed slightly. No one said anything else as I mopped the snot from Lorrie and Pete's noses with her scarf.

"I'm leaving." Randy's voice was steel-cold. "And they're coming with me."

"No," Mom breathed. "Randy, no."

"You can't do that!" My own voice was high, furious.

"Keep out of this, you snotty half-breed." He glanced momentarily at me in the mirror and turned his attention back to her. "Listen, you lying bitch, I can't change their blood, but I can damn well make sure you don't have one more second of influence over them."

He jammed the brake on, and the car slammed to a halt, throwing everyone forward.

"Get out."

No one moved.

"I said, get *out!*" He jumped from the car, raced to Mom's door, jerked it open and yanked her out. She stumbled, half-fell, then righted herself as Randy pulled the seat forward and focused his blazing, blood-shot eyes on me.

"You, too. Go join your squaw mother."

I pulled Lorrie and Pete against me and tried to lift them with me as I maneuvered my legs through the door and onto the frozen ground. Suddenly Randy's hand clamped onto my arm. He dragged me past him, wrenching Lorrie and Pete away and shoving them back into the car. His blow against my back sent me staggering against Mom as he jumped back to the driver's seat. Mom followed him, reaching toward the car door as he slammed it shut. The car roared into life and lurched forward, forcing her to let go, then stopped, turned around, pointed back toward us. Mom rushed at it as it passed, reaching for the back door handle, grabbing it, running with the accelerating car.

"Stop! No!"

I caught a glimpse of Lorrie's contorted face against the glass of the side window, heard their terrified cries. The car gathered speed. By then Mom was being dragged, her feet bumping against the ground, her arms and torso pressed against the door. Then, thirty yards up the road she fell free, rolling over and over as the car raced off, hesitated, and fishtailed again, its lights zigzagging from side to side. As I ran toward her, I heard the crunch of metal against a wooden fencepost as the taillights disappeared. A series of enormous dull thuds boomed through the night sky; then there was a huge crash, the tinkle of glass, and silence.

I kept running, racing past Mom, who was trying to struggle to her feet as she sobbed in ragged gulps, blood trickling from cuts on her face. My feet crunched toward the edge of the road, through the snow-pocked weeds to the broken fence. At the bottom of the steep embank-ment, in the middle of the craggy rock-filled gully the car was resting on its right side, its wheels spinning slowly.

The only sounds in the vast silence were the hissing of escaping steam and the trickle of liquid from beneath the car. I ran back to Mom, who was lying on her side, her eyes half-closed. As I dropped to my knees, she raised her head and let it fall onto her left arm, which was stretched out at an odd angle. For an instant, I saw Bell, blood seeping from his head. Then it was her again.

"Mom!" I shook her shoulder. She lay inert, her breathing raspy, her eyelids twitching. I got to my feet and ran once more to the gaping hole in the fence.

As I slid down the gully, a dark shape moved inside the car. For a crazed instant, I was convinced a bear had somehow forced its bulk through the broken side and was preparing to feast on whoever—or whatever—remained. Locked onto the grisly image manufactured by my imagination, I rushed forward just as Randy's arms and head emerged from the space that had been a window. Jagged edges of glass caught his jacket and pants as he hoisted his torso and jumped free. At once he leaned over and struggled with one door, then the other. I pulled and tugged uselessly with him, afraid to look into the black void from which no movement or sound escaped.

"Hurry!" His voice was high, practically a scream. I knew what he was thinking: would the car catch on fire? He jumped onto the side, squatted, and slowly lifted the back door, his jaw clenched, pulling air in and out in grunting gasps, the muscles of his wrists and hands writhing.

"Help me, goddamit!" His voice was still whiskey-thick.

I crawled up alongside him. Slowly the door lifted until finally it stood open. I held onto it to keep it from closing while he reached in, his upper body disappearing, his rear end jutting high for a moment against the stars, until he slid back, half-kicking, half-swimming, holding in his arms a small, still shape.

"Oh, god." Randy's face twisted as he carried Petey several yard away from the car and gently put him down. Immediately he climbed back up and dove in again. He took longer this time, cursing, banging against something, cursing again. I craned my neck to peer over my shoulder, straining toward the white blur of Petey's face. I thought I could detect the twitch of an arm, heard a faint whimper. Randy hoisted himself out again and swiped at his eyes.

"You go in. You're smaller, you can reach her."

My heart lurched.

"Wh—where is she?"

"Where do you think, you idiot?"

I must have recoiled, because he went on more calmly, "There's something pinning her down. I'll pull it up, and you can pull her out from under it."

"Is she. . . ?" My throat closed on the words. Randy seemed not to have heard. I moved until I was crouched over the open space.

"Wait." Randy, unmindful of his hand, quickly picked the remaining shards of glass from the window, then helped me slide feet-first into the car.

"Don't step on her." I prodded underneath me gingerly with my feet as Randy held my arms, lifting the weight from my legs.

"Let me go."

As I fell I threw myself to one side and scissored the front seat with my knees, grabbing it and hoisting myself to lie along its now-vertical back. From there I wrestled with what was left of the back seat. Randy's arms brushed past me, his head level with mine.

"There!" He pulled up the compacted frame and cushioning of the back seat to reveal Lorrie lying underneath, her head bent at a horrible angle, one arm thrown across her face, her knees pressed against her chest, one sneaker missing. I tugged at her, maneuvering her until she lay tight against me. Randy wrapped his arms around both of us and kicked backwards, his pungent breath hot on my face, hoisting us in a mockery of birth past the gaping window up into the night.

As he stood with her small broken body and placed it gently on the ground next to Pete, Mom screamed and threw herself toward them. Randy pulled her away, yelling at her not to move them, holding her as she sank to her knees, still screaming. How she'd managed to crawl down the gully with a sprained ankle and a dislocated shoulder, we never quite understood. Her keening filled the air for what seemed hours but was actually only a few minutes, until a passing car spotted the overturned Chevy and went to summon help.

Eventually an ambulance loaded a crying Pete and an ominously still Lorrie aboard. Mom, who wouldn't let go of Petey's hand, was chair-carried on with them. Randy and I followed in the police car, to the waiting room of the hospital in Great Falls. Jess, notified by the police at my request, reached us soon after. And there we sat, not speaking, not looking at each other, in the harsh light of the waiting room, listening to the echoing footsteps and hushed voices, preparing ourselves to hear from the doctors whether our world had survived for us to continue to trample on, or whether what we had taken for granted was changed forever.

FINALLY THEY CAME, THE doctors, and took us to a small room, where we listened to words that at first formed no pattern, then suddenly clumped into phrases that would echo in my dreams. Other than her ankle and injured shoulder, as well as some bruises and the shock, Mom was okay. Petey had a broken arm and some fairly severe internal injuries, but they held out hope of a complete recovery.

Lorrie was dead.

She'd been barely alive when they brought her in, they told us. Her neck was broken, and she had a severe concussion that had caused her brain to press against her skull. If she'd lived, her brain would have swollen like a crazed balloon until, with nowhere to go, it would have turned on itself and squeezed the life out of the millions of cells that made her who she was. If she'd lived, she'd have been paralyzed from the chest down, a partial body whose soul was forever asleep.

They told us this, and then they left.

Everything looked the same, and everything looked different, the light too bright, expanding in the space behind my eyes until I grew dizzy and grabbed Jess' hand. I tried to imagine Lorrie in a wheelchair, fed through tubes, her body growing older without her experiencing it, her consciousness absent, and suddenly, unable to bear it, I shut my eyes and clapped my hands over my ears.

"I'm glad she died." I thought I'd whispered the words to myself, but my voice must have been louder or the silence greater than I'd imagined, because Jess put her arm around me just as Randy sprang from his chair, leaned over me, and tore my hands away. He brought his face close to mine and grabbed my hair. His lips were pulled back from his teeth, and his eyes were crazed.

"If you ever say that again, I'll fucking kill you!"

Before I could react, he yanked his hands away and raced out of the room. I turned to Jess.

"Lorrie wouldn't have wanted to live like that."

"You can't know that." Her voice was quiet, but I heard a tiny quaver in it. "Any life is better than none at all."

I stared at her as if she'd said something in Chinese.

"That's stupid! You sound like some tight-ass Sunday school teacher!"

I knew I wouldn't be able to contain myself, so I pushed through the doorway and started tromping down the hall, not knowing where I was going.

"Win!" I didn't stop. I looked briefly into each room, scanning the anonymous faces, moving on, until I saw Mom lying very still on a narrow bed, her face turned away toward the dark window. Randy had knelt next to her and was clasping her hand, his cheek resting on the edge of her pillow, his voice an indistinct murmur, too low for me to understand, but clear in its urgent pleading. His words flowed like a river, bathing her in the waves of his love and his need, crumbling the ground beneath her feet. Any second now, I knew, she'd fall.

Instead she pulled her hand away. Without thought, I found myself hurtling toward Randy, bending over him.

"You shit!" The words tore my throat. "*You* killed her!"

For a moment he didn't move. I tried to repeat my words, but I couldn't find my breath. Then his head dropped onto his chest and gruff barking sobs erupted from his throat, a sound so shocking I stepped backward, bumping into Jess who stood behind me.

I felt Jess' hand on my arm. I tried to repeat the words, but my own sobs blocked them.

"Come on." I let her lead me down the hall, dazed, to a room where Petey lay breathing quietly as if he were asleep in his own bed at home.

"He's going to be fine."

Jess' voice was firm and confident. Gratefully, I surrendered to her belief, not needing to understand how she knew, simply convinced she did. I rested in that conviction throughout Lorrie's funeral, as Mom sleepwalked, dry-eyed, refusing to be comforted, and Randy's bloodshot eyes, leaking tears, followed her while she looked right through him. And it sustained me through the long days that followed as Randy kept vigil beside Pete's bed, never leaving the hospital, catnapping on chairs, barely eating, until the doctors pronounced Pete out of danger, until Mom was sent home and Randy disappeared, this time for good.

CHAPTER 18

THE WINTER SANK ITS teeth into the land with a vengeance after New Year's. Keeping the ranch just barely limping along involved an unremitting battle against cold, against fatigue, against icy needles that cut against the skin without quite breaking it, leaving it red and raw. The cattle were constantly hungry, bawling in the pasture and the pens, stomping in the barn. The chickens huddled despondently on their nests and hardly laid anything for weeks on end. Although not much new snow fell, the wind would drift it against the rises during the night and rearrange it all the next day.

Each morning we chopped the ice that had formed on the watering tanks and brought the milk cows out of the barn and into the pasture, where they spent the day huddling together against the cold. I helped Jess load hay onto the beat-up truck Selby had loaned us, and trek out to the pasture to toss it to the cattle, who'd be grabbing at it even before it hit the ground. We'd take note of which cows seemed near calving so we could get ready to move them to the barn, where we could keep an eye on them.

After school, Jess and I tackled the laundry, dragging the soaked sheets and towels down to the cellar, struggling to drape them over the lines where they'd drip onto the beaten-earth floor. Around four Mom would come back from the hospital, where Pete was still recovering, and we'd help her start supper. If I was lucky, I'd finally get to the piano and practice single-mindedly for a half hour before and after supper, pouring my anger and longing into the swells and currents of the music.

Then I'd sit in the kitchen, in front of the open oven door, doing my homework. No matter how long we left the heater on, the living room never got warm. Then out to the barn to check on the pregnant cows, knowing we might need to get up in the middle of the night if one was in labor. Finally we'd dive into our beds only after layering sweaters over our nightgowns and wool socks on our feet, then wait for our bodies to warm the sheets enough for us to sleep.

And all the time it felt as if Lorrie was somewhere in the house, just around the corner, waiting in the next room, about to run in from outside. I bit back her name just before I called for her, or referred to something she'd done, a wave of relief washing over me that I didn't have to see that anguished look on Mom's face. The empty space left by Lorrie's absence grew denser with the passing days as it dwindled into a compact mass, something we avoided, like a wounded animal left to heal itself on its own.

At school I felt set apart, as if a sheet of glass stood between me and the world. When I looked at the Indian kids, I thought I saw a flash of recognition in their eyes, but no one said anything. I kept my head down, did my assignments, avoided everyone, especially Corinne, who never looked directly at me anyway, and went straight home after school.

I noticed Marjorie watching me, though she tried not to do it when she thought I was looking. If she didn't want to talk to me, I sure wasn't going to approach her. Then, my second week back, as I left history class, there she was, waiting for me in the hall, taller than I remembered. I nodded to her as I walked past.

"We are sorry about your sister."

Her voice was low, almost formal. Unexpectedly my eyes filled with tears. No one else had even alluded to Lorrie's death, and I wondered, absurdly, if the class had elected Marjorie to be their spokesman. She fell into step beside me.

"Maybe you can come over one day after school."

I stared at her, astonished and confused. Why was she doing this?

I didn't want anyone's charity, not even—especially not—an Indian family's. Yet I was ashamed of that thought, too. I fumbled for the first that popped into my head. "I can't. I have to go home."

She nodded and began to turn away. I reached out and touched her shoulder. "It's just—There's so much to do." I found myself mesmerized by her unwavering gaze, babbling idiotically about the cold, the cattle, the chores, the fences toppled by the snowdrifts, the frozen pump, the leaking roof. Finally I broke off in mid-sentence and leaned against the wall, suddenly exhausted. Marjorie stood silent, then nodded once more and walked off. This time I let her go.

Two days later, as I was stomping my boots clear of snow at the kitchen door, a car chugged into the drive and stopped, foiled by a newly fallen heap of snow. Three heavy-jacketed figures peeled themselves from the opened doors and pushed their way toward the house. My heart jumped as I recognized Bell's cold-reddened face in the lead.

"Hey, stranger." He grinned at me, and I grinned back, flooded with happiness I hadn't realized I'd missed, the way a pang of hunger announces that you've forgotten to eat all day.

"You know Bronson. And this is Sam." He gestured at the other boys, one of whom I remembered from the Halloween dance as Marjorie's partner. The other was vaguely familiar: one of the Indians outside the sheriff's office, maybe.

"Okay, point the way." Bell read the confusion on my face. "The roof first, huh? Then the fence." He glanced up at the porch. "Where's the problem?"

"Up there." I pointed to a spot over the kitchen door.

"You got a ladder somewhere?"

"In the barn."

He buckled on a tool belt he'd been holding. "Show me." He jerked his head at Sam. "Get the shingles." He was already striding toward the barn.

I slid on my boots and struggled after him down the flattened snow path. Once inside the barn, I pointed to the ladder leaning against the far wall.

"Bell, listen. You didn't have to —"

"Grab it." He pulled the ladder away from the wall and lowered it. I took one end and we trotted it over to the back of the house and slid it in place.

"Go on, we can take it from here."

I backed away as Bell and Sam climbed to the roof and caught the shingles Bronson threw up at them. Dazed, I pushed my way onto the rear porch, unlaced my boots, and entered the kitchen. Mom was standing at the sink, dish towel in hand, arms akimbo, her expression unreadable.

"Do I know them?"

"You've met Bell at Roone's. Those are his friends."

"Did you invite them?"

"No."

"Then why are they here?"

"They came to help out, I guess."

She folded the dish towel carefully and laid it on the drainboard. "We don't need their help."

"Yes, we do!" I shrugged my coat off and threw it onto the back of the chair. It slipped onto the floor. Mom seized it and flung it at me, her face scarlet.

"I don't want anyone knowing our business!"

"Be quiet! They'll hear you," I snapped. "Everyone already knows, anyway!"

"Knows what?"

"Everything!"

Mom took three strides toward me and seized my shoulder.

"What did you tell them?" She shook me hard, three, four times, then suddenly let me go and sank into a chair and let her head fall into her hands.

"Oh, god. Oh, god." She rocked back and forth, half-whispering, half-moaning. I knelt next to her and rested my head on her shoulder, my arm around her waist.

"It's okay, Mom. It's okay."

A sudden banging overhead jerked us upright, our heads tipping back to stare at the ceiling, soaking in the hammer strokes raining down on us, mingled with deep guffaws and shouted words, like light after a storm.

THE THREE BOYS CAME back the following day, and the next. Bell came by himself almost every day after that, the rest of the week and the next. Mom slowly unbent and became, if not really welcoming, at least friendly in a restrained way. On Friday afternoon, as I was standing at the kitchen window, I saw her go out to stand next to his car. Quietly as I could, I slid the window open, just in time to hear her offer to pay him for the work he'd done. He refused her so abruptly, in such a tight voice, that Mom was taken aback.

"I didn't mean to insult you," she said. "You've worked hard, and I appreciate it."

"I'm not doing it for money." He slammed the trunk lid harder than he had to. "You should know that."

"If you took all the things I should know but don't," she answered tartly, "they'd fill a barn."

Bell laughed and reached for the car door. Mom's next sentence stopped my breath. "One thing I do know. You're doing this for Win."

I ducked to one side and tipped my head just enough to hear without being seen.

"Yes. But not just that."

"If you won't take money, maybe you'll take a meal with us."

I peeked out again as Bell straightened and looked at Mom quizzically. She said something to him I couldn't quite hear. Bell's eyes widened, and he grinned broadly at her, nodded, and followed her to the back door. I shut the window stealthily, even though I knew they knew I'd been listening to every word.

Supper was awkward. Jess was staying in town that evening and Pete was still in the hospital, so it was just the three of us. As we spooned in the thick stew, mopping it up with limp slices of Wonder bread, we kept up chatter about the hard winter weather, its effects on the neighbors and their animals, reports we'd heard of cattle freezing in place, our hopes for a break in the cold. Over dessert—homemade spiced applesauce—Mom questioned Bell about how he was doing in school, who his teachers were, and why he'd quit the basketball team. He shifted uncomfortably. I was annoyed.

"You know, Mom. He works for Selby."

"You're such a fine player," she went on. "Headed for being the star of the team. It's a pleasure to watch you."

Bell flushed and dropped his eyes. My annoyance increased tenfold: Mom had managed not only to allude to his family's poverty, but she'd said to his face what I felt but had never dared utter about his physical beauty. She'd stolen my thunder and embarrassed him at the same time.

"Mom, just drop it!"

She ignored me.

"You should go back to the team." She leaned forward, the light from the overhead globe catching the tip of her nose so it cast a shadow over her upper lip. Bell's hands began tearing his paper napkin into thin strips. He wouldn't look at her, or at me.

"Mom, for god's sake, he *needs* to work! Don't you get it?"

Her eyes never moved from Bell's face. He crumpled the paper into a ball and threw it onto the table.

"They don't want me there." Thin, metallic words.

"That's crazy! They're losing all the time without you," I protested, hating his bitterness. He turned his narrowed gaze on me. "If you were there, they'd be winning."

"That's right." His mouth tightened. "They'd rather cut off their nose to spite their face."

He picked up the balled napkin and began to pull it apart again. Mom placed her right hand on his, forcing him to stop.

"You owe it to us not to quit."

Whom did she mean? The town? The team? Her and me? Or was she drawing a circle around Bell's race and then, astonishingly, including herself in it? Was I inside it as well? And did I want to be?

"It isn't that easy."

"I know." Her voice was quiet, barely above a whisper. She withdrew her hand and sat up straight, touched her hair, and folded her clasped hands in front of her on the table. For slow minutes, we listened to the hum of the refrigerator, to the drip of the kitchen faucet that Randy had promised a thousand times to fix, to the rattle of the glass in the window frames, to our own breathing. My agitation, my irritation at Mom, my anxiety about whether Bell would like me less after Mom's intimacies, all slowed, melted, faded into the fragrant air, leaving me solid, heavy, at peace.

AFTER DINNER, BELL AND I washed the dishes. Mom consideratelyleft us alone, claiming she was tired and had to lie down. Our hips bumped as we stood at the sink, hands grazing as we handed plates back and forth. Finally, feigning a sudden interest in showing off our freezer, I lured him into the pantry, where we pounced hungrily on each other. I licked his mouth, tasting traces of spiced apple, as he ran his fingers up and down my back, grabbing palmfuls of my ass, my shoulders, the backs of my thighs.

He pinned me against the freezer, tipped my head upward and slowly ran his lips down the side of my neck, pausing every inch or so to close his teeth lightly on my skin. A wire of flame shot along my neck, through my nipples and down to the cleft between my legs. I let out a sound somewhere between a groan and a muffled scream. Startled, Bell almost dropped me and drew his head back.

"Are you okay?"

I could see his grin flashing in the reflected light from the kitchen as I giggled helplessly, setting him off, until, convulsed, we staggered against the shelves, knocking over a box of Bisquick and a can of peas. Knowing that any noise suggesting breakage would be sure to attract Mom's attention, I shushed him, and we lurched like drunken bears into the kitchen.

Bell barely managed to slide his impassive mask on before Mom was there, frowning slightly, accepting with raised eyebrows my reassurances about the state of the pantry. Bell hastily thanked her for supper, retrieved his coat, and headed for the door. We watched him wave once to us as he slid into the front seat and gunned the car down the road.

I followed Mom back to the living room as she picked up the pile of mending and began threading a needle, squinting in the lamplight. I wanted to say Bell's name, to hear her compliment him, properly impressed with his grace. Yet I also wanted to blow up at her, to let her know her opinion mattered to me not at all. I mourned for the loss of Bell as my secret, exposed now to her inscrutable judgments. I craved her approval yet hated my own need for it. Just as I was about to vent my irritation on her, she surprised me. "Play something, Win." She nodded at the piano. "That Chop-in thing."

I sat down and played the E-minor nocturne, its bittersweet arpeggios honeyed with lover's farewells in moonlit gardens. I turned to her.

"Does he like your music?"

"The first time he heard me play, he said I sounded as good as Roone."

Mom folded the shirt she was working on, sticking the needle into the faded fabric.

"I hope you understand what you're letting yourself in for."

I didn't answer. After a while she nodded as if I'd asked her a question she'd been waiting a long time to hear.

MARIE

January 18, 1971

How can I explain it to them what it's going to be like? Being part one thing—Indian—and part something else, it's as if you have to grow a special set of antennae like bees or ants have. They're always humming and turning and flickering, picking up signals that other people don't quite hear. My girls don't know this yet, but they will, and knowing what lies ahead makes me ache for them. They'll see shadows in corners that others don't see, shadows that might mean danger. They'll always be on the alert, they'll never really relax, not all the way. When people make one of those digs, those little remarks about "Cheys" or "lazy breeds," you think, They mean me, but they don't know it. If they did, they wouldn't say it, not to my face. They'd have to say it about me behind my back, because I wouldn't even be invited in to sit where I'm sitting, in their parlor or their kitchen. And then, just for a minute, you feel like your whole life is a lie. But you go on—you make yourself stop thinking that way, and you go on.

When my mother married my father, her parents disowned her. To her father, it was as if she'd never been born. He tried to get her marriage annulled, wiped out. He went to a judge and declared that she was crazy, that she hadn't the judgment to know what she was doing.

He actually got her put in an asylum for a while. But she was smart. She fooled those doctors into thinking she'd come to her senses, and as soon as they let her go, she ran off with my father. So then her father wiped her out of the family, erased her name from the family Bible, and refused to let anyone mention her name again.

That one time, after my parents had a big fight, she stuck William and me in the car and drove two hundred miles back to her parents' home. I'll never forget it. We were starving. We hadn't eaten anything but Cokes and Mallomars since lunch. When we drove up at nine o'-clock at night, my grandmother came out onto the porch, this little gray doll, and her face lit up, and she started down the steps crying, "Linda! Oh, Linda!"

But before she got to the car, the screen door opened, and my grand-father stepped out and yelled, "Stop!" and my grandmother froze.

He pushed right past her, and leaned in the car window, and stared at us for what seemed to me like a year. His eyes were like ice. His face twisted up with rage and hatred, and he said, "Get your goddamn half-breeds off my property."

My grandmother cried out, "Oh Samuel, no!" and made a move toward us. He just looked over at her, and she stopped dead in her tracks, like a hare in a field when a hawk floats over it.

"You married a filthy Indian and that makes you one, too," he went on. "I never want to see you again." He turned and went in.

My grandmother managed to slip us some bread and meat before we left. Just before we were off grandfather's land, Mama stopped the car and got out and told us to eat the food. She wasn't gone long, maybe five minutes, and as we drove off again, I saw something from the corner of my eye. When I turned to look, Mama said, "Just look ahead, Marie! Don't look back!" And I did, but not before I'd seen the burst of fire blaze up against the night sky. As far as I know, my mother never saw either of her parents again.

In high school I told people my father had been an Italian musician who'd run off when I was a baby, and that was why I had dark hair and olive skin. No one contradicted me to my face, but I think they all had their doubts. And when I got married, Lee knew from the begin-

ning, and it didn't matter to him, but it did to his family. When they found out, they treated me like dirt.

And then, right after his funeral, they wanted to take Win away from me. Her skin was so fair, and her hair was just like my mother's, so they tried to persuade me to let me give them to Lee's brother and sister-in-law to raise. They weren't interested in Jess, because she was too dark. I remembered how Mama had told me how her father had had her locked up in the loony bin, and I was afraid of what they might be able to do to me. So I pretended that I'd consider it.

The very next day I packed up and snuck off as fast as I could with the two girls. I went as far away as I could, which was only to the other side of the state, and I never heard or saw hide or hair of them again, until now. And now I feel like someone who thinks they've beaten cancer feels when the doctor tells them that it's back and, guess what, they have only a month to live.

If I had to do it again, I guess I wouldn't hide who I am from Randy like I did. But then I think, if I hadn't, there might never have been Pete, or Lorrie. Still, maybe the reason Lorrie isn't here any more is because of how I hid it. I don't know any more what's right. I've made so many mistakes, I can't tell anyone else what to do. I just hope they'll have it easier than I did. But I doubt it.

CHAPTER 19

I HATED GOING TO the hospital in Great Falls to see Pete. Every time I came through the swinging door, the smells of antiseptic mixed with acrid traces of frightened bodies—blood, sweat, urine, so faint I might have been conjuring it up—hit me in the center of my chest. I tightened my muscles so as not to let my distaste show, to not turn and run back out the door.

Then I'd see Petey, his eyebrows dark slashes in his unnaturally pale face, so quiet the first few days that he seemed to be sleeping even when he was awake. He came back slowly, fretful with pain, impatient at the arm exercises he was supposed to practice, not understanding why his body wouldn't do his bidding. He kept bombarding us with questions that made Mom wince: Where was Lorrie? Where had she gone? And Daddy, why wasn't he there, too? Mom answered patiently for a while, then got up and left abruptly. I searched for words that never provided him sufficient reason for their absence when he needed them so badly.

Then one day Pete announced proudly that his daddy had visited him yesterday, and the nurse confirmed it. After that, we could tell from the new stuffed animal or a fresh box of cookies when Randy had been there. I never saw him, but I suspected Mom had. She refused to answer questions about it, or about the occasional phone calls at home she'd hang up on quickly, saying, "Wrong number."

Pete got better fast once this started. When he finally came home at the end of January, I rejoiced for both him and myself. The evening before, while Mom stayed in town to be at the hospital as early as possible the next morning, Jess and I baked a chocolate cake with peppermint frosting, Pete's favorite. It was the first time Jess and I had been alone together for weeks. She'd been looking drawn and tired, dark circles deepening under her eyes. She'd started biting her nails again, a habit she'd broken several years before, when she began setting her hair and using lipstick. I'd tried to question her, but she'd cut me off with meaningless reassurances.

As she carefully spread the creamy white frosting, I pounded red-and-white-striped peppermint balls between two sheets of waxed paper.

"How's Collie?" I asked casually.

Her mouth twitched. "Fine." Saying nothing more, she stepped back to let me sprinkle the flaky bits onto the icing, then fit the top layer precisely onto the bottom one. I dropped a large blob of frosting onto the middle, and she swirled it with the knife in widening semicircles.

"He hasn't been out here much," I went on.

She glanced at me briefly. "So what? Who wants to come out here anyway?"

"Well, Bell does."

She threw the knife down hard enough that a glob of icing landed on the table.

"What are we doing, playing 'My boyfriend is better than yours'?" Her voice was tight. "All right, you win! Are you satisfied?"

She stomped out of the kitchen, eyes glinting, slamming the hall door. I finished sprinkling the cake, popped a few fingerfuls of leftover icing into my mouth, and crept down the hall. The door to our bedroom was closed. I tapped on it and, when Jess didn't respond, went in quietly and sat on the edge of my bed. Her back was turned to me; her hair glistened in the lamplight.

"Jess?"

No answer. I stared out the window, past the dim reflection of my face, into the solid darkness of the night. A memory hit me: myself at seven, sobbing inconsolably about the chocolate milk carelessly spilled onto my brand-new yellow-and- white dotted-Swiss Easter dress, the one I'd spent months praying for, almost passing out with ecstasy when Mom handed it to me. And Jess comforting me, slipping the dress off over my head, working soap carefully into the stain, patiently rubbing the suds into the fabric until the brown stain disappeared and my life was mended.

"Is it about Lorrie?" I knew it wasn't.

To my surprise she rolled over. "Nothing's the same. It's all gone." Her eyes were wet. I lay down and put my arms around her. She buried her face against my shoulder, wrenching my heart with her sobs. After a while her crying slowed, then stopped. She rolled onto her back, wiping her face with her fingers, and stared at the silver stars we'd pasted on the ceiling years before in our own version of constellations, their paper spokes peeling now, curled into withered spiders.

"It doesn't feel like before," she whispered. "He says it's because he's got to buckle down and bring his grades up. That he's behind because of basketball practice, all those games. But that isn't it."

She closed her eyes, and for a moment I could see the face she'd have when she was old.

"It just feels like, even when he's with me, he isn't really there." She turned her head toward me. "You know how, when someone's telling you a long boring story that you've heard a million times, and you're trying real hard to look interested, but you're really aching to just get out of there as fast as you can?"

I nodded.

"Like that." She began to shake her head slowly from side to side. "I can't bear it. It makes me feel ugly. Like that demon lady with the snaky hair, who turned men to stone."

"Medusa." I propped myself onto one elbow. "You're not ugly, Jess, you're beautiful. *He's* a stupid ass if he doesn't love you."

A smile flitted over her face and was gone. She resumed her close study of the ceiling. I seethed with useless empathy, aching to make her world whole again.

"Jess, he's not worth it. No guy is. Look at Mom."

Her body stiffened, and she frowned.

"Remember how we always wanted her to stop putting up with Randy's bullshit? To tell him off?"

"*You* wanted her to. *I* wanted to kick his butt myself."

"Well, she should have. And she never did, until. . . ." I let the sentence fade into silence. Lorrie's presence hovered suddenly in the air, an enigmatic fable whose moral we were supposed to figure out.

"So kick Collie's."

"I can't." Jess' voice was a whisper. "I need him."

Angry heat rose in my chest.

"What for?" I glared at her. "You've got us. Isn't that enough?"

"No."

"Why not?"

She took a deep breath and seemed to sink slightly into the mattress. Suddenly I dreaded what she was going to say. I hated what I saw happening to her, my proud, defiant sister alchemized into a trembling rabbit.

"Because I'm pregnant."

I wasn't so much surprised as stunned, as if I'd opened the door on a black-cloaked messenger announcing a long-expected death sentence. She scanned my face for a reaction.

"Are you sure?"

She nodded.

"How long?"

"About two months, almost three."

"What are you going to do?"

Instantly I knew that was the wrong thing to ask. Jess' brows drew together and her lips turned down at the corners. "Shit! If I knew that, I wouldn't be here now!" She pulled herself to a sitting position and wrapped her arms around her knees.

"Well, what do you *want* to do?"

"I don't know that either! If Collie—" She broke off and fell silent, her profile stern.

"Does he know?"

She shook her head. "Nobody knows. Except you, now. I shouldn't have told you." She threw me a withering look. "And you better not tell anyone."

"I'd never tell!" I breathed, indignant. Pride slowly filled me at Jess' having picked me, even inadvertently, as her confidante. More than ever I wanted to be useful, resourceful, and reliable, able to provide her with just the right strategy. Only I couldn't think what it was. Stumped by my ignorance, I was saved by my silence as Jess began to talk in rapid bursts.

"I don't want him to know. I don't want anyone to know. Everyone thinking I'd caught him with the oldest trick in the book. I *didn't*! We were always so careful, except for just twice, when we had too much to drink. Oh god, if I could just go back and change that! I'd do anything to change it!"

She dropped her head in her hands, her words muffled by the curtain of her hair.

"Mom will kill me if she finds out. And people will look at me like I'm a half-breed slut, a dirty tramp who can't say no. Oh god. And Collie already can't stand being around me. What will he think when he knows?"

Her nails dug into her scalp. I grabbed her wrists and pulled them down.

"Jess, maybe you don't have to have it. You could—there are ways. I've read about it."

She looked at me as if I'd suggested she drive an ice pick through someone's heart, which in a way I suppose I had.

"I can't," she whispered. "I couldn't."

Yet even as she protested, I saw something flare in her eyes, a kind of embarrassed complicity, like that of a child who agrees to play an outrageous trick on a friend.

"I'll see what I can find out," I assured her, without the faintest idea where to start.

FOR THE NEXT THREE days I racked my brain during school, during my chores, while I practiced or helped Petey practice walking, searching for ideas, discarding one after another. Any adult I approached might inadvertently or deliberately let Mom know something was up. The notion of doctor-patient confidentiality, when it came to parents being kept in ignorance of their daughter's hanky-panky, was still years away. Friends my own age were as ignorant as I was, plus not likely to be much more close-mouthed than the adults. I imagined humiliating scenes in which one person after another immediately assumed the "friend" I inquired for was me, or figured out it was Jess. Finally, in desperation, I asked Jess about using Leila as a resource.

"Are you kidding?" she protested. "Leila can't keep a secret for two seconds. I might as well publish it in the newspaper."

Did I want to help her, really? I knew about abortion, as a concept, but it seemed a procedure as foreign to my everyday life as polygamy or cannibalism. I flipped back and forth between images of fish-like embryos with inflated heads, floating in a murky red sea, and scenes of Jess and Collie naked, sweating, her head thrown back, her mouth open as, face pressed into her neck, he rose and fell above her. I'd assumed at some point that they were—what? All the labels seemed either crass—"getting it on, "doing it," "screwing"—or too technical—"having sex", "intercourse"—or watered-down , euphemistic—"making love," "going all the way." So I'd blacked out any phrase as soon as it jumped into my mind, clicked the image off like a TV show I didn't want to watch.

Until Bell came along.

The things we did together changed everything. I wasn't watching anymore. I understood now, in my body, why Jess would have no choice but to lie down with Collie, how her skin tingled when he touched it, how the center of her opened, pulling like a magnet toward him to fill that empty space. Yet the more I understood, the more I'd turned away from her. I wanted to keep what was happening to me unique, like Columbus glimpsing an undiscovered world, or an astronaut stepping onto the dusty moon: No one had ever been here before me.

The truth is, I'd been scared: scared that, if I let the truth about what Jess and Collie were doing sink in, the barrier would drop and I'd be helpless to stop myself from doing what my body urged, and I'd be swept toward the inevitable catastrophe that now had Jess in its grip. Now, because I could no longer shut out what I knew about her, I'd eaten the apple too, and I saw before me my own impending fall.

I decided to retreat to the high ground of research. Any books with relevant information were kept in a special hands-off section of the library, accessible only with the blessing of the librarian. I couldn't think of any plausible reason why I might need to consult *Ideal Marriage: Its Psychology and Technique* by Theodore van de Velde, M.D. In the encyclopedia I turned to the entries on "abortion" and "birth control" and read them, heart pounding, shoulders hunched forward, my finger marking another, innocent entry, ready to flip to "abstract art" or "Borneo" at a classmate's approach. They were of little help, though, focusing as they did on historical narrative and technical description couched in a faintly disapproving tone. I ended up knowing a lot more about the mechanics of the reproductive system, and nothing about how to find a doctor who would do what needed to be done.

On Thursday, as we filed out of history class, Mrs. Isaacson called me to her desk and asked me to come and talk to her after school. At three o'clock I pushed open the door to her classroom.

"I'm worried about you, Win," she declared as I stood in front of her desk. Her head was cocked at an angle as she scrutinized my blanked-out expression. "You haven't been paying attention in class, and you've forgotten two assignments."

I stared at the floor, trying to find the courage to speak.

"Is it about your sister?" Her voice had softened. "I'm so sorry about her. I know it takes time to get over something as upsetting as that."

"It's not that. I mean, it *is* terrible, but that's not why —" I stopped and glanced at her.

"Is it about your father?"

"He's not my father!"

She looked so startled I almost laughed.

"He's my *step*father, and I'm glad he's gone."

"But it must be hard on your family, your mother. I can tell how distraught she is."

I must have looked puzzled.

"I've seen her a few times at the hospital."

"I didn't know that. She never said. Actually she never says much." She leaned back.

"Then perhaps you don't know that apparently no one except me and Mrs. Grafton has ever dropped by to see her. Not even the minister." Her voice was tight. I stared out the window at the speckled grains of dust floating in the air. Did she know why? If she did, that meant everyone in town had been talking about us, in excited voices tinged with satisfaction: Did you hear? Thank God that isn't me.

"Win. Most people don't question what they're taught to believe. They don't want to stick out, so they go along with the crowd. But some people have the courage to stick up for what's right. I saw *you* have that courage, at the board meeting. You aren't the only one."

She began gathering papers into a pile and sliding them into the briefcase that lay open on her desk, then shrugging on her coat. I walked with her through the empty corridors. Just outside the heavy main door, she stopped to wrap her plaid scarf around her neck against the cold air.

"Drop over again sometime, if you'd like."

She walked off and I watched her tan sheepskin coat move down State Street.

THAT EVENING, THE PHONE rang while Mom was putting Pete to bed. I picked it up.

"Hello, Win." Randy sounded far away, with the rush of wind, the whish of cars, and the blare of a horn behind him. "How are you doing?"

"As if you care."

"I do. More than you know."

I fished for words to express my contempt and came up empty. "What do you want?" I said finally.

"I'd like to speak to Marie."

"What for?"

"That's none —" He stopped himself abruptly. "That's between her and me."

"Why don't you just get lost? We don't need you."

Before I could hear his protest, his angry retort, I slammed the phone down.

"Who was that?" Mom was standing in the doorway, frowning.

I shrugged. "Wrong number."

"Let me handle my own business, Win," she snapped, hands on her hips.

"Mom, you wouldn't let him come back, would you?" I pleaded. "You couldn't!"

"That's something for me to decide, not you."

She went over to the TV, switched it off, sat down heavily in the chair—Randy's chair—and let her head rest against her right hand. After a moment she sighed. "Every time I think about him—every time I hear his voice—all I can see is him lifting her poor little body up out of that car. All I can think is how he killed my baby, my sweet little Lorrie."

She let her head fall back onto the chair back. For a moment she looked dead, her face immobile, her eyes sunk into her skull. I knelt in front of her and put my head in her lap, and for the first time since Lorrie's funeral I cried, her hand stroking my hair, my tears wetting her skirt.

I PLAYED MY HEART out at my lesson that Saturday. When I finished, Roone was quiet a moment.

"How are you feeling about the competition?" she asked. "Do you still want to go?"

"Sure I do."

"All right. I checked with Marie, and it's fine with her, too. You'll need permission from your principal."

"I already got it." This wasn't true, but if the prestige of the event didn't convince him, I was ready to take off without it.

"All right. We'll leave two weeks from Wednesday, in the morning." She went over the arrangements yet again, my attention only sporadically on what she was saying. As soon as I could, I excused myself and ran to the shed to tell Bell I'd meet him in an hour. Then I took off for the Isaacson place, and in ten minutes I was sitting once again on the cream-colored sofa, Vivaldi on the stereo and a cup of spicy tea in my hand. I decided to plunge in. "I want to do a paper on birth control," I said firmly.

Mrs. Isaacson, her legs curled underneath her in the flowered armchair across from me, set her cup onto the coffee table and looked at me quizzically. "Why?"

"No one talks about it, but girls can really get stuck if they don't know how to get it. And then, if they don't, they can end up having to do something worse."

"Do you mean abortion?"

I nodded, sipping from my cup, making sure I didn't choke. She gave me a long, shrewd look. "This isn't really about a paper, is it?"

I said nothing. Was she another mind reader, or was I a really bad actress?

"Are you interested in where you can get a diaphragm? Don't worry—" my face was hot by then— "I'm all in favor of kids being prepared. And you're right not just to hope the boy will have a condom."

I couldn't look at her. Suddenly she stood up and crossed to the shelves that lined the far side of the room, scanned the rows of books, and pulled one down. Then she came back and handed me a large paperback with a red and white cover, on which I saw a large circle with a plus sign attached to its lower rim, a murky photo of women's faces, and the title *Our Bodies, Our Selves*. "You can borrow this if you like. It's got lots of information in it."

I sat with the book in my lap. It was now or never. "Will it tell me. . .does it say where someone can go if they need—if it's too late for birth control?"

She started, then sat down slowly on the sofa next to me. I rushed on before she could say anything. "It's not for me, honestly. I mean, maybe the birth control part, but not—about the other."

"I never thought it was." She took a deep breath and stared past me. After a long time she shook her head.

"I wish I could help you, Win," she said softly. "I can't. All I can tell you is, don't let your friend go to a back-room abortionist. It's not worth the risk of dying for. Okay?"

I nodded.

"Promise me, Win."

I promised.

BELL REACHED TO ADJUST the car heater, his torso tipping me upright briefly, then put his arm around my shoulder again. The purring heat had steamed up the windows. We were sitting inside an opaque bubble pungent with the aroma of sweat and pine air freshener, listening to "Light My Fire" with half-closed eyes.

"Bell?"

He grunted.

"How's Collie?"

He looked at me, brows lifted. "He's OK, same as always."

"No, really."

His voice tightened. "What do you mean?"

"I mean, why hasn't he come out with you sometimes, to see Jess? He never does."

Bell shifted his body, sliding his arm away and placing his hands on the steering wheel. He stared through the frosted windshield as if he were driving full speed into an ice storm. "I guess he just got busy, with practice and all."

I let out an exasperated snort. "Bell, come on, talk to me. What the hell is happening? Jess is really upset about it." I could tell him that much.

He continued to stare straight ahead, his mouth compressed into a thin line. I put my hand on his arm and almost jerked it away from its vibrating tension. It felt like a live electric cable. "Bell, help me. What's going on with him?"

"How the hell should I know?" The words came out in a husky rasp. He turned to me with a sudden jerk. I barely recognized the stony eyes, the expressionless face.

"See for yourself."

Without waiting for an answer, he started the car. I held my breath as we shot down the icy streets, side-slipping through corners and jamming to a halt in front of the Two Elks. Bell jumped out, ran around and jerked my door open, then frog-marched me by the elbow up the steps.

Overheated air filled with loud laughter and pounding music enveloped us, as if we'd fallen into the cotton candy machine at the circus. For a moment I couldn't move. Faces turned toward us and voices dwindled away, as if someone had turned the radio volume down. The music suddenly pulsed rapidly, loud-soft-loud-soft, and I realized what I was hearing was the vibrating drum of blood rushing in my ears. Then everything flattened and eased; people resumed their conversations, the music brightened, and Bell led me to a corner booth where Collie was sitting across from two boys whom I only vaguely recognized.

"Hey, Col." Bell nodded at Collie's blanched face and surprise-widened eyes. He slid onto the bench next to Collie and motioned me to sit next to him. For a moment no one said anything, all of us circling the table with our eyes like a bunch of suspicious poker players.

"Hey, Bell," Collie finally said.

Collie's two friends frowned. The one at the end shoved himself upright and slipped off the bench.

"Too much Chey blood at this table for my taste," he gibed. The other boy rose too and joined him. They stared at Collie, who wouldn't meet their eyes. His face, if it was possible, had grown even paler. Bell motioned for me to change to the bench they'd vacated and slid in with me, leaving Collie alone. Collie raised his eyes to Bell's, and in his tormented expression I saw everything I'd already known but hadn't wanted to understand.

His two friends shifted from foot to foot impatiently.

"Come on, Burns," the shorter one barked. "Let's go."

Collie began to rise.

"Can I talk to you a minute, Collie?" My voice was gravelly with apprehension. He sank back against the padded back of the booth.

"I'll be out in a minute, guys." The two wrinkled their faces in distaste, muttered something, and stomped off. I leaned forward slightly, feeling Bell's hand against my thigh.

"Jess misses you," I croaked, then brought my voice down half an octave. "She doesn't know I'm here. She'd kill me if she finds out I told you. But it's true."

Collie turned his head away.

"She needs you," I whispered. "Please."

Collie cleared his throat.

"You want to come back with us? For supper? Bell's coming." Bell stared impassively at the half-empty, abandoned beer glasses.

Collie opened his mouth and shut it, his shoulders sagging. He shook his head and began to rise, then looked at me and sat back down, grabbing a menu. "Give me a pen."

After a second's hesitation I rooted through my purse and handed him a pencil. He scribbled on the back of the stain-streaked paper, folded and re-folded it until it was the size of a dollar bill, and handed it back to me.

"Give that to her."

He slid out and stood up.

"Nice seeing you, Win. Take good care of Ding-Dong here." For the first time he smiled faintly. "*Hasta la vista*, Chief."

He turned away. I cocked my head at Bell, but I already knew from his wryly pleased grin that some dangerous corner had been safely turned.

I was very restrained. I actually managed to wait until we got back at the ranch and I scooted into the bathroom before I read the note. *Thank you*, I breathed, refolding it and slipping it to Jess a few minutes later in the kitchen as she spooned the mashed potatoes into a bowl, watching her face bloom with the radiance I'd missed for so long.

CHAPTER 20

OLLIE BEGAN COMING OUT to the ranch too, though not as often as Bell. They helped us feed the cattle and milk the cows, haul the garbage to the dump, and patrol and mend the fences where the cattle had leaned against a weakened post and pushed it over. In the mornings it was up to Jess and me to break open the ice crusts on the water tanks so the cattle could drink. We kept the tank pump running at night, so the pipes wouldn't freeze, but that meant water overflowed and froze into a slick around the tanks, so I'd take a bucket of sand down with me and sprinkle it around, to give them better purchase. Sometimes the best we could do was open a hole on one side of the tank. Then the cattle would jostle and butt each other as they jockeyed for a spot, only to be shoved aside by the next thirsty comer.

We knew that Mom tried to hide from us the depth of her worry about our finances, poring over the stack of bills, deciding how much of which ones she could afford to pay each month, how long before the gas or the electricity would send us a cut-off notice. Every few days she commissioned us to do grocery shopping after school, letting Jess drive the car in for the day, handing us a pared-down list with annotations about buying the cheapest brands, the eternal potatoes and macaroni. On the way home, if it had snowed, the car would barely make it over the rise just after the gate. If the first try failed, I'd get out and let Jess back up and race forward as I held my breath, then let it out in a white puff so dense it seemed solid.

If Bell or Collie had come out too, they'd often stay for supper. Those meals were islands in a somber sea. Although Jess and I had gathered Lorrie's toys and books and had put them away on the back shelf of a closet, every so often a cushion turned over, the corner of a rug flipped back, would reveal a red barrette shaped like a tulip, a Ballerina Barbie's toe shoe. Then her presence would break over the room like a wave, knocking us off our feet and drenching us with sadness that lingered for hours.

By contrast, when the boys were there, Jess would sparkle, laugh at nothing, as Collie or Bell sent the four of us into fits of giggles. Pete pretended to understand our jokes, yelling, "Ha ha *ha*!" in imitation of some favorite cartoon character, which made us laugh even harder, until he banged the table with his spoon and pretended to fall out of his chair. Mom's face softened at our antics; the parentheses etched around her mouth, and the parallel ridges on her forehead, would fill and fade, and for a few moments I'd be happy.

But I'd had to confess to Jess my lack of success in finding a solution to her problem. True to my promise, I tried to make her swear she wouldn't get an abortion. For one thing, I was afraid she could be arrested for breaking the law; for another, I didn't want her to end up dead.

She only shrugged. "Don't worry about it," she said. "Whatever happens, I'll be okay."

I tried over and over to get her to go into specifics about what options she was considering, but she evaded, scoffed, and finally snapped. "Leave me alone, Win!" she scowled at me. "It's *my* problem, and I'll handle it." So, as Collie seemed firmly in the picture again, mentally I handed the matter back to him.

One afternoon, as Bell and I were driving back from checking on the few cows that were getting pretty near to calving, snow started to fall, and by the time we reached the house it was thick enough that we could hardly see ten feet in front of the truck. I'd noticed a reddish-yellow ring of light around the moon the night before, which often meant a change for the worse in the weather. When we came into the kitchen, Mom was filling the kerosene lanterns, so I knew she'd gotten word this was going to be a blizzard.

"Jess called. I told her to stay in town tonight, but she wanted to come back," Mom announced, screwing the top back on the kerosene can and wiping the lamp bases. "Roads won't be safe."

I glanced at Bell.

"You'd better stay on the couch here," she went on, apparently addressing him though she didn't look his way. "I wouldn't want you ending up stuck in a drift and freezing to death."

Again Lorrie's shadow flitted over us. Was I always going to flinch, I wondered, when I heard that word?

"Win, go fill the tub." When the power went out, we'd need not only light but water to flush the toilet. Mom was already pulling down jugs she'd fill with drinking water.

"Bell, you could fetch us more wood for the fire and get one started? Then call your mother."

Immediately he left the kitchen. In a few minutes he reappeared, carrying an armload of logs.

"Take a look at the trees out front," he breathed through cold-reddened lips. Mom and I peered through the living-room window at the deep blue forms of the bare-branched willows. It took me a moment to see the fluttering motion of dozens of small birds flying in and settling on the branches to join those already huddled there, seeking shelter from the storm.

"This'll be a big one," Mom predicted.

It was. Jess returned just before dark, reporting that the radio had announced the governor had declared the western part of the state closed and ordered the highway patrol to arrest anyone driving on the Interstate as of ten o'clock.

We got halfway through supper before the power went out. Pete let out a whoop when we lit up the lamps, then groaned when he realized there wouldn't be any TV. But Bell charmed him by using his hands to throw shadows on the wall as he told Pete a story about a wolf, a bird, and a devil. He even got me to accompany the twists of the plot, and the appearance of different characters, with appropriate piano music: galumphing bass chords for the wolf, staccato bursts in a minor key for the devil, and fluttery arpeggios for the bird.

"Do another! Do another!" Pete insisted, and Mom didn't protest, so we did. In the background we could hear the howl of the wind and bursts of icy snow spitting against the windows.

"Soak up the heat," Mom said in the glow of the firelight. "We're going to work like crazy tomorrow."

WE DID, AND THEN some. By morning, snow had stopped falling but was still blowing and piling up in scalloped drifts. To reach the cattle, we fought our way through sudden sheets of icy crystals that stung and cut our faces. Luckily we'd put the cattle in the larger enclosure, where they were standing up to their bellies in muddy snow, hardly able to move. We wrestled hay bales into the sheltered corner against the barn, fighting the wind that tried to wrench them from us and blow them away. A thin skin of ice made it impossible to grab anything without it slipping from our grasp. Even though we wore long underwear under pants and sweaters under our heaviest coats, we were chilled through by perspiration that froze as soon as it popped out.

I thought of Randy: Where was he when we actually needed his help? I hadn't been fully aware until he was gone how much hard, relentless labor he'd put his back to every single day. That didn't exactly even the scales, but it did make them just slightly less lopsided.

By then the cars and truck were completely blanketed over, only the faintest mounds suggesting where they sat under the enormous drift that filled the yard. We took turns shoveling a path between the house and yard, and when we stirred up the gravel that lay at the bottom, birds flew down from the trees and pecked furiously, searching for grain. Jess finally wheedled some old popcorn kernels from Mom that she threw to them, and they swooped down by the hundreds until they formed an undulating black-brown-carpet against the snow.

After lunch, wearing a new set of dry clothes, we set out in the truck to feed the yearling heifers that had stayed out in the far pasture. The wind had died down a bit, but it was still freezing cold, and the wire was frozen onto the bales. Even once we'd cut it with wire-cutters, it took every bit of strength for us to pry it away from the hay. As soon as we heaved the bale over the fence, the heifers started tearing it to pieces. Several were missing, so we drove along the ridge on the southern side. Still didn't see them. Finally we checked a little gully at the far end, and there they were, huddled together for warmth. We shoved them up and out, and they seemed glad to join the others and make up for lost time.

On the return trip I sat out in the truck bed, watching the back of Bell's and Jess' heads as we bobbed and bounced over the ruts, thinking how much I loved both of them, and how glad I was they accepted each other. Just then Jess' profile turned to Bell as she laughed at something he'd said, and he grinned back at her. I was struck with a surge of anxiety so strong I had to look away. When I turned back, Bell was ruffling Jess' hair carelessly, the way you'd mess a child's, just for a moment. Jess pushed her head against his hand, and he withdrew it, and they both faced forward again.

I couldn't squeeze in enough breath to fill my chest, and my throat felt dry, as if every drop of moisture had been sucked out of my body. I tried to calm myself, repeating over and over that this was nothing, that Jess loved Collie, that Bell was Collie's friend, that he'd never harm him or me that way. All it did was keep me hanging on the narrow edge of tears.

All my life I'd envied things about Jess: her smooth skin, her hair, her graceful body, her poise, her two years' head start on adulthood. These were threads, I now saw, that formed a part of the fabric woven of all my feelings about her, all we shared and felt about each other. I might not like the color of any one thread—a repellent lime green, perhaps, or a flashy neon orange—but the overall pattern was pleasing.

This jealous rage was as different from that envy as the tropics from the Arctic. It was a hand clawing at that fabric, tugging and pulling at its delicate weave, threatening to rip it apart. I hated Jess, I hated Bell, and I hated what I felt. A tangle of images throbbed in my head: hands tightening around Jess' throat; heavy boots stomping Bell's face; slashed bodies spilling entrails onto the frozen earth. And then the images thinned and blew away like mist rising from a stagnant pond, leaving behind a rancid stench.

As the truck jolted to a stop I jumped down and headed for the back door, then veered off toward the barn, ignoring Jess' and Bell's calls: "Hey, where are you going? You'll freeze!"

I kept plowing forward, tears now leaking from my eyes, my head held stiff. I was no longer cold; humiliated indignation stoked my blood. I wouldn't have been surprised if steam had risen from my skin and smoke from my ears. I knew I was overreacting, but I couldn't make myself stop.

Just as I reached the barn door, Bell's black-gloved hand seized my upper arm and spun me around.

"Leave me alone!" I kicked at his shin, missed, and buried my foot in a pile of snow. Couldn't I do anything right? I threw a punch at his shoulder, and he grunted in surprise and put up his hands as I lashed out again and again.

"Cut it out, Win! What's the matter with you?"

He warded off my blows, reaching out to grab me like the terrified calves we'd rope into submission at branding time.

"I hate you, you shit!" The words exploded out of me in an ecstatic flash. "I hate you both! Go screw yourselves!"

I had never uttered the word before; I hardly realized I knew it. But when I needed it, there it was.

Bell stepped backward, his eyes wide in shock. *"What?"* As soon as the drawn-out sound left his mouth, he began to laugh, slowly at first, then full voice. Enraged, I rushed at him full-tilt and caught him off guard. He fell over onto his back into a snowdrift, grabbing my coat and pulling me on top of him as he fell. I kept kicking and pummeling him with my arms, half-sobbing, half-choking, only dimly aware of what I was doing. He managed to get hold of my shoulders and flip me over, pinning me down. His legs pressed onto mine as he propped himself onto his elbows and looked down at me. Wordless screams burst from my throat, subsiding into ragged sobs.

Jess' bewildered face appeared over his shoulder.

"Are you okay?" Her voice was anxious. I thought I detected a trace of guilt in it. My fury re-ignited.

"Stay away from me, you bitch!" Another word I hadn't known I had in my repertoire.

"Let me handle this," Bell said quietly. Jess' face disappeared. After a moment Bell sat up, slipping his legs to the outside of mine, still resting his weight on my knees, his hands around my wrists, and pulled me to a sitting position.

"Man, you're a real spitfire." His bare fingers were cool against my burning cheek; at some point, he'd slipped off his gloves. He stroked my hair gently. The memory of what I'd seen through the truck window flashed over me, and I began to cry again, this time like a hurt child. He wiped my tears, rose, and pulled me up against him. As I leaned on him, he murmured my name over and over, swaying slightly back and forth, his arms around me. I wanted to hear him explain, reassure me, laugh it off, but I'd be damned if I'd tell him what was bothering me.

"What's the matter?" He tipped my face up toward his. "Were you cold back there, while we lived the life of Riley up front?"

This came too close to the truth for comfort. I tried to pull away from him. He gripped my arms tighter and leaned over and kissed my cheek, running his warm mouth slowly up and down, over and over. Then he placed his lips over my ear and breathed out very slowly. My neck started to tingle furiously until I was ready to tear my coat off.

"Hey, I've got an idea," he whispered, his breath a hot roar against my ear. "Let's go into the barn. Right now."

He grabbed my hair and pulled my head back so I could look into his eyes.

"Whaddya say? It'd shock the pants off everybody." His eyes creased into inverted half-moons as a grin spread across his face.

I couldn't help it; I laughed, angry at myself for laughing even as I yielded to his soothing. He hoisted me over his shoulder as easily as if I were as light as I suddenly felt, and began to carry me toward the barn, singing loudly.

He grabbed the gray goose by the neck,
Flung a duck across his back.

He didn't mind the quack, quack, quack
And the legs all dangling down, oh.

I kicked and beat on his back in mock protest until he turned and trudged back to the house, both of us shouting at the top of our lungs:

Down oh, down oh,
The legs all dangling down, oh!

As soon as we got back inside, Jess pulled me into the pantry.

"What in the world got into you?" she asked in a whisper, hands on her hips. I mumbled an apology. She wasn't satisfied. "Come on, you acted like you'd decided we were Simon Legree!" she went on. "You can't just pop off like that for no reason!" She peered at my face, frowning.

"Oh, and *you* never do?" I countered, hoping to deflect her. She shook her head in exasperation. "I'll ask Bell about it, then."

"Don't you dare!" I warned her, my voice rising, and we both cringed. Mom was moving in and out of the kitchen.

"I'll tell you later," I murmured, pushing past Jess and emerging into the kitchen, clutching the first thing I'd put my hands on, a bundle of seed packets rubber-banded together. Mom gaped at them.

"Kind of early for that, isn't it?" she asked.

I flung the bundle onto the table and marched to the hall. "I've got to practice," I announced. In the living room, Bell was winding his newly dried scarf around his neck as Petey pulled at his leg, imploring him to play with him.

"Gotta go, big boy." Bell smiled down at him. "My ma needs me, just like yours needs you." He glanced at me. "I'll be able to make it okay, once I get onto the road."

As Bell slowly pulled on his black gloves, working the stiffened cracked leather down his fingers, his hair gleamed in the light, falling forward and throwing his dark face into shadow. As I looked at him standing there, long legs planted on the old red-and-yellow braided rug, his teeth glinting in a grin, I felt an attack of hunger for him as keen as a starving animal. Yet I couldn't move, embarrassed and astonished by my body's erratic demands.

I don't know what passed over my face, but Bell moved toward me. He stopped as Pete threw himself at him, protesting, leaning against his legs and winding his arms around Bell's thighs, face against his crotch. This was even worse. I couldn't help imagining myself exactly where Pete was, and my skin flamed as hot as if were actually there.

Bell inched gently forward, edging Pete's tiny feet backwards until they both stood directly in front of me. His arms reached around Pete's head and clasped my waist, and for a moment we stood there like a lopsided sandwich. Then Petey looked up at Bell.

"Are you an Indian?" he asked in a high, clear voice.

For a moment Bell was silent. He took a deep breath. "You bet."

"I'm an Indian, too."

Bell glanced at me, then down at Pete. "I know. Part of you is, anyway."

"Which part?" Pete pointed to his head. "This part? This one?" His chest. "This one?" He wiggled his leg.

"Part of all those parts."

"My Mom is an Indian. And Jess is. And you are, too." Petey butted his head back against my waist. "Everybody is an Indian! Everybody!" He swayed back and forth, rocking us along with him as he chanted, "*Ev'rybod-y in the world!*"

Out of the mouth of babes, I thought, as the three of us swayed together. If only it were true.

THAT EVENING, AS JESS and I lay in bed, listening to the wind rattle the windowpanes, the lamp between our beds softening the contours of the room, happy again and feeling benevolent, I gave Jess a stripped-down version of what I'd felt in the truck. She looked at me as if I'd accused her of being a vampire. "You're nuts, Win," she finally decided. "You *know* about Collie and me. And Bell and I have been in the same class for years. We're friends, because of Collie and because—we just are."

"How can you be friends with a boy?" I wondered. She humphed knowingly. "I mean, maybe when you were a kid. But now, don't you

. . .doesn't he. . .isn't it hard when. . . ?" I trailed off, exasperated at not finding the eloquence I needed.

"When you're attracted to each other?" Jess flashed me the superior smile of a worldly-wise woman. "It just adds flavor, that's all. You don't have to *do* anything about it. And if you already have a boyfriend, then you're not really all that interested, anyway. It's no big deal."

I narrowed my eyes.

"Before you went out with Collie, did you and Bell ever go out?" I knew they hadn't. "I mean, did you want to?" A more intense pang of fear. "Did you—do stuff together? After school?"

Jess gazed at me a long time.

"Win, once you're with someone, what they did before you is gone. It's over. You can't think about it, or you'll drive yourself crazy."

She reached out and pulled the lamp toward her to blow out the flame. The dark fell over us like a mist.

"But *did* you?"

Her bed creaked as she settled onto her side.

"Wouldn't you like to know."

I stared up at the ceiling, flopped over onto my stomach, then almost immediately onto my back.

"Jess," I pleaded. "Help me. Even if you have to lie."

"For God's sake, Win." In the tartness of her voice, laced with a hint of mockery, I heard the ring of truth. "How could I? He was an *Indian*."

TWO DAYS LATER, A Chinook began to blow, and the drifts melted into gushes of water that ran along every path and draw. We slogged around in hip or gumshoe boots, through thick mud and slush instead of snow. A week after the blizzard, you wouldn't have known it had ever happened.

CHAPTER 21

A S THE PIANO COMPETITION drew closer, I practiced every minute I could find. Roone and I had decided on my program: the Bach *Prelude and Fugue in E major* to demonstrate my Baroque technique; the first movement of Beethoven's *F minor sonata* for all-round mastery; and because I loved it so, Chopin's *Nocturne in A minor*. Even Mom got sick of listening to the pieces over and over, and Jess threatened to go back and live in town if she heard them one more time. And the mysterious wrong numbers continued.

Several times I caught Jess throwing up in the morning. Once I managed to deflect Mom's attention by pretending to turn my ankle, just as Jess turned pale and ran for the bathroom. She thanked me later, but she still wouldn't answer my questions about how she felt about her pregnancy or any plans she was making with Collie. Finally I lost patience. "Just don't forget to invite me to the wedding," I snapped, and deliberately put the problem out of my mind. Let her come to me when she was ready, I decided.

Two days before I was to leave, as school ended, Bell was waiting for me outside the front door. This wasn't unusual now. Most of the white kids had drifted back into a casual, distant connection with me. But no one invited me to join them between classes, or to drop over to their houses after school. Corinne was part of a trio now, hanging out with Judy and Liz, and our friendship seemed like a story about someone much younger whom I didn't know very well any more. So I depended more and more on Jess and Collie and Bell, moving away from the fringe of a group from which I'd been cut adrift into one I didn't feel quite ready for.

As I ran up to Bell, I was struck with how tense he looked, holding himself stiffly rather than slouching against the low stone wall as he usually did.

"Come on," he urged me and marched off in the direction of his car without waiting for me to catch up with him.

"What's the rush?"

He got in, and I slid beside him as he started the motor.

"Your sister's over at Frances'."

For a moment it didn't register. "My aunt."

Marjorie's mother. The medicine woman. Fear ran a finger down my chest.

"What's wrong?" My voice was shaky.

He didn't answer, his eyes fixed on the road, the skin around his lips white and taut. In five minutes we stopped in front of the small white house, its neat flower beds now a muddy mix of mush and dried-out stalks. As Bell pushed open the door without knocking, Marjorie looked up from the sofa, where she sat reading.

"Hey." She nodded at me, put her book aside, and stood up. She seemed taller, her long hair pulled away from her face into a braid, emphasizing her dark eyes. Before I could ask her anything, Frances entered from the kitchen, her face calm and grave. She was carrying a small pile of dish towels.

For a moment no one spoke or moved. Then Frances took my hand and led me into the kitchen. Starched green-and-white checked curtains altered the pallid sunlight falling on the small Formica table and shining on polished apples in a cracked yellow bowl. I caught a glimpse of a plastic tub in the sink containing a tangled cloth soaking in pinkish water.

"Your sister is bleeding," Frances stated simply. "What is inside her is deciding whether to come out."

"Why? What happened? Is she okay?" I gripped the back of a

chair.

"It's what she wanted."

Suddenly an image sharpened into focus, as if I'd looked through a pair of binoculars: Jess had gone to Frances for help. Which meant that Bell knew, too.

Why hadn't it occurred to me to ask Bell for advice? Because Jess would never have wanted me to tell him, I was sure of that. Yet she'd turned to him herself, knowing his aunt was a medicine woman, with ancient knowledge of herbs and roots and purges. Or else she'd turned to Collie, knowing he'd go to Bell.

It didn't matter anymore. I had failed her, and I'd make it up to her now.

"She can stay here," Frances was saying. "But she should be at home, where her mother can care for her." She shook her head slowly. "The daughter needs the mother's strength."

"She won't do that. She doesn't want Mom to know."

Frances nodded. "I understand."

"Please, can I see her?"

"Let me see how she is first."

Frances left the room and in a few moments came back, carrying a small enamel basin with a crumpled twist of stained cloth that she slipped into the plastic tub.

"Come with me." I followed her through a door at the far end of the kitchen, across a short hall, and into a dark, narrow bedroom where Jess lay on a single bed, eyes shut, her face as pale as the pillow. The lowered blind darkened the room to a dusky gray-blue. Frances motioned with her head for me to approach Jess. As I did, Frances left the room, closing the door behind her.

"Jess?" I whispered, my voice barely audible. Her eyes opened, and she turned her head very slowly toward me. In two steps I was kneeling by the bed, my head next to hers.

"Don't look so scared." To my immense relief she sounded like her normal self. "I just hope this works."

"Why didn't you tell me?"

"No point in you worrying, too." Suddenly her brows wrinkled and her eyes squeezed shut as she brought her knees up and curled over onto her side. Her hands clenched tight and she let her breath out in a hiss. I scrambled to my feet.

"I'll get Frances."

"No." She lay there panting, then groaned and curled her body even tighter. Finally her muscles relaxed and she sighed. "It's just like really bad cramps, that's all." She tried to smile. "No big deal."

"Where's Collie? He should be here with you." Helplessness had made me angry, and Collie was as good a target as any.

"He doesn't know."

"What? That you're—sick?"

"Anything."

I struggled to fit this new piece into the puzzle. No sooner than I put it together, it seemed, than I had to pull it apart. "But Bell knows. And Marjorie."

"It wasn't supposed to happen like this." Her voice sounded normal again. "The stuff I took was just supposed to bring on my period, a real heavy one, so I could just stay home like with bad cramps. But it came on out of the blue this morning, right before English class. All of a sudden I was all bent over in the hall. I couldn't even stand up! Luckily, Bell's in my class, and he took me to the office and got permission to drive me home. They thought. We came here—wait a minute."

She grimaced and curled up again, clutching her knees to her chest. A thin, drawn-out whine escaped from her clenched teeth as she rocked her body back and forth. When the cramp passed, her body went limp, and she lay still.

"Bell doesn't have to be here," I declared. "I'm staying here with you."

"No, you're not." Her eyes popped open and she grabbed my hand. "If you don't go home, Mom will suspect something and track me down. They may have already called her from school. You have to tell her something."

"Like what?" I was indignant. "You know what a bad liar I am. I'd rather stay and take care of you."

"You can't!" To my dismay, she began to raise herself onto her elbows. "I'll leave and go home myself if I have to."

"Oh, that'll really keep it a secret!" I could see she was in no shape to go anywhere, but I wouldn't have put it past her to try. I pushed her shoulders back until she lay flat. It was frighteningly easy to do. "Where does Mom think you are, anyway?"

"You've got to tell her I'm staying with Leila. And make sure she doesn't call there, either."

"How am I supposed to do that?"

She shrugged and narrowed her eyes at me. "And you're going to that competition day after tomorrow, like you planned, you hear me? Just do everything like normal."

"Why is the competition so important?" I asked. "Mom's going to find out about this somehow, anyway."

Jess hoisted herself onto one elbow and grabbed my collar. "Win, I swear to God, if you tell her, I'll never forgive you!" she muttered. "Never!"

Before I could answer, she gasped, and her features squeezed together in pain. She gripped my collar so tightly I was pulled forward, my face practically touching hers, her breath hot against my cheek. A square of light suddenly fell over the bed, my shadow in the middle. I looked over my shoulder at a tall silhouette in the doorway.

"Jess?" It was Collie's tentative voice. He took a step into the room. "Why didn't you tell me?" He stood towering over me. I rose, slipping out of Jess' loosened grip, and backed away.

"Collie." Jess began to cry softly. "I'm sorry."

"Jess, don't."   He bent toward her, his face hidden in shadow, his hands trembling. I turned to leave.

"Win." I stopped. "Promise me you'll go." I hesitated. Should I follow her instincts or my own about what would help her most? "Promise me. Please."

I couldn't bear the pleading, the abjectness in her voice. I was trapped in the next-to-last scene of *Gone With the Wind*, with Jess as the dying Melanie begging me, a repentant Scarlett, to take care of her son. If I stayed with her, that would surely guarantee her safety. Yet how could I refuse her?

"All right."

Jess' face softened, and her eyes closed. I turned and hurried into the hall, where Frances stood waiting.

"Will she be okay?" My voice was shaking.

Frances nodded. "Whatever happens to the baby, she will be fine."

I hadn't the least notion how she could be so sure, or why I should believe her, but I did, just as I had believed Jess when she told me Pete would recover. Wrapping that assurance around me like a warm blanket, I could leave that house and go home to whatever faced me there.

ALL EVENING I WAS as cheery as a Salvation Army Santa. I used my apprehension to fuel a jittery excitement that I blamed on the upcoming competition—something I'd later learn to call "test anxiety." I was fairly confident that Mom bought my act, as well as my casual explanation that Jess had decided to stay in town to study for a test the next day. I practiced—not very well, but I assumed Mom couldn't assess the nuances of my technique—and played with Pete without being asked.

After she put him to bed, as I was finishing my math problems at the kitchen table, Mom pulled out a chair and sat down across from me. "All right, Win," she said heavily. "Tell me what's going on."

I kept my gaze on my book. "Nothing's going on."

"Don't lie to me." I'd never heard such cold anger in her voice. I was used to quick outbursts from nowhere, exasperated bluster, yes, but not this dead-calm certainty. I put my pencil down.

"What's going on with Jess?"

"She got sick at school, and she decided to stay in town. It's probably just a twenty-four-hour bug. She was afraid she'd throw up in the car on the way home."

Mom looked at me with scorn.

"Then why didn't she just say so?"

"She didn't want you to worry."

Mom slapped the table so hard with her palm that I jumped. "Is that the best you can do? Try again!"

I opened my mouth but nothing came out.

"You're pitiful. Both of you. Now tell me the truth."

I began to shake, first invisibly, inside my belly, then in my hands, and finally my throat. "I can't. I promised."

Mom turned briefly toward the dark window and faced me again. "All right. I'll ask questions, and you answer them. Is Jess in some motel right now, with Collie? Is that why she didn't come home?"

I shook my head vehemently and sincerely.

"Is she really sick?"

I nodded just as fervently.

"Was she afraid to come home? Afraid to face me?"

I offered a more tentative nod.

"Afraid I'd guess what was wrong?"

I gave her an even smaller nod. Mom paused for what seemed a long time. I knew suddenly that she hated her own next question, as afraid of hearing the answer as I was of providing it. "Is she pregnant?"

The room grew wider and colder as I rooted for words that would appease her without breaking my promise to Jess.

"I don't know." That much was technically true. Maybe by now she no longer was.

"Has she told you she might be?"

I hesitated and shrugged, not meeting her eyes. I ached to stay loyal, but I knew I couldn't lie again.

"Win. Did she tell you she might be pregnant?"

After a long, miserable moment, I barely nodded.

"Oh, god." I heard a whispered sigh as Mom leaned forward, her arms in a V in front of her on the table. "Oh, Jess."

A long silence followed as I held my breath. Mom's head sank onto her cradled arms. I felt dizzy, as if sparkling grains of sand were floating behind my eyes. I wanted to run from the room, bury my head underneath the bedclothes, make time run backward. Instead I went over to her, put my arms around her, and held her tight until she found her voice again.

MARIE

March 1, 1971

Oh, God, I've been afraid of this ever since I can remember—ever since I had Jess, that's for sure. I look at her, and I think how dangerous it is to be a woman. To have to wonder, will she be like me? Will Win?

Win's got my mother's temper, always has, ever since she was a baby. For a while I thought, She's the one. She's got the taint. She even looks like her, with her flaming red hair and pale skin. Not her face, really, but everything else. Jess, with her quiet ways, how she holds things to herself and keeps herself calm, no matter what: That's my father. Or so I thought. It isn't so simple. I see that now.

My mother was so headstrong. She wanted her own way. If she got something into her head, there was no stopping her. It didn't matter to her who thought what about it. And one of the things she wanted was men—men, and her own pleasure. I hated it then, and it makes me cringe to remember it even now.

The first one was my father. No stopping her there! And when she left him for good, it was all right at first, living with Aunt Beulah and her husband Gerald, and their three kids, in Billings. Mama helped run their store for quite a while. But it got awfully crowded, three grown-ups and four children in five rooms over the store. And Beulah kept throwing out digs about how Mama had brought it on herself by marrying an Indian. Oh, that would get Mama mad! But it was their house, and we were beholden to them, so she'd mostly hold her tongue.

She knew she had to find a way to earn more money or she'd never get William back. So she started taking courses at the local college to become a teacher, and wham, in three years she had her credential. In that respect, her pigheadedness paid off. But she began going stir-crazy, and she started staying out almost every evening. She had classes, and choir practice, something all the time, and Beulah started getting suspicious.

I remember the evening when it all started. Mama was out as usual, and Beulah threw out a snide remark about Mama's gallivanting around. I didn't like it, and I told her that Mama was just trying to get independent so we could move out and not crowd them up so much. Beulah just sniffed in that high-and- mighty way she had that Mama hated, and said, "You can call it independence. I call it something else."

When I said I didn't understand, she wouldn't explain. A few days later, after I'd gone to bed, I heard their voices rise, then fall, then rise even louder from the kitchen. Finally Mama stomped into our room, slammed the door, and threw herself onto the bed, not caring if I woke up.

"That goddamn sneaky bitch!" she hissed. I was blown over; I'd never heard her use words like that. She lay there, muttering "That bitch!" over and over.

I sat up. "Mama, what is it?" I wanted to calm her down.

She slowed her breath. Her eyes were glittering in the tiny light from the alarm clock. "Beulah's always been jealous of me. She wants to show me off to the whole town as her repentant sinner. Well, I'm sick of her, of trying to please her! She thinks she's got me under her thumb, but I'll wipe that self-righteous smirk off her face so fast she won't know what hit her."

"What do you mean, Mama?" I asked. "How will you do that?"

She got up to undress. Usually she wouldn't take her clothes off in front of me, but this time she peeled them off slowly, baring her smooth white skin, glowing in the moonlight like fresh cream, turning so I could see her small breasts and the brush of hair between her legs. I was embarrassed, yet I couldn't pull my eyes away. As she slipped her night-

dress over her head and smoothed it over her hips, she smiled at me. But she didn't look happy, she looked mean.

"I'll do it with this," is what she said.

Then she got into bed, rolled away from me, and wouldn't say anything more.

AFTER THAT, I WATCHED *Mama whenever I could. Something had shifted in her, made her sway when she walked. She looked taller, and her breasts seemed fuller. While before she'd been surrounded by women, now she seemed to move alone. Men followed her with their eyes, smiled as she passed, walked over to her, leaned close to catch her words, her laugh that made me think of chocolate. She began wearing lipstick and a trace of rouge, and little pearl-and-rhinestone earrings.*

One day she showed me a pair of shoes she'd bought in Kelley's: bright red with straps over the instep and curved high heels that made her ankles look too delicate to hold her up. That Sunday she wore them to church, and I could see everyone glancing at them. She pretended not to notice, but she kept crossing and uncrossing her legs, swinging her foot very slightly as she sat up front with the choir. I knew Aunt Beulah was looking at her from the way the lines around her mouth got deeper, and I knew Mama was in for another lecture over Sunday dinner.

But she didn't care, and, wouldn't you know, it didn't stop her. I have no idea where she met them, but men kept calling for her, different men. They'd take her on long walks, or out to dinner, or to a picture show. She got more and more reckless; she stayed out later and later. She'd show off bracelets and silky stockings and perfume that somehow mysteriously appeared, who knew from where.

Once I saw her walking with a man I didn't know, in the middle of town. I'd gone to buy some notebook paper at Regent's, and I looked up, and there, with her back to me, so close I almost bumped into her, was Mama. I recognized her dress, a silky green-dotted white one that clung to her hips and moved with her as she walked. The man walking alongside her was tall, in a pin-striped suit. As I watched, I saw him lay his hand flat on Mama's bottom.

I was so shocked, I almost let out a screech. Lucky I didn't. Mama just slipped her own hand behind her, right over his, and held it there a moment before sliding his with hers in front of her, so she could take his arm and rub her hip against his. He leaned his head toward her, and I could see his nostrils flare.

"You smell so good I could eat you," he said to her.

I expected her to rear back at that, but she didn't do anything like that.

"Just hold your horses," she said. "You'll get fed soon enough." And they both laughed. And then, right there in the street, they stopped and kissed, a long, long kiss. I saw their tongues move in and out of their mouths, saw their saliva glistening in the sunlight.

I couldn't stand it. I turned and ran in the other direction. That's when I knew for sure what my mother was doing.

SHE JUST COULDN'T STOP *herself, I guess. Or else she didn't want to. When she got hired as a teacher, and we moved to Miles City, she toned it down a bit, because she didn't want to lose her job. But she just did it in a less showy, more sneaky way. I hated her for it. I hated having to baby-sit William, whom she'd got back, almost every evening, with him so angry at being taken away from the life he'd gotten used to. And then I had to put her to bed when she finally got home, drunk and mussed up, smelling of whiskey and sweat and whatever man she'd been with.*

Eventually she got married again, to that dull, prissy businessman named Oliver Lucas. I'm not real sure why she married him. Maybe she was tired of living hand to mouth on a teacher's salary. But I don't think it stopped her catting around, not completely, though it slowed her down some. They'd fight terribly about it sometimes. I swore to myself, That's never going to happen to me, to be a slave to my body, or to a man's power to set it on fire.

That's really why I married Lee. He was safe. He was as sweet as pie, and he loved me so much he'd do just about anything I asked him— except stand up to his family, as it turned out. I got him to love me, not by giving in, but by holding back. The truth is I wasn't ever tempted, not by Lee. I wasn't really tempted by any man, not until Randy came along. And then my false pride about my uprightness came back to slap me in the face.

I'd always told myself I was completely different from Mama, because I kept pure when she didn't know the meaning of the word. But now I wonder. Virtue is real easy as long as there's nothing around to tempt you. In the end, maybe we're just two sides of the same coin, my mother and me.

CHAPTER 22

HAD A HARD time sleeping that night, plagued by a recurrent dream in which I was walking through a beautiful twilight garden only to see, dimly at first, then clearer as it emerged from the shadows, the shape of a huge animal—elephant, tiger, buffalo with long curved horns. In each dream a different animal advanced, silent, menacing, its approach slow and relentless. I'd look around wildly for an escape, waking just as I realized there was none.

I went through classes in a daze. Mom had dropped me off at school and left a suitcase, carefully packed two days previously, at Roone's, where I was to spend the night. I knew her next stop would be Frances' house. Petey regarded it all as a bonus outing, though he worried it might include an unannounced visit to the doctor. He'd become understandably leery of anything medical. Mom was close-mouthed, receding again into aloofness. I wasn't even tempted to mention Jess, or anything else she'd unexpectedly revealed the night before.

The moment school let out, I headed to Frances'. As I hurried down Elm, I heard Marjorie behind me.

"Wait." I stopped to let her catch up. We walked on side by side. "Your sister was much better this morning."

"Thank you." I shifted my books to my other arm. "I was on my way to see her. I won't be around for the next few days."

"Good luck." Somehow the word had gotten around about where I was going and why. We walked on in silence, heads pulled into our shoulders against the cold.

"You will see Bell." She stated it as a fact. I was indeed supposed to meet him at Roone's in about an hour, and he was to stay and have supper with me and the Graftons. "Please tell him to come by our house later."

"Sure." I knew Bell had practically lived at Frances' for the last several years, studying and eating supper there, only returning to his mother's to sleep. It was one of the subjects he wouldn't talk about, beyond the few cryptic remarks in which he'd painted his broken home life in dingy colors of drunkenness, squalor, and misery. "Wouldn't he do that anyway?"

"Not anymore."

She walked without glancing right or left. Her blank expression suggested nothing, but suddenly it dawned on me how profoundly the change in Bell's routines created by his relationship with me might have altered Marjorie's as well. Especially since the accident. But what about before that, when he began working for Selby? Did Marjorie blame me for any of it? Did she resent me for drawing Bell's attention away from her? Did she feel about me the way I'd felt, so briefly, about Jess that day in the truck?

I could think of no way to ask her or to set it right if she did. And I wondered if this was the real reason I'd avoided her and felt so inexplicably uncomfortable when she was around.

Tingling with self-consciousness, I climbed the steps to her house and stepped aside to let her enter first. I knew immediately that something had changed. The house felt empty.

"Mom?"

There was no answer. Marjorie put down her books and walked into the kitchen. A moment later she returned and handed me a folded piece of paper with my name on the outside. I opened it.

Winona —
   We have gone on home. Don't worry.

Have a great time and play your best.
Love, Mom

And at the bottom, in Jess' scrawl:

Thanks a whole *lot, Judas!!*

CHAPTER 23

THE CONCERT HALL WAS bright and uncomfortably hot, less from the central heating than from the way my heart was racing. We were on the campus of the University of Montana, in the Arts building. We'd been given a tour of the campus that morning by a young woman with long, stringy black hair, wearing an ankle-length striped cotton skirt that looked as if it had been made from a tablecloth, and wooden clogs that could have stepped out of my old copy of *Hans Brinker*. She'd told us she was studying classical archeology, a subject I'd never heard of before. We'd tramped from building to building, visited the enormous library with its reading room filled with students bent over books spread on the long oak tables. They looked serious and impossibly glamorous. I'd known instantly that I wanted to live there forever.

I sat with a serenely poised Roone in one of the front rows, along with the other contestants and their teachers. The four judges sat in the same area, clumped together on the far right. They all had notepads on their laps. Behind us sat the audience, none of whom I knew except for Selby, who'd decided to accompany us, and Mr. and Mrs. Allen, the couple at whose house we were staying. There were all sorts of people, young, old, well-dressed or in casual clothes, scattered in groups in the high-ceilinged hall, listening intently.

In my green skirt, white Peter Pan-collared blouse, and freshly shined leather pumps, my hair swept up in a French twist, gleaming from the styling gel Roone had used to arrange it, I felt like a country bumpkin come to the big city. Discreetly I mopped the perspiration from my forehead and upper lip with a limp Kleenex, more nervous by the minute. According to the program, I was scheduled sixth of seven contestants in the twelve- to fifteen-year-old category. So far we'd heard a chubby twelve-year-old boy race through an easy Mozart *Sonatina*; next, a tall blond girl, even skinnier than Corinne, murdered a Schubert "Musical Moment" and then, as I agonized in empathy, totally blanked out after the first few bars of "Für Elise." Next, two identical twin girls in frilly pink dresses, their brown hair permed into fat ringlets, attacked Mozart's *G major Sonata*, twin number one performing the first movement, and twin number two the second. I waited in vain for an unannounced triplet to appear and polish the piece off.

Instead we were listening to an older girl, with eyelashes so dark she must have been wearing mascara, whom I sized up as my first serious competitor, finish a piece by Brahms, one I'd never heard before. She was good, and the piece was hard, with lots of complicated chords and arpeggios. But she smeared all the notes together like a water-splashed ink drawing.

"Know how I'm always telling you to go easy on the pedal?" Roone whispered to me as the girl lifted her hands from the keys. I nodded, glancing at her. Even in that crowd, Roone was a standout, in a bright green silk blouse that brought out the coppery tones of her mahogany skin. Her tiny diamond ear studs shimmered in the light with every movement of her head. She was by far the most elegant woman there; sitting beside her, I felt like a wiry mutt plopped down next to a pure-bred Afghan hound.

The girl began her second piece, Bach's *D minor Prelude*. To my ears it sounded mechanical, her left hand pounding the repeated bass notes too loudly, without the lightness needed to make the music "dance," as Roone had so often put it. The insistent pulse of the rhythm reminded me of the gallop of a horse, and suddenly I saw Jess riding Battle, the pony we'd owned years ago, her hair streaming behind her, a triumphant shout ringing from her lips. What was she doing? Where was she now? My stomach, already low, sank even further. All morning I'd pushed her image away, unable to consider how furious she might be at me or to ponder what Mom had revealed. I promised myself that, like Scarlett, I'd think about that later.

The older girl stood up and bowed slightly to enthusiastic applause. Roone put her hand on my shoulder. It was my turn. "Win, remember," she whispered. "All that matters is the music and what it's saying." She patted me gently. As I rose and slipped past her, she added, "You play beautifully, and I'm proud to be your teacher."

Every breath I took as I walked down the aisle, climbed the steps to the stage, and seated myself on the bench, reaching down to adjust its height, opened me deeper and wider. As I held my hands over the keyboard, I imagined Roone and Mrs. Isaacson standing just behind me, each with a hand on my back, the warmth of their touch coursing through the muscles of my shoulders and arms, and down into my fingers, as I began to play. And I played first one piece, then the next, for them and for everyone I loved—Mom, Jess, Bell, Pete—the music a golden filament linking my heart to theirs. When applause broke over me, I realized I'd nearly lost awareness of where I was and who was listening. I stumbled to my feet, almost forgetting to bow, and hurried off the stage.

Roone said nothing as I took my seat. Then she put her hand over mine and turned her face to me, her dark eyes shining. I saw there the look I'd always waited for from Mom.

"Thank you," she whispered.

This was what Mom must have meant in that now-long-ago revelation in the dark of my room after Marilyn's visit. To be the vessel that brings this satisfaction to someone else is the most glorious feeling on Earth.

It didn't matter when the next contestant, a boy so young he must barely have passed the lower age limit, gave a stunning rendition of the first movement of a Schubert sonata and a Rachmaninoff etude, the latter light-years beyond my abilities. Even when the three finalists—myself, the older girl, and the boy—were recalled successively to perform our third selections, I played, not for the audience or the judges, but for Chopin, spinning through the notes his garden in moonlight, the nightingale singing in the cool depths of the forest. Once I knew I couldn't possibly win, I played even better, released from any last vestige of anxiety. As I expected, the boy won first prize. Then the head judge called my name.

"Miss Winona Daggett of Redmond, second prize in the junior division. Her teacher is Mrs. Roone Grafton."

I stood up, and Roone rose briefly too. Then she pointed me toward the stage, where the judge pumped my hand like a handle and presented me with a sealed envelope. Back at my seat I tore it open and pulled out a check for $200.

"I didn't know there'd be money prizes except for first!"

"I didn't tell you," Roone laughed. "Close your mouth before you swallow a fly. I didn't want to make you more nervous than you already were."

Selby came over to us and reached out his hand.

"Way to go, Win," he beamed. "You were the best in my book." Mr. and Mrs. Allen added their words of praise. As we made out way up the aisle and into the lobby, I was greeted and congratulated by one smiling face after another. I ended up feeling like something of a minor celebrity as we marked the occasion by going to dinner at one of Missoula's fanciest restaurants, so highfalutin the menu was written in French. We got some funny looks—two black couples and a white teenage girl. But I was beyond caring; in fact, I relished it. See, I thought, I'm not who you thought I was or who you want me to be. I can be whoever I want.

BACK AT THE ALLENS' I called home. I'd spoken only very briefly to Mom the night before, just long enough to make sure Jess was all right. Jess hadn't wanted to talk to me. I listened to the phone ring three, four, five times, before Mom answered.

"Mom, I won second prize! There were seven kids, and one was a genius—no one could have beaten him except maybe Mozart, or Van Cliburn. But I was next. And I won two hundred dollars!" I paused for breath.

"Good for you." Mom's voice was flat, without expression. Instantly I felt deflated, then angry.

"That's a lot of money. At least I thought so."

"It's fine, Win. I'm real glad you won."

"You don't sound glad."

"I am." But she sounded preoccupied, distant. The hell with her, I decided. Here I'd gone through the biggest ordeal and the greatest triumph of my life so far, and she didn't care.

"Can I talk to Jess?" I made my voice cool, unforgiving. A long silence followed. I became uneasy.

"Mom? Is Jess okay?" Still nothing. I clutched the receiver tighter. "Say something!"

"She's gone."

"Gone? What do you mean?" Terrifying images formed and dissolved: Jess on a hospital bed covered with blood, her face like stone, colorless as paper.

"She's disappeared. She went to school today, but she never came home."

"Where'd she go?"

"I don't know. Nobody knows. Or they won't say." I heard her point an accusing finger at me.

"*I* don't know anything about this. Honestly. Not this time."

After another long pause, she sighed, "Just come on home, Win," and I heard weariness, a sadness so deep I drew back from it, resenting it yet pulled toward it.

"Doesn't Collie know where she is?"

"He's gone, too. I think they've run away together."

Bell, I thought. He must have known, and he didn't tell me. No one tells me anything. I'm just the little tag-along baby sister, the naive would-be girlfriend. A fury of indignation began to build in me, only to career over the edge into self-accusation. Had I actually brought my exclusion on myself? I wondered. Had I placed myself outside the realm of their trust and earned Jess' enmity too, thanks to my childish inability to evade the truth, to dissemble, to lie?

Then worries about Jess flooded over me. Had they decided to find a doctor who would perform an abortion? Would I ever see her again? Next, a surge of anger—she'd managed to upstage me at my hour of triumph!—followed by guilt: She's vanished, and all I can think of is myself.

That, I resolved, was going to change.

ON THE DRIVE HOME, I could feel myself drawing tightly inward like an umbrella furling shut. Roone could sense that something was bothering me and asked a few leading questions, but I kept my answers bland and unrevealing. Jess' life was hers to reveal or not. I was determined to practice deception, or at least concealment.

When I walked through the door, Mom hugged me hard. I could feel her ribs right under her skin, and her face looked frighteningly gaunt. I checked my memory carefully. She couldn't have lost so much weight in two days, yet somehow the change had escaped me until that moment. In a flash I saw I had taken her unchanging presence for granted, the way a child accepts as a given that which is essential and irreplaceable, and assumes it will be there forever. Now I clung to her in fright, trying to hold the pieces of her solid reality together.

"Any news?" I asked.

She shook her head.

"What do you think she—"

"I don't want to talk about it, Win. It makes me too angry."

She bit her lip and disengaged herself from me. As I helped her dry the supper dishes, I found myself chattering about the competition, the college savings account I planned to open with my prize money, in order to distract myself from the bewildered pain in her eyes. Finally I ran out of topics, and we sat at the table quietly, listening to Petey strike random notes on the piano, filling the empty house with noise.

"He wants to be like you," Mom said. "He's been playing with that piano for two days straight."

I shrugged and winced as Petey hit the keys with both hands.

"Your father was really musical, you know. You get your talent from him. He was always singing or humming something. And he could play the guitar real beautiful. All he had to do was hear a song one time, and he could play it right off."

She stared at a spot a few feet to the left of me. I held my breath. This was more than she'd ever been willing to tell me before.

"Go on," I encouraged her.

"About what?"

I bit my tongue at her obtuseness. "About—him."

She shrugged. "I already told you. He was a nice man, but weak. He couldn't say no to anyone, least of all to his mother." Her eyes narrowed and her mouth tightened. "She'd say jump, and he'd jump. Didn't matter if he was in the middle of a meal, or sound asleep, or if his kids needed him here."

Suddenly she looked me directly in the eyes. "That's why he died. His mother rang up, middle of the night, because she had a sick headache and she was out of aspirin, and she needed Lee to bring her some. 'She's in awful pain,' he said. I tried to get him to stay home and wait till morning because the roads were awful, all slick and icy. 'No, no, I've got to go,' he said. So he did, and a truck hit him head-on and he ended up with the steering column jammed so far through his chest it almost came out his back."

I must have turned pale because she got up and came over to me and put her hand on my shoulder. "I'm sorry, Win. I shouldn't have told you that."

"It's okay. I'd rather know than be kept in the dark, like a. . .a mushroom or something. Or Count Dracula."

A smile flickered across her face.

"My daughter, the vampire."

The smile faded as she took her hand away. "That reminds me." She left the room, and returned in a moment with an envelope she placed on the table. I stared at Marilyn's now-familiar angular handwriting. The envelope was addressed to me.

"I sent her a Christmas card," I muttered.

"You can write whoever you want," she shrugged. "It's a free country, last I heard."

She began stacking the dishes and putting them away as I opened the envelope. A photo was tucked inside a note card. I slid the photo onto the table and stared, mesmerized, at the five of us, shoulders touching, standing on our front steps: Randy, Mom, and me in a row, and in front, Petey, leaning back against Randy, and next to him, Mom's hands on her shoulders, Lorrie, her face round and pink with excitement, so alive and present in the world that I gasped for breath. Instantly Mom was beside me.

"What is it?"

Mutely I pointed at the photo, and she in turn froze before its spell. I remembered the moment, just before lunch, when Marilyn had herded us out the front door to snap her camera at us. "One for the family album," she'd said. How was it possible that things could change so quickly, so completely? There we were, innocent of what the next hour would bring, stupidly unconscious of the great good fortune we'd possessed, of how all our animosity—Randy's flare-ups, Jess' poker-faced rebellion, Mom's infuriating roller-coaster moods—added up, not to misery, but to happiness.

Mom reached down and brought the photo closer, her face as immobile as if it, too, had been transformed into a snapshot of itself. For five, ten unbearable seconds she stood there. Then she handed the photo to me and walked out of the room and down the hall. I heard her bedroom door close.

It took a few minutes before I could bring myself to read Marilyn's note, and when I did, I gave silent thanks that Mom hadn't seen it.

> *Dear Win,*
>
> *I thought your family might enjoy this souvenir of our 'reunion.' It was a day I'll never forget. You were all so friendly I was overwhelmed. Surprises like this one are so much fun, don't you think?*
>
> *By the way, I found out something else through the Bureau: your great-aunt, Moon Little Deer, who is your mother's aunt, still lives on the Lame Deer reservation.*
>
> *It would be fun to meet her, too. She must remem-*

ber all sorts of interesting things about your family.
I hope we'll all see each other again soon.

My very best to everybody, and give Petey and sweet
little Lorrie each a kiss from me.

Marilyn

CHAPTER 24

O VER THE NEXT TWO weeks I did my damndest to track down Jess, hampered by ignorance and a strange paralysis of the imagination. Everyone I asked—discreetly, for the most part—claimed to have heard nothing. Bell insisted Collie had left him in the dark, and Leila's indignation about Jess not having clued her in seemed genuine. What else could I do? I wondered. Run advertisements in every newspaper in Montana? Hire a detective, assuming I knew where to find one? I even called one I found in the Great Falls phone book, but his fees were out of my league.

It seemed to me that, despite their facile congratulations about my prize money, everyone was looking at me with pity, as if they were speculating about the next blow fate would level at our family. At home, Mom grew increasingly silent. She'd decided that, with Jess gone, taking care of the herd was simply beyond our abilities, so she'd sent most of the cattle to the Brickers, our nearest neighbors. They agreed to care for them, along with theirs, in return for getting to keep half the proceeds when the calves were sold at the July auction. She let me know that someone—presumably Randy—was paying the mortgage, so we didn't have to worry about losing the ranch, at least for the moment. And she kept herself occupied with the chickens and the two milk cows and by baking cakes and dried-fruit pies that she took to the Redmond general store, where they sold well.

She produced one of her prize concoctions, a German chocolate cake, for my fifteenth birthday. We celebrated it quietly with a dinner of all my favorite dishes: mashed potatoes, fried chicken, and store-bought tartar sauce, a peculiar addiction I'd acquired in fourth grade. Mom's present, a beautiful lilac cotton nightgown trimmed with white lace threaded with light-blue ribbon, made me wonder where she'd found it. That afternoon Bell had given me a bottle of Evening in Paris and a gold ankle chain from a jewelry store in Great Falls. I loved the way it glinted against my skin, and I hated covering it up with a thick white sock. That night I put on the nightgown, patted on the cologne, and arranged myself on my bed, ankles coyly crossed, imagining scenes of ungovernable passion between Bell and me, until the cold forced me under the covers.

Keeping back fifty dollars, I'd used my prize money to open a savings account for my college education, or for the emergencies I worried about lying in the dark: our family thrown off the ranch, our belongings stuffed into the car, the three of us hitting the road, bound for—where? Part of me wanted to run to Mom for reassurance that we'd be okay no matter what, that I didn't have to carry the burden of this worry. The other part refused to add the weight of my fears to what she already had to bear.

One afternoon, as I left school and walked down Maple Street toward the cafe, hoping to see Bell or Jess, there stood Randy on the corner. Before I could turn around, he walked up and grabbed my arm.

"Win." He looked awful: pasty-faced, clothes hanging off him, rusty stubble covering his face. His clothes smelled musty. "I need to talk to you."

"Forget it." I pulled my arm away and walked back toward the school. Randy fell into step beside me.

"How's Marie?"

"She's okay. We're all okay."

"I need to see her." I glanced at him, at his slumped shoulders, his thinning hair. "We need to be together. You have to believe me."

"*We* don't need *you*. Nobody needs you." I tried to inject all the contempt I'd felt toward him in the past two months into my words.

"Pete's my son. He needs me, you know that. And Marie—we belong together." He grabbed my arm again. "Tell her—"

"I'm not telling her *anything* from you!" I shouted. "You're a drunk and a coward, and because of you—"

"I don't drink anymore," he interrupted. "I haven't had a drink since the funeral."

"Big deal." Again I snatched my arm away. "Just leave us alone."

"I can't." He wiped his forehead with a mittened hand. Despite the cold he was perspiring heavily. "I'll do anything I have to to get her back. To get you all back. You don't understand this yet, but once you really love someone, you can't stop loving them just because you're supposed to."

He stopped as I kept walking, staring straight ahead.

"She's in my bones." His voice followed me as I hurried away. "*Tell her, Win.*"

Like hell I will, I vowed. Let her find out some other way.

THE VERY DAY I decided I had to look for a part-time job—assuming there were any—Bell took me to Selby's shed and announced that he planned to take an open-ended leave of absence from school and from Redmond. He was set to leave in two days, on Saturday, as soon as he got his car into shape.

"But why?" I protested, shocked and hurt. We'd been meeting regularly, after school and on Saturdays after my lesson. We'd hang out at the Two Elks, where people generally left us alone, barring a few unsuccessful attempts at provoking a fight, or at the Wagon Wheel, a decrepit Indian bar at the edge of Indian town, where at first I got the same kind of looks Bell had in the cafe. After a while the Indians seemed to accept my presence, perhaps grudgingly admiring my stubborn persistence, which they may have interpreted as loyalty. The truth is, we had almost no choice. Bell refused to take me to his house, and I no longer felt comfortable going to Frances'. Bell never asked me why, so I assumed he had figured it out or was too diplomatic to ask.

"Why do you want to leave now?" I repeated. "What about school?" *What about me?* I wanted to add.

"That can wait." He stared past the workbench with its built-in circular saw, his hands resting on his knees. "Something big is going on."

"You mean the war?" Over the last three years, several boys had left Redmond for Vietnam, none younger than eighteen, therefore none I knew well. I couldn't believe Bell would go, and he wasn't eighteen yet.

He let out a derisive snort. "More like the war at home. The one right here."

"What do you mean?"

He turned his cool gaze on me, more remote than I'd seen in months. "You wouldn't understand."

A cold wind rushed into the space that had torn open between us. "I might," I said tentatively.

He stared at me a moment, then sat down on the bench and lowered his eyes. "Never mind that. That's not the main thing." He pointed to the empty bench beside him and I sat down. "I'm going to see Collie and Jess."

"But. . . . How did you find out where they are?"

"Collie called me a couple of days ago and said they needed money. I'll take them what I've got."

"Where are they?"

He shook his head. I gripped his arm hard. "Tell me! I've got a right to know!"

He smiled wryly. "You couldn't keep a secret from your mother if your life depended on it. Everything's written right there on your face." He put his palm against my cheek. "I love that about you. But it sure can get you in a lot of trouble, you and anyone else who needs to stay hidden."

An idea shot through my head like a blast of air. "I want to go, too."

He stared at me and laughed shortly. "You're nuts."

"I've got money, too. I want to see her. You can leave me there with Jess, and I'll go back myself on the bus. Please, Bell, I have to see her."

My voice was trembling, and I fought to bring it under control. Bell was frowning at me, not unkindly, but with intense concentration, as if judging something about me on which my entire future might rest.

"If you don't take me, I'll tell your mother about it."

A second's silence, and then he let out another short laugh, a harsh bark without a trace of humor. He stood up abruptly. "You think she'd care? You think she'd get off her barstool? Or stop bringing home the skins she fucks for booze money?"

I sucked in my breath. No one had ever deliberately used that word in conversation with me. Bell turned away from me and rested his arms on the workbench and leaned forward, his head bent. I got up. "Bell—"

"Half the time she doesn't know or care if I'm around or not. The other half she screams at me to help her, take care of her, bring her whiskey, or get out of the house." He straightened and took a deep breath. "So I might as well get lost. What's here for me, anyway? Except you." He looked at me directly. "And we won't be together much longer."

I opened my mouth to protest, but he held up his hand. "You know it's true."

But I didn't. All I knew was how much I wanted to lean against his body, to feel his hands on my back, his warm skin flush against my face. Everything my orderly mind had collected—the life that lay ahead of me, college, music, travel to every country in the world, rooms I'd live in that, no matter how I tried, I could never see him sharing—flew about like feathers in a windstorm. I crossed and stood in front of him, slipping my arms around his waist, raising my mouth to his, letting my hands wander underneath his belt, pushing my body against the bulge at his groin. I wasn't being coy; there was nothing I wanted just then except not to be away from him.

In turn, his arms went around my waist and he pulled me tight against him, gripping the back of my blouse, kissing me harder, running the fingers of one hand along my breasts. He pulled my hair with his other hand until my head tipped back, and licked my throat, my ears, as my breathing grew shallow and rough and my knees buckled.

Suddenly he shoved me away. I stumbled backward, my calves

thwacking against the bench. I clutched at the work table behind me to keep from falling.

"No." He was panting, his eyes narrowed as if I were an enemy, a wild animal he had to keep at bay. "Not here. Not until I have—something."

I let myself sink onto the bench and hung my head, suddenly ashamed, frightened of the humming heat we brought to life so easily, tingling with frustration. He took a step toward me and placed one hand on my head. I leaned my face against his belly.

"All right." His voice was hoarse, almost unfriendly. "I'll take you there. We'll leave Saturday."

That was all we said as we left the shed, crunched through the snowy back yard, sat quietly during coffee and cookies with Selby and Roone, negotiated the icy roads in Bell's Chevy to the ranch. But we both knew a promise had been made, that we'd crossed the border into treacherous territory we could only visit, not own.

And an image of the map I'd studied carefully in the days after Marilyn's last note kept rising in my imagination. Lame Deer and the Cheyenne reservation lay only about eighty miles beyond Billings.

I SNUCK OUT OF the house early on Saturday morning to meet Bell's car waiting at the road, the fifty dollars I'd kept aside in my purse, the tote bag I'd smuggled past a still-dozing Mom the day before now in his trunk. I'd left a note for Mom where I knew she wouldn't find it until we were long gone. Collie had an older cousin in Billings, it turned out, who owned a garage and had offered Collie a job. Jess and he were living with the cousin until they got enough money together to rent a place of their own. Jess was looking for a job too. And, Collie had told Bell, she was still pregnant.

"When will they get married?" I asked as we rolled onto the highway, the sky still dark, the moon crisp and bright overhead. "Did he say?"

Bell shrugged lightly.

"Are they going to stay in Billings? Not come back to Redmond?"

"Hey, they just got there two weeks ago. Give them a chance."

"What kind of chance? Working in a grimy garage, having a baby in a tiny apartment, stuck in one little town all your life?"

"Hey, Win." Bell's eyebrows creased into a frown. "Some people, that's exactly what they want. A place of their own, a family, a job to go to. Maybe *you* don't like the idea, but they do." He glanced at me briefly. "Not everyone is you. Thank god."

He grinned, then arched his back, rotated his head to relieve his cramped neck.

"That's probably why we like each other. We're both off the beaten track, right? You're headed off to college, book learning, music, ideas coming out of your ears. Once you're out of here, I can't see you settling in one place for a long, long time."

"And you?" I countered. I realized I'd rarely heard him talk about his future, in what direction he wanted to set his course. He'd dropped out of basketball, which might have opened the road to an athletic scholarship, without much of a backward glance. But what had taken its place, besides me and the time he'd devoted to helping my family—and that, it was now clear, he saw as no more than temporary?

"Oh, I'm out of here. There's going to be a camp set up in Pa-Sapa, the Black Hills. What you call Mt. Rushmore. AIM is organizing it. They did one there last fall. Of course, no one out here reported it. But AIM is growing. It'll turn things around for us. It's got to. And I'll be part of it."

He noticed my startled expression.

"Yeah, that's right. I'm a bad-ass angry skin. That surprise you?" He snorted contemptuously. "That's all you hear about it on Whitey's radio. According to them, we're out to overthrow the government and kill every white man west of the Mississippi."

It was true that I'd heard some scathing reports about the American Indian Movement's ungrateful attitude, its determination to break every law on the books. Its unlawful occupation of Alcatraz had been played up by the newspapers and radio the year before. That the judicious, restrained Bell I knew was a member, applauded their tactics, and was ready to participate in their rebellion confounded me.

"They've got it all wrong, as usual. They make us sound like crazies and criminals, when it's them who've broken every treaty they ever made. They don't tell you the real story, about what's really going on, how the whites frame skins like Russ Means or Dennis Banks and stick them in the iron house because they're getting people to really listen and take us seriously. All we're doing is trying to get back to what we once were. What we'll be again."

His voice had deepened, and his words, freed from self-consciousness, flowed in a passionate current. I wanted to be swept along by them, but the fierce expression in his eyes turned skeptical when he looked at me, as if I were a rock against which he was prepared to break, rather than a wave in his torrent. "I feel bad for you." The words slapped against me, stunning me. "You don't know who you are, and I do."

He paused, listening to the hiss of the tires, the sputter of radio static interspersed with a woman's voice wailing along with a tinny guitar. "I think I know what you're going through. It's sort of how I felt before I hooked up with AIM. Like you woke up one morning and discovered a new part of yourself that had been there all along, but hidden. Quiet. And now it's alive and awake, and you don't know what to do with it. Like—like a third eye. Or a pair of wings."

He grinned, pleased by the image.

"You've got to decide what you're going to do with this new thing. It makes you weird—everyone else with smooth backs, and you with your strange new wings hanging out there. Are you gonna try and stuff them back where they came from? But you can't. Not forever. That's what your mother tried to do, and look at what happened." He nodded once. "They just popped out again, when she didn't expect it, and there's hell to pay.

"You might as well not fight it. You're different. And that means you'll never be in just one world again. You're not a bird, and you're not just an ordinary human being. You're a freak of nature."

It wasn't just me he was talking about, I realized. It was himself, too. It was as if someone had turned off the stove just as my indignation reached the boiling point.

"So are we angels?" I asked.

"Us?"

"Well, you're one, too. Part of you in one world, part in another."

"I know which world I belong to. Do you?"

I had no answer.

"Hey, maybe you're the next step in evolution," he offered. "If you can find your way, you'll be ahead of us all."

"I've never heard you talk like this," I ventured. This new Bell might take some getting used to.

"Surprised?"

"Yes. It's not just what you're saying. Usually you don't. . .all those words—"

"Didn't expect me to be such a windbag, huh?" He grinned. "It's getting away. Like when you take off your shoes after a hot, hard game. Feels good, doesn't it?"

He reached over and took my hand. We drove for several miles, smooth and steady, as if we'd sailed unexpectedly into a calm inlet out of a windy sea. This was the right time, I decided. "Bell, listen."

"Hm?"

"I've got an aunt I've never met, on the Lame Deer reservation. I just found out last week."

He said nothing.

"She's my grandfather's sister."

He still said nothing.

"I want to meet her. I want you to take me there."

He turned and raised his eyebrows at me in a silent question. I nodded. His face broadened into a wide, pleased grin that lit up his face like moonlight.

"Are you kidding?" he said. "I wouldn't miss this for the world."

BY THE TIME WE reached Billings, it was dark again. We'd had clear, cold weather the whole way, the roads dry, straight once the hills disappeared behind us, after Butte, with the sky stretching hugely overhead from horizon to horizon, making for a fast, easy trip. We stopped at a gas station in the center of town, and Bell went into the lighted office. The ear-muffed attendant inside pointed to the phone fastened to the far wall. Bell dialed, spoke briefly, dialed again, ran back, and slid into the front seat.

"Shit, that guy must be an Eskimo," he gasped, breathing on his reddened hands. "They're coming to meet us here." He grabbed the back of my neck. "Warm me up quick, before my fingers fall off."

His hands were so cold I shrieked, and we tussled briefly, giggling like grade-schoolers, slipping back to childhood, revisiting the last place I'd felt completely safe.

A few moments later a car's headlights lit the dashboard, and Collie's green pickup pulled alongside us, Jess' smiling face at the passenger window.

We all spilled out, laughing, hugging, slapping backs. Jess held me close for what seemed a long time.

"It's so good to see you," she murmured into my ear.

"Then you're not mad at me?"

"For what?" She laughed, "I was when I heard Mom at the door that day. But now everything's different."

She did look different to me, subtly but clearly, her face soft and relaxed, slightly fuller, the strained dark edge gone. Her movements were slower, her old gracefulness returned. I remembered the last look I'd had of her, writhing in pain on Frances' bed, and relief washed over me, making my eyes sting.

"Don't cry, stupid." She wrinkled her nose at me in mock disgust. "What's to cry about? Dinner's waiting."

"Let's go before we freeze our asses off," Collie called from the other side of the car. As I turned to open the car door, Jess put her hand on my arm.

"You can drive back with me, and Collie'll go with Bell."

She led me back to the pickup. With a wave to Bell, I climbed into the seat, avoiding the hump of broken spring. Jess backed up expertly and followed Bell's taillights, closely at first, then slowing down as they sped away. Now she seemed more subdued.

"I wanted us to get a little more time to talk." She brushed her hair back from her forehead in the familiar gesture I hadn't realized how much I'd missed.

"How's the baby?"

"Fine." She put a hand on her barely swelling stomach and returned it to the steering wheel.

"I brought you some money." I scrabbled in my purse for the envelope and opened it, fanning out the bills.

"Where'd you get all that?"

"I won it, Jess! I came in second in the competition. This is the prize money—well, some of it. I kept the rest of it in the bank. I couldn't withdraw it without Mom's signature."

Jess smiled and gently pushed away the money. "I can't take this, Win."

"Yes, you can. Bell told me you need it."

"He shouldn't have told you that."

"Why not? Is it something else you think I'm too young to know about?"

"It was supposed to be private between Collie and Bell."

"Why? Don't you think Bell and I *talk*?" Honesty got the better of me. "Actually he wasn't going to tell me at first, but I wormed it out of him. And he couldn't stop me from bringing the money."

I stuck the envelope in her coat pocket.

"How'd you manage to get here? I'll bet anything you didn't tell Mom."

"I left her a note."

She sighed.

"I just feel like I'm a bad influence on you. Here you are, running off, handling stuff you shouldn't be dealing with."

"Stop treating me like a baby!" My voice was shrill and discordant, startling me almost as much as it did her.

She eased the car to a stop. "Win. Are you—being careful?"

I didn't know whether to laugh or cry. I knew her question was about sex. Part of me was flattered that she assumed I'd joined the exciting club she herself belonged to. Another part wanted to hide my face, to remain hidden and private, to conceal from her what I didn't yet know.

"I don't want to be nosy, I'm just—I don't want you to have to go through what I did. Not that it hasn't turned out fine for me," she added hastily. "But you're not me."

"If I hear that one more time, I'll scream. I'm always careful. Haven't I always been, when it counts?"

She pursed her lips and nodded, guiding the car back onto the road. "Here we are."

She pulled behind Bell's empty Chevy in front of a tiny house, more like a cottage, its paint peeling, gutters sagging, blinds shut, the boards on the porch uneven and splintered. As I reached for the door handle, she grabbed my arm.

"Listen, I almost forgot. There's something I wanted to tell you."

"What? It's cold out here." I shivered theatrically. "Tell me quick."

"It can wait." She slipped out of the car and hurried up the walk. I followed her through the front door into a tiny living room that seemed packed with furniture and bodies: Bell standing next to a broken-down brown Barcalounger, Collie slumped onto a burnt-orange tattered tweed sofa.

Everyone kept the conversation light and playful during dinner, which consisted of macaroni and cheese and canned peas. I kept stealing quick peeks at Jess' belly. Obviously she—they —had made a decision to have the baby. . .and then what? Collie seemed content enough, though it was hard to tell how much his exhilaration came from Bell's presence, the buddy he hadn't known how much he'd missed until he suddenly reappeared.

After dinner, as we sat around in the living room, Jess asked the obvious question. "So how long are you here for?"

"Just tonight," Bell replied.

"Back to school, huh?"

"Win wants me to take her someplace."

Jess and Collie looked at me.

"To see Aunt Moon. Mom's aunt," I sputtered. "You know, her father's sister. She lives over in Lame Deer."

"You're going on the Rez?" Collie sounded incredulous. Bell's face tightened.

"Hey, I'm from Pine Ridge, remember? That's where I'm headed, after we see your aunt." That was directed at Jess. From the way Jess turned her eyes away, I could tell they were still tiptoeing around that particular sleeping tiger.

"Look," Bell went on smoothly. "Everyone's gotta do what they've gotta do. You gotta settle down and get a job. I gotta go be a blood. Join the AIM, see the world." He uttered a humorless snort of laughter. "Don't worry, I'll be in touch. And I'll bring Win back here before I take off."

"Great, so we'll see you again." Jess smiled at him, then at me. "Listen, you guys. You must be ready to crump out. I have a hard time keeping my eyes open after nine."

She hesitated, looking over at Collie, who wouldn't meet her eyes. "Where do you want to sleep?"

Neither Bell nor I said a word. I hadn't been able to bring myself to say directly to Bell that I wanted to be alone with him, and I certainly wasn't going to say it in front of Jess and Collie.

"Well, there's the couch here," she went on. "It unfolds into a double bed. And there's a cot in the closet. You can set it up in the kitchen. I left some sheets there on the TV. Make up your mind, and we'll see you in the morning."

Jess turned toward the doorway, then came back and put her arms around me. "Don't worry," she whispered. "It's more fun than you can imagine." I felt my face turn beet red as she slipped her arm in Collie's. "Come on, big boy," she said to him.

Collie threw Bell a quick nod, half-amused, half-complicit, and left the room with Jess. I looked uncertainly at Bell, who stared back impassively. Now that this momentous decision about my life was firmly in my hands, I wanted to throw it back like a hot potato. Only no one seemed willing to catch it.

"Up to you," Bell murmured.

My heart began to pound unevenly, and my throat was suddenly as dry as sand. I realized I was staring at the floor. It took all my courage to raise my head and look at him, at his deep eyes sunk in shadow, the flat planes of his cheeks highlighted by the overhead lamp, his solemn mouth, his long legs, his hands thrust deep in the pockets of his jeans. And I knew that, if I didn't leap into this abyss after what I wanted right now more than anything in the world, I would never forgive myself as long as I lived.

CHAPTER 25

W HILE BELL REGISTERED IN the office and paid for the room, I shivered in the Chevy, slumped down in the seat, watching the green and orange neon letters flicker, sputter, fade out, and catch and glow again, spelling out *Sleeping Giant Motel*. Bell had found out from Collie that, unlike many others, they rented rooms to Indians, though how they'd have reacted if they'd seen me with him we weren't eager to find out. Two other cars were parked in the lot, along with a truck so ancient its color had faded to a dark wash, and a Volkswagen camper decorated with haphazard multicolored designs of butterflies, clouds, and flowers undreamed of in nature. I tried not to think of who else might be inside these rooms, concentrating on remembering Jess' expression as I'd said goodbye. She'd never asked anything else or come out of their bedroom when we slipped out the door, and I loved her for it.

Bell slid back into the car and drove to the far end of the row of symmetrically aligned doors and windows that studded the one-story pea-green building.

"I asked for the quietest room," he muttered, guiding the car into the last space. "For privacy."

My face grew hot again, an occurrence by now so frequent it felt like my normal condition. Bell pulled our bags from the back seat, unlocked the front door, and stood aside to let me enter the darkened room. It smelled of mildew and pine room freshener, with undertones of Lysol and of something pungent and mysterious, animal-like and musky.

He flicked on the wall switch, and the fluorescent fixture on the ceiling flickered on, revealing a double bed covered by a faded yellowed-white chenille spread, its tufts worn down to nubs. A multicolored hooked rug covered the ugly brown-and-green-speckled linoleum between the edge of the bed and the door to the bathroom. On the far side of the room, a shade with one long tear down the middle covered a window, the radiator below it hissing and clanking like an angry dragon.

He put down the bags, crossed to the window, and pulled the flowered drapes hanging on either side across it, hiding the tattered shade.

"Turn on the lamp," he said, nodding at the end table next to the bed. As I did, he recrossed the floor and switched off the overhead light. The small rose-colored shade cast a soft light over the pillows and the walls, and suddenly the room was transformed from repulsive to almost homey, from a place where my imagination conjured up white-coated doctors with gleaming instruments who lurked in the corners waiting to perform unspeakable acts, into one where whatever was to happen would happen between me and the Bell I loved.

I sat down on the edge of the bed. He tossed his coat onto the chair in the far corner and sat next to me. He unbuttoned my coat and laid it behind me, then leaned toward me. I felt his breath hot on my nose, then the familiar, velvety pressure of his mouth. He slid his hands onto the sides of my cheeks, then down my sides. I wrapped my hands around his waist, kissing him back, pushing my chest against his.

"Open your eyes." His voice was low, urgent. I hadn't realized my eyes were squeezed shut. He held me away from him.

"All right?" He was giving me this last chance to turn back. But if I went forward, how could I promise not to try at some point to withdraw from what might become—what? Unbearable? A line from a song I hadn't realized I remembered popped into my head, a song Randy had often sung when Jess and I were small, until Mom decided— a year too late—that Jess, at least, might be catching on:

> *"Cheer up, my girl, what ails you*
> *Will never kill," said she.*

Jess had explained it to me: A mother is reassuring her daughter about what has just happened to her on her wedding night. At the time I barely understood what the words meant. Now I repeated them to myself like a prayer: It can't kill me. It can't be all that bad.

So I nodded and Bell slid his hand under my sweater, pulled it over my head, undid my bra, my jeans, undressed me carefully, his eyes washing over my skin, my breasts, leaning forward to lick my eyelids, my ears, my neck. In turn I unbuttoned his shirt, slid it away from his shoulders to reveal his smooth-skinned chest with its nipples, twins to my own, puckered and taut. I brushed my fingers over them, and he drew in his breath. He rose, and I slipped my hands behind him, caressing the globes of his buttocks, burrowing my nose into the concavity between his ribs and his waist, the swell of his crotch humming between my breasts.

I looked up at his blood-darkened face, his lips slightly apart. His eyes were fastened on me, waiting, I knew, for what I did next: slip his belt free from its loop, unbuckle it, work the button of his jeans open, and slowly lower the zipper. I was petrified and fascinated; I wanted to keep looking and at the same time to curl up, eyes hidden, slipping free from all responsibility for what was happening. I slid his jeans and shorts down his hips and jerked backward as the purplish cylinder of his penis with its half-tunnel veins slipped free and pointed upward at me.

My expression must have registered my astonishment, because Bell laughed, and the sound released me.

"Your eyes are practically popping out of your head," he grinned. "Not what you thought?"

I'd felt it before, but we'd never gone further than groping and stroking inside our clothes. Now I couldn't take my eyes from it, overawed by its size and its odd dissociation from all the other angles of his body. I reached out and touched the tip tentatively, then pulled my hand back: It was moist.

"Wait a second."

He fumbled for his jeans and fished in the pocket for a foil-wrapped square that looked for all the world like an Alka-Seltzer packet. He tore it open and pulled out a circle of amber rubber which he unrolled down the length of his penis until it coated it, changing its color from purple to a pinkish-beige.

"Go ahead, touch it. It won't bite."

I cupped my fingers around its sleek circumference, feeling it grow from tepid to warm. He pressed my shoulders gently, guiding me backward onto the bed. He stroked my thighs, brushed me gently, then more firmly, between my legs. Suddenly my own body took over, arching against his hand, my thighs gripping tight, my pelvis thrusting over and over against his fist until I shuddered uncontrollably as I had so often at night in my bed as I imagined us doing exactly what we were doing now.

Even as my thighs relaxed, I felt him ease them apart and push himself into me. It hurt; then it hurt more, and then even more. Just as I was about to call out for him to stop, he slid completely in, bringing his pelvis flush against mine, letting out a sound between a gasp and a sigh. He lay still a moment; then his hips began to move, slowly at first, then faster, until I knew he wouldn't be able to stop if an earthquake brought the roof down on our heads. I grabbed the mounds of his buttocks and felt the muscles clench and unclench, listened to the rasping breaths against my ear grow louder and louder until he stiffened from head to toe and groaned. His body heaved in slow undulations, three, four times, flexed tight once more, then relaxed and settled heavily onto mine.

I watched him as his breathing grew slower, more regular, sensing my own blood ebb and flow, his heart thump in rhythm as it eased, feeling proud of myself, awed and envious at his loss of control, pleased to have caused him pleasure. I worked one arm free from his weight and stroked his forehead, smoothing the long hanks of hair away from his face and tucking them behind his ear. He opened his eyes and smiled at me.

"Win. Win-ta. Beautiful Win."

Slowly he eased his hips away from mine.

"No." I pushed against him.

"I have to."

He pulled his body away and reached between us. The rubber made a sucking sound as he freed himself and dropped it over the side of the bed. We watched each other, touching here and there in astonishment, my finger on his cheek, his hand on my shoulder. There, I thought, it didn't kill me. I'm glad I did it. I even enjoyed it. I even want to do it again.

Being young and healthy, of course we did, then again when we woke up during the night, and again early in the morning, our pleasure finally brought to a halt by my soreness, our ravenous hunger for food, and the fact that our small supply of condoms had run out. By the time we were dressed, it was full daylight, and the parking lot was empty. We stopped at the first cafe we saw and bolted down platefuls of ham and eggs, toast, home fries, and coffee, until our stomachs felt as satisfied as the rest of us.

As we drove away from Billings and turned onto route 90 toward the Crow reservation, I kept stealing glances at Bell. He didn't look different, yet he did. Or was the change in my vision? My body felt fuller, as if I were pressing outward against my own skin. This is me, I said to myself, the me Bell touched, wants to touch again. I slid closer to him, let my hand rest on his thigh, drunk with wanton daring. He lifted his arm and slid it around my shoulders, smiling slightly at the expanse of snow-encrusted dry grass, interspersed with blackish strips of willows in the gullies, that stretched endlessly on either side of the road.

At Crow Agency we stopped to visit the Custer Battlefield monument. The rolling plain opened before us, covered by dried stalks of winter-brown grass flecked with frozen clumps of frost. The wind whipped our hair and died down, only to lash us again.

As we walked among the grimy gray-white headstones, the carved names of Custer's regiment half eaten away by eighty years of wind-driven snow, hail, rain, and grit, the connection between us thinned and snapped. Bell strode ahead of me, pulled into himself like a turtle into its shell, hands sunk in his pockets, eyes narrowed against the wind. I wanted to go and stand next to him, our arms linked against the world, but I couldn't. I didn't dare. I thought I knew what he was thinking: all that had happened to his people, their slow destruction by mine.

But were they really mine? It didn't seem fair to include me. Why were we here, anyway, headed where we were headed, if not to connect me with the part of myself that included him? As I tried to summon up the will to walk over to him, realizing I needed even more courage for this than for what I'd done the night before, he stopped and turned his head toward me.

"This is where we made them sweat," he announced. He pointed to a spot about a hundred yards away. "That's where they rode right into the trap. It never occurred to them we could out-think them. They never learn."

I joined him, staring at the hummock of grass, imagining the column of blue coats, their horses rearing as a rain of arrows and bullets tore into them, bodies falling, men frantically reining their mounts into a circle, cut down again and again, brown-skinned riders racing into their midst, knives flashing, blood pouring into the grass.

"Why does it have to be that way?" Even to my ears the question sounded childish, a futile protest against a force as inevitable as gravity. Bell threw me an impatient look and turned back to the car. I matched my stride to his.

"They deserved what they got," I said. "For all they did to. . ." I didn't know how to finish: To you? To your people? Mine? Us? He stopped.

"You know, they told themselves for years how bloodthirsty we were, calling us savages, sneaky, thieves, killers. But who killed who? Who stole from who?"

He swept his arm over the wide stretch of land and sky.

"Once this was ours. All of it. Now it's theirs, except for the tiny piss-poor bits they let us have. And they hate us for not being grateful."

His mouth pinched into a tight line. After a moment, he took a deep breath and looked at me.

"It's not fair to expect you to be part of this. You've grown up in your world. When I look at you, I see a white girl. And you look at me and see an Indian. Even though now I know you've got almost as much Indian in you as I've got white in me. Oh, yeah," he answered my frown of surprise. "My mother's grandmother was half white. Her mother was raped by a soldier. And my other grandfather had a white father who married a Sioux woman when he came here to settle. Lots of that out here."

He nodded slowly.

"But no way can I be part white, the way *you* can decide if you want to be part Indian. You get the choice, I don't. The white world doesn't want me, except to help fight their fucking wars. Don't expect the skins to be happy to see *you* knock on their doors."

My chest felt as if it were filling with stones that weighed on my heart so painfully I almost cried out.

"Why do you hate me?" I managed to say. "I thought we—" Once again I couldn't finish.

Bell's eyebrows drew together in shock and for a moment he seemed paralyzed. Then he grabbed me tight against him, his chin resting on my hair. "God, Win," he whispered. "I don't hate you."

"Then why are you so angry at me?"

"I'm not. It's not you. It's—" I felt him pull the wind-whipped strands of my hair from his mouth— "I guess I wanted you to be prepared for how they think on the Rez. So you'd be ready. Not just for that, but—" he hesitated, then tipped my head back to look at him. "I guess I'm getting us ready to not be together."

The stones in my chest grew heavier. Until that moment I'd managed to forget his plan not to return to Redmond.

"You don't have to go."

"Yes, I do. I know what will happen to us if I stay."

A blaze of illumination shot through me.

"No, you don't." I pulled myself away from him. "You *don't* know, and I don't know, and *that's* what you can't stand. Not being sure. You'd rather make it happen than wait to see if maybe it won't."

He looked away from me, tightening his mouth. I'm braver than you, I thought. I'm willing to bear not knowing, though the pain is as heart-burning as jealousy, and you're not. Coward. Appalled by the realization, I tried to take the thought back, but I couldn't. I saw his face harden as he absorbed the words I'd spoken and caught an echo, perhaps, of those I hadn't. For a moment I came close to despising him, seeing him shrink under my contempt, darken, grow thin and raggedy, pitiful and helpless, and then I couldn't stand it. I wrenched my vision back through sheer force of will, and suddenly he was Bell again.

For who was I to judge, really? First walk a mile in someone else's shoes, the old saying went. He'd had to walk his whole life in mine, while I had only begun to slip his on. I reached for his hand. "Maybe you're right," I said. "Why wait around to be hurt?"

He shook his head and reached up to smooth his hair. "It's not you I wonder about," he said quietly, "as much as the rest of the world. No one can stand up against it forever. Look what happened to your own grandparents."

I stared at him in astonishment.

"Oh, yeah." He smiled wryly and took my hand, swinging it as we began to walk toward the car. "We know. You think your story is just yours, but it isn't. It belongs to us, too."

I knew he meant: to our people. Ours. I was part of who he is, and was, and would become, and he part of me, no matter what else would happen to each of us in all the years ahead. The stones left in my chest rolled away, and the blue air, the sensuous undulations of the plains, the crystalline sky, expanded to fill the space their absence left behind.

CHAPTER 26

N O FENCE, NO GATE, no line marked our entry onto the Crow and then the Cheyenne reservation—only a small faded sign you'd miss if you happened to be turning your head to say something or to fiddle with the radio dial as you zoomed by. If you were paying attention, you might have noticed that, once inside, the metallic flashes of gold and silver beer cans, the glistening amber and green bottle shards along the roadside, grew more frequent. Shreds of crumpled Pampers stuck to fences and bushes. Every so often we passed a ramshackle house or cabin, usually with the skeletons of two or three rusted cars and trucks, or abandoned washing machines, standing forlornly in front, a wobbly TV antenna bent sideways over the tarpaper roof. In one place a brown-and-white horse galloped in parallel with us until he was brought up abruptly by a fence. Here and there deserted stands announced *Indian Crafts For Sale*, manned now by ghosts. Everything seemed increasingly meaner, poorer, shabbier.

Noticing this made me intensely uncomfortable. The poverty and squalor oppressed me; consciousness of my own relative privilege made me squirm, knowing I'd done nothing to earn it. And what about Bell? He was very quiet. Should I pretend I didn't see what I saw? Or should I simply not comment on it? Perhaps he would know what I noticed, even if I said nothing about it. That thought both comforted me and made me uneasy. He seemed to be joining the ranks of those who, like

Jess and Mom in her sharper moments, could insinuate themselves into my brain.

"How are we going to find her?" was what I finally chose to say. "I don't have an address."

Bell smiled briefly.

"No addresses needed out here. Everyone knows where everyone lives."

Two kids, brandishing sticks and chasing each other around a yard, flashed by.

"Did you ever want to live on the reservation?" I asked. He didn't answer. Was this a stupid question? Insulting? I realized again how little I knew. At least I did know he was a Lakota, from the Oglala branch. "Sioux" was what the French called the Lakota when they misheard the enemy Ojibwa's name for them—'cutthroats'. Just as I was getting ready to kick myself, he rolled his window down. Cold air rushed across our faces.

"I've got about a hundred cousins and aunts and uncles out on Pine Ridge. Been there lots of times, summers mostly. Not lately. My mother grew up there. It's in South Dakota. That's where the name 'Dakota' comes from."

"Why isn't it 'Lakota'? Like 'North Lakota,' 'South Lakota.'" I couldn't help grinning at the unfamiliar lilt of it, as if I'd heard my name mispronounced by a foreigner.

Bell didn't smile back. Maybe he thought I was making fun of him. "Whole damn place should be 'Lakota'," he muttered. "'The United States of Lakota.' From the Mississippi to the Rockies, and down to the Rio Grande."

"But what about the other tribes? The Apaches and the Hopi and the Navajo and the Cheyenne?" My tribe. "Wouldn't they each want their own piece?"

"They used to fight each other all the time over it. Except the Lakota and the Cheyenne. *They* never fought, not since Whitey showed up."

I felt a small jolt of pleasure at this unexpected ping of harmony, as if a silver cord vibrated between us.

"They did what everyone's gonna be doing now—they got together to fight the real enemy," he continued, rolling the window back up till only a few inches were left open. The wind whistled through the crack like a distant flute.

"And yeah, I've thought plenty about living on the Rez. When I'm there, I can relax. Really relax. Everyone's like me. No walking on eggshells. And I know, no matter how far I fall, I won't disappear, like I could outside. People take care of each other on the Rez; they share whatever they have, even if it's next to nothing. And that's just about what it is, nothing."

He reached into his shirt pocket and, to my shock, extracted a cigarette and a matchbook, and took his hands off the wheel to strike a match.

"You don't smoke!"

"Seeing is believing." He held the cigarette next to the window. "This is why I don't live there."

"What?"

"This." He rolled the cigarette between his fingers. "All there is to do here is smoke and drink. You hang around a while, and something creeps in and takes you over. Kinda like those Pod People." We'd seen *Invasion of the Body Snatchers* one Saturday afternoon in January. "There's no jobs, and even worse, if you try to find one, or get something going, like a business or a project, people look at you as if you're selling out to Whitey. You get no support. You're just an apple."

"A what?"

"Red on the outside, white on the inside."

"What do you mean?"

"Lots of skins see anything that gets you ahead as telling them they're not as good as you, that you put yourself above them. It's the down side of sticking together, putting the tribe ahead of each separate person."

He shrugged lightly, inhaled, flicked the ash onto the floor between us, and glanced at me apologetically. He seemed both older and less accessible than before, and at the same time more vulnerable in his self-consciousness.

"Bell." I put my hand on his thigh and slid closer to rest my head on his shoulder. I love you, I wanted to say. *I believe in you.* I'll fill you up, I'll make you believe in yourself. Yet I couldn't say it. I couldn't ask him to do for me what he couldn't do alone.

"Things aren't always going to be like that, though." He interrupted my train of thought. "That's why I'm going where I'm going. Not just for me. For the people, so they'll see. And when they see, they'll change."

His words sliced the air. Maybe he was persuading himself as much as me, I realized. Still, for a moment I envied him. Unlike me, unless you counted music, he had a cause, a passion greater than his own personal history, even though he might be clinging to it with the wishful desperation of a rodeo cowboy on a bucking steer.

THE TOWN OF LAME Deer turned out to consist of a collection of a few buildings, some tacked together from pieces of weathered wood and some of rain-streaked concrete. We stopped in front of the general store. Bundled-up Indians sat on the steps in the weak winter sun, mostly old, some young, quite a few with beer cans in their hands.

I realized I was more scared than I'd thought. I already knew what it felt like to be stared at with curiosity, with bewilderment, even with hostility, both by myself and with Bell. But only when surrounded by people like me, of my color, and knowing not too far away lay the refuge of my family. Not here. I felt again the angry eyes of the Indian kids outside Dr. Elwood's office that night of the dance, heard the anonymous voice warning me to stay away. My color—my skin, my hair—meant I couldn't hide. Here, I was the other, the different one. In 'my' world I belonged because people couldn't see the Indian part of me. Here the same thing meant I didn't belong.

"What's the matter?" Bell had already gotten out and slammed his door shut. "Come on."

He walked pulled my door open. I took a deep breath and slid out, hoping my legs would hold me up, which they did, barely.

After the outside light, the windowless store was blindingly dark. Slowly I noticed tiers of shelves piled randomly with boxes, cans, jars, and stacks of clothing. A large red Coke machine stood opposite us, next to a glass-doored refrigerator case full of beer. A large iron stove with a protruding flange on all four sides, surrounded by five chairs, took up the center of the room, radiating heat. The figures in the chairs were all men.

Everyone looked at us silently.

"Hey," said Bell.

"Hey-ya." The man who spoke sat nearest the counter on our left. He seemed to be the youngest of the lot, which meant he wasn't yet sixty.

"We're looking for someone. Hope you can tell us where to find her."

"Who's that?"

Bell turned to me.

"Melinda Little Deer."

After a long silence, the man spoke again. "No Melinda here."

"You called her something else, didn't you?" Bell asked in a low tone. I nodded.

"Aunt Moon."

If it had been possible the room became even quieter, as if my words had laid a hand on everyone's chest and stopped their breath.

"Aunt Moon," the man repeated. "Your aunt?"

"Great-aunt, really. My mother's father's sister."

Suddenly one of the old men got up, limped toward me, and peered at me intently.

"Jesus Christ," he breathed. "If you don't look exactly like Frank's wife."

Now they all began jabbering to each other, partly in English and partly in their own language. I glanced questioningly at Bell, but he shook his head.

Finally the first man waved his hand, and they fell silent. "We welcome you, Frank Little Deer's granddaughter. Your aunt lives out by Cedar Creek." He proceeded to give us a complicated set of directions, all of which passed through me as though he were still speaking in his native tongue. I was shaken by the contrast between their apparent acceptance of me and Redmond's continuing unease and ambivalence. Bell thanked him, took me by the elbow, and steered me toward the door.

"Tell us your name."

I turned back to them.

"Winona Daggett." I paused and corrected myself. "No. Just Winona."

Silence.

"Wehnona?" The way the man said my name made it sound as if he doubted it belonged to me. He repeated it thoughtfully and said something to Bell, who nodded silently.

Outside the light was fading and the air had grown colder. I shivered as we drove away, beyond words. After a while, Bell glanced at me. "Who gave you your name?" he asked.

"I don't know. Mom said once it was a family name. I don't know whose."

Bell lit another cigarette. I wondered if he was more rattled than he'd seemed in the store. "In Lakota, if you give a girl the name Wenonah it means she's perfect. The ideal Lakota maiden. Happens maybe once in anyone's lifetime. A girl who never gets mad, always puts others first, never puts herself forward." A smile crossed his face. "Guess your mom was hoping the name would rub off on you." The smile grew. "Guess I've been hoping the same thing." His grin widened as he looked at me and shook his head.

"Oh, well. Even Indians make mistakes."

He threw back his head and laughed, a deep, sustained, contagious belly-laugh that washed over me and swept me along with it.

BELL STOOD TO ONE side as I knocked at the door of the weather-beaten cabin that stood alone on a grassy rise under a sky darkening to deep blue at the far horizon. It had taken us two hours and three wrong turns that ended in open prairie or sandstone washes to finally find the place. To the right the land sloped down to a small draw filled with bare cottonwoods. The stream that would run through it in summer was frozen now. A cold wind hummed along the ground, rustling the dry grass, and cut through my coat like a knife.

I heard a few hoarse barks, then footsteps, and the door was opened by a short, stocky woman whose body nearly filled the doorway's width and left a few feet empty over her head. She was wearing a stretched-out brown cardigan over a faded blue-and-yellow striped dress, ankle socks, and battered tennis shoes. Except for the laugh wrinkles around her deep-set eyes, her broad brown face was nearly unlined. Pure-white hair was pulled into a bun at the nape of her neck. Her eyebrows were nearly black, which gave her face an air of alert concentration. Her mouth and nose were both wide and generous.

Something about her made me want to smile, although her expression was calm and impassive. A large shaggy brown-and-tan dog poked his head between her hip and the door jamb.

"Yes."

It wasn't a question so much as a call for explanation. A flicker of surprise or excitement sparkled for a moment in her eyes and then vanished, like a curious face peeping for an instant from a curtained window.

"Aunt Moon. I'm Winona. My mother is Marie. . . ." I hesitated a moment: Moon might not know Mom's married name.

"Little Deer." A smile bloomed on her face, her white teeth gleaming. "Frank's child. Come in. Welcome to my house. This is Buster." The dog thumped his tail against the floor.

I introduced Bell, and they exchanged a few words in Lakota.

"This sure is a happy day," said Moon as she seated us at a rickety Formica table and set the kettle on the stove. "Marie's daughter is in my house. But not Marie. How is she?"

"Pretty well." I realized I had no idea at what point she'd stopped getting news from or about Mom, who was so close-mouthed it could be last month or twenty years ago. We waited for the water to boil and the steaming coffee to be placed before us. Then Moon seated herself across from me and stared hard at my face.

"Tell me about Marie. And about you."

"Where should I start?"

"Go back ten years. When you were four. The last time I heard about you."

"That'll take quite a while." I glanced nervously at the window, at the nearly dark sky.

"I want to hear all about her, and you. And then you can hear about me, if you want."

"But. . . ." How long would that take? Even as the question raised itself, she spoke.

"You'll stay here tonight."

She pointed to the worn sofa covered with a multicolored cotton quilt. Other star-pattern quilts hung on the walls. "Nowhere else to stay anyhow."

I opened my mouth to protest, but Bell intervened. "Thank you, *unci*." Later I learned from him that this meant "auntie," a term of respect used with any older woman.

Moon looked at him. He dropped his eyes.

"Are you married to her? She's awfully young for that." I felt myself blush.

"No, *unci*," announced Bell. "We're friends. Good friends."

A pause, then laughter rumbled from deep in her chest.

"Oh, yes. Very good friends." Her eyes snapped at me over the rim of her cup. "Excellent friends." She waved a hand toward our cups. "Drink, drink. Our best reservation special, made by Mr. Maxwell House himself." Again the rumbling chuckle. "Start with what happened after Marie married your father. What was his name?"

"Lee Reynolds."

"Yes, Reynolds. That's your name, too?"

I didn't answer. Instead, while Moon retrieved various items from the cupboards, mixed biscuit dough, and heated a pot of stew, I told her what I knew about how my father died, Mom's flight from her in-laws, her remarriage to Randy, the birth of Lorrie and Pete, our life on the ranch, and finally Lorrie's death. There I stopped, suddenly exhausted. I hadn't mentioned the real reason for Randy's departure, nor Jess' pregnancy and her flight to Billings. Even if I'd wanted to, I didn't know how to do it without telling someone else's secrets.

We sat a while in the silence, the windows now black, light from the overhead bulb glistening on Bell's hair, Moon's back to us as she slipped the biscuits into the oven.

"We knew that Marie got married the first time. We weren't invited, but we knew."

"Mom said her father had died before that," I offered as an excuse.

Moon turned and gave me a searching look I couldn't interpret. "Yes, he was dead by then. Your mother knew me only when she was a girl. Not once her mother and father lived apart."

I nodded.

"She never told you about us?"

"Not till just a few months ago. That's when—when we found out we had Indian family."

Moon's entire body grew still. The only sounds were Buster shifting himself on the floor, and the wheezing hum of the refrigerator. Sadness rose through the deep lines suddenly visible around Moon's mouth and the dark circles under her eyes, as well as something close to anger. She hesitated, then came and sat down heavily across from me and folded her hands in front of her on the table. They were big and puffy, work-roughened, the joints swollen and the skin dark and puckered.

"I'll tell you something about your grandfather Frank," she said. "He loved his children more than anything in this world. He loved them more than books, and he loved books like a crazy man, ever since he was a child in the mission school. He loved them more even than his wife, and he loved *her* more than was good for either of them."

I considered this; it fit with what I'd heard from Mom.

"Yes, you may already know this," Moon went on. Wonderful, I thought, another mind-reader in the family. "What you don't know is how hard he fought to keep his children, to get them back and have them live with him again. Your grandmother was like a princess who needed them around her, but your grandfather was like a trapped grizzly who sees her cubs stolen away by a hunter. He fought in the white man's courts. He fought with his words. He fought by coming again and again to see them, even when she slammed the door in his face. He went to jail for them, and then he lost his life for them."

She stood up slowly and turned back to the stove. Apparently the story was finished as far as she was concerned. I looked over at Bell, whose gaze was fastened on the far wall, then back at Moon.

"What do you mean? How did he lose his life?"

"That's not my story to tell," she answered, stirring the pot. "That belongs to your mother. You must ask her."

My mouth opened, but once again Bell intercepted my question. "Can we help you set the table, *unci*?"

I shoved his shin with my foot, but he didn't flinch. He got up and took three plates and a fistful of silverware from the dish drainer and began to arrange them on the table.

"Lay off," he murmured close to my ear as he reached past me. "She's said all she's going to say about it."

How did he know? I wondered. But I decided not to force the issue. It turned out he was right. For the rest of the evening, Moon stuck to stories about how she and my grandfather had been snatched from their families and imprisoned in the Jesuit-run Le Sabre boarding school, where they were forbidden to speak their own language and were beaten if they did, constrained by endless regulations, and subjected to the discipline of nuns and priests as strict as the toughest drill sergeants. They'd learned to read and write English, but at the price of their own tongue. Her stories were fascinating enough that I lost sight of the earlier one she'd left hanging, with my grandfather teetering on the brink of the grave.

Later that night, lying on the lumpy sofa bed Moon had opened for us, pressed together by desire and a sloping mattress, preternaturally conscious of Moon asleep—we hoped—in her tiny bedroom just beyond the paper-thin wall, Bell and I tried to refrain from reaching for the once-secret parts of each other we now longed for and knew where to find, then succumbed, holding our breath, moving as slowly and silently as we could. We only succeeded in sharpening our pleasure to near-unbearable intensity, so that when I came, Bell had to press his hand over my mouth to stifle my cries, and I had to wrap the pillow tight as I could around our heads to muffle the groans torn from so deep within his chest that my own body convulsed yet again, like a violin string resonating in sympathy with a bass chord.

It seemed hours before we grew quiet, sweat cooling, breathing nearly normal. Only then did I become conscious of a high, reedy voice singing a tuneless melody that seemed to come from nowhere, from the stars outside. It took me a moment to understand that it came from Moon. At that I pressed my face to Bell's chest and clamped my hands over my ears, moaning with embarrassment. He pulled them away gently.

"It's okay," he smiled. "She's singing the wedding song."

CHAPTER 27

WE TOOK OUR TIME driving back, stopping for lunch in Crow Agency. Then we found a back road cut-off to Hardin so deserted we saw not one other car for close to twenty miles. Halfway there, we pulled over onto a small rise and walked a hundred yards into a stand of scrub pine. There, on a ratty blanket Bell kept in his trunk, perhaps for other similar occasions I didn't want to think about, we made love under the low-bending trees. When we were done, I couldn't make myself loosen my grip on Bell's shoulders, and though I willed myself not to, I began to cry. I tried to hide my tears by burying my face in his neck, but of course he felt them.

"Don't," he whispered. "I'm not going away forever. I'll be back. I just don't know when."

"But I need you now," I protested, like a child on her first day of school calling after her mother as she walks away.

He leaned his head close to mine and wiped my cheeks, my nose, with his hair. "No you don't," he said softly. "Not as much as you think."

"Oh, yeah?" I was immediately indignant. "Listen, if I say I need you, you damn well better believe it!"

Even as I said it, this sounded so ridiculous that I began to laugh. That set him off, and we collapsed together, laughter pulsing shakily through our chests. After a while, he grew serious again.

"Win. It isn't just you who feels like that."

He rolled away from me, once again pulling the rubber off carefully and placing it on a nearby tuft of grass. Suddenly I was flooded with gratitude for his mindfulness and with foreknowledge of the loneliness that lay ahead for both of us. For a moment I saw how our lives were about to flow now on their separate courses, young and resilient as we were.

I reached over and took his hand, and we lay back, watching two cedar jays hopping in and out of view among the branches overhead, leading their mysterious bird lives, oblivious to us below.

BY FIVE O'CLOCK WE were back in Billings at Jess and Collie's place, the boys trading one-liners and zingers while sipping beer and watching the football wrap-up on TV. Jess and I shut ourselves in the bedroom and sat side by side on the big bed, leaning against the wobbly wooden headboard.

"So what was she like?"

I gave Jess a quick account of our visit to Aunt Moon, including her description of our grandfather's schooling and the brutal battle between our grandparents over Mom and the uncle we'd never seen.

"There's so much out there we still don't know," I concluded. "Like, what happened to Mom's brother? He just disappeared."

"The way Mom did, from Dad's family."

"And what about the mysterious way Mom's father died?" Calling him 'grandfather' felt odd, artificial. "Do you know anything about it?"

A shadow flitted over Jess' face. "I don't know. I remember, once, Mom let something slip about it, as if it wasn't like he had a heart attack or been in a car accident. Something worse."

"Like what?"

"I don't know. Something she wasn't going to talk about."

"Well, that covers just about everything, doesn't it?"

We grinned at each other.

"I'll make her tell me when I get home."

"Oh, sure," Jess snorted. "She'll be so mad, you'll be lucky if she talks to you at all. I mean, you slip away with your boyfriend and stay gone for four days. Then you show up without him, looking like a cat that's been living on cream. *And* you've gone and looked up her aunt that she's kept quiet about for ten years. It'll be a month before she'll even look at you, let alone tell you anything."

"You'd be surprised what she's told me," I answered, deciding to ignore the cat-and-cream remark.

Jess wouldn't let me rest until I'd recounted Mom's version of her mother's loose behavior and easy morals. That kept her quiet for a few minutes.

"If that's true," she finally pronounced, "I bet she'll go completely nuts about what you've been doing."

"What do you mean by that?"

She rolled her eyes. "Oh, come on, anyone can see it. You and Bell can't stop touching each other. You're always bumping thighs or knees, or shoulders, or whatever."

I felt myself blushing yet again.

"Hey, don't bust a gut about it. I told you it was fun." She poked me in the ribs. "Wasn't I right?"

I nodded, and a grin spread across my face. Jess started laughing, and then we were rolling helplessly on the bed, convulsed, shrieking, gasping for breath, until Collie shouted, "What's going on in there?" from the other room, which only made us laugh harder.

When we finally calmed down, Jess put her hands behind her head. "Win. The thing I wanted to tell you. It's about Mom."

I sat up. "Is she okay? Have you—did you tell her where I was?"

"She already knew, stupid. You left her a note, remember?"

"I mean about Bell."

"She knew that, too. Or guessed. She knows about it from experience, too."

I winced. I didn't want to imagine Mom doing what I'd done, or who she'd done it with.

"Win, she's going to let Randy come home." I stared at her. "She told me a few days ago."

"Told you? You've been talking to her?"

"Yeah. I called her about a week ago. She doesn't know where we are, just that I'm all right."

"And it's okay with you if he goes back?"

"It's not up to me, or you either. She loves him, and he's crazy without her."

"He's crazy, period. Look what he did. Mom told me she can't forget it."

"She won't ever forget, but I guess she's ready to forgive him. He's sorry, really he is. He even begged *me* to forgive him."

"You've talked to him?" I croaked. "How many times?"

She shrugged. "He sent us money for the deposit here. That's how we were able to rent this place. He's visited us once, too."

"He stayed here?"

"Yeah, on the couch. We had to be real quiet that night." She giggled and poked me, but I sat stiffly, maintaining an indignant distance. She reached over and took my hand.

"Win, we've hated him for so long. I'm tired of it. I want to stop, and if he's really trying, why not meet him halfway?"

I snatched my hand away.

"You can do what you want. I can't stop Mom from letting him come back, but I don't have to like it."

Jess sighed. "You don't have to. Just give him a chance."

I sniffed.

"He's here in Billings," she went on. "Mom sent him to drive you home. He's going to come home with you."

For a moment I was speechless.

"No! Absolutely not!" I spluttered. "I will not sit in a car for six hours with that creep! One or both of us would end up dead."

"Haven't you heard anything I just told you?" Her voice was pleading. "He's different. He won't pick on you like he used to."

"What's he done, got religion?" I sneered. "Anyway, I don't care. Maybe *you* can forget what he used to be like, just because he's acting all squishy and mealy-mouthed. Not me!"

Jess clasped her hands over her belly. I caught a whiff of her freshly washed hair.

"Win, she's as skeptical as you are, but she's ready to give it a try. She aches for him. I can hear it in her voice. She misses him the way you're going to miss Bell."

I gaped at her in disbelief. How could she twist the knife in me like that? How could she use her knowledge of what I felt about Bell against me, in defense of Randy, of all people? She must have seen this in my eyes, because she stopped, then let her head fall onto my shoulder.

"I'm sorry, Win," she murmured. "I don't want you to be unhappy. Just let him make it up to Mom."

"Maybe she's not ready yet." I was weakening. "She's the world champion grudge-holder."

Jess nodded.

"I know. But when she gave him this chance, he was in his truck heading here to get you in about two seconds."

Without warning her face changed, as if she'd heard a distant bell, the way a dog perks up his ears at a supersonic sound. She grabbed my hand and placed it on her belly.

"Feel that. The baby kicked!"

Something tiny, a miniature mole tunneling beneath Jess' flesh, rolled against my fingers. Astounded, I stared at her belly, then at her beaming face, and the remains of my resistance crumbled. Next to this force driving the universe through her, and Mom, and through Bell and me, my anger of a moment before seemed like something from long ago.

"CAN YOU DO ME a favor?" Bell whispered some time during the night. "Stay in touch with Marjorie and Frances."

I was so full of the feel of him, his skin and blood and bone and muscle becoming familiar, fitting into mine, that I agreed without a tinge of uneasiness. At that moment I felt only compassion for Marjorie, as for anyone denied the privilege of receiving him into her body and riding with him to nirvana.

"I'm not going to show them your letters, though," I insisted.

"I'm not much of a letter writer, Win. When you hear from me, you can tell them how I'm doing. And they can tell my mother. I just. . . ."

He stared at the ceiling, his hands behind his head. "It feels like I'm getting in a boat, about to start a long, long trip. And all the people I care about are standing on the shore, watching me go. If I know they're all there together, even when I can't see them anymore, I'll be okay, no matter what happens."

I pressed closer to him. "You care a lot about Marjorie and Frances, don't you?"

"Frances is like a mother to me. More than my own mother ever was. And Marjorie. . . ." He hesitated, and my heart lurched. "We grew up side by side. We drank from the same cup."

He rolled over and put his hands alongside my face. "When you talk to her, you will be talking to me."

My heart did another nose-dive.

"Do you love her?" I managed to whisper.

He smiled. "Not the way you think."

"What way, then?"

"Like a sister. Like my sister."

I stared at him.

"Haven't you already guessed?" he said softly. "Frances adopted her when she was small."

"Why don't people know about it?" I asked.

"They do. *We* do. Whites don't care what Indians do with their kids."

In a flash, everything made sense. I'd attributed their striking resemblance to their being from the same tribe, second cousins—even, I was ashamed to admit, to their both being Indian. His eyes never left mine as I absorbed the gift he was giving me. "I always liked Marjorie," I finally managed to say. "Right from the first. Now I know why."

EVEN TODAY, ACROSS THE stretch of twenty years and all that has happened since then, I can hardly bear to remember the anguish I felt, like a cord constricting my throat, my guts, my heart, when I saw Bell's car turn the corner down the street, a final blast of his horn cutting through the gray morning air. A separate self, standing beside me, watched

Randy arrive, listened to him greet us in self-consciously hearty tones and put my bag behind the front seat of his truck. Someone else, not I, said goodbye to Collie and clutched Jess so hard she grunted in protest.

"Maybe you can come again when the baby's born," she breathed in my ear. "Maybe you'll be here for it."

I knew that was her oblique way of asking for my help. I nodded over and over, afraid that, if I opened my mouth, I'd let out a wail that would stop their hearts. Then I climbed into the cab and stared fiercely at her transparent, rosy face, her long hair loose, Collie at her side, as they waved to me, and tears began to slide down my cheeks.

Randy, who had appeared freshly shaven, just after breakfast, in clean clothes that fit, had the sense to keep quiet for the first several hours. If he'd so much as opened his mouth, I'd have jumped out the door without a second thought. As it was, he contented himself with listening to the radio, changing to a new station when the one he was listening to faded into staticky noise or began to bore him. I kept my face turned away and tuned my attention to some remote screen on which I ran scenes from the last two days over and over. When he stopped for lunch, I stayed in the truck until he entered the cafe and I could run to the restroom and cry at last.

When I climbed back into the cab, though, the smell of the hamburger and fries he brought back and laid on the seat between us began to chip away at my determination. Finally I couldn't stand it any longer, and I opened the greasy bag and began to eat.

"Be my guest," Randy said. "Didn't know if you wanted ketchup, so I stuck some over on the side."

"Thanks." The first grudging word I'd addressed to him. He began to whistle along with the song on the radio, a rambunctious high-kicking version of "Lonesome Cowboy." I winced.

"Want me to change the station?" I stared at him in disbelief. This was incomprehensible. I decided to test him. No one was allowed to touch the radio in his truck. Gingerly I reached for the knob, and sure enough he pushed my hand away roughly. Then he caught himself. "Go ahead." I touched the knob, and he let me search the dial until I found a station playing "Born on the Bayou." He snorted, took a deep breath, and forced his face into an imitation of a smile.

"Well, Merle Haggard has those guys beat by a mile," he said when the song ended. "But whatever greases your griddle, I guess."

I flushed, remembering Bell's fingers slick with my juices, insisting to myself that Randy couldn't possibly know, wouldn't be hinting at this, and convinced he was. Not only that, but he knew I knew he knew, and I couldn't stand it. I settled my face into a mask, like the ones on the cover of the Shakespeare we'd used in English.

"Listen, Win," he said. "I know damn well what you and your boyfriend have been up to. It's not gonna do a bit of good to try and stop you, I know that. You're a lot like me. If anyone tried to stop me from doing some damn fool thing, I'd just turn around and double it in spades. Know what I mean?"

I kept quiet, which stopped him for a moment.

"Until I met Marie, I was a crazy fool hell-bent on killing myself without knowing it. She saved my life." He paused a moment, as if deciding whether to go on. "When I met her, it was like door opened to a new place, and if I could walk through it, I'd have a chance to live in a warm place with people who loved me."

He stopped abruptly and turned away, rolled down his window, and spat. That gave him an excuse to drag a bandanna from his pocket and wipe his mouth. I saw him use it on his nose, his face still averted.

"Do you remember how you used to run right at me whenever I came through the door? You were just five, the cutest little thing I ever saw, with red curls all over your head, and a wise-mouth to beat the band. Jess was a lot quieter. She took longer to warm up to me, but finally she did. And we were a family, the first family I'd had in twenty years. It felt—it felt like. . . ." He cleared his throat, once, twice. "It felt like I'd found my little sisters again, and they were welcoming me home."

He blew his nose noisily and fell silent, watching the road.

"And then Lorrie came along, and Pete. My own kids. I'd never thought I'd have kids, and there they were, so beautiful, so loving.

"And then it began to slide downhill. First you and Jess turned against me, just like my sisters had. Then things on the ranch got shaky, and we were more and more in debt every year. It seemed like I couldn't do anything right, and I got angrier and angrier, and I started back on the bottle, like I'd done before. I know I took things out on all of you, and each time I hated myself worse. It felt like a giant hand was pulling me out of that warm, good place and back into the night I'd come out of, and there was nothing I could do to stop it.

"Then Lorrie died—"

He stopped and again rolled the window down, spat, and wiped his mouth and nose. "I don't remember much about the funeral or the days at the hospital, and when I left, all I knew is that I was out of my mind. I wouldn't wish how I felt then on my worst enemy.

"When I came to my senses, I knew I'd lost it all. All I had to hang onto was that I had to find a way to make it up to everyone I'd hurt. Not so I'd be forgiven, but so I could live with myself. That's when I went on the wagon. I got a job and saved up some money to send to Marie, and I set about finding Jess and helping her, too. If I've got a second chance at what I know I want more than anything in this world, I'll do whatever I need to make it last. I'll beg forgiveness of everybody I've hurt. I've already squared it with Jess. I'd like to do that with you, too, Win."

He held out a hand. I sat unmoving.

"I'm sorry for what I've done to you, Win. I can't believe I ever treated you like my stepmother treated me. I hope —"

His voice cracked and once again he blew his nose and stared through the windshield.

Don't go on, I begged him wordlessly as the long stretches of gray sky and dry-blown prairie rolled past the dirt-streaked window. I don't want to hear this. I don't want to feel bad for you. I don't want to cry any more, especially about your sad life. I don't want to like you.

But it was already too late.

AS WE TURNED INTO the rutted lane toward our house, its windows were glowing yellow against the dark. The tires crunched on the gravel, and the engine gurgled and clanked as Randy switched the ignition off. For a moment the silence roared in my ears. Then the door was thrown open, and Mom's figure was silhouetted against a sheet of light. The truck creaked as I stepped down, straightening my stiffened legs, and slowly approached her. Without a word, she grabbed my arms and pulled me to her, hugging me tight, then held me at arm's length. She shook me briefly, hard.

"Jesus Christ," she said. "You gave me such a scare!"

"I'm fine." All I wanted to do was escape to my room and go to sleep. "You got my note."

Mom nodded as we studied each other's faces. I saw fear, recognition, dismay, relief, all pass over her. What did she read in me?

"Are you hungry?" I had to smile at the eternal coded plea of motherhood: Are you all right? What can I do?

"We ate in Helena."

"You go on to bed, then. It's late. We'll talk in the morning." She patted my shoulder.

I walked down the hall and turned, remembering the bag I'd left in the truck. Mom was gazing at Randy, who stood just outside the door, his arms hanging at his sides.

"Marie." His voice was low, full, ardent. In it I heard tones—desire and hope, seduction and fear—I wouldn't have picked up four days before, as if my range of hearing now stretched into the supersonic, like a bat's.

Mom didn't move. Randy took one slow step toward her and stopped, trying to get close without spooking her. I could feel the icy air between them shiver into liquid with the heat suspended between their bodies. Potential energy, I thought, that's what I'm seeing. Energy poised on the brink of force, two magnets quivering between attraction and repulsion.

I turned away and walked into my room and closed the door as quietly as I could. Just let me fall asleep, I prayed, before they start singing.

THE NEXT MORNING I found Mom alone in the kitchen, sitting at the table in her fuzzy blue bathrobe. Randy, I guessed, was still asleep, with Pete curled in their bed next to him, having crawled into Mom's bed as he always did at first light. Before Mom could start in on me about my shortcomings and lapses of judgment, I handed her a bundle from Aunt Moon. She'd given it to me when we left, telling me sternly it was for Mom's eyes only.

"What's this?"

I explained, describing as vividly as I could my impressions of Moon, retelling her stories, deflecting, I hoped, Mom's attention from the rest of the picture. It had occurred to me that maybe she didn't know Bell had been with me, since I hadn't mentioned him in my note. I didn't really think she was fooled, but I rattled on, and she listened quietly, seemingly absorbed by my words. Outside, the clouds hovered low, and a few heavy flakes began to drift past the window. The yeasty smell of biscuits filled the air.

Finally I fell silent. Mom gazed at the folded bundle on the table for a while and shook her head.

"I don't know, Win. It's happened too soon for you. You're still so young." She took a huge breath and let it out slowly. "But it's good it happened with someone you love. Once you know how it's supposed to be, you'll never settle for anything less."

Of course my face burned at this. When I was able to look up, she was staring at me.

"How was Randy with you?"

"What do you mean?"

"How'd he treat you?"

"Okay, I guess," I shrugged.

"He says he's changed," she went on, "and I think maybe he has. He seems different, like something's eased up in him." She sat back, her eyes still fixed on mine.

"Win, this is important. Did he give you a hard time, like he used to? I have to know."

I stared back at her. What would she do, I wondered, if I said he'd berated me, called me a slut, slandered Bell? Would she toss him out the door? Could I have that much power over her life?

She shook her head slowly, her shoulders slumping, and stared at the floor. I opened my mouth to lie, but I couldn't do it. "He was nice to me," I breathed.

She lifted her head, her eyes suffused with happiness. "Really?"

"He let me pick the station on the radio."

Mom smiled, unexpectedly reached over, and hugged me briefly.

"Thank you, Win," she whispered. "Thank you."

After a moment, she began unwrapping the bundle I'd brought her from Moon very carefully, as if it contained something infinitely breakable. The yellowed cloth fell open to reveal a thick circle of multicolored dots, patterns of red, yellow, white, and black beads on a leather armband.

Mom sat motionless. She reached out and touched it gently.

"My bracelet," she whispered. "The one my father kept for me." The one he told her he'd give her on her wedding day, I remembered.

Her eyes began to fill with tears. In a moment, I knew, she would rise and leave the room, hiding her pain as she always did. Instead, to my astonishment, she put her hands over her face, and for the first time in my life, I saw my mother cry.

MARIE

March 28, 1971

    Whenever I think of my father, at first I feel so warm and good, like a baby wrapped by her mother after a bath. And then I trip and fall into an icy lake, with the water closing over my head. Moon wouldn't tell Win; she said it was my place to do it. But I don't know if I can, it makes me hurt so much to remember that my father died because of me. I didn't kill him, but I might as well have, the way I saw it then. And sometimes I still do.

    It was because of Mama. After she married Mr. Lucas, we all breathed a sigh of relief, thinking, Well, that's over, she'll settle down now. And at first she did. She liked having a man around, and there was something between them, for a while, anyhow. With her, it seemed nothing could last. There was some awful devil of restlessness in her, something drawing her to mess up whatever she had, to heat it up and see how hot it would get before it burst into flames.

    Maybe she was born before her time. I've thought that sometimes. She needed more room, more to do than teach a bunch of restless kids, or, even worse, sit at home and bake and clean. That's what Mr. Lucas wanted her to do, so she stopped teaching and slipped her moorings in the same way she had before. She began sneaking around, meeting other men in secret, leaving hints for him to find. Often enough I'd find them and hide them first—things like a love letter, a new piece of jewelry, panties that smelled of sex while Mr. Lucas was away on a business trip. But often enough he found them before I did. And then they'd fight, real ugly fights, with him calling her a whore, and her screaming how he wasn't man enough to satisfy her.

It tore my heart open to hear it. "Why didn't you just stay married to Papa if all you were going to do it switch to fighting someone else?" I'd ask her.

"Because of this," she'd say, and hold up the new silk dress or the fur coat he'd brought home for her, or pat the seat of the shiny Buick she was driving now. And she'd smile, like she was pleased with herself. But I could see the contempt in her eyes. Whatever had gone on between her and my father, even when she was in a fury about what he couldn't give her, I don't think she ever hated him the way she began to hate Mr. Lucas, for being able to best him every time.

Well, my father got wind of how things were between them. He'd never stopped coming to see us, William and me, even though he didn't come very often, there being two hundred miles between Lame Deer and Fort Peck. William had come back to us when Mama got her teaching job. She'd threatened to use the law against my father, and the law was on her side, as it always was when it was a case of white against Indian, and Papa knew it. But William was never happy with us. He ran away a lot, usually just for a day or two. One time he actually hopped a freight to go back to the reservation, but, wouldn't you know, the brakeman found him a couple of stops down the line and telephoned Mama to come and get him.

Anyhow, this time Papa got serious. He even went and talked to a lawyer, and he told Mama he was fixing to declare her an unfit mother. Mama pooh-poohed him and said not only did he have nothing against her, but she knew her children would never turn against her. She was right when it came to me, but not William.

"I want to live with Papa," he yelled at her one time. "I hate this house, I hate Mr. Lucas, and I hate you, and I hope you both die!"

Mama's face turned chalk-white at that.

"You've turned my son against me with your lies!" she screamed at

Papa, and right there she telephoned the sheriff and had him arrested, claiming he'd tried to kidnap us. And even though William and I denied it, they hauled Papa off to jail. That was when I understood right to the marrow of my bones how the cards were stacked against you if you were Indian, and how I'd better learn to deal myself a different hand.

WE DIDN'T HEAR ANYTHING from Papa for a long time after that. First he was in prison for a while. They didn't even have a trial because the judge hit Papa with some trumped-up accusation Mama made about how he'd tried to steal her car. We heard he'd been released, but months went by, and no word from him. Then one day I got a letter from him—such a beautiful letter it made me cry. I still know it by heart.

> *Singing Bird, my daughter,*
>> *My heart is always with you, and with your brother. A child needs both her mother and her father, and when one is missing from her life, it is as if she tries to shoot an arrow from a bow with no cord. If you tell me you want to see me, I will come, even if the judge and all the lawyers say I must not. I will wait to hear from you.*
>> *Be well.*
>>> *Your father,*
>>> *Frank Little Deer*

> *This put me in a terrible spot. If I wrote him how much I longed to see him, he would get in trouble with the law again. If I didn't, the thought of the pain I would cause him was unbearable. Mama decided for me. She railed on and on about how, if I had a speck of gratitude for all she'd done for us or a smidgen of understanding of what I'd be getting both him and myself into if I didn't, I'd tell him in no uncertain terms to stay as far away from me as he could. And if I didn't, she'd never look at me again.*

> *So I said that's what I'd do, and she made me write it on the spot, and she took the letter and posted it herself that very day. I cried myself to sleep that night, and the next and the next. And then I sent him an-*

other letter in secret, telling him the first one was a lie, that I not only wanted to see him, I wanted to leave Mama and go live with him and William somewhere Mama couldn't ever get to us again. I wrote it out of bitter anger at her for having forced me to say what I hadn't meant. And because of that anger, I ended up writing a different thing I didn't really mean either.

More weeks went by with no sign from Papa, and I began to think he hadn't received my second letter. Perhaps, I thought, Mama had managed to somehow get hold of it; maybe she and the postmaster were in cahoots. Any man might be one of her lovers, as far as I could tell.

Then one evening in late June, a few days after school was over for the year, and I was sitting on our front porch waiting for my friend Nancy to come over to supper, I looked up and saw my father standing by the bushes that marked the end of our lawn. Usually I could hear the rattle of his old beat-up car coming down the street, but this time he appeared like a ghost out of nowhere. It wasn't until he said my name that I really believed it was him. Then I jumped up and ran to him and threw myself into his arms. He held me real tight and looked long and hard into my face. "I've come to take you and William with me," he said. "That is, if you want to come."

Suddenly William came banging out the front door and ran as hard into him as I had. "Papa! Papa! Can I come live with you?" he kept saying, over and over.

"Go get your things," Papa told us. "And tell your mother to come out here."

We ran inside and found Mama in the kitchen. When I told her who was waiting for her, she froze a moment, then took off her apron and walked out without a word, pure rage in her eyes. William and I stared at each other. "Let's get moving before she can stop us," William whispered, and we ran to our rooms to pack a few things as best we could.

As I was dragging a satchel out from the hall closet into my room, I heard voices raised outside in anger, and when I looked out my window, Papa was holding a big piece of paper in front of Mama's nose. She glanced at it, turned, and walked back to the house, real stiff, her face like concrete. *Praying she wouldn't bust in on me, I started stuffing things helter-skelter into the satchel as I heard her head for the bedroom she and Mr. Lucas shared, then a moment later walk back down the stairs. I was just closing the satchel when a great "boom!" went off in the front yard. By the time I got outside, Papa was lying on the grass, and Mama was standing next to him with Mr. Lucas' gun in her hand.*

I ran over and knelt next to Papa. Blood was oozing out of a hole in his chest and running down and pooling underneath him. There was a piece of paper clutched in his right hand, the paper he'd been showing Mama. His eyes were closed, and awful wheezing, bubbling noises were leaking out of his mouth. I was afraid to touch him for fear I'd hurt him worse.

By then, William was kneeling next to me. He looked up at Mama and croaked at her, "You killed Papa! You killed him!"

Mama stared at us calmly. When she spoke her voice was as smooth and cold as a sheet of iron in the dead of winter. "I had to do it. He was going to kill me."

And that's the story she stuck to after she'd shoved us into our rooms and the sheriff arrived, when the lawyers talked to her, when the police questioned her. She told them Papa was a terrible drunk, and that he'd been drinking before he showed up that evening, and that when he got drunk he'd lose his temper and become vicious. I knew none of that was true, and so did William, and we were ready to say so, but, wouldn't you know, they never asked either one of us a single question about it.

Before they took his body away, though, I worked the paper loose from Papa's hand and read it. It was some kind of official document from a judge, and it said that Papa had the right to visit us regularly and have us visit him over the summer, and Mama would get in a whole lot of trouble if she didn't let him. Even with that, and even though they didn't find any weapon on Papa, not even a knife, they let Mama go free. It still makes my blood boil when I think about it. Everyone knew that an Indian was capable of anything if he got mad and drunk enough, and that Mama had the perfect right to defend herself.

I never forgave her for it. William hardly spoke a word to her af-

terward, and he ran away and disappeared a couple of months later. She really slid downhill after that. She got to wandering around downtown in her slip, propositioning men on street corners, then staying up all night, singing hymns and insisting Mr. Lucas and I get up and sing along with her. God, she embarrassed me. When she jumped up one Sunday in church—she still went every Sunday, and I had to help wrestle her into a respectable outfit first, instead of the outlandish get-up she wanted to put on—when she stood up in the middle of the announcements and started to harangue the congregation about how the Whore of Babylon had seduced Jesus and got pregnant with their secret child, who turned out to be the Queen of England, who then gave birth to her, Mama—well, the deacon of the church told us she was no longer welcome.

So what could we do but have her committed? She went off to the state asylum in Billings, and she's been there ever since. As soon as I graduated high school, I married Lee, your father, and I thought I was well out of it.

But as long as I live I won't forget how she got down on her knees the night before she was to leave. "Please, Marie, please don't let them stick me in that loony bin! Let me stay with you!" Clutching at my legs, her fingers clenched up so tight in the fabric of my dress I had to tear it to get it out of her hands. Like a scene in a movie, only much worse because of the tears running down her face, streaking her makeup. And the terrible fear in her voice, and her eyes begging me, as if I could raise her from the dead if only I wanted to. I had to run from the room so she wouldn't see how guilty I felt. But it was her or me. I wanted my own life, not one where I was caretaker to a crazy woman I didn't even like. So I let her go.

I visited her pretty regularly for a while, until Lee died. Every time I went, she hardly recognized me, or maybe she just pretended not to, staring right through me the whole time I was there. Then once I moved with my kids, as far away from Fort Peck as I could get, I stopped going. I put her out of my mind. As far as I was concerned, she was gone. I didn't see her, only sent her one card each year, at Christmas. Then two years ago, the card came back, marked "Deceased." I'd thought I could make her and my whole past disappear. And now, the past has come back to haunt me and everyone I care about.

But I've learned something. Until I had to turn around and face it, let the chips fall and try and clean up as best I can, I'd lived my life in fear of what could happen one day. And that made me a coward, like a deserter hiding in the trees, afraid to make a sound in case he's discovered. Bad as everything got, I like it better now. I can't say I wouldn't undo it, if it would get Lorrie back. I know I'll wrestle with that till the day I die. All I can do now is put the best of her into my life, so I can live like I'd have liked her to, free and open and brave.

CHAPTER 28

F OR THE NEXT FEW weeks, my whole world was drained of color. The sky was always gray and flat, and the ground alternated between frozen lumps of dirt and a muddy gumbo that stuck to my shoes. Food didn't taste good, and nothing fit right. I forced myself to do the bare minimum in school, and the ranch kept me more than busy, with the end of calving getting us up at all hours to help with a difficult birth, digging the truck out of drifts we'd plowed into while feeding the stock hat were left, cleaning the bathroom floor when the pipes froze up as they did every year.

In a way I was grateful for the endless sequence of tasks that unrolled before me every day, that gave my body, if not my mind, something to occupy itself with. Only when I sat at the piano did everything disappear except the music, and the veil that lay between me and the world lifted and I could fly.

"Look," Mom said one day, pointing into the sky. "The geese are heading north."

Randy followed her gaze. "Well, I guess we've made it through another year." He nodded energetically. He'd been so damn cheerful since his return, I could hardly bear to be in the same room with him, his mood a complete 180 degrees from my own. I could see he tried to tone it down around me, but he was so happy he kept whistling "Hey, Good Lookin'" until I thought I'd go crazy. He'd touch Mom whenever he got near her, little pats on her rear end or arm that made me ache inside.

I haunted the post office in town, hoping for a letter from Bell, and finally I was rewarded.

Pine Ridge Reservation, South Dakota
April 10, 1971

Dear Win,

How are you doing? Sorry this took so long, but I'm not much of a writer, like I told you. I'm here on the Rez at Pine Ridge, staying with my cousins, all six of them, in their little two-room shack. And you thought we were crowded at Billings! I sleep on an old mattress in the kitchen, along with Henry and Cricket (he's called that because he can't quite talk yet, so he chirps and thinks he's talking).

Everyone here is dirt poor, even worse than in Lame Deer. Somehow the Sioux get the shortest end of the stick every time. The wind blows right through the wall, and no one has any money even to buy tar paper to nail over the holes.

On my way here, I went back through Lame Deer and visited your Aunt Moon again. She's still doing real well. She said to say hello to you, and that she's really glad you looked her up. Did you know your mom wrote Moon? The letter got there just before I left. Moon told me your mother had lost her way, and to find herself again she had to find her, Moon, and she did that by sending you first. I told her no, the whole thing was all your idea, that your mom had no idea what you were up to. Moon just smiled and said everything was working out like it was supposed to.

There's stuff happening here and all over. We're still

holding Alcatraz. You've probably read about it. AIM has started a survival school out in Minnesota to help Indians fit into white society without becoming white. I'd like to see one set up here, one on each reservation. There's a local guy, Russ Means, who was born here on P.R. and grew up in Oakland, who started AIM in Cleveland. He organized the demonstration last fall at Paha Sapa (what you call Mount Rushmore). There may be another one this year, and guess who wants to be part of it—me, that's who. Gives me something to look forward to. People around here mostly just sit on their butts and starve, and someone's got to do something about it.

This is an awfully long letter, the longest I've ever written. Hope you're impressed. You can write to me here if you want (I hope).

*C.Y.K., * Bell*

P.S. Do you miss 'singing'? I sure do.
*P.P.S. * That means "consider yourself kissed" (and then some)*

Of course I read the letter twenty times and sat down to answer the same night. I poured my heart out to him: how I missed him, how bleak my life was without him, what a boring and petty existence I led. Then I re-read it and decided it sounded like one long whine. Over the next few days I rewrote it, trying to capture for him the color and texture of all the small events, pretending he was there sharing them. In trying to make them sound interesting to him, I found myself observing them more closely and searching for the right words to describe them. And as I did, they began to come back to life and regain the freshness they'd lost for me as well.

And then things began to occur that gave me plenty to write about.

THE WHOLE SCHOOL WAS gathered in the gym for a Friday pep rally for the high school basketball team's game that night against their biggest rivals, the Winchester Wolverines. Kids were screaming, waving blue and gold pom-poms, sound bouncing off the walls, and the cheer-leading squad was running off the floor, sweating from a series of gravity-defying routines. Suddenly a whole row of kids in the back of the bleachers stood up and spread out a long white banner, holding it up into the air. In big red letters the words *Indian Rights! Support the American Indian Movement* seemed to fill the room.

Everyone grew quiet as they puzzled over the words. Once again all the kids in the back row were Indian, and one of them was Marjorie. Thanks to Bell, I knew about the movement and supported it, at least internally. Another part of me wanted to hide and not be tested yet again.

The Indian kids began to chant "A-I-M! A-I-M!"

After a few seconds, all sorts of white guys started yelling, "Shut up, red trash!", "Go to hell!", "America, love it or leave it!", and someone started a spitball barrage. Then two or three rushed at the banner and started trying to tear it up, but it was made of cloth, not paper like they'd thought. The Indians pushed back, and a serious fight loomed in front of us.

"All right, all right, break it up!" Mr. Sajarsky's voice boomed over the P.A. system. For a moment the din ebbed; then pandemonium broke loose. Three teachers ran up, pulled the kids apart, and shoved the Indians down the benches toward the door. The Indians didn't fight back, but some of them sat down and refused to move. The teachers got most of them out the door, leaving the sitters to face a screaming mob. I was frightened for them; no one seemed to be trying to protect them.

Then Marjorie leaned over and said something to them, and they stood up. "We're leaving," she shouted. "But it isn't because we're scared. Indians are treated unfairly at this school and every place in Montana, and until that changes, we won't stop!"

She turned and marched down the steps, and all the remaining Indian kids followed her, shouting "A-I-M! A-I-M!"

As they reached the door, Jim Fulton turned and yelled back at us,

"Who's with us? Who's not afraid to join?"

Marjorie was staring straight at me, but I couldn't make myself move. Her eyes were fierce, challenging. I looked down at the floor, then back at the mob of faces, searching for an ally, trying to read their thoughts. An image of Bell pacing through the grass of the Custer battlefield flashed through my mind, his shoulders hunched against the cold and the burden of his world. Oh, hell, I thought, what do I have to lose? and slowly stood up.

Marjorie's eyes flashed as I started down the risers. Everyone else stared at me. As I passed him, Steve Harper stood up, and then out of the corner of my eye I saw Liz Tennant stand too, and then I couldn't see more because I was walking out the door right behind Marjorie.

There, we ran into Mr. Sajarsky rooted right in the middle of the hall.

"Get back inside," he barked, his face bright red. I hadn't seen him that mad since the school board meeting. "Anyone who leaves is suspended. *You* can leave if you want." He pointed at the Indians. "*You,* turn around and go back." This to the rest of us. We all stood uncertainly.

"We're all going." I barely recognized my own voice.

"If they want to ruin their records, let them." Mr. Sajarsky took a step toward me, and involuntarily I stepped back. He turned his head toward the Indians again. "You all get going! You're out for a week!"

I tried to slip past him, but he grabbed my arm so hard I found finger-shaped bruises when I undressed that night. He planted his stocky body between the Indians and the rest of us. Two other teachers who had followed us out-flanked him on either side.

"Go ahead," I said to Marjorie, not sure if were more a coward or a shrewd tactician. "We'll talk later."

"I'll call you," Marjorie shouted to me. Then the Indian kids, stiff with self-consciousness, walked out the front door.

OVER THE WEEKEND, MARJORIE filled me in on what they planned to do, and Mrs. Purdue and three other parents passed on rumors to Mom and Randy. Mom insisted on driving me to school on Monday, and when we got there, a big crowd of kids and adults was milling around in front, led by Marjorie and Frances along with the Indian kids and most of their parents. A line of five troopers and the sheriff blocked the front steps, Mr. Sajarsky at their head. It looked like a replay of a picture I'd seen of the Arkansas governor and his soldiers keeping Negro kids out of the high school there.

"All right, let's have order," the sheriff boomed through a megaphone. "All you kids come in, except those who're suspended."

A few kids started up the steps, urged—and in some cases pushed—by their parents, and the troopers let them through. Most stayed back, reveling in the novelty of a change in routine. Mr. Sajarsky turned and said something to the teachers standing behind him, and they filtered into the crowd, pressing the white children to enter the building.

Frances stepped forward.

"All our children belong in school," she stated in a clear, firm voice that carried over the crowd. "They weren't breaking any law, and they shouldn't have been suspended. If you let in the others, they enter, too."

"They were inciting a riot!" Mr. Sajarsky cried.

"They were attacked."

"That's right! Let them in!" various Indian parents shouted. As the Indians moved toward the steps, the troopers linked elbows, forming a phalanx.

Mrs. Isaacson's blond head appeared behind one of the troopers, whispering something in his ear. He let her through.

"I don't support this suspension," she announced. "Free speech is a right for everyone. All children enrolled in my classes are welcome to attend."

She moved down the steps and began greeting the Indian kids, waving others forward, gathering them in a group around her. Catching my eye, she motioned to me to join them. As I started toward her, I felt Mom's hand on my shoulder. I tried to shrug it off, thinking she wanted to keep me back, but she was walking alongside me. As we reached Mrs. Isaacson, Mom stopped and looked directly at her.

"Thank you," she said, and patted my back gently as I joined the group.

Others from Mrs. Isaacson's classes joined, one or two, then a small troop. The sheriff looked at Mr. Sajarsky, eyebrows raised. You could see the contents of Mr. Sajarsky's brain boiling behind his eyes.

As Mrs. Isaacson walked up and stood in front of the troopers, the sheriff moved aside and nodded to them. Their ranks opened and we slipped through quickly. The sheriff shrugged. "I got no idea which are in her classes," he apologized. "I'll let you sort the whole thing out. Let me know if you need me."

He motioned the troopers to step aside. Slowly the rest of the kids milled up the steps and through the doors, discussing loudly the oddest start of a school day any of us had ever known.

THE MORNING'S EVENTS PERMEATED the whole day. Most teachers tried to keep as close as possible to the normal routine, but at every opportunity someone brought them up. Mrs. Isaacson simply jettisoned the assigned work and led discussions about free speech and the balance between individual liberties and the need for social regulation and safety—issues most kids hadn't spent two minutes thinking about until then, when they found themselves whirled into a tornado they couldn't escape.

Everyone wondered, in crowds, in small groups, in pairs, what Mr. Sajarsky would do. He seemed to have vanished from the school, but no one believed that to be permanent. At home, Mom said little, but Randy made up for her reticence.

"You're pissing into the wind," he told me as we sat around the table after supper. Petey was already watching TV in the living room. "In my day, you'd all have been thrown out on your ear, and given a good hiding. That teacher's been a troublemaker from the word go, and she's gonna get smashed for it. I don't care if she's Abraham Lincoln in skirts, they won't let her get away with this."

"But she was just supporting our right to say what we think!" I objected. "That's what America is all about."

He shot me a contemptuous look and shook his head. "Boy, have you got a lot of waking up to do." He lit a cigarette and leaned back in his chair. "What's written in those history books of yours, and what goes on in the real world, are different as a convent from a whore-house."

"Don't talk like that, Randy," Mom spoke up.

"Why not? She knows enough about it by now. Don't you, Win?" He narrowed his eyes at me.

"What does that have to do with it?" I countered. "If people don't stand up for their rights, that's when they're taken away. Like the Jews in Germany."

"Something that teacher of yours probably talks a lot about, huh?" He pulled deeply on his cigarette and let out a stream of smoke.

"Why shouldn't she? She knows a lot more about the world than you do!" Randy's face twitched at that, but I kept going. "We should all be treated the same, and instead whoever isn't the right color or religion is picked on and treated like dirt."

Randy lurched forward and smacked both hands onto the table, his face mottled. "You listen to me," he snapped. "*I'm* white and I'm a Christian, and no one's ever given me a goddamn break for it in my entire life. Except your ma." He glanced at Mom, who looked down at her own clasped hands. What break was he referring to? I speculated. Did he wonder if Mom had married him, overlooking his obvious flaws, in order to hide behind the screen of his race? Did that matter less now than his love for her as she was?

"I've finally figured out," he went on, "that what's important in this world is money and the power to keep it. If you've got money, you get respect, you get the good jobs, and then you get even more money thrown at you. Me, I work like a slave at some boring crap job, and the boss can fire me for no reason except he doesn't like my ugly face. I break one stupid law, and I'm thrown in the clink. You think that happens to the ones with the dough? You bet your ass it don't."

He glanced at Mom, but she was still staring at her hands.

"Whether you're black or red or white or purple with green stripes, them that has gets more, and them that don't get shit."

He sat back, took a last drag on his cigarette, and stubbed it out in the pool of gravy on his plate. "So pardon me if I can't get too excited about free speech rights for Indians. Words are cheap. You wanta change things, get hold of something the big guys want enough to pay for. And be sure you have the guns to back it up, or they'll just take it from you, like they took the land from those poor Indians you love so much." He heaved himself up and took a deep breath.

"That's going to change," I insisted.

He gave a snort, half-amused, half-scornful. "Sure it will," he retorted, walking toward the living room. "On Judgment Day."

"That's right," I threw at his retreating back. "And Judgment Day's coming sooner than you think!"

I wasn't sure exactly what I meant by that. I just didn't want my enthusiasm quenched by the soggy cynicism that dripped from his words. As I heard his recliner creak and his voice soften as he agreed to Petey's request to sit in his lap, Mom spoke up.

"Don't let him put out your fire." There she went, mind-reading again. "We need young folks like you to move us forward." She looked straight at me. "Like you and Bell, and Marjorie."

I was startled. Which side was she on? And what if, instead of where I'd seen a world bisected into light and dark, it was woven into a multicolored pattern that shifted and flowed as I watched?

The next day I had to concede a point to Randy: Mrs. Isaacson had been fired by the school board for insubordination. Mr. Sajarsky had lifted all suspensions but put bad conduct marks on all the Indian kids' records, and on those of any white student identified as having defied his authority—including mine.

April 25, 1971

Dear Win,

Thanks for the news. Wow, Marjorie's sure a chip off the old block! It does make me a little upset not to be there now that the shit is getting stirred up, excuse my French. How's it coming out?

I got Bury My Heart at Wounded Knee. *Thanks for sending it to me. I started reading it the next day and read it straight through. Sometimes it got me so mad I had to run outside and chop the hell out of a stack of firewood. Where did you get it? Not in Redmond, I bet. I wonder who'll buy it. I guess they think someone wants to read it, if they printed it.*

If you read it first, you know a lot more about why people here are so mad all the time. Up till now, the madder an Indian got, the more of an asshole he made of himself, getting drunk and driving a truck into a tree. Now we're getting mad at who we should be mad at. Maybe people outside are starting to listen. A big maybe.

There's an AIM conference coming up in St. Paul (Minnesota), and I'm going, if the car holds up, which it may not. (Remember that noise the engine makes when it gets hot? Now it does it all the time.) Anyway, there's also going to be a Sun Dance in June here on the Rez, and I'll go to that too. Maybe I'll pierce there. That leaves a little time for me to come to Redmond. I sure could use a little singing practice, I can tell you.

Well, that's all for now. Write soon and give me the latest.

Love from Bell.

Marjorie came over to me the day after we'd learned about Mrs. Isaacson's firing.

"Some of us are going over to her house after school," she told me, falling in step as we walked toward the cafeteria. "Kind of like a study group."

"Who's going?"

"Dave and Jim, and Sam, we think." All Indians. "Maybe some others."

"What about Steve Harper? And Liz?" The ones who'd first joined me at the gym walk-out.

"If you want to ask them, go ahead." What was I, I thought fretfully, the bridge between the whites and the skins? I decided to ask them anyway, and they declined, as did the three or four others. At least at first. With every day the group got bigger and bigger as more kids, Indian and white, jammed the Isaacson's living room, filling chairs, sofa, and every inch of floor space. I begged off afternoon chores at home for the time being, promising double duty later. We read and discussed books, and articles from newspapers and magazines, brought in by different people and from Mrs. Isaacson's library.

"We don't have enough time for everything," said Jim the next week, on Tuesday, as several of us prepared to leave. "Why don't we come here at nine instead of going to school?"

"Great idea!" shouted Steve, and others agreed.

"Let's do it!"

"Strike!"

Mrs. Isaacson stood up and held up her hands. "Wait a second," she protested. "I can't go along with that."

"Why not?" Steve said. "We're learning a hundred times more here in a week than all year at school."

"I'm glad you're excited about what we're doing, but you belong in school."

Murmurs of disappointment mixed with a buzz of rebellious defiance from the more outspoken members.

"If you skipped school, you'll just bring a lot of trouble on yourselves," Mrs. Isaacson continued. "Plus the authorities will stop looking the other way about this group."

"They can't stop us from coming here!" cried Sam. "It's a free country."

"Free to those in power." Marjorie's retort drew knowing smiles from many. We'd learned a lot the past week, questioning authority to the point of suspiciousness.

"Maybe they can't stop you," Mrs. Isaacson went on, "but they can make it very hard on me. I'm protesting my firing, you know. And if I'm seen as supporting you in breaking the law, well, they'd kick me into the next county. The next state, more likely." She smiled grimly.

That stopped us. We'd never really considered how our actions might have consequences for her, an adult, someone whose status as a teacher automatically conferred power as far as we were concerned. I'd forgotten the lesson of the school board meetings: that she too was constrained by forces greater than her own.

"Okay," said Steve. "We want you to come back, and we'll do what it takes to make that happen."

But it didn't turn out that way. On Thursday evening, the board met again, behind closed doors. Mrs. Isaacson brought a lawyer with her, but when her contract was examined, she had no grounds for an appeal. She'd been hired on a one-year probationary basis, pending evaluation by the board at year's end, and could be terminated for misconduct at any time during the year. And that was that.

THE GROUP MET AS usual for a few days more, after which people began to trickle away. No one could think how to counter the board's decision. Our energy drained off, and inertia reasserted itself. By the following Wednesday, only Marjorie, Jim, Steve, and I sat in Mrs. Isaacson's living room, dejected and pensive, unwilling to admit that this was probably our last meeting.

"Listen, kids," said Mrs. Isaacson, her hands in her lap. "You've learned a lot from all this."

"Yeah, like that good guys finish last," Jim muttered.

"No," she answered firmly. "You take what you've learned from our reading and talk, and you go on and use it the next time."

"What next time?" Marjorie asked bitterly.

"There's always a next time," Mrs. Isaacson said matter-of-factly. "And a next, and a next."

"Will you help us?" I asked. "Can we still come talk to you?" I was sure she'd agree.

Instead she fell silent and stared out the window. "I would if I could," she said finally. "But I won't be here much longer. I'm—we're moving to Minneapolis next month."

My chest hurt as if a hammer had struck it hard. The others looked like I felt.

"My husband's taken a job there," she continued. "I'll try to get a teaching position in the system." She smiled briefly. "It won't help me if my reputation has preceded me. But it'll be easier in the city—more kids, more schools that need teachers."

None of us said anything for a minute. Then I spoke up.

"Lucky Minneapolis." I fished for my books and stuffed pencils in my purse in an effort to keep from crying. Marjorie rose and stood in front of Mrs. Isaacson.

"Thank you for everything," she said, holding out her hand. Mrs. Isaacson placed both hers around it. "We won't forget you."

Saint Paul, April 28, 1971

Dear Win,

I can't write much now. I'll tell you about the conference later. Sorry to hear about Mrs. Isaacson. If all whites were like her, we'd get somewhere fast. I'm re-reading Bury My Heart at Wounded Knee. *Have you read* Custer Died for Your Sins? *Get it!*

More later. Love, Bell

May 2, 1971

Dear Bell,

I'm really glad you liked Bury My Heart *so much. I think everyone in this country ought to be forced to read it, before they get the right to vote. And they should have to prove they've read it before they can graduate from high school. Of course, that would leave out a bunch of people right there, like Jess and Collie, or you. Aren't you going to school on the Rez? Doesn't AIM want Indians to get an education? I bet if Indians ran the schools, they'd put books like this on the top of their reading lists. I'll get hold of* Custer Died For Your Sins *as soon as I can.*

Selby and Roone say hello. I'm still taking lessons

and concentrating hard on music since the study group ended. I've decided that when I graduate I'm going to try and get a music scholarship to the U of Montana. Roone thinks I can do it. She says I should start learning a second instrument, one in an orchestra (guitar doesn't count), maybe flute or the clarinet, because they're easy to carry around. I love the sound of the cello best, actually. But you've got to hold it between your legs, which looks weird, and it's huge. Which do you like? Anyway, whatever I choose I'll start it in the fall, when I'm in high school. It's funny, a year ago 'high school' seemed like a far-away grown-up place to me, kind of shiny and glamorous, like New York or Hollywood. Now it's just the next stop down the street.

I really wish you could come back, even for a few days. Or maybe when school is out I could come visit you there, or we could meet some place in between, if I can find a good excuse for a trip. Maybe Billings to see Jess!

Love and kisses, Win

May 5

Dear Win,

What do you need a cello for? You've already got something huge to hold between your legs. Hope you don't have to guess what it is. Get ready to sing.

Bell

May 11

Dear Bell,

Oh god, I miss you so much. I thought I missed you before, but it's ten times worse now. Not that I wish *you hadn't come—I'm so glad you did. I wouldn't have missed those last two days for anything in the world. Thank God Mom bought my story—or seemed to— about visiting Jess, and thank Jess for covering for me. I guess she understands how it is. When I close my eyes I can still feel your hands touching me, and your mouth, and—well, you know.*

I know you gotta do what you gotta do, to quote Randy. I just don't have to like it. Or rather, I like it because it's so much you and it's something I really admire in you. But hey, there's plenty of Indians right here in Redmond, or Great Falls, all over this part of Montana. Why do you have to go so far away?

Okay, I'll shut up. I really just meant to tell you how much I wish you were here, right this minute, and how much I love being with you, and what I'd do if you were—

Hope this reaches you before you take off for St. Paul. Be careful, okay?

Love, love, love, Win

Pine Ridge, May 12, 1971

Dear Win,

This will be a short one. I don't think too much about the time we had together because, when I do, it gets me all fired up, and then I have to go play my cello before I can calm down. It sure doesn't make the same music without you, that's for sure.

Hey, I'm on my way to Alcatraz! Some skins at the conference decided to head out there and try to join the others on the Rock if we can. I could stay around here and help people learn more about Indian ceremonies and stuff. That's what the policy is now for leaders, to go back to their reservations and teach and get back into the old ways. But you know me, I can't sit still long enough for that, and besides I'm no leader, not yet. That's for the elders. Us young guys, we're ready for some warrior spirit. So we're off in a couple of days. If I can, I'll swing by Redmond and see you on the way. Hope it works out.

Love, Bell

May 20, 1971

Dear Bell,

Here's a poem I found in a magazine Marilyn sent me from Berkeley. (I changed it just a little.)

> "Love is the afterwards of the man:
> That he may walk where we have been
> and say,
> 'We were here.'
> It is the dreaming period,
> remembering the way it was
> —the time before he kisses you again,
> why he counts the stars.
> Love is the shape of the man
> and where his hands were."

I can't stop hearing the last two lines in my head, over and over. It says just what I feel.

You promised you'd call Marilyn to pick up your mail, so I'm sending this to her address. Of course you might already be on Alcatraz, in which case who knows if you'll ever get it. Probably I should come to San Francisco and stick it in a bottle and hope the tide takes it out to you.

No big news here. In July Mom and I will go to

*Billings to be with Jess until the baby is born, and a
week after. The plan is for Jess and Collie to come back
with us to Redmond and get a place on their own in
town, at least for a while. Mom and Randy hope they'll
come back and live here and help run the ranch, maybe
take it over one day. I don't know if Jess is ready to
even consider that, but who knows? Stranger things
have happened.*

*We wanted them to get married here, but it turns
out they went and did it already! I'm mad at them for
not waiting till I was there, but guess what, people don't
do things on other people's timetables, as we all know.*

Write me care of Jess and Collie.

Love, Win

San Francisco, Ca.

June 8
Dear Win,

Say hello to PFC Bell Youngman, US Army.

*I know, it sounds crazy, even to me. Here's how it
happened: We got to Frisco right at the end of May. I
drove straight through with three other guys from the
Rez. We hooked up with some of the local AIM people,
who told us there was no way to get out to the Rock.
Besides it looked as if they weren't going to be able to
hold out there much longer. They've been there since
November 1969. Well, that just made us want to get
out there twice as much and be a part of it before it was
over.*

*So that night we drove down to the Marina and
stole a boat—Alvin Dark Horse knew how to run one—
and headed out. Man, it was cold out on the water, even
though it's supposed to be summer, and we didn't really
know where to go. We tried to land somewhere, which*

was stupid because the island is a prison and they've made it just about impossible to land anyplace but where there's all kinds of guards. Of course, the actual island is full of skins now, but the police have boats patrolling the place. We'd cut the motor and were using oars, and we turned the lights off so they wouldn't find us, but they did anyway, and then the shit really hit the fan. We'd gotten pretty sloshed before we started, and the cops found pot on Al, so they hit us really hard with possession as well as felony burglary plus resisting arrest (because we called them names)—a real mess. They threw us in the tank overnight, and the next day they offered us a choice: Go to jail or join up.

We got AIM with our phone call, and the guy they sent over told us we'd never get away without doing some time. I sure didn't want to get stuck in prison. Plus I just turned eighteen and I've got a low lottery number, so they'll get me, unless I cross the border, and what would I do in Canada the rest of my life?

Even if I wanted to, there's no way I can get out of it now. So I'll make the best of it, I guess. I know they'll send me to Nam, which is totally nuts, me over there fighting for Whitey against the natives! Shit, when I think about that, I can't believe this has happened, and I'd give almost anything to be back on the Rez.

I keep thinking, though, about how in the old days, young guys had to go out and prove themselves as warriors before they were allowed to be men in the tribe. They learned things they needed later, how to defend themselves and their people. How to go on even when they were afraid. How to do what they didn't know they could do. That's what I keep my mind on, becoming a warrior. For some reason I've got to do it this way first, before I do it the Indian way. If I don't keep thinking that, I'll go crazy.

*They're sending us to Fort Ord for basic tomor-
row—no time for goodbye visits. As soon as I get there
I'll send you my address. Don't worry about telling
Frances and Marjorie. I'm going to call them myself.*
Love from Bell.

Fort Ord, California, June 19

Dear Win,

Believe it or not, this is the first chance I've had even
a minute to write since that postcard I sent you the day
I got here.

This place is awful. It's hot as hell every day, and
all we do is march and march, run obstacle courses, then
march some more, this time loaded down with a full
pack, about twenty-five pounds' worth. The sarge calls
us names, kicks us, makes fun of us—his favorite word
is "numbnuts," plus a few others I can't tell you. They
yell at you all the time, even while you're marching. Especially then. When they give an order, you better jump
to it right away. No point in thinking anything out—it
seems like they want us to forget how to think. And
that's what's happening. After a day out there, all you
can do is collapse and sleep, so forget using your brain.

The only reason I can think straight enough to write
you is that we're getting our first break, half a day to
rest, once we've cleaned our equipment and our bunks
and stuff. So count yourself lucky I still got an hour to
myself and can write this letter.

Jesus, Win, what am I doing here? I hate the way
they treat us, and I hate the war they're getting us ready
for, but I'm beginning to see how I could get too tired
to do anything but hang on and survive—just put one
foot in front of the other and forget where I am and
where I'm going.

The only thing that's OK here is that the guys in the unit are in it together. It doesn't seem to matter anymore who's white or colored or Indian—they dish out the same shit to everybody. If we'd met outside, I wouldn't have much to do with most of them, except this one, Jeff Sands—he's part Indian, Crow, and he's pretty much OK. But here, we're all becoming brothers in shit. Not a nice picture, but that's how it is.

Sorry to bring you down. I think a lot about you back there in Redmond, on the ranch, and about Frances and Marjorie, and Selby. And everyone and everything. Even school seems like heaven now. Say hi to your mom and Pete. Please write. Getting one of your letters feels like an ice cold beer after a month in the desert.

Love from Bell.

It took me a long time to really absorb what Bell had done, and what it meant. At first I mulled it over to myself, trying to join it to everything else I knew about him. Emotions battered me, like the cards that rained down on Alice in Wonderland: disapproval of his action, anger at the separation this would entail, remorse for not having tried to dissuade him from the Alcatraz adventure. Then I called and confided in Jess, who was properly sympathetic.

"Collie says, why doesn't he go AWOL?" she added, after passing the news on.

"And go to jail? That'd be worse."

"He could go to Canada."

"He already said he wouldn't do that."

"Ask him again."

"I'll think about it." We fell silent.

"What does Mom say?" Jess asked.

"I haven't told her, and I'm not going to," I stated firmly.

"Randy would probably agree about Canada, I bet."

"*What?*" I hooted.

"He hated Korea. He talked about it when he lived here, about Basic, and the night patrols, and how the grunts got all the flak while the generals and colonels lived easy."

"Well, I'm not talking to him about it, or about anything."

"Hasn't he been behaving himself?"

I had to admit he had.

"So when are you going to forgive him, Win?"

"Never. I can't. I won't. And I don't understand how you can."

Jess sighed. "We were so little back then," she said thoughtfully. "We don't have to keep seeing things the way we did." She paused. "You know yourself now that what we decided to hate him for way back then isn't so awful."

"I don't know what you're talking about!"

Another pause followed, which I broke. "Let's not talk about it anymore, okay?"

We went on to other things—the baby-to-be, Collie's job, my plans to be with them for the birth—but something about the last thing she'd said nagged at me for a few hours, until it was shoved aside by Mom's next move.

SHE CAME INTO THE living room that evening, after finally getting an unusually fussy Pete to bed, and sank onto the couch next to me to watch Randy doze in front of the flickering TV. I'd been pretending to read. Every so often I'd slip Bell's latest letter out of my shirt pocket and open it behind the book's concealing covers, then fold and pocket it again, as if it were a talisman against whatever would go wrong next.

Randy roused himself. "Pete down for the night?"

Mom nodded as Randy yawned noisily and stretched his arms and legs, feet flexed and fingers wide apart. When he was through, Mom spoke up. "I'm going to visit Moon."

Randy and I stared at her. She sat quietly, as if there were no more she needed to say.

"Who?" Randy asked finally.

"My aunt Moon. My father's sister. I've been writing her."

"And just where does she hang out?"

"Lame Deer."

"On the reservation? You following in Win's footsteps, huh?" He looked at me. Obviously he knew about that part of my trip from Mom.

"I'm taking Pete with me," Mom went on, ignoring his question. "We'll leave day after tomorrow. Now that school's out, Win can take over for me while I'm gone." She patted my hand. "I'm calling in your debt." This was double duty and then some, I rebuked myself.

Randy's face flushed and he clenched his hands. "You want to take my son to that god-forsaken hellhole?" The old Randy returns, I thought. I'd known it couldn't last.

"It's not a hellhole," I blurted. "She keeps her place clean. And she's nice and friendly. I like her."

Randy narrowed his eyes at me.

"Your opinion's not worth squat," he bit off. "We know what kind you like." He returned to Mom. "How long do you plan to be gone, Madame?"

"About a week, I guess, what with the two days each way to get there and back."

Randy shook his head slowly. "If anyone had told me last year that this day would come, I'd have laughed in his face and then knocked him cold." He *tsked* his tongue, rubbed his hair into a frizzled mess. "Live and learn, I guess." He stretched a hand out to Mom. "Let's go, woman," he said. "If you're gonna be gone for a week, I want to get some use out of you before you leave."

My cheeks burned, and I dropped my eyes as Mom rose and took his hand. I snuck a look as they left the room at Randy's hand slipping down to grab the taut roundness of her ass. Why them and not me? I asked myself bitterly. They've had enough chances to have grown tired of it, yet they want to go at it again. And I, who've barely had a taste of it, have to sit here alone and hope they'll be done by the time I try to sleep.

ONCE MOM AND PETE left, I was kept so busy I had no time to do anything but work, eat, sleep, and write a few paragraphs in an ongoing letter to Bell. The weather had been warm for over a month, with lots of rain, and the grass was plentiful. One day we gathered the cattle we'd gotten back and treated the calves and yearlings for lice, being careful not to get the putrid medicine on ourselves. Another day we branded a new bull Randy had bought, as well as eight new calves. Yet another we moved the cattle to summer pasture. I tended the garden every morning, weeding and watering the tender shoots of corn, peas, and lettuce, and setting out the tomatoes where they'd ripen best.

The meadows were thick with flowers: death-camas, Indian paint-brush, lupines, mustard flower, vivid dots of yellow, white, blue, and red in a sea of green. By eleven o'clock it was warm enough to make a huge pitcher of iced tea which we drank our way through till sunset, when cool winds blew through the open windows in all four sides of the house, saturated with the pungent smell of alfalfa. I'd sit on the porch after supper, watching lightning on the horizon or waiting for moonrise. Randy was occasionally terse or gruff, but in general he was even-tempered, even praising my erratic cooking and helping with the dishes and the laundry, things he never did with Mom.

We went to town one day for groceries and farm supplies. Of course I checked at the post office as I mailed my letter to Bell, only to be disappointed. Randy must have noticed my glum face as we started the trip back.

"Boyfriend didn't write, huh?" he asked, drumming his fingers on the steering wheel along with Johnny Horton's "Honky Tonk Man."

I kept a dignified silence. We drove a mile without speaking.

"Listen, Win," he said as the truck hit a deep rut and I barely saved my skull from a fracture. "I've meaning to tell you to thank your boyfriend next time you write, for helping out at the ranch while I was—away."

Suddenly I was furious, a Pandora's box unleashing its load of angry demons.

"Why can't you say his name? It's Bell, Bell Youngman, and he's worth ten of you! He came by every day, and he brought friends to help us, while you just hid away someplace with a bottle, afraid to face us!" I gritted my teeth to stop the flow of words.

"You don't think he came out of the goodness of his heart, do you?" Randy spit out. "He was trying to find a way to get into your pants, and it worked!"

"That's a lie! Sure he liked me, but he liked Mom and Pete, too. He felt sorry for us, and he did something to help us, not like all the others who sat around gossiping and turning their backs on us!"

I turned and faced his stony profile.

"You can't believe someone could do something just for someone else, do you? Not to get something out of it for themselves, like you." I drew myself up and turned away. "I feel sorry for you."

I hoped he'd yell back, unforgivable words. As long as I was this angry, I wouldn't cry.

When he spoke, his voice was unexpectedly gentle. "I tried so hard with you girls," he said. "We got on so well at first. Then when you began to turn on me, I still kept on trying. I couldn't believe what was happening. I guess I should have expected it, when girls hit a certain age, and being your stepfather and all, but I didn't back then. It felt like my sisters all over again."

"We changed because you started to be so mean!"

"No, you didn't. It was the other way around."

As soon as he said it, at the exact moment I was opening my mouth to object, I saw myself at eight, sitting under the cottonwoods down in the eastern coulee, as Jess explained to me, with her advanced ten-year-old knowledge, what Randy and Mom did together in bed at night. I heard myself, hands over my ears, yelling in protest, then, drenched with sudden clarity drawn from countless observations of the cattle, the dogs, the cats, even the goddamn chickens, that she was telling the truth. And then came our pact, sealed in blood we pricked from our fingers with Jess' new pocket knife, to hate and spurn Randy the rest of our days.

I dropped my face in my hands, unable to look at him.

"I know," he said, easing the truck into low gear for the hill that signaled we'd soon be home. "It's like turning a corner and seeing yourself in a mirror you didn't know was there. You see the way you really are, before you've had a chance to put on the face you recognize."

He's right, I thought, and at the same moment was struck by another realization: We don't forget the times people hurt us nearly as fast as the times we hurt them.

WHEN MOM AND PETE came back two days later, all Pete could talk about was the motels he and Mom had stayed at, how he'd gotten to sit up in Mom's bed and watch TV, and how he'd saved all the little wrapped-up miniature soaps, which he proceeded to show us. The main thing that impressed him at Moon's was Buster, and how smart he was. About Moon, all he said was, "She can do magic tricks."

Mom wasn't much more forthcoming. "We talked a lot," she said. "There was a lot to catch up on." Then she threw out a thunderbolt. "Jess and Collie are coming back here."

"Here where?" asked Randy, squinting at her.

"*Here* here. In time for the baby."

"Well, thanks for talking to me first." Randy's voice was fierce. The old Randy rears his ugly head, I thought.

"Randy, that baby will be my grandchild, my first, and I want him here. I want them here. They won't live here forever, but they need to be here now. I hope you understand."

"Or else I know what I can do about it, huh?"

She said nothing. The room hummed with tension. Finally he took a deep breath. "I understand I ain't got much choice. You ask a lot, woman, you know that? Good thing you're worth it."

"So are you." Mom ruffled his hair, and he caught her hand and pulled her onto his lap.

"How did things go here?" she asked.

Randy and I looked at each other briefly. "Just fine," he said. "There was a little misunderstanding a few days ago, but we got that straightened out, right, Win?"

I agreed. Mom raised her eyebrows in her look that signaled, *Oh, really?*

"Moon may visit us in the fall," she went on. "Or I might go back to see her."

Randy sighed, and Mom put her hands on her hips.

"Well, I guess you gotta do what you gotta do," he stated. "Custer made a stand, and look what it got him. I know when I'm licked." This startled even Mom, and I almost fell off my chair.

"Maybe I should go away more often," Mom said when she recovered. "Absence really does make the heart grow fonder."

"You couldn't have said a truer thing," he grinned, kissing her cheek. "Hope you missed me where it counts."

I waited for the familiar revulsion at his crudeness to hit me, and when it didn't, a weight seemed to lift from me. The way her eyes lit up, her face grew rounder, her voice lighter, pointing to the young woman she'd been when she first met him, pleased rather than sickened me.

Randy nuzzled her neck, like a teenager high on beer in the back of a car.

"Stop it, Ran," Mom protested, pushing his head away and glancing half-apologetically in my direction.

"It's okay," I said, finally, gratefully, meaning it. "My turn will come."

Little did I know how soon.

Fort Ord, July 8

Dear Win,

I got the tape you sent. I took it into town the one day they let us out of here, and I found a music store where they let me play it. I loved hearing you play—I closed my eyes and imagined you sitting at the piano, your hands flying around the keys, with that funny little half-smile on your face you get when you're happy (the one you got a few times flat on your back, too). No one here has a reel-to-reel, but I'm gonna keep the tape with me wherever I go, on the chance I'll find a place to play it again. Tell Roone thank you from me for helping you make it.

They're shipping us out two days after we've fin-

ished Basic, meaning on July 20th. Can you believe it? We get two days in San Francisco, and then boom, gone. No time for a visit home. They must be getting desperate over there in Nam. Jesus, I hate the idea of not seeing you before I leave, but there's nothing I can do. Can you send me a picture of you?

Congratulations to Jess and Collie for little Bell. Glad they're back there. I'm going to send them a present from Frisco. I'm pretty knocked out they gave him my name. I'll try and make it something he'll be proud of.

Love, Bell

I didn't beg or plead. I just told Mom I was going, that nothing could stop me from this last chance to see Bell before he disappeared into the jungle for God knows how long.

"You're so young," was her sole objection. "You're too young to be in so deep. I wish—" she didn't finish.

"I've got the money for the bus," I countered, hoping to deflect her thoughts. "All I need is to get to Great Falls. There's a bus every day at ten-thirty, and it connects in Butte with a direct bus to San Francisco."

"And what next? San Francisco's a big town. You don't have any idea where to go."

"I've already talked to Marilyn. She'll pick me up in Oakland. I can stay with her in Berkeley."

I didn't mention that Marilyn had offered to stay with her own boyfriend for the two days and let Bell and me use her place.

"How exciting," she'd exclaimed on the phone. "My little cottage will be your love nest!"

Mom pursed her lips. I got ready for a struggle, but all she said was, "I don't like that you went behind my back, Win."

"I'm telling you now, aren't I? I could have just snuck away like before, but I didn't."

"So now you're making me part of your plan. Guess I can't win."

She heaved a huge sigh. "All right, I'll tell Randy you're going to visit Moon again. I can hear him now. 'Why can't that girl stay off the reservation?' She smiled at me and grew serious. "You be careful, Win. On the bus, and in the city. And use something, you hear? I don't want another of my babies with a baby."

"I'm not a baby! And neither is Jess."

She frowned sharply.

"And don't worry, I *am* careful," I went on. "I promise. *We're* careful."

"You better be. All it needs is one mistake."

"Mom, I'm not stupid. If I did get pregnant, I'd get an abortion."

I forestalled her shocked reaction to what seemed to me an eminently reasonable idea with repeated assurances of my level-headed prudence, until she relaxed enough to agree to drive me to Great Falls the next day. As she got up to leave my room, she leaned over and put her hand on my shoulder.

"Be careful of your heart too, Win," she breathed. "Don't give it all away just yet."

But how could I follow such advice?

THE BUS RIDE SEEMED like a series of monotonous yet mesmerizing TV episodes—travelogues of the Rockies with their peaks still covered with snow, level stretches of scrubby high desert, the Sierras rising abruptly, then easing down into the Central Valley, interspersed with dream-scattered sleep and rest stops during which I staggered into neon-bright cafes and dirty bus stations to grab a sandwich, a Coke, a Snickers or Hershey bar. Then back to stare out the window at the landscape flying by, a backdrop for my fantasies of Bell and me laughing, coupling, crying, flying, as I slipped again into a restless doze.

By the time I stepped off the bus, I was so dazed all I could do was let Marilyn take charge of me until I collapsed at her place onto a pull-out sofa bed and slept for the next ten hours. As soon as I woke, it was time to leave for the post where Bell's unit would be let loose. Gulping a cup of coffee and gnawing on a bagel—my first ever—I sat next to Marilyn as she navigated the endless streets of Oakland, through the gates, answering the guard's questions with careless ease. Then we stood with a small but eager crowd of girls and women, sprinkled with a few fidgety children and crying babies, staring at a chicken wire gate through which would walk—soon, we hoped—our heart's desire.

The gate opened, the first men—they looked like men to me then, though now I'd see them as boys so young their faces had hardly had time to sprout whiskers—sauntered through, some joking with each other, some scanning the crowd. Five, fifteen, thirty, and then there was Bell, duffel on his shoulder, army fatigues crinkled around his legs and torso, saying something quick to the man next to him, who threw back his head and laughed. His beautiful black hair was gone, cut down to a fuzzy stubble that made him look like a convict on a Wanted poster.

For a moment I drew back, tempted to duck behind Marilyn, let him pass by, and take the next bus back to Montana. Then he saw me and stopped so suddenly the next man bumped into him. His eyes registered shock, then confusion, then certainty, and then he grinned so wide the sun gleamed on his teeth. He dropped his duffel, took a step forward, then he was running toward me and I toward him, and then all I knew was that this was what I'd been living for.

INTRODUCTIONS, EXPLANATIONS, DRIVING, WITH us in the back seat, unable to let go of each other's hands, Marilyn's pleased eyes on us in the rear-view mirror. A stop at a drugstore. On to Berkeley, Marilyn leaving us with a promise to drop by the next morning. Then, before she'd finished going down the steps, we were on each other. Mouths, hands, skin on skin, his teeth finding the sensitive place on my neck that drove me into a frenzy. Pulling him into me, rising to meet him. Grunts, sibilant liquid noises, shouts and cries, gasps, easing then toward fullness, the luxuriousness of amplitude. Knowing we had time now, as much as we wanted, the vast horizon of two full days stretching as rich and expansive as a century.

We made love over and over, with breaks to raid the refrigerator and to spin the dial of the radio, awed by the range of choices and the diversity of sounds available for our enjoyment. I chose a station and we coupled again as Joni Mitchell's then-unfamiliar high, pure voice, one I would come to know almost as well as any, sang of ladies of the canyon.

"I'm sorry, Win," Bell whispered into my hair afterward.

I tried to pull away, but he held my head steady. I raised a hand to his face to find it wet. My heart sank. Was he going to tell me—I couldn't imagine the rest.

"Sorry for what?"

"For being so stupid. Getting dragged into this. I'd give anything to be staying here."

Relief made me easily sympathetic.

"It's done, Bell. It'll be okay."

"Okay? I'm gonna be stuck in the middle of a fucking jungle, in a crazy war I don't believe in, risking my life for nothing!"

He rolled onto his back and stared at the ceiling.

"What about going to Canada?" I offered hesitantly. "Other guys have done it."

"And never come back? No way."

"They say there'll be an amnesty some day."

"When? When I'm fifty? And how would I even get there? The MPs would find me first."

"There's people who would help. I bet Marilyn knows how to find them. Berkeley's full of war protesters, she told me. She could—"

"Win, I can't. I'm going to Nam, I know it. I've got to get through it, that's all. Then I'll be free. I can live my own life. I'll have earned it."

"You can live it right now, just the way you are. You don't have to do this to earn it." I put my hand on his chest and decided to pull out all the stops. "Look, you made one bad decision, like you made a wrong turn on a trip. That doesn't mean you should keep going and get more and more lost. You can turn back and find the right road again. No one would blame you for getting off a road that leads nowhere."

He turned and stared at me, then laid his hand gently on my cheek. "That's true for you, maybe," he said softly. "But I've got to do it this way. I made the decision, and I'm responsible for what comes with it. It's like I signed a contract, I guess. I gave my word. As soon as I carry it out, I can get back to the right road."

There it was, the part of him I loved so much, something strong and solid in him, like the cedar roof beams of a house, or the straight tall trunk of a pine.

"You're nuts," I said, laying my head on his chest, listening to the steady thump of his heart. "You're nuts, but a beautiful kind of nuts."

His laugh made my head bounce.

"That makes two of us," he said. "Guess we're made for each other, huh?"

I voiced my agreement without any words.

NOW AND THEN, DURING the night, the next day, I'd look at him and open my mouth to try again: Don't go. Stay here, dammit, stay with me, I'll go to Canada with you, I'll tie you up and lock you in a room for the next four years if I have to. And then my heart would turn around: I loved his certainty, his knowledge of what was right for him. Now I wonder—was it knowledge, or was it determination not to be a coward, a judgment cobbled from half-truths and passionate conviction? If the war didn't hurt him, he was right. But what if it did? When does caution become cowardice? Why can't we know the future when it really counts?

July 29, 1971

Dear Win,

I still can't believe you did it. When I saw you standing at the gate of the post, I almost stopped breathing. Tell Marilyn I'll get down on my knees every day for the next ten years and thank her. And you too, for spending two days and nights on the bus to get there. I hope it was worth it for you. It sure was for me, and then some. I'm getting a lot of ribbing from the guys about what a Romeo I must be, to have such a pretty girl come halfway across the country to see me off. I told them you came from a long line of headstrong women who do exactly what they want, just try and stop you, and why would I want to, anyway?

It was great to see Berkeley, too. What a town! I'd like to go back some day. Those weird guys on Telegraph Avenue, stoned and banging cymbals and drums were something else. And the Hairy Krishnas (funny name for a bunch of baldies) clapping and jumping up and down reminded me of skins who get high on chanting the old songs.

Hope you got back okay, and that you stopped crying before your bus left Oakland. Please don't worry about me too much. You can bet I'll keep myself as safe as I can—no John Wayne crap for me out here. Whenever I get a break, I go down to the mess hall and get the sarge to play your tape on their tape deck, and I think about you.

Anyway, we're already out on the front line. I can't say where or give you any details. I'll just tell you it's hot as hell here—worse than during basic because it's so goddamn wet. Dry season here just means a little less wet than other times. Between the snipers and the mosquitoes and the leeches and foot rot, there's no rest for the wicked. So far it's mostly boring. We sit around waiting for something to happen. We've been out on patrol a few times, which means we slog through the mud and rocks and sopping trees and vines, wondering when we're going to get shot at, or when someone's going to step on a mine. So far it hasn't happened. The only guys who've had real trouble are the ones who get KOed by heatstroke and have to be stretchered out—more work for the rest of us. One of them went nuts and tried to strangle the guys who *were carrying him. And that's life in the good old Army.*

That's all for now. Like they say here, hasta la vista until next time.

Bell

I relaxed a bit after this letter. Boredom was okay; boredom was terrific. If Bell's war could consist of tedious day after tedious night until his sentence was up, that was fine with me. I felt bad for his having to endure the discomforts of the jungle, but who really cared about leeches and mosquitoes, as long as mines and mortars stayed out of sight?

So I wrote him about the doings of our small world, our own August hailstorms and the break-in at the Two Elks—four high-school kids in search of after-hours booze—and my own low-key preparations for high school. And of course about Little Bell, his moods and his many accomplishments, like smiling, burping, holding his head up.

September 3, 1971

Dear Win,

I thought I was scared before, but now I'm really scared. We all are, but we don't talk about it much. You can only stand it so long, then you sort of blank out.

We had our first death, Jim Sully, a big tall guy from Arkansas. He got shot by a sniper yesterday. He was filling his canteen at the river while we were on patrol when, bang, right through the neck. He didn't die right away, he bled to death as we dragged him out of range and back into the jungle. Every time I close my eyes I see him staring at me while his blood pumps out, like he's asking, "Why me? What did I do? Why?"

And now we all know that it could happen to any

one of us, any second, for no reason other than bad luck, you're in the wrong place at the wrong time. And there's nothing you can do about it. You can be careful, don't take any stupid chances, keep your head down and all that crap, but it doesn't really matter in the end. No matter how much you do things right, there's no guarantee you'll survive.

I shouldn't talk like this to you, Win, but I've got to tell someone. Please don't think bad of me. I'm not going to crack up or go AWOL, and I know being afraid isn't the same as being a coward. I'm going to stick it out, but I want you to know I hate it. I'm afraid it's going to turn me into someone I don't like, and that you won't like either. Someone who doesn't know how to feel anything but hate, or nothing at all.

That's why I'm so glad I have you. When things get bad, I take out your picture, the one of you holding little Bell, you squinting at the sun, your red hair blowing all around so I can almost feel the breeze coming off the Eastern front. And then I know I'm still me, and I can feel, and what I feel is love.

Win. I don't know any more what could happen between us when I come back—I'm not as sure about anything as I was once, a long time ago. I think back then you were right, I was scared to hope that things could be better than I was used to. Now, even with what's going on here, I see it just might be different one day. What I do know for sure is that you are one of the best things that's ever happened to me.

I love you.

Bell

Then there was only waiting, a postcard that said nothing, waiting, writing lighthearted letters in which I hid my fear under gossipy chit-chat, another three-line postcard, and more waiting. Until one day, as

I leafed through the four-page weekly *Redmond Gazette*, a headline caught my eye.

Redmond, Montana, November 3, 1971

REDMOND YOUTH KILLED IN VIETNAM
Bell Youngman, private first class in the 8th Battalion, 2nd company, United States Army, was killed near Cho San, Vietnam, on October 29th. Mr. Youngman was a resident of Redmond and attended Redmond High School, where he was an outstanding forward on the school basketball team, the Grizzlies. Services will be held when his body is returned to his mother, Ruby Youngman.

CHAPTER 29

'D THOUGHT IT HAD hurt when I saw Bell drive away from Jess and Collie's, when he left me after our two-day reunion in Redmond, when he put me on the bus in Oakland. But next to what I now felt, those were love-taps, a baby's bumps and bruises as it learns to walk. Now the pain was so great it hollowed me out. It hid deep in a dark cave, sucking me from the inside, leaving my outer self dry and dead, able to walk and talk but without real sensation.

After the first few days, during which I stayed in my room, crying, reading and re-reading Bell's letters, refusing to go to school or talk to anyone, even Jess, I decided I had a choice. Since I couldn't find the ruthlessness to kill myself, I had to rearrange my past to make it so Bell disappeared. I had to take all the evidence of my senses, my whole memory of him, and blank it out as if it had never happened.

So that's what I set out to do. On the fourth day I came out of my room, dressed in my new blue sweater set I'd bought to start high school, sat down at the table with a startled Mom and Randy, and reached for a piece of toast.

"Looks like you're going to school," Randy hazarded. "Want me to drive you?"

"Not unless the bus breaks down on its way here," I answered, dividing the toast into quarters so it would look like I was eating.

"Are you sure you're ready to go?" Mom asked. "You could stay home a couple more days, if you want."

"I'm fine," I insisted, crumbling the toast and biting off a corner. It stuck to the roof of my mouth. "I'll be fine if you'll just leave me alone."

Mom and Randy looked at each other briefly and back at me. I swallowed, chewed another corner of the toast, stood up, put on my coat and boots, picked up my books, and marched out the door.

I was dreading the solicitude I was sure I'd encounter from classmates and teachers, but no one said anything. An eerie silence seemed to surround me as I sat in class, walked the halls. It reminded me of the first days after the Harvest Ball, or after the school board meeting, after the infamous report. But those times I'd hated my segregation; now I craved it. I did my work, answered the teachers' questions, turned in my papers. At home I did my chores, helped Mom when she asked, and pretended not to hear her questions about my state of mind.

But I couldn't touch the piano. I was afraid of what might happen if I heard the notes he'd listened to, the plangent chords pouring from under my fingers and directly into my heart. I'd been in my room the first Saturday, and no one reminded me about my lesson. But the next one was two days away.

"Aren't you going to practice?" Mom asked me as I shucked beans for supper.

"I'm taking a break," I answered, dumping the tips onto the plastic tablecloth and tossing the beans into the blue bowl.

"For how long?"

"I don't know. As long as I feel like it."

"Does Roone know? You'd better call her."

"I already did," I lied. Roone would figure it out fast enough, I guessed. I supposed she'd be disappointed, but what was a little disappointment next to the heartache I was locking away? I was holding myself as far from anything that might unlock the door to that cave as I could, and that included music, and therefore Roone. I avoided anyone who might try and comfort me, or make well-meaning, sympathetic inquiries about how I was doing. If only I could be whisked off to a place where no one knew what had happened, I thought, I'd be safe. I could act out the part of an ordinary high-schooler, untouched by tragedy, uninteresting to the point of invisibility.

Well, it worked, at least in the sense that people left me alone. I got a note from Roone inviting me to resume lessons whenever I wanted, and to drop by anytime before that. I got another, from Mrs. Isaacson (how had she found out?), inviting me to visit or call her in Minneapolis, and expressing tender solicitude that would have reached me if I'd been even half there. But I wasn't.

The one I hadn't counted on was Marjorie.

I hadn't been in touch with her since I got back from my trip to San Francisco. I figured from what he'd said that he was writing to her and Frances, and I wanted to keep his letters to me private. In the fall, Marjorie didn't appear to be around. I learned from Jim Fulton that she'd gone to live on the Pine Ridge reservation with a cousin, and was attending the high school there. So when I looked up one day just before Thanksgiving and saw her standing across the street from the high school steps I'd just walked down, my stomach lurched as if I'd seen a ghost.

Even if I'd wanted to avoid her, I couldn't, with her eyes fixed on mine. I crossed the street slowly. She was thinner than I remembered and a little taller, her body smothered in a navy pea coat several sizes too large for her. Her hair was cut almost as short as a boy's, making her dark eyes look huge. She was holding a paper bag clutched in front of her. "Hey," she said softly.

"Hi," I answered. "Are you back for Thanksgiving?" As soon as I said it, I wanted to bite my tongue. I knew Indians didn't celebrate Thanksgiving; to them it was an anti-holiday, along with Columbus Day. To hide my embarrassment, I stammered on: "I hear you're in school on the Rez?"

She looked at me a long moment. "It's where I have to be," she said finally. "Lots of AIM there." She paused. "Bell wanted to go there, but his mother needed him here, so he stayed." Another pause. "Then he met you."

All the things I hadn't known, would now never know, about Bell exploded in front of me, as if I'd been yanked out from a dark room to stand blinded in the light. "But then he left anyway," I whispered. "He should have stayed here. We should have made him stay."

She shot me a scornful look. "He was going, so he went." She turned her face to the west, narrowing her eyes at the pale sun, and in that moment, I saw Bell's face in hers, and I loved her like a sister, like a mother, like a lover returned from the dead. Without realizing it, I'd grabbed her hand.

She looked at me again. "I came home for the funeral."

My stomach lurched a second time. "The—Bell's funeral? When?"

"It was yesterday."

"But—" I stammered, dropping her hand. "Why didn't anyone tell me? Where was it?"

"In the Catholic church. His mother's church. But he'll be buried in the Pine Ridge cemetery. He's on his way there now."

"No!" My voice was shrill, harsh. "Why didn't you let me know?"

"You wouldn't have wanted to be there."

For a moment I couldn't catch my breath, as anger paralyzed my throat.

"That's not it," I managed to say. "You didn't want me there, did you? Me, a white girl, sticking out like a sore thumb. Didn't you remember I'm part Indian?"

Marjorie stared at me, narrowing her eyes. "Not everyone who's Indian is Indian," she said. And at that moment her resemblance to Bell seemed hateful, a mockery, like a clumsy painting of a beautiful face. Her eyes softened. "Bell wouldn't have wanted you to be there," she said. "He didn't believe in that religion. It meant nothing to him." Now it was she who took my hand in her own icy one. "Nothing important of him was there."

"That's not true," I countered, near tears. "Frances was there, wasn't she?" Marjorie nodded. "And so were you."

"You have what's really important of him," she said, "and so do I, and so does my mother."

She placed the paper bag in my hand.

"He wanted you to have these. They were sent here from Nam with his body. They were the only things he saved."

She turned, then stopped.

"Come over and see us sometime."

As she moved down the street, I opened the bag. Inside was a flat box, with "Win's piano music" written on it. And a bundle of letters held together by a rubber band, addressed to Bell in my handwriting.

As soon as I got home and found myself alone for once, I sat down at the piano and, without consciously choosing to do so, played all the pieces I'd recorded for Bell, over and over, tears streaming down my face. As I played, in my mind's eye, I began to see him in a booth in a record store near the base, sitting near a tape deck in the mess hall at the front, listening to these very pieces, and for the first time I felt I had a piece of him back. Sobs burst from my chest, and I crumpled over the keyboard, my cheek resting on the cool ivory.

"Win, honey." Suddenly Mom was sitting on the bench next to me. I hadn't even heard the car drive up, or the front door open. She ordered Pete to his room in a tone that he recognized as not to be argued with as she put her arms around me.

"Go ahead, honey," she murmured, rocking me in her arms, and I did, for what seemed hours. When my sobs diminished to gulps, then sniffles, she wiped my face with the bottom hem of her old purple cardigan.

"I know you don't think you'll ever feel better," she said, stroking my disheveled curls. "Right now it hurts so bad you want to die. But you won't die. It won't kill you, I promise you."

For some reason, that reminded me of the song that had popped into my head in the motel room in Billings as I watched Bell reveal himself to me for the first time, and I started crying again. Again Mom held me, rocked me, stroked my hair.

"Win, it's the crying you don't do that can kill you," she said finally. "It kills your spirit. When Lorrie died—" she paused a moment, reluctant, I sensed, to revisit that place, then plunging ahead. "That's how I felt, too. I wanted to die. But I couldn't. I had to go on, for you and Jess and Pete. It's the ties to the living that pull you on, that let you let go of the ones you lose."

"I don't want to let go!" I gulped. "I won't!"

"You don't have to, not yet," she reassured me. "Just hold on tight to the ones who're still here."

Something eased in me then, though I started crying again, letting her rock me on a river of grief toward her bruised and healing heart.

"Do me a favor, Win," she asked after I grew calmer. "Play me that Chop-in piece?"

"I can't," I began, reluctant to mix Bell's presence with anyone else's, the living with the dead.

"Lorrie loved that piece, you know," Mom went on quietly. "When I hear it, I can feel her here with us. Please play it for me."

I stared at her: Was she trying to trick me, to lure me out of the magic circle that encompassed only Bell and me? But I could see it written plain in her eyes: She'd been where I was. She needed something from me almost as much as I needed her. So I played as I never had before, for myself and for Mom, as Lorrie and Bell and all those we both had loved and had lost, gathered round us in the lowering dark.

EPILOGUE

THE PALE LEMON-AND-PINK STREAKS of cloud on the eastern horizon tell me daybreak is here, hinting at the Montana summer day to come. A tentative bird calls, then another, then silence again, nature pressing the snooze bar for a few moments before the air fills with their song.

Carefully I stuff everything—letters, manila envelopes, cardboard boxes, photos, the journal I've spent the last hours reading—back into the trunk and shut the lid. Not the bracelet, though. I study its ridged, bead-stubbled diamond shapes awhile, stroking them with my fingers, then work it over my large-knuckled hand, overdeveloped by the exercise of playing piano, letting it come to rest just above my wrist. Perfect in size, its worn leather sits smoothly against my skin. I'll keep it with me, maybe give it one day to the daughter whose face I don't yet know, the daughter I'd given up hoping for.

I rise and walk back to the kitchen, turn the flame on under the half-filled coffee pot. Soon I'll have to shower, get dressed, stand in front of the blunt bathroom mirror and decide whether to try and draw a prettier, younger face on my everyday one, with its indented line between scraggly brows and pale skin dotted with faded ghosts of freckles.

In an hour, they'll arrive to pick me up, Pete and his wife Jennie. Jennie is Liz Tennant's younger sister—Liz, who followed me as we walked out of the gym, and joined Mrs. Isaacson's outlaw study group. They've been married for five years—no kids yet, but Jennie is pregnant. They live in town, where Pete is a mechanic, a really good one, headed toward owning the garage one day. He's been coming out here to help Jess and Collie on the ranch when he can, mostly for the grain harvest and when the cattle need to be sorted and shipped.

Jess and Collie live with their two younger kids, twenty-year-old Lee and sixteen-year-old Lorraine, in a house about a mile away that they built eleven years ago on the southwest corner of the ranch. They've done their best with this place, taking over the bulk of the work from Randy and Mom. But even with all of them working long days, summer and winter, the place has never reversed its long slow slide into debt. Farm machinery costs so much, and a drought year or a late hailstorm can wipe out what little has been put aside. Borrowing means heavy interest payments that never let up, even if the income from cattle sales goes way down.

Of course I'm no help, living as I do in San Francisco. I come back only on holidays. I did become a musician. I teach piano and cello, and play in a chamber orchestra. I love it there, but I miss it here, too. I'd feel stabbed to the heart if I couldn't come back and ride under this great stretch of sky, feel the sweet sting of the wind in my face. L.B.— that's what we call Little Bell since he started objecting, when he was nine, to being called "Little"—is out in San Francisco too, studying film of all things. He's had a passion for photography since he was ten, then he got hooked on movies, toting around his Super-8 everywhere. He made a bunch of funny little films his last year of high school, of family and friends doing silly things. In the last one, everyone was wearing a totally inappropriate hat—Randy in a flowered bonnet of Mom's, Jess in a turned-around feed cap, Mom in a much-too-big Stetson, Collie in Lorraine's deely-boppers, the kids in fright wigs—all sitting in the front yard here, sipping tea.

All these years we felt sure that, sooner or later, the ranch would make it, until Mom got sick two years ago. She got a cough that wouldn't go away; then she started having trouble breathing. When we finally dragged her to a doctor, he told her she had congestive heart failure and she had to take it easy. On top of which Randy's long-ago drinking, plus the smoking he never could give up, finally caught up with him. He's a real bulldog, refusing to slow down even when his liver is killing him, which is exactly what's happening.

It was this last winter that made it clear we couldn't go on this way. Randy got sick, and when they operated on what they thought was an infected gall bladder, they found his liver was riddled with cancer. All they could do was sew him back up, dose him with chemicals, and send him home. "Home" meant moving in with Collie and Jess, since they can't manage by themselves anymore, much as they hated to admit it. Collie built an addition so they can have their own room and bathroom. Jennie's parents, who own the next ranch over, have agreed to buy our land so they'll have some money for the doctor bills, and Collie will work for the Tennants now. He won't talk about it, but I think it must be a blow to him. Of course, he wasn't really working purely for himself before, but for Randy and Mom as well, and Randy's no angel, even if he's not the devil he once was. And Jennie's parents are part of our family now. So maybe less has changed than it seems.

That's why I'm here, helping pack the house up, now that Mom and Randy aren't living here. Soon everything that hasn't already been moved will be gone, sold or discarded. I'll take the trunk over, and Mom and I will go through it together. All the questions she wants to ask me but never quite does will flutter up from the raggedy bits of cloth, the yellowing paper, the faded photos: Are you happy? Aren't you lonely living by yourself? Are you still stuck in the past, remembering Bell?

I haven't told her yet about Uri. We've been together for almost three years, and after so many years of being alone, I can finally see how the shape of staying with a man, with him, fits into my life. He's nothing like Bell on the outside. He's Israeli, short and stocky, with curly hair and a bright quick voice that jumps up an octave and stumbles all over itself when he gets excited. He's far from perfect; he's got a quick temper, for one, though he never deliberately uses it to hurt anyone, and he's impatient at anything he perceives as stupidity, which, since he's smart, is a lot. But I can talk to him about anything and we are best friends. I have to struggle not to compare him to Bell, to the shimmering memories I still have of him, against which Uri can't measure up, because no one can.

I remembered Bell constantly all through high school, through the unhappy romances and tempestuous love affairs that succeeded one another in an unsettling march during and for many years after college. For a while I immersed myself in finding out all I could about Indians, or Native Americans, as I learned to call them. But it was always "them," not "us," not "me." I never went native, trying to live in the Indian way, hugging a set of foreign garments tightly to me to try to transform myself into someone else, as I've seen some do. Somehow I realized that I could never leave off being white, and that made me angry, because it kept me separate from Bell.

It was Marjorie who took over where Bell had been stopped. She got involved with AIM, participating in the actions at Wounded Knee, then studying to become a nurse and helping set up health clinics on several reservations, one right at Pine Ridge. And I envied her for being able to share more of who Bell had been than I ever could.

But over time I grew to understand that Bell wouldn't have expected me to be anyone other than who I was. He'd just begun to see the path his hopes, his life, could take, when he was killed, and some of his dreams passed on to Marjorie, not to me. What he'd seen, though, was my own future, clearer than I had, and in the end that's what he gave me: the courage to follow my own heart's desire. His appreciation of my music fueled my spirit, my ambition and my determination to become who I was meant to be. It's what Mom said to me, so many years ago, about Lorrie: Our precious dead become our guides. They are like the stars shining above us, remote and brilliant, compressing and focusing their light on us like the rays of a diamond, looking down with all-encompassing understanding, no longer involved in our human life that goes on implacably without them.

As I watch the sky fill with radiance as the sun reddens the fields and touches the trees with fire, I find myself pulled back into a dream I had the night before I left to come here: I'm standing on a snow-covered hillside, the sky filled with thick gray clouds studded with small patches of blue. In the distant valley below I can see a group of huts, wood smoke rising above them. The people in those huts are all gathered around a woman who is about to give birth. Directly in front of me lies a line in the snow where white gives way to deep, rich brown dirt. And I know that, if I cross that boundary onto the bare ground, at that very moment I will die, and then instantly I'll be reborn as the baby about to come, fresh and new, into this world.

I lift my foot. I hesitate, and stand paralyzed, filled with enormous fear and excitement.

I step over the line.

CPSIA information can be obtained at www.ICGtesting.com
Printed in the USA
BVOW041028151112

305593BV00001B/52/P